THE DISAPPEARANCE

THE DISAPPEARANCE

Efrem Sigel

THE PERMANENT PRESS
Sag Harbor, NY 11963

For information, address:
  The Permanent Press
  4170 Noyac Road
  Sag Harbor, NY 11963
  www.thepermanentpress.com

Library of Congress Cataloging-in-Publication Data

  Sigel, Efrem.
    The disappearance / Efrem Sigel.
       p. cm.
    ISBN-13: 978-1-57962-180-3 (hardcover: alk. paper)
    ISBN-10: 1-57962-180-5 (hardcover: alk. paper)
       1. Missing children—Fiction. 2. Couples—Fiction.
    3. Marital conflict—Fiction. 4. Massachusetts—Fiction.
    5. Psychological fiction. gsafd I. Title.

  PS3569.I412D57 2008
  813'.54—dc22   2008040482

Printed in the United States of America.

2 3 4 5 6 7

For my sons, Jonathan and Matthew

Acknowledgments

Special thanks to:

Judge Dyanne Klein of the Newton, MA District Court and Sgt. Dennis Marks of the Massachusetts State Police for patiently answering questions and providing perspective on legal and sentencing matters and on police procedures.

Larry Weissman for his keen editorial suggestions and expert professional assistance.

Lewis Mandell, dean, professor and Cub Scout mate, for reading and commenting on early sections of the manuscript.

Kathryn Lang of SMU Press for warm words of encouragement and advice at a critical juncture.

Judith and Martin Shepard of The Permanent Press, wise and gutsy publishers.

And especially, to my wife, Frederica, for reading chapters, drafts, more chapters and more drafts with patience, frankness and tact.

Chapter 1

He calls it running toward the light. He is jogging along the bend where the big gray rock rears up on his right flank. Now the road straightens, tunneling between close-standing sugar maples on either side. Leafy branches nearly touch overhead; they form a canopy that shelters as it darkens. It is early morning; after a night of spring drizzle, miniature dots of moisture cling to leaves and tree trunks. The sun, peeping above Miller's Needle to the east, angles a shaft of light through the tangle of elderberry and sumac up ahead, just beyond the passageway through the trees. Tiny specks of crystal shimmy in the cool air, as the light goes to ground in a splash of gold.

He is only a few hundred yards from the end of the road, and if he has run many miles, he often slows to a walk here to enjoy the whisper of a breeze on his arms, the pleasurable ache as muscles in his calves contract. But not on the rare mornings when light hangs suspended in the air. No matter how far he has gone, he must speed up, must run toward the light, knowing its ray is the balm that will quiet and soothe. But though he can run toward it he can never arrive. At the point of illumination the beam has vanished, leaving an instant of warmth as he peers ahead toward another shaft of light, descending like a ladder between now and before.

It is always the way it looks in the late afternoon sun that defines The Hollow to Joshua Sandler, as if a deep golden hue, taken from an inexhaustible supply, has been spread over the grass with wide and silent rollers. The sun rarely strikes that side of the lawn to the west of the house full on. Two massive sugar maples with gnarled trunks and a vast spreading canopy of leaves block the direct light. In mid-summer the leaves are dark green and large as a man's hand, too dense for the sun to pierce

The trees stand by the side of the road, and by coincidence or design, the needlepoint that hangs in the downstairs bathroom depicts just such a house, also with two trees in front of

9

it. On that needlepoint is embroidered the motto, "Let me live by the side of the road and be a friend to man." Sometimes in the grip of the black despair, rage and fury that take hold of him after Daniel's disappearance Joshua wants to rip the framed needlepoint from the wall, stomp on it, break it into shards. Once or twice he does take hold of it and twist it this way and that as if to mash everything in his bare hands—the frame, the glass, the fabric, and most of all, the words.

The house in which the needlepoint hangs in its glass frame is like the picture in the needlepoint: a massive but graceful colonial, close to the road, which is how they were placed in those days, before paved driveways and Jeeps with snowplows. The house sits on two and a half acres of lawn, healthy, sturdy grass nourished by the snows of winter and the ample rainful of spring and autumn. Before the disappearance, Joshua liked to stroll barefoot on the large expanse of lawn to the west of the house, where the late afternoon sun bathed it in a golden green. He is a man who is always on his way to or from someplace, always finishing up one task and thinking of the next, but at this hour his heartbeat slows as he makes a circuit of the property, moving from light to shadow and back to light, the rays of the sun dissolving whatever is bitter or discontented within him.

What you notice first about Joshua is his springy hair; it is the color of dark sand with specks of carrot and seems to be constantly in motion. Then, the orange freckles that populate his face, the thin lips and the brown eyes that are always bubbling, often with mirth, sometimes with anger. His hands are large and competent, which becomes evident as he slings a basketball from right to left before putting it on the floor, darting to his side and rising like a high-board diver, straight up, heels together, pupils narrowed to focus on the basket. He can shoot from either side but the left hand is stronger, and a tad steadier. In a pickup game he is pure energy; once you know this you can understand why Joshua in the office or in someone's living room gives this impression of someone about to leap out of his work clothes and cut to the hoop in nothing but his underpants.

The house is in the Town of Smithfield, not in Smithfield proper but in The Hollow, a tiny hamlet of 60 souls about two and a half miles northwest of the town to which it belongs. Smithfield itself has 500 residents spread out over 50 square miles. Bordered by the other hill towns—Northway, Woodfield,

Cooperville—it is an insignificant geopolitical entity at the far edge of Adams County in western Massachusetts.

Yet despite this small size, and the fact that Smithfield has only a general store, a hardware store, a garage, a town hall and a church, the residents talk of The Town as if it is a giant force in their lives. They complain that The Town has stopped using salt in winter (state regulations, a bunch of Boston politicians who couldn't find their asses in a snowstorm) and the roads are often rutted ice from January to the middle of March. They grouse that The Town has yet to replace five of six white cement posts, knocked over when Billy Parsons smacked into them with his dad's truck; the posts serve as a guardrail where Route 33A veers sharply left, to reveal the vista of an eroded hillside plunging into the Northway River.

Besides the icy roads and the knocked-over posts, there is also the matter of the public street lamps, two on the main street in Smithfield, one on Old Route 57 in The Hollow; they're no longer being lit at town expense: the budget won't allow it. Things aren't the way they used to be, the old-timers complain; every year the taxes go up but we get less for our money.

Joshua and Nathalie have had their own run-in with The Town; nine years ago Joshua had demanded that the town selectmen put up a sign at either end of Route 57 at the turnoff into The Hollow, warning motorists to go slow, that young kids were playing in The Hollow.

"Oh, there's no need for that," said Carl Puckett, president of the selectmen. "There's never been a sign like that."

"Well there sure is a need for one now," said Joshua. "There are four kids all under the age of five and if one of them wanders off a lawn and onto the road and gets smacked by a car roaring by at 50 miles per hour it's going to be on your head."

Pause. Puckett was, and still is, a very wide, upright man whose neck seems to merge into the humpbacked mass of his torso. Joshua was holding the phone in a perspiration-laden fist; he'd been out whacking weeds and trimming the rough grass at the edge of the raspberry patch.

"On my head? On the parents' head," said Puckett. "We're not responsible for watching your kids."

"Do you want to have an argument after a child gets hit by a car about whose fault it is, or do you want to spring for a few dollars now to see that the accident doesn't happen?"

11

Another pause, then Puckett said, "You haven't lived here long enough to be making requests like that."

He might have said, you people from New York haven't lived here long enough, but it didn't matter; Joshua heard the omission as if it had been spoken.

"I'm not aware that the laws are written one way for people whose grandparents lived here and another for those of us who moved in a year ago."

After that conversation he wrote a letter. When he got no answer he called again, and when Puckett told him the same thing he wrote another letter with a copy to his lawyer, a genial but sharp-minded fellow in Collegeville. A month later, one day in April, a long-haired kid drove up in a pickup truck and hammered two "Go Slow Children" signs into the ground, one at either end of the road through The Hollow.

The Hollow is nestled in a jog of Route 57, the main east-west route. Coming west from Smithfield, you turn right onto Main Street, which the old-timers called Old Route 57, you drive through the village on a half-mile loop and then rejoin Route 57. Along the way you pass a collection of two dozen houses dotted on either side of Main Street, as well as straggling up on both sides of the intersecting road, Northway Road, which meets Main Street a quarter of a mile from either end of Route 57. Northway Road climbs steeply from the intersection of Main Street and after a hundred yards it enters a pine grove; at that point the asphalt ends, and turns into a narrow brown dirt road, snaking steeply past state forest land, like a cart track in the Carpathian Mountains.

Joshua and Nathalie's place is one of the oldest in The Hollow. Heading west on Main Street, you pass the group of houses in the center of the village, then some woods and a bridge. Just beyond the bridge in a graceful curve of a shallow, fast-flowing stream, stands their house. Built in 1805 or so, the brass numbers over the front door proclaim, it is a federal style colonial; on either side of the front door are very long clapboards—15 or 16 feet long, stiff and knotted with age, like a farmer's fingers that have known too many cold mornings.

Dan disappears on a Thursday in August, six days before his 14th birthday and almost exactly one year since his Bar Mitzvah at a synagogue in Mamaroneck, New York. There is no place to have a Bar Mitzvah in Smithfield. On Main Street in Smithfield, opposite the town hall, sits a Congregational Church; in The Hollow there is a separate Congregational Church, to which the minister drives at 11:00 A.M. on Sunday to conduct a service identical to the one he has presided over an hour earlier in Smithfield. The old ladies come down to church from their homes on the Northway Road or on the Hawes Hill Road, a rugged dirt road at the other end of The Hollow. They dress in lilac and pink, with a sprig of lily of the valley in their white hair.

The day Dan disappears, Joshua takes the Jeep to Smithfield to buy some things at the Smithfield Hardware—100 feet of agricultural fencing, 14 four-foot metal posts, nails and new wire clippers. He wants to replace the rusted chicken wire fence that's become an eyesore along the back of the lot. The property ends at the river bank, and the bank plunges down quite steeply through brush and low-growing weed trees, willow and poplar, to the rocks and sparkling water of the Northway River. Joshua loads the back of the Jeep with three barrels of kitchen garbage and household trash, including a huge wooden storm window that must weigh 25 pounds, even missing half its glass.

At the last minute Nathalie decides to come along. She's been kneeling in her garden, watering petunias and coleus and geraniums at the edge of the vegetable plot. The Big Boy tomatoes are staked as high as Joshua's chest; they have sinewy trunks that are an unnatural green, a green that seems to exist only on tomato plants or in drawings of frogs in children's books. It is nothing like the green that the kiss of the sun lays down on the side lawn in the long shadow of the maple trees, all golden and smelling of clover.

She comes skipping up to the Jeep as he is about to put the key in the ignition. Afterwards Joshua pictures the way Nathalie lay her arms on the driver's side, his door, with her slim fingers resting on the opening where the window slides up. Her arms are tan, her fingernails caked with dirt. Thinking of her face, how sun-washed and carefree, is about the worst memory he has of that day.

The day is warm, pleasantly warm. The air is dry. Even at noontime the sky is the blue of outer space, of daydreams.

"I'm coming."

13

"To the dump? I mean, the compactor?"

Since the mid 80s, dumps in small towns in Massachusetts—those sprawling, smelly, picturesque dumps—have been replaced by compactors, green boxcars into which you slide your garbage by pushing it down an incline. A solid waste disposal company collects the compacted garbage and transports it to some other state. Going to the dump used to be an adventure; going to the compactor is like a trip to a crematorium.

"I'll go with you to the hardware store. Then I'll walk down and see Terry. I made him some brownies yesterday.

"He's doing poorly, isn't he?"

"He'll be happy for the visit. And the brownies."

Nathalie darts inside and calls to Daniel, who is up in his room, and he yells down, "Okay, mom, see you later," and that is the last time either of them speaks to him.

Terry is Terrence McBurnie, Daniel's great friend, who would come to cut the lawn and turn over the beds and who would get down on his hands and knees and play horsie with a delighted three-year-old when Dan was barely out of diapers. Except when he's with kids, Terry is serious and unsmiling, a wizened man, brown as a dry leaf in November, slow-moving, but with ropey, sinewy arms that harken back to a time when he'd been a lumberjack, handyman, potato farmer.

And convicted killer. When Terry was 21, his stepfather woke up one morning after a drunk, demanded money from Terry's mother, and began smacking her on the top of the head with a heavy skillet. She'd had other beatings from him, but this would be the last.

Terry came running into the kitchen by the back door, carrying the axe with which he'd been splitting logs by the woodshed, and found his mother slumped against the stove, blood running down the side of her face from the deep cut that had opened at the edge of her scalp. She was blubbering and barely able to walk. "Wait here," Terry said, settling her into a chair.

His stepfather had just stumbled into the front yard on the way to try to start his truck when Terry caught up with him, raised the axe and severed his head, cutting it off the way you prune a wayward branch. It was the only violent act he ever committed.

For his crime Terry served 28 years in a state prison before being paroled.

A year after his release Terry came back to Smithfield and landed a job as the janitor at the local grade school. No one believed him a threat to the children; those old enough to remember the case swore that Terry had gotten a raw deal. He passed the next 20 years cutting the grass, raking the leaves, trimming the roses, spackling and painting the classrooms, patching the roof, polishing the wooden banister in the hallway. At the end of the day when the youngsters filed onto the school bus, a few of the little ones running into the arms of mothers who'd come to pick them up, Terry stood beaming, all aglow with reflected happiness.

Terry had retired from the school just about the time that Nathalie, new in town, had asked old Grace Flint if she knew someone who could mow the lawn. Grace is the white-haired widow who lives up the Hawes Hill Road about a mile from the center of The Hollow. She drives an old Ford pickup, the same one her husband had owned until, 13 years before, he fell off the roof of the church during a painting party, broke his neck and died enroute to the hospital. When the truck starts, Grace is able to get out to the store or to the weekly afternoon meetings of the Ladies Benevolent Society, where the women sip tea and wrap bandages for World War III.

Grace had come by one day to introduce herself, leaving the pickup outside, its engine running. "Don't think I'm wasting money by leaving it on," she twanged. "If I shut it off the damn thing might not start again." Then she smiled darkly. "Nathalie, why are you painting your house shit-brown? A house in Smithfield should be white. Lord knows they've been white for two hundred years."

"This one was every color but white," Nathalie said. "When Josh and I scraped the old paint off we found blue, red, gray and pink."

"That's because people lived here who had no respect for the place," Grace Flint said. "Now you people, even though you're from New York, you keep it all nice and tidy."

Nice and tidy doesn't apply to Grace's own house. Her front yard is like the ghost of a tag sale in a sun-bleached western town. An old vacuum cleaner, a Ford Pinto with no wheels, a chipped white washing machine, a stack of four truck tires obscure the walkway to the front door. Two panes of the living room window are out and have been patched with cardboard and rags. Inside, the dust is piled in irregular ridges on the floor, like a model of a mountain range.

Nathalie got in the habit of walking up the hill to Grace's place to bring her little goodies, and she asked if Grace knew someone who could help her with mowing, gardening, odd chores.

"Do you mean the gruntwork?" Grace asked. "Gruntwork is the 99% of gardening that makes the mental work worthwhile. Are you looking for someone to do the gruntwork?" Grace never said anything without giving you a lesson about it.

Nathalie smiled. "Yes, the gruntwork."

"The best person is Terry McBurnie. He has a strong back and is honest as the day is long. He won't exactly talk your ear off, but I don't suppose you're looking for companionship."

"Where do I get a hold of Mr. McBurnie?"

"I'll see him in church tomorrow and ask if he's interested."

Sunday afternoon, Terry McBurnie came by. When Nathalie saw his weathered face, she immediately thought of him in Indian terms, as a man who had seen many winters.

He introduced himself formally and called Nathalie Mrs. Sandler, and for the eight years that Terry worked for her that's what he called her, Mrs. Sandler. Often when he came to the house to turn over the beds or mow the lawn or pull the ivy from the maple trees at the back of the property, Nathalie would be in the big living room playing the cello. On a summer's day the sound would drift out the front window through the folding screen as if it were being squeezed out of a rich dark piece of furniture, the sound flowing through the dark colonial interior like wine oozing from the press. Now and then Terry McBurnie would pause for a few seconds at the end of a row, if he were mowing, or when he'd finished a ditch, if he were digging, and let the music wash over him.

"You play very beautifully," he told Nathalie.

"Thank you. You like the cello?" she asked.

"I like music. I like nice music, not the stuff they play these days."

"Do you play?"

"Not anymore," he said. "I played piano when I was a boy. My mother taught me."

"Was she a music teacher?"

16

"No, Mrs. Sandler, but she loved music and she played whenever she could. She would have liked the way you play."

From time to time if she looked out the side window, where the wing of the extension to the house made an el, she'd see Terry propped up on his spade or pitchfork, dreamy, just listening. When Daniel was little, something about Terry drew the young boy to the silent man, with his gaunt, erect dignity, and he would run outside and follow him around and beg to be allowed to push the mower.

"When you're big enough and strong enough, you can help," Terry always said. That moment arrived soon after Daniel's 10th birthday. For two years he helped Terry push the mower around the large lawn, until, when he was just short of his 12th birthday, he began to do it himself. Terry had started to fail. Parkinson's deprived him of his ability to walk a straight line or handle the chores in any semblance of order. No longer able to drive or navigate without help, he wound up in the senior citizen housing in the center of Smithfield.

Every now and then Nathalie makes a trip there with brownies or apple crumb cake. Terry brightens to hear her tell what flowers are coming into bloom, or how tall Dan is getting. Occasionally she'll bring the portable CD player so he can listen to the cello music that he likes. On this day there is an alertness to him. They took us for a ride this morning, he tells her. In the van. How nice for you, Nathalie says, and thinks, too bad Dan didn't come along to visit.

When they get home from the dump around 2:00 that Thursday they unload their purchases and Joshua puts the big aluminum trash can inside the garage and Nathalie goes around the side to verify that some of her day lilies are ready for cutting. She still has the visit to Terry in her mind. She calls, "Dan? Dan?" as she ducks into the shed for her cutting shears. The door is slightly ajar and she wonders if Dan can be lurking in the corner of the shed; there are times he'll fool with a chisel or make a tiny bird house out of the scraps of wood lying around under the workbench. The light is off and the darkness has a warm, moist feeling to it, as if an animal is there, silently breathing.

When she comes out with the shears, Joshua is kneeling by the badminton net, reattaching a cord to the plastic orange tent peg in order to hold it rigid.

17

"Seen Dan?"

The sound seems to issue forth from his mouth in a twisted, roundabout way because Joshua is facing the road with his back to Nathalie, but he is directing his question back around his neck toward her ears.

"No. Did he say he was going out with Sam or any of the other kids?" Sam is Sam Bonacio, who lives three houses away at the other side of the street.

"He didn't tell me," Joshua says. He gives a few whacks at the peg to reanchor the line. "I'd like to know where he is, I thought we might play tennis after lunch."

"Did you talk about that with him?"

"Yeah, I mentioned it and he said, 'Well, maybe.'"

"Just humoring you," Nathalie says. The two of them, father and son, used to do everything together but in the past year a gap has opened, and now it seems as if day by day it widens.

Two days later when Joshua finally, really accepts that their son is missing, he replays the conversation in his mind, just as he replays everything that happened that day. It's when he gets to Nathalie's words, "Just humoring you" that his brain starts to buck, like a car that won't go into second gear.

"Maybe he's out riding his bike," Nathalie says. Dan loves to race up Route 33A toward the state forest. There he hops off the bike in the shade where the campsites nestle under the pine trees, and walks to the man-made dam at the end of the swimming area, where water plunges down a four-foot drop.

Joshua checks the garage. "His bike is there," he says. "Maybe they went up to The Shadows to go swimming." This is a natural swimming hole about half a mile up 33A. A big humpbacked sloping rock, its glacially made indentations like a series of Welsh valleys, rises out of the river at that spot; although the river is as narrow here as elsewhere, barely 12 feet across, in this spot it is deep enough to dunk your entire body.

But Joshua knows Dan is unlikely to be at The Shadows. He and Sam and the other boys in town typically stop there after a long bike ride and come back with chests glistening, hair dripping wet because they'd plunged in without suits or towels, swimming nude and then using their T-shirts to dry themselves.

Nathalie says as much. "Probably he'd have taken his bike." She pauses. "Maybe they went messing around in the woods."

This statement by Nathalie hangs there between them, and Joshua has a chill as he listens to it, a chill on a brilliant sunny August afternoon when the temperature is in the low 80s.

At about 3:30 Nathalie makes her first phone call. She calls Pat Bonacio, whose house is at the end of the road just before the intersection of Main Street and 33A.

"Hi, it's Nathalie. Have you seen Dan? I thought maybe he was with Sam."

Sam is with a friend up in Northway, Pat says.

"Have you seen Dan at all today? We were in town for a couple of hours and since we got back we haven't seen him."

Pat says she gave Sam a ride to his friend's house in late morning, loading his bike on the roof rack so he could ride back. Then she went shopping in Hartsfield. She likes to go to a supermarket on the northern edge of town, it's set in the notch of the surrounding hills. From the parking lot you can look through a gap in the mountains and see all the way to Vermont.

"You haven't seen him at all?" Nathalie persists.

"No, not at all. Is something the matter?"

By this time Joshua has been up to The Shadows by car, and then beyond, to the Lexington Park campgrounds. Kids are frolicking in the river. Adults are in the shade outside their tents, sipping lemonade and beer and watching portable TVs. He asks the ranger on duty if he's seen a 14-year-old with a serious expression, a compact, well-built kid, about five foot three, close-cropped light brown hair, brown eyes. No, the ranger says, no one's come up here, just the kids whose families are at the campgrounds.

Joshua asks if maybe the ranger was on break and could have missed the boy.

"I've been right here," the ranger says, annoyed. The ranger is sitting on a white lifeguard's chair. In the river, which is barely three feet deep, nothing more serious than a splashing contest between a couple of eight-year-old boys is going on.

What is it about the uniforms they wear that enables them to feel superior to you, Joshua thinks. He's having none of it.

"My son is missing, he's 14. Sometimes he rides his bike up here. Please think really hard about whether you've seen him or anyone from outside the campgrounds or anything at all unusual." The tone of his words brings the ranger up short.

Now he turns and gets a good look at Joshua, looks too at the photo that he proffers. And shakes his head, no.

"Here's my phone number. If you see or hear anything, please call me right away."

He drives back to The Hollow very fast, the six miles of narrow winding road flashing by in about 10 minutes. Nathalie is on the phone when he comes in.

She cups her hand over the receiver. "I've called the police."

"Who?"

"The chief of police in Smithfield. You know him, Art Sammons. He's coming over here."

"Okay," she says into the phone, "as soon as you can." She turns to Joshua.

"The chief of police in Smithfield?" It's a cruel joke; their son is missing and the person who will look for him is the chief of police in a town of 500 people.

"He knows his business, Josh. We have to start somewhere."

In the meantime he sets out to go door-to-door in The Hollow. The Blakelys live opposite; he's an actuary with Bay State Life in Hartsfield. On weekends he and his wife take their English Springer Spaniels to dog shows. There is no one home. Greta Wilding lives in the adjacent house, a deaf lady in her 70s who has seen nothing, heard nothing.

Next to Greta are the Bonacios. Pat Bonacio comes to the door; she wears her dark hair cropped very short, and on the sides, where it glides over her ears there are strands of silver. She's lean and active, always mowing the lawn on a riding mower or getting up on the ladder to clean out the gutters and patch holes with mesh and tar. Her husband Steve is on the road, putting in a 60-hour week on his beer delivery route, which takes him through Massachusetts, Vermont and eastern New York State for one of the major brewers. When he comes home after a week of work he'll sleep all day Saturday. Steve is a small, scowling man with a dark shadow from his heavy beard.

"What's the matter?" Pat knows right away, it's the expression on Joshua's face.

"We don't know where Dan is. He hasn't been home all afternoon. Do you know anything about where he is? Does Sam know anything?"

"Come on in." Pat tries Sam at his friend's but he's already left. "He'll be home soon," she reports to Joshua. "I'll ask him as soon as he gets in. Then in a little while I'll ask him again."

When he asks what she means, Pat shrugs. "You know, kids," she says. "Sometimes you have to ask a few different ways before you really get the story."

A cold drink? Pat offers. Iced tea? A coke? No thanks, Joshua says. He walks the 50 yards back to the house, approaching it from the west at half past five as the dipping sun fireballs the crowns of the two large sugar maples. On the eastern side of the trees are long, deep shadows across the front of the house. On the western side the lawn is bathed in that magical golden light that only comes in late afternoon. Joshua reaches the front door with the sun warm on his neck but his chest cold as a meat locker, thinking about what Pat said. Kids: sometimes you have to ask a few different ways before you really get the story.

Chapter 2

On the day that Dan disappears, Art Sammons, the chief of police in Smithfield, answers Nathalie's phone call himself. Sammons used to be in security at the mill; the mill is what they call the paper plant on the river in Hartsfield, the aging factory town about 20 miles away. That plant had shut down eight years ago, as had another factory that made surveillance systems for fighter planes. Papermaking had gone south, aerospace had gone west. Now Sammons is the security officer at a shopping mall east of town, home to an eight-screen movie complex, a supermarket, a toy store, a discount clothing outlet. Where manufacturing had once provided jobs with overtime, pensions, four-week vacations, the mall stores offer 25-hour-a-week minimum wage work and no health insurance.

Most of the calls that Sammons gets in Smithfield are from people whose riding mower is missing from the garage or whose neighbors have moved beyond shouting at each other and are throwing dishes or breaking windows; in the country these sounds carry far.

When Nathalie reaches him, he says he'll be along as soon as he finishes clearing some brush at the woodlot behind his house. Nathalie pictures a chain saw, an axe, a dusty pickup truck. When he arrives, barely 20 minutes later, he is driving a spotless beige Oldsmobile.

"Did your son leave any note?"

"No," Nathalie says.

"Any sign of a hasty departure, like an article of clothing on the floor or a refrigerator door open or a phone off the hook?"

"No."

"Have you checked the places he usually hangs out or called the other kids he hangs out with?"

"Yes. My husband went up to The Shadows where he sometimes swims—there was no one there. He hadn't been up to the state park, he hadn't been with the Bonacio boy, Sam. I called the Bartlett house, sometimes Dan hangs out with Bobby Dawes."

"What did they say?"

"Bobby says he hasn't seen Dan."

"And his mom? Ellen?" Ellen, now the wife of Tim Bartlett, used to be married to Robert Dawes, Bobby's father.

"She's still working; she'll be at the movie theater till about 9:30. That's what Bobby says, anyhow."

She mentions to Sammons that Dan usually hangs out either with Sam or with Bobby. She can recall one time a month ago when all three of them were together but in the telling it seems trivial, as if the unease she felt that day has nothing to do with the reality of what has happened now.

"Uh huh." Sammons says. He is making notes in a pocket notebook. Nathalie is surprised at how carefully he writes, how neatly dressed he is in clean work pants and short-sleeved tan shirt with collar. He's a man who fills out his clothes: six two at least, his belly snug against a wide leather belt. Nathalie sits opposite him at the kitchen table, now and then reaching up a hand to smooth her chestnut hair. She looks at Sammons out of dark eyes that seem swollen and protruding with terror. Even in a tiny village like Smithfield, she thinks, a policeman must see a lot of suffering: hunting accidents, logging accidents, heart attacks, fires that leave people homeless, all the accumulations of a lifetime turned to cinders.

"I don't know why, but I feel something terrible has happened."

"There's no reason to think that, Mrs. Sandler. Let's take it one step at a time."

But she can't get the premonition of tragedy out of her head. Already her anxiety is becoming an omnipresent, suffocating wrap.

"Tell me something about yourselves," he says. "You don't live here, full time, do you? Where do you live? What do you do for a living?"

"We live in Mamaroneck," she says. "In New York. My husband has his own business. I'm a musician. A cellist."

"For the New York Philharmonic," Nathalie says in answer to his next question.

Her voice is soft but even in her sadness and fear there's no ignoring the timbre of her voice, with its sensuality, its discipline, its perfect pitch.

23

Sammons tells her they will do whatever they can to find her son. In the meantime, he urges, carry on with your life. Practice your music. Eat when it's time to eat, sleep when it's time to sleep.

She looks at him as if he is mad. "I'm serious," he says. "I know you think I'm crazy, but I mean it."

At that moment Joshua comes in, just back from his sixth or seventh trip on foot to the intersection of Main Street and Route 33A. Each time he stands there looking up the road as it winds toward the Shadows and the state forest, hoping that Daniel will emerge from the bend in Route 33A and bounce toward him, jogging the last quarter mile, swinging his arms in that way he has.

No sign of him, Joshua says, and asks Sammons if there have been any accidents on the roads, any other reports of missing kids or adults. No, Sammons says, not yet, but we'll be checking. He says we as if there is a whole police force instead of just him, a solitary 220-pound man with hands the size of shovel blades.

"I know something has happened," Nathalie says. "I know something has happened."

"I hope not," Sammons says. And then he asks, "Why do you say that? Was there any warning of something? Has he said anything in recent days to make you think there was something afoot?"

"No, no, nothing like that. But I know something has happened, Daniel would never be away this long without keeping in touch. That's the kind of kid he is."

"When did you realize that your son was missing?"

"Josh and I came back from Smithfield about 2. He'd bought a couple of things at Smithfield Hardware and I paid a visit to Terry McBurnie."

"Terry McBurnie?"

"You know him?"

"Sure I know him," Sammons says. He explains that McBurnie's mother used to babysit for Sammons when he was growing up. Sammons must be 45 at least, maybe 50, and it is hard to imagine him as a kid. And he talks for just a minute about how devoted Terry was to his mother and how hard he worked as a teenager to bring a few dollars into that sorry household. Sammons asks about Daniel, what kind of boy he is, what his interests are, and he lets slip, in a neutral tone, that he has two daughters and two sons; the eldest son is married; the youngest son, only 17, is still at home. He takes the car now and then, Sammons says, and that's when his own worry starts. He has brown eyes that are liquid and a voice that is melodious, a warm tenor's voice.

"Mind if I go through the house? It's just that I might spot something you hadn't noticed."

He walks through the house with Joshua and Nathalie, room by room. In the bathroom the towel on the towel rack hanging on the door, the lower one, is Dan's. His red toothbrush is in the toothbrush holder. Sammons spends a few minutes in Dan's room, taking it in. On the floor next to his low bed is a dog-eared *Sports Illustrated* and a Travis Magee novel. On top of the bookcase is the Bible, and when Sammons opens to the bookmark he comes to the page with Dan's Bar Mitzvah portion.

"Is that Hebrew?"

Yes, Joshua explains, that's the five books of Moses in Hebrew and English, and for his Bar Mitzvah last year Dan read a section from the Torah scroll.

Sammons nods. He has heard about Bar Mitzvah but never knew what was entailed. Fingering the *Sports Illustrated*, he asks if Dan plays any sports. Soccer and baseball, Joshua says. And hiking and rock-climbing. Tennis, Nathalie adds.

"I'm going to check out a few things," Sammons says when he comes down. "I'll be back in touch in an hour or so. If Dan shows up or you hear anything, call me."

Something about Sammons, a bedrock reliability, provides Nathalie a dollop of comfort. Beneath his placid surface she senses someone who likes to get to the bottom of things.

No sooner is he gone than Joshua is jumping up again; he wants to check the river bank, he wants to cross over the stream to Torvald's land on the other side, he wants to cruise in his car back and forth between their house and the main collection of two dozen dwellings in the center of The Hollow.

"Josh, please," Nathalie says, but her husband bursts out the door to the garage, leaving her alone.

Nathalie shivers; the house feels empty, as if marauders have swept through it, taking her most valuable possessions. She goes into the big living room, where she keeps her cello; the room

25

is rarely used, except for her practicing. The wide pine boards, stained blond, gleam up at her accusingly. It was only yesterday that she vacuumed the floor; everything is spotless and she longs for the disorder of an adolescent boy, leaving daubs of mud, discarded T-shirts redolent of perspiration, cookie crumbs and peach pits as he sweeps through the chambers of their lives.

She opens the closet and sees the instrument, its dark wood, the delicate work around the bridge, the strength of the strings. In this moment its beauty offends her and she can't bear to look at it, let alone take it in her hands. Nathalie remembers that she has orchestra rehearsals Monday and Tuesday, a concert at Lincoln Center Tuesday night. How can I pick up a cello bow? she thinks. Sammons' words of advice come to her—eat, sleep, practice the cello—and in her mind she angrily tells him off. Who do I call to let them know that I can't possibly play? she thinks. Who do I call to let them know that my life is on hold?

Chapter 3

Afterwards, in the days and weeks when it comes clear that Dan is not coming back, Joshua struggles to understand how. How could it have happened? How here in Smithfield? He and Nathalie had bought the house 11 years ago at a time when everything was going so well: she had her dream job, they had their son, Joshua had taken over the business from his dad and was making a big success of it. Nine summers here, idyllic times for Nathalie and Daniel, with Joshua coming up every weekend; then he met Bob Franco who had this idea for a resort called Tall Pines, and everything started to go bad.

Nathalie and Joshua met through a high school friend of Joshua's, Lisabeth Adams, a funny, overweight bass player who knew Nathalie from Curtis.

When Joshua saw Nathalie for the first time she was standing on the sidewalk across from Lincoln Center, in front of the record store she'd named for their rendezvous. She was inspecting the jewelry display of a street seller, holding a necklace festooned with silver-spangled triangles and with blue and rose stones. She hefted it in her hand with an appraising smile on her lips.

"Nathalie? I'm Joshua. Are you buying or selling?" Seeing her in the pale October sunshine, he was glad he'd called.

"Who wouldn't love to be buying?" she asked. "What do you think?"

"Nice. What's he asking?" Joshua pointed to the seller, a bespectacled black man in a purple and gold chenille shirt. "But wait," he said. "Wouldn't it get entangled in the cello?"

He liked her laugh, liked her slim frame and the chestnut hair with its wine-red highlights. She wore it evenly trimmed, just above her neck where it turned under to give the effect of a living pelt that moved when she moved, dipping and rising with the bend of her neck.

They strolled to the restaurant he'd picked out, a low-ceilinged place with live jazz. As they waited for their table, hearing the first notes of a Miles Davis arrangement, Joshua snuck a sideways look at her. Her slender, very straight carriage made her seem brave and alone. When they were each clutching a wine glass, Joshua asked about her family and she told him she had a sister, Barbara, who contracted leukemia at age 10—a treatable form, thankfully, but still an ordeal for child and parents.

"Either my parents were ignoring me to concentrate all their attentions on Barbara, or they were smothering me, the healthy child, with over-protective, loving anxiety. They tried to build this cocoon around me. I rebelled; I was determined to do what I wanted, not what they wanted for me. The cello was my idea, they wanted something feminine, like the flute. After-school swim team was my idea too. My mother said, you can't do both cello and swimming and I said, 'Oh yes I can.'"

Joshua took her to dinner once more, but the next time he called, the message on her machine said she'd be away for a few months. He forgot about her. One day in March the phone woke him up.

"Hi," a voice said. "It's . . ."

"Nathalie?" His clock said 6:30.

"Am I calling too early?" She'd flown in the day before from Copenhagen, where she'd spent four months playing with a chamber music group. She'd been up since four.

"It's the time change," she said. A pause. "I've been thinking about you."

The sound of her voice, warm, melodic but slightly melancholy, filled him with a longing to see her.

"Meet me for coffee?"

After they'd been going out a few months Joshua had invited Nathalie to spend a long weekend at an inn in Waitsfield, Vermont, a five-hour drive from Manhattan. As he drove, she sat looking straight ahead.

"Have you been there before, to this place?" she asked.

"To Waitsfield? Once," he replied. "Seven or eight years ago. A friend and I were hiking the Long Trail and we got off the trail in Waitsfield to have a meal and to get provisions. It was so pretty, I never got it out of my head."

She asked about the Long Trail and he told her how a couple of hikers had the idea in the early 1900s for a footpath that

28

would go from the Massachusetts border to Canada, 270 miles in all, how people began donating land and volunteers offered to make the trail. He told her how the Green Mountain Club maintained the trail, how there were shelters every six to ten miles, how much food you could carry and where you stopped to reprovision.

As he talked he stole a look at Nathalie to see if she was bored. The air-conditioning worked intermittently, the car was hot and Nathalie looked as if she wanted to be anywhere but in a dun-colored Plymouth Valiant with bad shocks, bouncing over twisting Route 89 en route to central Vermont.

"I spent a summer in Vermont," she said. "At Marlborough, at the music program there. I remember practicing the cello in a practice cabin in the woods with a cool breeze coming in through the little screen window and wasps buzzing around under the eaves. I always took it as a kind of commentary on my playing that I attracted those wasps. Saturday nights we'd have concerts and parents would come up, if it was your parents you'd be both pleased and embarrassed that there they were, sitting on those rough wooden benches surrounded by teenagers in their dirty T-shirts and shorts and bare feet."

"Why embarrassed?"

"You know, everything your parents do makes you ashamed at that age."

They rode in silence for 20 minutes, which stretched to 30 minutes, 40 minutes and finally he got off the highway to stop at a little crossroads village for gas. Nathalie disappeared into the bathroom for a long time and Joshua imagined she was crawling out through the window and escaping around the back, to a path that bordered the meadow where he knew, though he couldn't see them, that black and white cows lay with their legs bent under them, hugging the perimeter of shade along a fence and swatting uselessly at flies with their long tails. Perhaps she had made her way to a phone to figure how she could hitch a ride to the nearest Peter Pan bus stop and thence back to the city.

But no, here she was pulling open the passenger door of the Valiant; the door creaked from where the frame had been knocked off-center in a collision with a panel truck.

"Hi," she said, and gave him a brave smile and touched his hand with her fingers, and the next hour passed quickly. Then they'd arrived and she'd seen the slope of General Stark Mountain, its spine covered thickly with fir trees, plunging into the gorge of the Mad River. Nathalie hadn't known there were such mountains in the east. She was enchanted by the way the sun set on the ridge of Mount Ellen, like an exotic fruit, some combination of an orange and strawberry shooting rays of gold, crimson and yellow at them.

Early the next morning they walked behind the inn through the sweet-smelling grass toward a shimmering pool. Drops of heavy dew lay on every blade, like diadems etched by the morning sun. Joshua and Nathalie were alone in the inn, not a single other guest, no one but the sharp-eyed proprietress. It was mid-June and though the temperature that day would be in the high 70s, their skin tingled with the crispness of the air.

Standing by the clear water of the pool, Nathalie proclaimed, "It's so perfect. I'm going to go in." She walked to the deep end. She removed her cream-colored shorts and pink top, unfastened her bra and stepped out of her panties. She gave Joshua a smile that was shy and bold at the same time. Then she dove. Her body cut through the water cleanly; her intake of breath, a little pouf, was the only hint of how cold the water must have been. Joshua couldn't take his eyes off her white body with its dark nipples and well-formed breasts suspended over the pool just before the moment of impact.

She swam back and forth easily, 12, 15, 18 times. The pool barely rippled as she swam, her arms slipping in and out of the water like porpoises. Joshua watched dumbfounded at her athleticism. He had seen her play the cello on stage and had been struck by her presence, graceful and assured. Now she had the same transcendent quality to her, as if by dint of this activity that she loved, she'd left the earthly plane. Her skin glowed; her beauty was like a bell ringing, clear and insistent.

She came out of the water and he took off his T-shirt and dried her in it, rubbing softly and then faster until her flesh sparkled, as if bits of sunlight were embedded here and there, in her hair, in the hollow of her neck, in the soft curve of her back. Then she put on her shorts and top and they strolled hand in hand back to their room, actually an entire wing of the inn which they had to themselves, and they lay down on the bed, its sheets and pillows twisted this way and that as if they'd spent a night in hand to hand combat.

The night before they had been awkward and distant, alone together in a bed for the first time. They spent the night huddled stiffly against one another, more like stray dogs than lovers. When Joshua had tried to remove Nathalie's nightgown she stiffened. Not now, she said. Joshua's nerves were jangled from the long drive and the anticipation of the weekend, from wondering how he and Nathalie would get along, and when she all but pushed him away it was a confirmation of what a bad idea this must have been.

Now he lay on his back, his head against a pillow, his knees braced, his penis long and curved, and she lowered herself onto him, tickling his chest with her hair and teasing his lips, slipping him her tongue, softly, tantalizingly, while he kept his hands clasped behind his neck, refusing to caress her, as her body inched closer and closer to his.

That weekend established a rhythm to their sexuality together, a togetherness that alternated between carnal and tender, between exuberant and brooding. Nathalie set her alarm for six because she wanted to be showered and practicing by seven. But usually she would wake at 5:30 and use the extra half hour to ready her instrument and bow, and look over whatever music she needed for the day's rehearsals or teaching. She'd skim scores the way Joshua scanned the business pages, picking out passages that needed special attention.

Often he would wake with her and pull her to him, stroking her bare arms, her neck, her strong white legs; it became a game to try to get her to give up her schedule, to let him spread her thighs and bring her to climax there in the half-dawn of a winter's day.

"You're ruining me," she said. "My work ethic, my timing, my devotion to the music, they're all fleeing like birds going south."

It wasn't true; never had Joshua met a woman like Nathalie, so intent on her career, so in love with what she was doing. She'd already auditioned for at least half a dozen orchestra slots, traveling to Tampa, Phoenix, St. Louis, even to Göteborg, Sweden. She was a finalist three times but never caught the golden ring. Then, three months after the weekend with Joshua in Vermont, a miracle happened: a substitute slot opened up in New York—a cellist recuperating from hand surgery—and Nathalie won the competition for the eight-month position.

"I can't believe they're paying me to play with musicians of this caliber," she confided to Joshua. "If they only knew that I'd be willing to pay them."

"Don't let the union find out. They'll boot your sexy little ass right out of there."

The Philharmonic gig was extended four months, and when a full-time position as second cellist opened up she competed and won it. In December, just after she landed the job, they got married, a proper suburban wedding in Ridgefield, New Jersey. Light snow fell, dusting the bride's wedding dress with flakes of white powder as she dashed from the car.

Nathalie was 27 and playing with one of the world's top orchestras. But she never took her good fortune for granted; she seemed immune to the cynicism that leaked from the pores of her older, fellow musicians. The day Nathalie got the call about the full-time position she practiced an extra hour; she did the same the day after and the day after that.

"What are you doing?" Joshua asked. "Isn't four hours a day enough?"

No, she said. It's not. Her right arm grew so strong that she could sling a 40-pound bag of peat moss as if it were a box of Kleenex. By this time they'd bought their first house, a three-bedroom cape. Nathalie immersed herself in gardening books and then embarked on a spring-long project to uproot everything from the rear border of the tiny backyard and to replant it with viburnum, oak leaf hydrangeas, clusters of purple and pink bleeding heart. She was never happier than with her hands covered with dirt, bits of leaf and twig sticking to her arms and streaks of brown perspiration covering her neck and arms.

Joshua twitted her for adding another sweaty, thankless avocation to the one she already had—"at least they pay you for practicing," he said—but she said no, he had it all wrong.

"Gardening is so much easier, you stick the plants in the ground and they stay put, it's not a fight with your body to force your arms and shoulders to do things that God never intended them to do. Here you only have to find the right spot

and the right mix of water and sun and food and they thrive by
themselves."

She gave him a sly smile. "Not like children," she said. He
might have guessed that she had a timetable for that, too. By
December, a year after the wedding, she was pregnant.

Chapter 4

When Dan was born on the 16th of August during a sticky heat wave, everything changed again. Nathalie had endured an anxious pregnancy. What if they had a child destined to be ill like her sister Barbara or worse, a child crippled at birth by physical deformity or mental incapacity? She read books, haunted medical lectures at Mt. Sinai looking for evidence of this or that infant malady.

Not only was Dan perfect, but his birth was easy. Three hours of labor and out he popped. Edie, Joshua's mother, said, "You're made to have them. Two or three more will be no sweat."

He was an unusual baby. She saw her friends, fellow musicians, worn to a frazzle by the routine of nighttime feedings, up at one, nurse the baby, put him down, listen to him cry, up at 2:30, more feeding, more fretting, back to sleep at four, finally the baby is sleeping soundly but it's time for the mother to get up, to rehearse, to do the work of daytime.

After nine weeks Dan settled into his routine: he took his last feeding at 11:00, promptly fell asleep till 5:00, at which point he was up for the duration. At four months old he was goodnatured, curious about the world, responding to light and sound; Nathalie sang to him at all hours, played music, let him close thumb and middle fingers around an unsharpened pencil and smack it against the slats of the crib in a rudimentary but still recognizable drum roll.

When Daniel at 10 months began refusing to take a morning nap, Nathalie could often induce a state of wakeful bliss by sitting him in front of the speakers and putting on a Beethoven piano sonata.

By age 20 months he was already manipulating his own portable CD player, progressing from nursery rhymes to Burl Ives to her beloved Dvorak.

Dan got his first instrument at three, a simple wooden recorder; at five he was taking violin from a fellow Philharmonic musician and getting an introduction to cello from Nathalie. By the time he entered first grade Dan's worldliness surprised all who met him.

"Is that the business page you are looking at, grandpa?" Dan said one day to Nathalie's father, Dave, who was studying the stock tables. Soon the boy was asking for an explanation of the Dow Jones and figuring stock price percentage changes on the same scratch pad he used to calculate up-to-the-minute batting averages.

When he was in third grade Nathalie got a call from Dan's teacher, Mrs. Lynch. She didn't understand how Dan was getting the answers on her pop arithmetic quizzes. She was afraid that he was stealing glances at the paper of Bettina Caruso, who sat next to him; the two of them were first and second in the class.

"Are you saying that my son is cheating?"

"No, Mrs. Sandler, but where is his scratch work? Math is a series of steps—you do the steps, you get the answer. I need to see his steps."

Nathalie asked Dan about it and he said, "I don't need to put down all those steps. I get the answers in my head."

Nathalie and Dan and Mrs. Lynch sat down together to talk about math. "Dan, can you show Mrs. Lynch how you get the answers without writing anything down?" his mother asked.

Dan shrugged. Give me a problem, he said. Mrs. Lynch gave him one and then another, and another and another. Dan did all four problems in his head; not a single one took him longer than three seconds.

"All right," said Mrs. Lynch. "All right. We're going to have to see if we can find something that challenges Dan." She arranged for a math resource specialist to give Dan two hours a week of private instruction. Mrs. Lynch divided her own class into three groups and used Dan as a tutor, rotating him between the medium and slow kids.

He kept up the violin and cello until age 10. Then he asked his mother, "Am I ever going to be as good as you?"

"What a question! You're only 10. You've got a long way to go."

"Yeah, but when you were 10, were you better than I am?"

"Maybe I was," Nathalie said; she could never hide the truth from him. "But you're learning a foundation, a set of skills, a way of listening. Whether you continue in music or not, those skills will be a part of you."

The fact that he could never play as well as his mother settled it for him. He didn't mind putting in a maximum effort if there was a chance for a maximum return—a way of calculating that he inherited from Joshua. Besides, although Dan loved all music from rock to classical to jazz, performing left him cold. In place of the music lessons he took up track and cross country in junior high; went on a modified Outward Bound at age 12, climbing mountains and surviving in the Anza Borrego desert with water and a compass. He was getting taller and stronger, his summer tan lasting well into October.

Nathalie could see the changes in him. Previously he would argue with her when she forbade him to do something. Now, he had a tendency to act without asking.

The incident that brought this home vividly occurred in the seventh grade; it was the fall semester, about 10 weeks after Dan's 12th birthday.

Dan had brought home one of those school forms that parents must sign, a permission slip for a trip to the Museum of Natural History in Manhattan. Nathalie had been off early that morning, a Monday, to give a lesson at the conservatory. Her car was parked in front, the cello strapped in its case; the motor was running and she'd come back in to get some sheet music as Dan waved the permission form at her. "Have your father sign it," she said and dashed for the car.

Five minutes later Joshua left to get his train. As he went out the door he shouted up to Dan, who was on the second floor, "Bye, Dan, lock up, put the alarm on." By the time Dan called, Dad, Dad I need you to sign something, Joshua was around the corner, fast-walking the nine blocks to the station.

He always traveled at that speed, especially on a Monday—he'd burst into the tiny office on Madison near Grand Central, wave to Gert, who was usually on the phone, and grab the lists of auctions that had come in from a fax service they subscribed to. The business was simple: buying, then reselling used office furniture to dealers in the city, Westchester, Long Island, Jersey and Connecticut. In fact, Joshua almost never bought anything without having already sold it to these customers, pocketing 10% of the selling price as his commission. Joshua would go as far afield as Rochester or Baltimore or Pittsburgh, but he preferred not to travel more than three hours by car; that way he could go and come back in a day, hating to stay in dreary low-ceilinged motel rooms or in aging downtown hotels.

In the days when his father was alive, Max had managed three-quarters of an acre of desks and chairs from the cement-floor warehouse on Third Avenue in Mt. Vernon, in the midst of an area where drugs were retailed like ice cream. Max, a bear of a man with a barrel belly and arms and legs to match, had had a heart attack after lifting a desk by himself and Joshua and Joshua's mother had put their foot down, no more lugging desks and file cabinets, no more carrying a handgun in his briefcase when he walked to the local branch of Chase Manhattan to deposit a couple of thousand dollars from the day's sale. We'll just broker the stuff, Dad, no inventory, no retail space, no druggies looking to rob you on your way home, Joshua explained.

An old line office supply store, all wood and steel and plastic, got transformed under Joshua's astute management into an information business, with faxes, computer accounting, e-mail. The fat retail markups were gone but so were the inventory, the trips to the bank lock-box and best of all, the warehouse.

Along the way he got to know a few contractors and developers and soon was participating in their deals, as well as buying property on his own in Westchester. He had an eye for how to turn the neglected into the sought-after. Real estate development brought him into contact with the local elected officials; he found himself in front of the mike at public hearings. The local Democrats even talked to him about a run for county legislature but Natalie hated the idea. She wanted their privacy and reluctantly Joshua put the idea on hold.

That night at supper Nathalie turned to Dan to ask how the trip had gone.

"Fine, the dinosaurs were really cool."

"Dad signed the permission slip okay?"

No answer.

"Dan? What permission slip?" Joshua said.

"The one they gave us at school."

"If mom didn't sign it, how did it get signed?"

A long pause and then Dan said in an aggrieved voice, "I had to sign your name."

A few days later, Joshua thought about what he'd done at that moment and concluded that he had over-reacted. Severely over-reacted. But at the moment, stunned by what he'd heard, he stepped to within an arm's length of the boy. And Dan, sensing that his father was about to erupt, flinched, turning his head slightly and raising his left hand as if to protect himself. Joshua's arm went out, seizing his son by the left shoulder.

"Why? Why did you do that?"

"Because I wanted to go, and because you didn't hear me calling to you, you left before I could bring the permission slip down. Mrs. Tomashefsky has a fit if we don't bring those back—she won't let us go. Kids have to sit in Mr. Ruffino's office all day when their class is on a trip and they don't have permission. It's boring."

Everything Dan said at that moment grated on Joshua's nerves, the mealy-mouthed explanation, the way the boy looked to one side and refused to face him head-on.

"What the hell does that have to do with anything? Because of the consequences you do something that's just plain wrong—just wrong on all counts? You could have asked Mrs. Tomashefsky to call at work and I'd have given permission on the phone, or faxed her a letter of permission to the school."

"They don't do that . . ."

"Don't tell me what they do or don't do," Joshua said sharply. "What you don't do, ever again, is forge my name on a piece of paper. And to make sure you learn your lesson, you're grounded for the next week. No going out of the house to visit friends, no friends coming over, no TV."

When Joshua thinks about that night, it's as if he were standing in a cold white fog, the kind that seeps under your mackinaw to wrap itself around flesh and bones. He doesn't regret the punishment he meted out, but he would give anything to take back the words, and not just the words, the tone of voice, the anger, the self-righteousness.

The awkwardness between him and his son lasted a few days and then he and Dan were on good terms again.

The real fight they'd had came a few weeks later, when Dan brought home his final report card with the B in Social Studies, even though he'd been pulling an A all the way through the term. Dan confessed to having neglected to do a homework assignment the next to last week of class. What's more, he'd been late in turning in a research paper to his Social Studies teacher and then failed to take advantage of the opportunity to revise the paper and thereby earn an improved grade. He'd settled for a B on the paper, even though other kids were, by the alchemy of extra effort, turning B's into A's.

Under Joshua's questioning, Dan told this story in an exasperating way, dodging up one conversational alley and down another, never moving in a straight line and offering up one after another of the "You know, I mean" phrases that his father couldn't stand. Afterwards Joshua and Nathalie had had words about the confrontation.

"I don't give a damn about his getting a B if that's the best he's capable of," Joshua said. "What I object to is his getting a B out of laziness or sloppiness—that's inexcusable."

Nathalie protested that he was being too harsh but Joshua wouldn't be swayed. So he'd had an argument with Dan, then an argument with Nathalie, then a second argument with Dan. At that point, Dan, sullen, determinedly uncommunicative, had lashed out.

"I can't be perfect just because you want me to be," he yelled at Joshua. "I'm not perfect. I just have to be me."

Looking at Dan at that moment, Joshua had been so aware of him as a person in his own right and not just as their son; he'd looked at his thickening lower lip, at the way the light brown hair at the front of his head stood straight up, refusing to be tamed. He'd trembled a bit to hear Dan's voice, altering day by day as puberty took hold, begin to croak from the effort to assert himself.

When he thinks of his missing son now, the image of this older, more assertive boy superimposes itself on the picture of Dan's baby face, until, by a flux of will, eyes shut and temples clenched, he forces the newer image to dissolve and brings back the Dan of memory and myth, the Dan who at six years old had greeted life every day with a grin as bright as an egg yolk.

Chapter 5

Joshua can't get out of his head the feeling that all the trouble started with Bob Franco and Tall Pines—that there's some connection to Dan, if he can only figure out what it is.

Franco is a songwriting genius who's knocking out one award-winning film score after another. He went to college in Collegeville and fell in love with the area, so much so that four years ago he bought a rambling white Victorian where a former U.S. senator once rocked on the porch. Then came his idea—more than an idea, an obsession, really—to build a resort on 220 acres straddling Smithfield and Northway.

Franco's lawyer, Len Stern, told Carl Puckett what a good deal this development would be for the town. "After all," said Stern, "he's won two Oscars and he could invest his money anywhere in the world but he wants to invest it in Smithfield."

Twice married, Franco now lives alone, though various female and male friends, including a lean young actor, have shared his Santa Monica beach house for months on end.

"I read the papers," Puckett said. "I know all about him."

Puckett knew that real estate investment meant more tax revenues, but there was a negative: new people coming to Smithfield, the sort of people who are up and down the streets of Collegeville, with its crafts fairs, its health food stores, its bookshops, its three Japanese restaurants. Those same people might descend on Smithfield if the resort is built.

It's Len Stern who introduces Joshua to Franco. It turns out they both went to Bronx High School of Science, where Franco spent more time in jazz band rehearsals than in the lab. "I remember you up on stage," Joshua says. "Long hair, quick hands on the piano."

"At least I still have the quick hands," laughs Franco, his head closen-shaven and nearly bald. After Bronx Science and college, he landed in LA, playing clubs and writing songs. There he met Stuart Lee, a promoter who got him a recording deal and later, a contract to write a film score.

Franco, seeking partners, takes Joshua and five other potential investors to see 220 acres of woodland and pasture on a westward-facing ridge opposite Miller's Needle, a 2200-foot mountain. The property has most recently been a camp. A ramshackle building houses the camp administration and the remnants of the kind of store you come across in Appalachia: torn wrappers, traces of potato chip dust and a meandering, malodorous trail of squirrel droppings.

After the camp's regular six-week session the camp owners used to rent out the cabins to young men in their 20s who came to fish the seven-acre lake, toting a couple of days' bait and a month's worth of beer. Franco ushers his group into one of the cabins, painted a fading white and littered with crushed beer cans and empty whiskey bottles. The window is broken and on this late October day, the air inside feels a lot colder than the outside temperature of 42 degrees.

"Jeez, what a shithole this place is," says one potential backer, a Collegeville restaurant owner.

Now, outside the main lodge, Franco contrasts the sorry state of the camp with his vision of Tall Pines. He's a tough guy who's climbed Denali, Kilimanjaro, the Matterhorn; he never quits. Despite the chill, Franco wears lightweight blue jogging pants and an orange sweatshirt with a pull string at the neck; the breeze tugs at his Red Sox cap.

"Look at the hills, the beauty of the dark green pines. Imagine a January day, cold and still, sunlight glinting off those branches, now covered with snow from an overnight fall. White powder everywhere. A brand new lodge with stone fireplace big enough to stand in. Your own cabin, done in red cedar, its fireplace stacked and ready; all you need do is touch the match."

As Franco paints his word pictures, Joshua is struck by the suddenness of change, how it disrupts old behaviors and spawns new ones. These hills with their mass of pine trees, capped by the iron gray sky of late autumn used to be where rowdy young men drank beer by the case. Where deer hunters stalked their prey the first week in December, when an inch of new snow covers the ground and the air is so cold you can cut it and stack it like wood. Can it now be a refuge of wholesome exercise and pampering, with cross-country skiing, a spa, and a list of fine wines? It's a transformation no one could have foreseen, but apparently Franco has a head for business—no surprise in Hollywood, where entertainers sound like businessmen and businessmen masquerade as artists. Cross-country skiing is booming and this spot averages 77 inches of snow each winter. Yes, Joshua nods, yes, this could work.

Still, he warns Franco of the difficulties he faces in getting approval from the town.

"With all the money this will mean to the town? Money they don't have to do a thing for?"

It's not just about money, Joshua says, as he gives Franco example after example. Why did they permit Joe Burnham to keep disassembled tractor-trailers parked in his front yard like so many pieces of artillery? Or the Smithfield Garage to operate a smelly oil change pit 10 feet from the grassy green where the war memorial stood? Why did they harass poor Jack Cerniak, who was trying to expand his B&B on Main Street but had a run-in with the building inspector over what kind of smoke detectors to install?

"Don't look for these people to be rational," he warns. "They'll stall you to death."

Franco submits his proposal in March. One delay follows another, until finally at its October meeting the board takes up the project. During the meeting Joshua tries to keep a straight face each time Puckett refers to Franco as "the gentleman from Collegeville"; he might as well be describing a Noel Coward dandy in tux and black tie, escorting the ladies to supper.

The vice chairman of the Selectmen is Mary Shaw of the Smithfield Shaws, who are sensible and business-minded, unlike the Northway Shaws, who are reckless and spendthrift. Albert Sims, Phil Wright and Tony McMartin round out the Board of Selectmen.

Mary trained as a bookkeeper. "Excuse me, would you mind going over that one more time," she says, pushing the glasses up over her tight steel and wheat-colored curls.

When Franco tells how guests at the resort will do their shopping in Smithfield, Mary hoots, "Shopping? A can of soda pop at the general store, some busted old table at Granny's Antiques?" It falls to McMartin to ask the technical questions:

42

the square footage of the lodge, the roof pitch, the setbacks from the road. McMartin is knowledgeable, a freckled Boston Irishman, a builder who inherited property in Smithfield and wound up moving his family there.

"Where will the people come from for this inn?" Puckett demands. "From New York?" As he says this his eyes swivel among the spectators before lighting on Joshua, his nemesis.

"Wherever they're coming from we're happy to have them," Franco responds.

"Any foreigners?" Puckett asks. "You know, Germans, Italians. Japanese?"

"What are you afraid of, Carl, Pearl Harbor here in Smithfield?" asks Albert Sims. A long, grizzled, ageless fellow, he looks as if he'd been squeezed through a tube, a process that has left the gray hairs on his neck turned up in a curl. Sims lives alone in a farmhouse up the road. His first wife ran away to California; he buried a second one 11 years ago. The tanned, webbed skin on the back of his hands is like paper that has been folded and refolded.

"Pearl Harbor?" Franco is taken aback.

"You didn't know that Albert here is a Navy vet? Stationed at Pearl in 1941?"

Mary Shaw is grinning at him. Franco, prepared to be grilled about parking, traffic flow and restaurant closing times, is suddenly being given a history lesson. He recovers his poise. "You must have been a brave man, Mr. Sims."

Albert laughs, a maniacal laugh. "Brave? I was so scared I crapped in my pants."

Franco totes up the benefits to Smithfield: more tax revenues, more local business, a beautiful resort in place of an eyesore. "One improvement project stimulates others," he says.

"Oh, so we need improvement? You fellows from Collegeville or Boston or wherever you're from are going to improve and beautify our town, is that it?"

"Since when is making things look better something to apologize for?"

"Yeah, well," Puckett says. "Any more questions? Phil?" Phil Wright hasn't said a word. His droopy eyebrows tell everything about him.

After Puckett opens the floor to public comments—four speakers in favor of the project, four against—Wright finally

43

opens his mouth. He moves to defer a vote until after the January Town Meeting, at which residents eat homemade donuts, vote on the town budget and generally sound off.

Franco and Stern fume at yet another three-month delay but the motion passes.

Franco has spent $65,000 on studies and consultants and is running out of patience. He gets his buddy Anne Curtis, the local state senator, to devote half a day to going up and down Main Street, ostensibly soliciting votes for her third re-election campaign. At each house she asks, "What do you think of this idea for this Tall Pines resort? You know, a clean, modern place with beautiful cross-country trails, instead of that dump where those guys gather every August to drink and make noise?"

She brings along Smiling Bill Tuohy, the Republican committeeman for Smithfield. At each stop Tuohy releases one of his famous tight-ass smiles, as if paying extra for each millimeter that the corners of his mouth turn up from horizontal. When the residents ask Tuohy for his opinion of Tall Pines, he says, "Can't hurt. Might help."

Two days before the Town Meeting on January 11th, Joshua gets a call from Franco.

"I'm going to fax you something they're circulating in Smithfield."

It's a flyer that was delivered to every mail box in town. "Stop the invasion of Smithfield," it reads. "Stop Tall Pines." It goes on to rant about out-of-towners with different lifestyles. "Come to the Town Meeting and make your voice heard," it concludes. "This is our town and we can keep it that way."

Joshua thinks of the day, 15 months ago, when they stood shivering in the cabin with the crushed beer cans, looking up at the stands of massed pines set against the rolling hills.

"Bob, we better take this seriously."

Joshua brings Dan with him to the town meeting—an education in old-fashioned New England democracy, he calls it. The meeting reveals plenty of support for Tall Pines, but also a vocal, if beleaguered, opposition. One of the speakers against the project was Johnny Lambert, who maintains the town machinery and does odd jobs for Puckett.

44

Another opponent, Tom Robinson, makes a living cutting, splitting and selling wood, tending the town cemetery and plowing town roads in winter. He lives up in the hills in a log home; he is a striking man, with arms as long as spears and black eyes that glow even in a darkened room. "Up there is some of the best deer hunting in the state," Robinson told the town meeting. "When the Watts family owned it they let us hunt, provided we respected the land. It's been that way long as anyone can remember. Seems like it ought to stay that way."

As Robinson spoke, Joshua scanned the crowd at the town meeting, recognizing many faces. About a dozen rows back, he noticed a flash of shiny black hair, twisted into a braid: a woman in a red shirt leaning forward to hear Robinson, the top button open to reveal a long slash of white neck. When she finally caught him staring, he reddened.

Later, she rose to say a few words in a low, cadenced voice. "Whatever we do, let's protect and nurture the land," she said. "Because once we spoil it we can never restore it."

A week later the Selectmen voted 5-0 to approve the project. Carl Puckett went along reluctantly when Tony McMartin, Marie Shaw and Albert Sims all came out in favor; of course Phil Wright followed Puckett.

Then, just before the March groundbreaking, Franco told Joshua about a late-night call: a harsh voice telling him, "We don't want your goddam resort messing up the land."

"Who's this?" Franco had asked.

"You heard me, we don't want your goddam resort. Just because you have a big fat checkbook, don't think you can buy up all the land and change the way things are." The man spoke in the flat twang of the western Massachusetts hill towns, all the shadings muted.

Franco is built like a bouncer; his large, shiny head and prominent knuckles accentuate the impression that you don't want to mess with him. He asked the caller for his name.

"Never mind about my name. All you need to know is we don't want you around here."

At Anne Curtis's request, the head of the state police for western Massachusetts, Charlie Burns, sends a trooper by to check on the site a couple of times a week. Franco, back from three weeks in Hollywood editing a film score, throws himself into the completion of Tall Pines. These dank April mornings are foggy, with spitting rain and blowing; nevertheless, by 7:00 A.M. he is walking the site in his muddy work boots, telling the foreman just how he wants things.

The acts of sabotage are random, minor, and occur several weeks apart. In the center of the macadam parking lot with its neatly painted yellow lines, someone has wielded a pickaxe to gouge out three irregularly shaped holes, each about the width of a large pie plate. Piles of two by fours disappear. Two back windows are smashed. Then, after the front door—a massive, weathered piece of oak—is installed, they find in crude letters across its lower panel a single word in orange paint: "Soon."

Franco takes to riding out to Tall Pines on the long June evenings, when daylight seems to stretch forever. Once or twice Joshua joins him there. They reach the site as the sun hangs level with the summit of Miller's Needle. Security is a lone night guard with a glass right eye. Franco threads his way between skids of lumber, roofing shingles and cinder blocks, skirting the dark woods where ski trails will be carved. The fading sun diffuses bands of pink through the living green fabric of maple, beech, oak and ash leaves. A breeze twists the high clouds this way and that as evening ebbs into night.

Sometimes in the car on the way back, Franco takes a call from Stuart Lee in LA, where the studios are pestering him and Franco for new scores, new collaborations, new ideas. Just a week ago, a producer dangled before Franco the opportunity to get in on a new musical in New York, both as investor and songwriter but Franco shilly-shallied.

"Come on, bubby," Stuart pleads, anxious to get Franco's head pointed once again in the direction of work, anxious for his 10 percent. "These chances don't come along that often. You've done film, you've done studio work, now Broadway is calling. You've got to do this."

"The timing isn't right."

"The timing isn't right? Who are you, Brando or Streisand? The timing is the timing. Either grab it or it's gone."

"I've just got to be here the next few months to finish Tall Pines."

"Tall Pines," Stuart snorts. "Tall pipedream, if you ask me. For Christ sake, bubby, this Tall Pines is draining all your creative juices. There's nothing left for the music."

He's right, Franco thinks; Tall Pines has seized his consciousness, leaving little energy for anything else. But he always finishes what he starts; threats or no threats he will see this through.

By the end of the third week of July, the main lodge is complete: 32 sleeping rooms, a restaurant with seating for 120, a bar with its long cherry countertop. The night before they are to hold a party to celebrate, Franco gets the second call.

"Don't think we've accepted your stupid resort. Just because you've got a roof over it doesn't mean a thing. The right mixture and that roof is blown to smithereens."

Franco has to stop himself from shaking. "What's your name?" he tries.

"No questions. I'm telling you, your fucking resort will never open its doors."

The next day at the 1:00 P.M. opening ceremony, Anne Curtis says a few words about how lucky Massachusetts and Smithfield are to have visionaries like Bob Franco. Carl Puckett speaks. "Congratulations," he says with a nod toward Franco. "We've gotten along in Smithfield for a couple of hundred years without resorts, but I suppose there's a first time for everything."

The crowd numbers two dozen: Joshua, Nathalie, other investors, the architect, the banker, Rosa Puckett, two more Selectmen. At the buffet lunch, Franco pops a champagne cork and fills the plastic cups. The date is July 10, four and a half weeks before Dan disappears.

That night Franco comes home to Collegeville to find that intruders have poisoned Arthur, his five-year-old brown Lab.

Joshua is stunned when he hears the news. "Your dog Arthur? Dead? Where? Where did you find him?"

"In the little pantry where we keep his water and food bowls. His tongue was stretched out toward the water bowl, as if he was desperate to flush his system of the poison." The few dried scraps of meat that were caked to the side of the food bowl tested positive for cyanide.

Nathalie, just coming downstairs as he hangs up, asks who was on the phone. Before he can answer, Dan walks in, his face

47

a fiery red from playing soccer at the field behind the school in Smithfield. In that moment Joshua decides to keep the news from Nathalie and Dan.

"Franco," he says when she asks. "Nothing much, just an update on the construction."

Joshua gives Tall Pines a wide berth for a while. He's taking a week's vacation up here and pares his daily routine to the essentials: early morning jogging; trimming dead branches from the trees along the river bank; tennis every other day with Len Stern, at Albie Moreau's old court high in the hills. And he reads—at the kitchen table, on his stomach in the shade between the maples. He's engrossed in *How Green Was My Valley*, haunted by the ominous slag heap growing taller and taller until it mars the beauty of the Welsh valley.

Nathalie practices three hours a day; tends her flowers; bakes. Dan keeps out of their way. He'd kicked and sulked and protested about spending any time in The Hollow this summer. No way, he'd said, it's boring. But the first three weeks of July they sent him off on a hiking and biking trip in Colorado and on his return—taller, sun-blackened, mellow—he agreed, grudgingly, to come for a month. Joshua sees him fly by on the bike with one or another of the boys; after supper he disappears until the fireflies are darting here and there in the moist darkness.

Joshua asks where the kids go every night.

"Oh, they've got some hideout on the state land off the Northway Road, a place with benches and stones for a campfire." Nathalie pauses. "He doesn't drink or smoke, if that's what you're worried about. He's always home by 9:30, which is the deal we made."

Four days go by without any word from Franco, but Nathalie is curious about the progress at Tall Pines and finally they pay a visit. The late afternoon sun is filtering through the canopy of tall oaks and beech trees, loosing its yellow warmth on the earth. Nathalie, in jeans and soft lemon shirt, her hair falling easily to her neck, spots Franco coming out of the construction office.

"Schedules, schedules," he says, making a joke of the stress that is scored on his face.

"What is it, Bob? There's something, isn't there?"

48

"Don't you know?" he says, before he can be warned off by the frantic up and down movement of Joshua's eyebrows. "About Arthur?"

"Nathalie," Joshua says.

"Damn, I'm sorry. I figured she knew."

"Knew what?"

"Bob's Lab, Arthur. He was poisoned," Joshua says, surprised at how calm she is.

"Oh, I knew there was something, the way you talked to me." And she plays back their conversation that hot day in the kitchen: her question, his pause, Dan's entry, and then, his lame explanation: Nothing much, just an update on the construction.

Joshua can never get used to the way she recalls every syllable, every word. When she is performing, the music on the stand is a prop; she quickly knows it all by heart.

"I knew there was something," she says. "I never figured it could be this."

Chapter 6

Usually it's only two of them, Dan and Bobby or Dan and Sam. That's what Nathalie thinks when she sees the three of them together two weeks before Dan disappears. One minute they're on their bikes, hair wet from a swim at The Shadows and the next, as she watches from the dining room, they've thrown the bikes down on the lawn and are clambering down the steps to the sculpted rock overlooking the river.

Bobby Dawes is a lusty 16 going on 20. He smokes. Drinks. Sneaks out in his stepfather's pickup for unauthorized joy rides on the back roads. In the past year, he boasts, he's had sex with the girls' gym teacher in the high school (undoubtedly a lie) and with the bleached blond who waits tables in the Taco Bell in the mall in Hartsfield (probably true), a 19-year-old who's already had one abortion.

Sam Bonacio is 15, a sophomore. Everything about him is dark, tightly wound. His eyes are a deep chocolate, his hair a thatch of black. Even with the other kids he rarely talks. Nathalie is tuned in to Sam, wondering what family urges will finally win out in him: the don't-ever-give-me-more-than-one-thing-to-think-about mindset of his uncommunicative father, or the can-do spirit of his sociable mother. The more she sees of the boy, the more she wonders if someday the internal fires will burst forth, setting off explosions.

At The Shadows the three boys skip stones, lie on their backs and squint at the speckled trout wheeling and darting in the deeper pools, then slide down smooth rocks into the swirl and eddy of the current. After a time it is Sam who speaks.

"Know what? Across the river here if you go right and straight up you get to a spot high up the hill, a nice quiet spot. It's all Torvald's land."

Edward Torvald, a secretive man who lives up the road in Northway, just over the line from Smithfield, owns several hundred acres all along 33A and dozens more acres fronting on Route 57 where it starts the long climb from The Hollow to the heights of Cliffmont, one of the highest towns in Massachusetts, elevation 2398.

"So?" Bobby Dawes asks.

"So nothing. It's a nice spot. And from there if you come straight down, you join up with the river right across from his house." Sam nods in the direction of Dan. The land across the river from the Sandlers is rocky, clayey hillside and ravine with a mixture of hardwood, pine and spruce.

Sam leads the way, wading across the stream, holding a sneaker in each hand, and then through the tangle of swamp grass in the marshy area on the other side of the river. Bobby curses as the brambles catch his bare, muscled arms. All three boys put their sneakers back on and begin to climb.

With Sam ahead of them, Dan, who is fleet and slim, teases Bobby to go faster as they hike up the ravines and through the tangled stands of pine and beech and maple and spruce. In five minutes the road, 33A, is completely hidden from view by the forest. The wooded hillside is a world onto itself, full of wild, prickly vines that grasp at clothing and fallen trees whose crumbling stumps now succor ants and chipmunks. They go higher and higher, Sam picking a path by habit and instinct.

All of a sudden there it is, a perfect rectangle of blue-green grass, as if someone had seeded, weeded and watered this miniature garden of Eden in the midst of the forest. Sam lets out his tentative smile, happy to be here, upset that he's given away his secret. Dan sinks down on the long grass, clasps his hands around the front of his knees, the fingers of one hand seizing the wrist of the other.

Bobby fishes his pack of Marlboros out of his tight jeans. He strikes a match off the brass zipper, lights up, inhales deeply.

"Here, pricks, have a butt."

Sam lights one of the cigarettes and takes a puff and then another. Daniel, shaking his head, says, "Those things give you cancer."

"Shit," Bobby says. "What are you, a fucking pussy? A 14-year-old kid scared of cancer? What do you know about it?"

"My great-grandfather, my mother's granddad, was a big smoker. He died of lung cancer. It was six or seven years ago. He was 77." Dan remembers a nattily dressed man with sagging pockets of flesh beneath his large blue eyes. Recalls how he would joke with waiters and waitresses, the way he would take a playbill from the usher in a Broadway theater and hold it

51

between his long fingers as if it were a rare object, like a thousand dollar bill. His musical ability: he played piano, violin, saxophone, had a deep bass voice, had toured with roadhouse bands as a teenager, later wrote radio jingles and popular tunes.

"Yeah? My grandfather drank himself to death. Jeez, I don't know how old he was, not that old. He was an airplane gunner in the Second World War, got shot down over France, got rescued by the frogs."

"Frogs?"

"You know, the Frenchies, the frogs. I saw a picture of what he looked like when he got back to England. Skinny as a piece of wire."

"Did he live near you?"

"He and grandma lived with us, in the back room. When he was drinking that room didn't smell too good. He'd throw up and grandma would wipe him off and put him to bed."

If Sam has any stories about departed relatives he keeps them to himself. He puffs away at the cigarette Bobby has offered. Sam takes no pleasure in it, but he's a kid who never shrinks from a challenge.

Bobby again appeals to Dan. "Come on, you want a weed?"

"Naaah," Dan says. And when Bobby and Sam finish dragging on their Marlboros and Dan has had his fill of the blue sky up above the canopy of the trees that border the natural meadow like an elaborate stockade planted from the heavens, Dan turns to the other two and says, "Let's go."

Before they can answer, Dan is on his feet and darting over the rocks, through the gate in the trees and over the many rivulets and brooks that seep out of the spongy undergrowth. Dan is nimble—he's a soccer player, midfield, a tireless runner. Bobby is bigger but slower. Once he nearly pitches forward as his foot catches an exposed root; one knee brushes against a tree trunk, causing another tear in his already frayed and splintering jeans. Sam keeps at Dan's shoulder until the slice of silver-gray river appears below. Then he pulls ahead and is easily first, through the swamp grass and across to the big rock.

Out of the woods the air is still, hot, and they are soon in the water, frolicking like young seals. After a while they hop on the bikes and peddle back to The Hollow. Here, down the steps from the Sandlers, the stream is much shallower. They sun themselves on the broad rocks on the far side of the riverbank just across from the Sandler property.

Nathalie comes to the top of the wooden steps.

"You boys decent?" She catches a glimpse of bare shoulders and chests.

"Just a minute," Dan calls back. They pull underwear and jeans over moist flesh.

"What is it, mom?"

"I don't suppose you want any, but I'm making cookies."

In a few minutes they are sitting on the front step, which is fashioned from a giant millstone. In the late 1800s, a sawmill in The Hollow had employed more than 300 workers. Back then, the owners of the house had tacked on a wing and turned it into a boarding house. Though the Sandlers are gradually refurbishing it, parts of the wing are showing their age; in one of the tiny bedrooms upstairs you can see bare lath poking through gaps in the plaster. The round stone in front of the house, below the wide first step, came from the mill. An eight-foot high dam across the river had provided the power to turn the machines.

Nathalie brings the boys iced tea and sugar cookies.

"Thanks Mrs. Sandler." Sam lowers his eyes, shy in her presence. Bobby Dawes looks at her in a way that makes her uncomfortable. In the kitchen she checks to see that her blouse is tucked into her shorts, that the straps of her bra are not showing. But she refuses to be intimidated by him, so she finds a reason to come back out.

"Anybody want to stay for supper?"

Sam says he can't.

Bobby says he has to get home to help his mom with some chores. "If my stepdad comes home and they're not done I'll catch hell." His stepfather, Tim Bartlett, has large, calloused hands, toughened from factory work and from chopping and splitting the wood they burn in the winter. He never raises his hand to Bobby unless he means to hit him, and when he does the boy can feel it for days. Again Bobby gives Nathalie a conspiratorial smile, one knowing adult to another.

"I'd advise you to do what your father wants," she says dryly.

The three boys get out the badminton rackets, whacking the birdie back and forth for half an hour, with cries of, "It's out,

53

my point" and "No, it's not, you blind mother," floating on the warm afternoon air.

The net rises up in the side yard where the grass is going golden green as the sun edges farther west, its rays beginning to light the far side of the maples. When next Nathalie comes out, Bobby and Sam have vanished. Dan is lying on his back near one of the maples. He is reading one of C.S. Forester's Horatio Hornblower novels as he slowly chews a long piece of succulent grass.

"Is Bobby gone?" Nathalie flops down in the grass and places her hand on Daniel's shin, which feels hot and sweaty from the exercise.

"Yeah."

"Sam, too?"

"Yeah."

"What do you think of him? Of Bobby?"

"He's okay." Dan laughs. "He tries hard to be grown up."

"Something about him . . ." The sentence hangs there, unfinished.

"Yeah, he thinks he's real tough." He gives her a look that says, it's okay, I can handle it.

Nathalie remembers the conversation the morning after Dan disappears, as she sits paralyzed at the breakfast table while Joshua handles the phones and dashes to the front door each time a car goes by. It was a summer day like any other in The Hollow, one of those weeks when she and Dan were alone in the country, and Joshua was working in the city, sleeping in Mamaroneck. And yet the picture of the three boys with their wet hair and their bikes on the lawn sticks in her mind.

That morning Sammons asks her about the kids that Dan hangs out with.

"Sam Bonacio and Bobby Dawes," she answers. "A couple of girls who live up the Northway Road—Melanie, Melanie Roberts, and a girl named Kristen."

Sammons knows them all. "I'll start with the boys," he says. "Maybe one of them has a clue."

Chapter 7

The night Daniel disappears they make a flurry of calls, to Joshua's mother, to Nathalie's parents, to Joshua's office manager, Gert, to Nathalie's friend and mentor at the Philharmonic, who happens to be first violinist and concert master.

"Nathalie, don't even think about those things now," he says—rehearsals, concerts. "Do what you have to do there. We'll talk in a day or two, hopefully your son will be back safe by then."

Before she can hang up Joshua is snatching the phone from her hands to make one more call to Sammons. The police chief had promised to alert the state police if Dan didn't return and now he assures Joshua that he has done so.

"If I have any word I'll be in touch, no matter what the hour."

"No matter what the hour," Joshua repeats. Now, in the upstairs bedroom with the soft bedside lamp, he and Nathalie look at one another across the shadows. An old house like this groans and creaks; downstairs the refrigerator strains, its compressor starting, then stopping. They try to go to bed, but to climb into the sheets knowing that Dan is not sleeping in his monk's cell of a bedroom around the corner from their room is intolerable.

Every half hour Nathalie nudges Joshua. "Did you hear something? Is that a noise at the door?" She wears the short pink nightgown, a diaphanous affair through which he can see her rounded shoulders, the white of her neck.

Joshua, clear-eyed, stares at the ceiling, perfecting his knowledge of it, searching out its cracks, his eyes tracing its uneven westward slope. A series of horrible pictures flashes through his mind: shadowy men from a van, swooping onto the lawn to snatch up Dan. An accident in the river that knocks Dan unconscious, to be swept through the rocks to the deeper water on the other side of the bridge. A beer-crazed motorist, not five years older than Dan, careening down 33A in a souped-up Buick at midday, missing the curve, smashing into the boy and mangling his body.

All these scenes are absurd, he knows, but no more absurd than the fact that their son is gone. By the dim glow of moonlight filtered across the ancient glass pane, Joshua rolls his eyes this way and that. When Nathalie starts and asks did he hear this, did he hear that, he says, no darling, no, I heard nothing.

Normally he is irritated by her ability to shut everything out, to find a quiet space inside herself where no one else is welcome, but during the long afternoon and evening and now as they lie sleepless beside each other he has told himself: no angry words, no menacing looks. Perhaps she senses this; perhaps this is the reason she looks as if she wants to dig her fingernails into her arms until she draws blood. The more effort that Joshua makes to master his natural impatience, the more her blood congeals in despair.

At 3:00 A.M. Nathalie falls asleep. Joshua dozes off, sleeps fitfully. He awakes to the sound of a heavy car, probably a station wagon, cruising down Main Street slowly, as if delivering newspapers in the suburbs. It travels from the west, from the Hartsfield direction, and comes to a stop near or on the bridge. Joshua wrenches himself out of bed, runs on wobbly legs to the window. He sees nothing. What he hears is the crunch of tires on the loose gravel of the bridge as the station wagon speeds away.

A long day passes, dream-like, intolerable in its duration. Joshua prowls the property incessantly, searching for clothing, hair, blood, belongings, any clue to his missing son. He sits on the rock looking at the river and the bank opposite. He walks in the woods, Torvald's woods, through a tangle of willows, fir trees, hanging vines that seem prehistoric, walking for a half hour at a time, in aimless circles. Already he has covered every house in The Hollow. At mid-morning he gets in the jeep and drives very slowly to Smithfield, a distance of five miles, looking at every house, every stopping point along the road. On Main Street in Smithfield he goes door-to-door.

"I'm Joshua Sandler. We have a house in The Hollow. I'm looking for my son, Daniel. He's 14 and has been missing since yesterday."

One lady with sparse, untidy white hair says, "You poor man, come in and I'll give you a cup of tea." It is 90 degrees today, a burst of hot air in midsummer, and Joshua isn't interested in tea. The woman has very few teeth. She is wearing a purple bathrobe that has gaping holes and dark stains, as if it had been worn by a stabbing victim. The woman and the bathrobe appear inseparable. When Joshua asks if she has seen or heard anything of his son, the woman says her son, too, has gone off and not come back. When it becomes clear that she is talking about someone who moved to Kansas City 12 years ago, Joshua backs off her rickety porch.

At another house, a hard-faced man in his late 30s or early 40s answers his knocks, wearing tight jeans, no shirt. He has a blue tattoo proclaiming U.S. Navy-San Diego on the right shoulder. His breath smells of sausage and onions. "Fucking kids," the man says when he hears what Joshua is after. "They never fucking do what they're supposed to."

No, Joshua protests, Dan is a good kid, a dependable kid.

"They're fucking all the same."

A freshly painted white house belongs to the Pucketts. Rosa is a part-time postmistress at the Post Office, across the street from the Smithfield Hardware. The Post Office adjoins the garage in town, in fact has been built as an addition to it. The regulars who come in to get their mail out of the boxes or to buy a roll of stamps are used to the smell of diesel oil fumes seeping in under the door. Rosa, a sweet-tempered lady in her 70s whose flesh sags loosely from the bones of her thin face, comes to the door wearing a full skirt and a long-sleeved blouse. She carries an item in her hand that Joshua recognizes only from old photographs: a feather duster.

"I know your wife," Rosa says warmly, "she's always coming in to buy stamps. Such a lovely woman. And a wonderful musician." Behind Rosa in the parlor he can see an upright Baldwin, its dark finish gleaming. Rosa sounds like a piano teacher, the way each word drops so distinctly from her lips.

"What is this about your son? Art Sammons mentioned it to me last night, a report about a missing boy, a family in The Hollow, and it broke my heart. I told Carl all about it."

"Right, Carl." It is Carl with whom Joshua had the run-in over the go-slow signs and now, more recently, about the Tall Pines project. At the Smithfield Fair, Carl takes up much of the front row of the grandstand as he watches the tractor pull. His thighs seem to meld together like gargantuan loaves of bread side by side on a vast baking sheet.

Carl has been a Town Selectman for 26 years. When he was a young man of 48, weighing about a hundred pounds less than what he weighs now, he was tearing into the Selectmen for not fixing the potholes; this was in June, two months after the last snows had melted, and you still couldn't drive down Main Street without risking a busted axle. A friend said, Carl, if you know so much about it why don't you run for Selectman yourself?

Why not, he said. Now every year Carl would wonder aloud whether this wouldn't be his last term as Selectman, only to decide in the end to have "one more go."

"It's our son, Dan, who's missing," Joshua explains.

"Yes, I've met Dan. I heard you at the memorial service for Albie Moreau, where you said a few words. That was a fine day in May, about a year ago. You spoke well."

Moreau was a much-loved pastor of the church in Smithfield, of French Protestant ancestry. Moreau had his own tennis court high in the hills off Hawes Hill Road, the court in a grassy meadow bordered by poplar and birch trees. The court was red clay; it needed tending and Moreau said you were welcome to come and play on the court if you rolled and swept it afterward. Dan would tag along, hit some balls with his Dad before Joshua's partner showed up. Later Dan would lie back on his haunches on the soft lawn, chewing on a piece of sweet grass and listening to Moreau's stories of his travels as an Army chaplain in World War II to Shanghai and Tokyo, Cairo and Trieste. Dan came to the memorial service and was proud when Joshua got up to speak.

Joshua makes no reply, standing on her doorstep, remembering.

"Your son, Dan," Rosa repeats. "Does he hang out with any kids here?"

"Sam Bonacio from across the street, along with his sister, Christine. And Bobby Dawes, who also lives in The Hollow."

"Sam, I don't know at all. How old is he?"

"A little older than Dan. He's a quiet boy, a serious boy." Since Sam's father is always on the road, Sam helps his mother with the mowing and weeding, and earns money working at one of the local dairy farms in haying season.

Joshua declines Rosa's invitation to come in out of the heat for a glass of lemonade. It is too much for him: a feather duster in her hand, a pitcher of lemonade on the kitchen counter.

"I don't know Sam," she says, almost to herself. "Bobby Dawes, of course, lives with his mother and stepfather. I know his father."

"What about his father?"

She purses her lips. "I don't like to gossip."

"Please! Tell me what you know." Tendrils of his orange-flecked, sand-colored hair come to life. He is wild-eyed, ready to break a window or slam a fist into her weathered front door with its black oval knocker.

"It has nothing to do with your boy. Robert Dawes is a rough one, that's all. The last I heard he was still in jail for beating up a man in Springfield during a robbery. It was armed robbery and assault and he got a long prison sentence, eight or more years as I recall. That was several years ago."

"You talk as if you know him. Do you?"

"He and Carl had words. Dawes punched Carl in the stomach and threatened to beat him up."

"Did that land him in jail, too?"

"Carl didn't press any charges. He just looked Dawes in the eye and said if Dawes ever threatened him again, Carl would shoot him. Dawes knew Carl had a gun and after that he just left him alone."

"And the son? Bobby?"

"Like all the kids here," she says, earnestly. "Angry at growing up in a town like this. Convinced that if they only lived someplace else, life would be different."

Rosa asks him to convey her greetings and prayers to Nathalie, and he drives away from the Pucketts' neat Cape, half of whose front porch is stacked with cut and split wood. He can't get the story about Bobby Dawes' father out of his head. On the drive back he stops at several houses on Route 57. One is a palatial home opposite Bugner Road, about a mile before the turnoff for The Hollow. Here everything is shut tight; no one answers the bell, or the pounding he administers to the door. Half a mile further on, he stops at a collection of peeling white-painted house, barn, shed and outbuildings nestled in a curve of the road.

Joshua steps down from his car, nearly stubbing his toe on the rusting wheel of a beached truck body, turning an oxidized orange-brown in the moist heat of the day. A dog barks, then a second. Joshua blinks from the brightness of the sun. At first thinks he has wandered into a junkyard but he soon sees that there is order. Busted headlights, the remains of a muffler and tail pipe, an empty 10-gallon drum and several worn tires are stacked compactly in the area of the truck carcass, perhaps awaiting a vehicle large enough to haul them away. Hardpacked sand with tufts of weeds gives way, as he moves toward the house, to an irregular but pleasing perimeter of soft grass bordered by orange day lilies.

The barking grows louder as he steps onto the porch, with its freshly laid, still unpainted planking. The door handle is new, and on the other side he can sense 80 or 90 pounds of angry dog hurling itself at the door. The buzzer, yet to be replaced, is stuck in the open position and his hard knock temporarily stuns the dog into silence. The dog resumes making noise but a lower-register noise, a growl rather than a bark. Perhaps, thinks Joshua, it is preparing itself for attack and dismemberment. Soon it is joined by another dog, smaller and very noisy, likely a terrier.

When his banging produces no answer, Joshua leaves the porch and moves to his left around the kitchen—he can see counters and a sink through the windows—whose exterior clapboards show evidence of recent painting. In front of the barn, three scruffy brown chickens peck their way around a sun-bleached, canvas-topped Jeep, faded but serviceable, like something out of the African bush; only the palm trees are missing.

He walks to the back shed, also newly painted, with a tidy corrugated roof. Here he finds a striking woman with long black hair, rangy, with capable hands, stepping over the sill into the yard beyond. She moves with a slight hitch, the hint of a limp in her left leg. Something about her is familiar, but he can't recall why.

She sees Joshua over her shoulder and nods, as if she knows why he has come. In her left hand is a squawking chicken, in her right a straight-bladed razor. She kneels on a flat, raised killing stone, her right knee planted in the middle of its black scaly surface. Stretching the neck of the chicken beyond the stone, she draws the razor across the neck from the underside. In an instant the head is tumbling into the beaten-down grass around the stone. Blood spurts upward. Her left hand holds tightly to the body of the decapitated fowl.

"Who are you?" Though the question is direct, her speech is slow, almost circuitous.

"Joshua Sandler. Have you seen my son, Dan?"

Her back is to him as she squeezes the last blood from the dead chicken. Now he notices a vat of hot water to the left, on another stone. There is some sort of stove inside the shed, he figures, maybe a wood-burning one; he can see the bright steel pipe exiting the rear wall and making a right turn upward to end in a triangular cap. The hot water makes clear that the slitting of the chicken's neck, however brutal and quick, was premeditated. She plunges the chicken into the vat, holding it there by a leg to avoid burning her fingers. Joshua comes closer and sees feathers and blood floating on the surface of the water.

Pause. "Slender guy, tanned, brown hair, always smiling?"

"Yes," he says, amazed, as she describes Dan.

Again she waits half a beat before answering. "I've seen him."

"Yesterday? Today?"

"Not for a week or so."

"Where did you see him?"

"In the woods."

"In the woods? Why do you go into the woods?"

"For plants, for firewood and kindling." Her voice is low and not at all harsh. He can't tell if she's 32 or 45. Joshua realizes that the woods behind her collection of buildings eventually join the woods behind his house, after meandering for the three quarters of a mile through a state forestry preserve, and then across the Northway Road onto more state land before reaching Torvald's property.

He asks how far she went in the woods—did she make it to the spot across the river from his and Nathalie's house, high above the remnants of the old dam?

"Yes," she says, "And sometimes I saw him and his friends at the campsite, the one they call The Preserve."

"Friends?"

She mentions Sam Bonacio, Bobby Dawes, a girl named Melanie, with wild, curly hair and her friend Kristen, who is blond and chunky. Two other kids who came occasionally, Doug and Caroline. And a boy from Northway who has a car.

"Northway? Who is that?"

"An older boy, tall, with mousse in his hair. He wears expensive clothes."

That must be Tony Bentley, Joshua thinks; his dad owns real estate in Collegeville. But who are Melanie and her friend? How does the woman know so much? Her hands are in the hot water now as she plucks chicken feathers. The water is pink, then red, with many feathers floating on top of it. The sun is beating down on his close-shaven head, making him dizzy, but the woman seems unaffected by it.

Chicken feathers float in the tub like confetti in puddles in the street after a big parade. The woman's back is straight and very powerful. It annoys him that she keeps plucking, but just then she turns to face him and he sees the beads of perspiration on her neck, under the coil of glossy black hair.

He asks her again, insistently, to tell him when she saw Daniel last.

"My son is disappeared, gone, maybe dead," he shouts. "I need to know when you saw him and how and with whom."

The look on her face is sympathetic and again she waits half a beat before she answers. "I'm sorry," she says. "I've seen him several times with the other teenagers but not for at least five or six days. How long has he been missing?"

"Two days. Since Thursday. Haven't you heard? It's been on the news."

"No, I haven't heard. I had to go to Boston Thursday night and just returned this morning." Again she says she's sorry, registering now what this father must be going through. Behind her in the tub of hot water under a hot sun, the feathers and blood give off the odor of a foul-smelling paste.

All of a sudden he recognizes her: the woman with her black hair in a braid, bending forward to listen when Tom Robinson spoke at the town meeting last January. He asks if she was there.

"Yes," she says. "I remember seeing you."

"What's your name?" Joshua asks abruptly.

"I'm Irina." A pause, then a smile. "People around here all know me. The nature-lover, the tree-hugger, that's what they call me."

Now Joshua recalls her plea at the town meeting to preserve the land. "I'm not from around here," Joshua says. I'm an outsider, he wants to shout, one of those New Yorkers, as the locals liked to call them. There are a lot of questions he wants to ask this chicken-plucking woman with the amazingly strong arms. She is wearing a loose-fitting top, made of polyester (it hangs like silk but can't be silk, Joshua thinks) and it rustles like a curtain in an open window as she works with her hands. Now he thinks, she's not in her 40s, mid-30s is more like it, her long bushy hair caught with a single tie in the middle of her back. He wants to ask, who else lives here? What's the reason for the front door that won't open or the two frantic dogs hurling themselves at it as if waiting for a rescuer?

Instead he says, "If you hear anything about my son, please call us, no matter what time it is. I'll give you my phone number." He prints the number neatly on a business card.

She swivels to get a good look at Joshua, then glances at the card. Her eyes are very blue, like glacier ice.

"Irina. Do you have a last name?" he asks.

"Loginov."

"Not exactly an old New England name. Is it Russian?"

She nods, her eyes now curious as well as sympathetic.

"I know where to find you," she says. "If I see anything at all I'll be in touch."

In two minutes he is back in The Hollow, unable to rest until he has traced a wide ambit in Torvald's land across the river, heading northeast before circling back to the west and south. Near the joining of Northway Road he comes on a small campsite that is part of the Preserve. He stands by the semicircle of fire-blackened rocks, visualizing the kids coming here on a July night to drink beer and to shuffle and stamp their feet in the leaves and twigs by the campfire. Dan, Bobby Dawes, Sam Bonacio, a wild-haired girl named Melanie, her blond, overweight friend, Tony Bentley with the mousse in his hair. Except for Dan, a group of small-town teenagers who gather here to curse their small-town lives.

At the house Nathalie tells Joshua that Sammons has come by; he says there is nothing new but he is working hard on the case. He tells Nathalie none of the details of what Irina has said, although he does fill her in on his talk with Rosa Puckett. Oh Rosa's a nice woman, Nathalie says; she gave me her recipe for double-chocolate chip cookies. Baking has always relaxed her, and Joshua wishes now that this was nothing but a placid summer afternoon, with the overwhelming smell of chocolate chip cookies filling the house.

In the mid-afternoon Sammons comes back, bringing with him a Lieutenant Wally Ford from the Massachusetts State Police; the DA in Collegeville has assigned him to the case. Ford has a greyhound face, thin, with hair that is gray-black, combed carefully across a ridged scalp that falls away sharply to each side, as if representing the continental divide. Ford asks the Sandlers to go over everything related to Daniel's disappearance.

"Listen, dammit, we've done this three times. Why are you wasting time sitting here with us when the answer to this is somewhere out there? Go interview the neighbors, talk to the kids, find the drivers who came through The Hollow between 10:00 and noon two days ago. With all these people there has to be someone who saw something."

Ford makes no apology, leaving it to Sammons to explain that every time he talks to the Sandlers he picks up some additional piece of information, some detail that, insignificant by itself, may lead them closer to what happened.

Again they go over the kids that Dan hangs out with, the places they go, as Ford listens intently, taking notes.

Nathalie says nothing. Since the disappearance she has seemed this way to Joshua, just this eerie disconnectedness, as if her ears are stopped up, cutting off sounds that her brain is used to processing. At one point he looks over at Nathalie, across the table from him, and tenders a hand to her. She looks at it as if it were a dirty sock lying at the curb. There is no emotion, no tears, nothing except reddish blotches on her cheeks and eyes that want to bore through everything in their line of vision.

The more they talk, the sharper Ford's face becomes. He is a different animal from Sammons; with his innate decency Sammons is someone you come to with problems, the family friend who knows what to do.

Ford is all business, and Joshua senses how impatient he is to get his feet moving, like an eager autumn hiker starting up a woods trail to conquer an unfamiliar peak. A thick, corrosive acid rises in Joshua, a terrible anger at whoever did this to his son and he wonders if these two men, the hulk of a fellow who works at the mall in Hartsfield, the greyhound with the sharp face and the small black eyes, are equal to the task.

Chapter 8

On day three at 8:30 in the morning the phone rings.

"Josh, Bob Franco here. I'm out of town, in LA, but I called home to check on a few things and I heard the news. Josh, how awful for you. What do you and Nathalie need? What can I do for you?"

Nothing, says Joshua, there's nothing we need except our son back. And then, "You're on the west coast? It's five in the morning, isn't it?"

"Never mind about that. I'm at the recording studio, I've been here all night. Listen, Josh, who's working on this? Have you got the state police involved? The FBI? You know, in cases like this it's important to move quickly, the best chance of finding Dan is right away." In the next breath Franco is offering to hire private detectives, commandeer helicopters, organize search parties.

"Bob, it's almost 72 hours since he disappeared. We're worn out over this, we're at the end of our rope."

"God, I wish I'd known earlier. I've been in nonstop editing sessions for two days and it was only this morning that I talked to Len Stern. He saw it in the paper. Look, I should be back in Massachusetts by the end of next week. You've got to let me help." He tries to reassure Joshua: "We're going to find Dan and bring him back to you and finish Tall Pines and make a great success of it and live happily ever after." Perhaps as these words leave his mouth he realizes how silly they sound.

Then Franco lowers his voice. "Josh, we know there are wackos out there. In Smithfield, I mean. What is it with this town?"

Joshua has been asking himself this very question. Why? Why here? Why this contrast between the peaceful landscape, all those hayfields and green hills and running streams, and this incomprehensible deed? How can he be at peace again with his neighbors—the people who work the fields and timber the hills, who drive their pickups up and down the winding lanes on their way to a job in Hartsfield or Collegeville; the people who stay

65

at home in their trailers, collecting social security checks, welfare checks, food stamp allotments—as long as each one he sees becomes a potential abductor or murderer?

And yet those same neighbors have been calling, bringing food, offering assistance. Grace Flint came chugging up to the house in her Ford pickup, bearing a cherry pie. Rosa Puckett drove over from Smithfield with a bowl of chicken salad and a tin of brownies. Pat Bonacio delivered lasagna, arugula from her garden, a twisted Italian bread from the bakery in Hartsfield. And Art Sammons organized a search party, 28 people who started at first light, 6:30 a.m. yesterday and went until late in the afternoon.

The searchers covered a quarter of a mile up the hill into Torvald's woods; a quarter of a mile on either side of Route 33A, scrambling through marsh and brush and along the stony river bank, looking for something, anything. They found a couple of squashed tuna cans, many styrofoam coffee cups and McDonald's takeaway bags, three socks, one pair of lady's panties, a snow mitten, condoms, someone's torn up cancelled checks from 1987, cigarette butts, empty Gallo bottles sticky from wine residue and raccoon urine, a page of anguished poetry, water-spotted and dyed purple by the elderberries that had fallen onto it. But there was no sign of Dan: nothing belonging to him, nothing belonging to any of his friends. Sammons himself took any object that might have been dropped by one of the teenagers around to each of them; all disclaimed any knowledge of it.

Joshua tries to keep this picture of town residents in the forefront of his mind: men like Norm Simmons, a plumber who lives in a spotless white house at the foot of the Northway Road and whose round, smiling face can be seen behind the serving line as he dishes out chicken with gravy at the potluck church suppers every summer; women like Pat Bonacio in sensible twill khakis, bandanas around their foreheads and liberal squirts of bug spray on their necks and arms, reporting for duty. Norm and Pat and two dozen others with knapsacks and rubber gloves had moved methodically along Route 33A, picking up trash, searching for clues.

Joshua wasn't among them. Sammons had told him in no uncertain terms not to join the search, saying his presence would distract the others; they'd be too busy offering sympathy or looking sideways at him to concentrate on their jobs. What Sammons was really afraid of, Joshua surmises, was that one of the searchers might find Daniel's remains; he didn't want that person to be the boy's father. So instead Joshua showed up at the end of the day at the debriefing center, which was the sanctuary of the Congregational Church building in The Hollow. There he went around shaking the hand of everyone who had helped in the search and listening to, but not hearing, their words of sympathy.

He can't rid his mind of this unreasoning suspicion of anyone and everyone. Why does he feel guilt at where his thoughts are leading him? How can he not regret the random impulse that led, more than 10 years ago, to their turning off the main road to the Berkshires onto this backwater? No sooner had they made the detour than they found the house with its pedigree, built in 1805, stenciled over the lintel to the front door, and the mud-splattered "For Sale" sign rooted in the front yard like a thorny shrub. Joshua stands there with his hand on the phone after hanging up from Franco, picturing the place as it looked when they first saw it. In brilliant October sunshine the house stood outlined against Torvald's wild hillside, as the Northway River bubbled just out of view below the riverbank. It was love at first sight; who thinks in such a moment about neighbors with evil in their hearts?

Ninety-six hours after the disappearance, Joshua's mother Edie has come up to The Hollow, driving all the way from Morristown, New Jersey, toting her chafing dish of pot roast and her determination to not let this thing, this grievous inexplicable thing, destroy her son and daughter-in-law.

Her maroon Cadillac now sits in their driveway, immovable, like a meteorite from space, announcing her presence. Edie, a young 71-year-old, moves like a massive cylinder; her shoulders, her breasts, her waist are all in the same plane. The only sign of age is her lack of suppleness. Grief and shock cover her face like a stain. When she arrived at noon she folded Joshua and Nathalie to her and proclaimed, "We're going to survive this, we're not going to let this defeat us." She is indomitable. In the past six years she has buried two husbands, Joshua's father Max, stricken with liver cancer, and the very wealthy, very secretive Wally Abrams, who dropped dead of an aneurysm while leaning over the counter to water his orchids.

Edie is a force to be reckoned with, she will be there with them, she won't let them wallow in despair and self-pity. How different Edie is, with her focused energy, from Nathalie's parents, Dave and Robin; her father in the darkened living room of their place in Long Boat Key, staring at the stock ticker symbols on CNBC as if they are subtitles that hold the meaning to an obscure Chinese film, her mother in the sunlit kitchen, endlessly soft-scrubbing the countertop with its diffused splotches of red from the cranberry juice that Dave pours—and spills. Good for the prostate, they told him, and he drinks it greedily, like a six-year old slurping his chocolate milk.

During this crisis Nathalie finds she has little patience for either of her parents; Edie, so direct, so strong, suits her mood better. Now, with her mother-in-law taking charge of the kitchen and late afternoon shadows rolling across the lawn, Nathalie's mind begins to fill with a jumble of thoughts: the kids Dan hangs out with here, the malicious adults who make threatening phone calls, sabotage a building site and poison a dog. She feels a kinship with Stuart Lee, Franco's agent, who has no patience for the project: she wishes she'd never heard of Tall Pines, she wishes she had never set foot in Smithfield or The Hollow.

The old-timers are opposed to Tall Pines and she and Joshua—and Dan—are the newcomers, the troublemakers, an easy target. Why has she not made this connection until now? Can it be that Joshua, so quick to grasp everything, has not made it for himself? Or is it another secret, like the secret of poor Arthur being poisoned, that he keeps from her until circumstances beyond his control force a disclosure?

From the refrigerator, where she has been dumbly putting away the jar of homemade salad dressing after supper, she turns, straightens, looks at Joshua. The words burst out of her mouth.

"How could you have fallen for that idiotic project, that Tall Pines? Something that brings out the worst in those stupid people in Smithfield? Not only did you invest our hard-earned money in it, but you were upfront and visible—a perfect target for the crazies who are out there. Couldn't you see from what happened to Bob how it might turn out, that something more precious"—here her voice breaks, but only for an instant—"than a brown Lab would be a casualty?"

"Nathalie, for God's sake. You've got no right, no right at all."

In his own hurt, Joshua lashes back. He is stunned because unlike him, Nathalie rarely loses her temper; oh, at times she gets cranky or edgy or indulges in a spate of nagging, but these moods never last long, a few hours, sometimes only a few minutes. Is it the tyranny of the cello that has taught her such control, or is it the other way around, that the trait of self-discipline, innate or cultivated at an early age, is what has enabled her to master the cello?

She is so different from Joshua. Joshua is the one who goes off in wild dashes of enthusiasm—witness the way he worked like a driven man to set up his business in the early days, how he fell in love with the Smithfield house and slaved for weeks that first summer to scrape and paint clapboards that hadn't been painted in 20 years, to pry out the putty from the old windows, re-point the panes that were good, replace those that were broken, uproot the poison ivy amidst the tangle of dead or stunted willows to the right of the house, in order to clear a path down to the stream. That's the way he is; he'll throw himself into a new idea at work and for three weeks will neglect everything else; he'll find a project in The Hollow and put his business on auto-pilot.

Not Nathalie. Nathalie's byword is balance. Hardly a day goes by—went by, before the disappearance—that she doesn't practice four hours at least, but still she maintains a spotless house. She keeps Joshua and Daniel in strip steaks, baked potatoes, cheddar cheese, fresh corn on the cob, red plums and butter pecan ice cream. Every day without fail she calls her parents in Florida and Edie in New Jersey.

Joshua makes fun of her for this ability to juggle, to never waste a minute. Fifteen extra minutes before they must get in the car to run an errand? There's Nathalie slicing bagels to freeze for another day, or peeling and salting the potatoes for tonight's supper. Thirty extra minutes after paying the bills but before she is to climb into bed? Time enough to unsheathe the cello in the parlor and practice the tricky part of a quartet. If

Joshua, sprawled on the bed upstairs with the TV clicker, hears this sound float up from the parlor, filling the house with its richness, like banana bread baking, then he knows that Nathalie has found half an hour and is putting it to good use.

"You've got no right," he says again.

"No right? No right? I've got every right, every right under heaven. Our son, Daniel, carried off, kidnapped or murdered and you say I have no right?"

"I'm knocking myself out, Nathalie, I'm thinking about nothing else, day and night, I sleep two or three hours a night. I'm doing everything I can and you want to blame me? Without even knowing what happened, where he might be, what caused this, what can be done about it—just like that you turn on me."

"Nathalie! Joshua! Stop it. If you could hear yourselves the way I'm listening it would break your hearts."

Edie, who can stand it no longer, interposes herself between them. She insists they all need to pull together, that there must be an end to this awful finger-pointing.

"What can it achieve? What good can come of it?"

"Mom, don't start in, it's not your place." He is grievously wounded by his wife's accusations; Edie's intervention only accentuates the crevasse that has opened between them. Nathalie falls silent, turning over Edie's words in her head.

Edie's expression softens; she comes to where Nathalie is standing and gently closes the refrigerator door for her. "Come," she says, putting her right arm around Nathalie's shoulder and leading her back to the kitchen table. Joshua, pacing the room, his feet in constant circular motion, stops, then takes a seat opposite Nathalie, with Edie planted in the middle. In his mother's throat is a low hum, and even Joshua can recognize the melody as Brahms' lullaby; she used to sing him to sleep this way.

"Okay, mom." Nathalie's words are the white flag being hoisted, though Joshua doesn't know if it is acquiescence or exhaustion that prompts her to speak. Her head sinks onto her right hand and in her chocolate brown eyes he sees a tide of helplessness.

It is this wretched blankness on her face that gives Joshua the feeling that everything is coming loose. Joshua knows that no matter how headstrong he can be, Nathalie has always teth-

70

ered him to reality by her grounding in the world around them, by her unspoken confidence in the direction of their lives. Now, looking at her across the table, he feels as if he is standing on a windswept island pier, watching a terrified stranger in the stern of a ship as it eases from its berth. Of course the pier is fixed in place; of course the island is immovable; why then does Joshua have this sensation that his feet, the pier, the entire island are slipping backwards, second by second, as the ship moves toward the horizon. In this instant Nathalie seems to him to be the stranger at the rail of the ship, her dark pupils filled with the dread of a journey she has not chosen.

Chapter 9

Edie stays until Wednesday, then leaves; she finds it painful to be around her son and daughter-in-law, preparing ample meals that no one wants. She tries to talk to Nathalie, but after her outburst, Nathalie retreats into a rough-edged, antagonistic silence. As for Joshua, there is no talking to him, either. Joshua cannot, will not sit still; after a half hour in the house he must be out again, bent on covering every mile of Smithfield's roads, accosting every person he sees, whether on foot or in a car.

Days pass; to Nathalie every 24 hours seems like a week. Every day the same, except that the tightening knot of anguish is different, more intense, more consuming: nights spent lying on the mattress as if on a wooden plank in a cell, or tromping downstairs at 3:00 A.M. to sit barefoot in the drafty kitchen, revisiting favorite recipes, the only reading she is able to do, as the evening breezes play upon her face and arms.

In late August, the air is alternately cool, or fragrant with the last fruits of the season, with the scent of the yellow floribunda roses and the harsh, cidery tang of rotting apples, brown mushy puffs that lie at the base of the three apple trees in the side yard. Nathalie wears jeans and the blue pullover, not bothering with her appearance, except to splash a few drops of lukewarm water on her cheeks. She leaves her thick chestnut hair in the tangle left by the overnight bout with her pillow; a quick run-through with her fingers takes the place of a proper brushing. She gags at the thought of what she used to do: 50 strokes in the morning, 50 at night the way her mother taught her. Neglecting her appearance is the way she gets revenge on . . . whom? Herself? Her husband? Anyone who might pass her in the street?

In white, mud-encrusted sneakers she drags herself out to the garden to pick the last tomatoes, plucking the suckers that sprout between the thickening stalks. She places the fruit in the yellow salad spinner, then takes the three-pronged gardening claw and works at the weeds, every one of them, from the border along the chicken-wire fence to the barely visible shoots that sprout daily in the shadow of the zucchini plants.

The ground at this hour, a few minutes before seven, is wet with dew but she pays it no heed, squatting in the mud, often working without gloves. Her fingers stiffen from the initial contact with cool air and sodden earth, but the movement of her hands in the moist, clayey soil, the balm of the sun when it has finally climbed to the point above the roof where it begins to warm her body, combine to loosen her joints. If she is lucky, the physical activity coming so soon after rising from her bed helps to shut her mind down, to banish all the horrible thoughts to a far corner of her skull.

She collects her tomatoes, tosses the weeds into her barrow with the large wheels, then moves on to the three apple trees. The ground is knobby with the fruit that has fallen, much of it brown and rotten. In past years she made applesauce, coring the apples, working the peeler until her fingers cramp up from the effort, until her sink is awash in the muck of peel and seeds and a fermenting, yeasty odor has spread through the kitchen. Now she has no energy or taste for applesauce; she saves the good apples only out of habit.

Nathalie has always relished the squatting in the earth, the feel of the dirt between her fingers, but day by day the slow march to the garden becomes harder. Even on sunny days a cloud hangs over her head. The seasons of the garden are ordained: this is the time for weeds to die, for tomatoes to be harvested, for apples to rot. Time for a teenage boy to eat and stretch and store up food for growth, not to be cut down like the brown and woody tomato vines. Once she looks up from the ground to see a shadow cross the lawn, and she remembers the syncopated ballet that used to be: Dan steering the mower with Terry's help, Dan with croquet mallet in hand, gleefully preparing to rocket someone else's ball toward the trees.

Afterwards Nathalie sips coffee and spoons plain yogurt with slices of banana into her mouth. This time is worse than the garden. She dreads these minutes alone in the kitchen, minutes that can stretch to hours of immobility and despair. She wants only one thing, to not think of Dan, but she can do only one thing, to think of Dan, to see him in bathing suit, shoulders sunburnt, racing up the stone steps to the front door; hears herself asking, Dan, did you dry off, worried about drops of water on her wideboard floors, hating the memory of asking that question, desperately wishing for nothing else but floor boards that stain, discolor, even rot from the dripping of her sunburnt son.

One morning she wakes to a choking feeling, as if a cord is being stretched inside her head from ear to ear, pressing down on the back of her throat. In the bathroom it is an effort to swallow a few sips of water. Her head echoes with a single sound: No. No, no, no, no.

She puts the glass down and drags herself back to the bedroom to begin the job of getting into her clothes. She slips into sandals, then slips out of sandals and into sneakers, barefoot, then decides she needs socks. She takes the sneakers off to put them back on, and only then begins the long march down the staircase.

Joshua is already gone and the downstairs is deserted. On the table she sees the crumbs from his English muffin, sees the ring made by his coffee mug on the red place mat. Everything about the house oppresses her. The tightness in her ears returns, more powerful than when she awoke. The house is crushing her. She has known solitude before. Solitude used to be her friend—for making music, for reading—but this is the solitude of life imprisonment. Every molecule in her body revolts against her fate.

The sound begins in her strangled throat, more as a clearing of the airways than as a word. "No," she manages, coughing out the syllable. "No. No. No." She has found her voice now and she plants herself in the center of the room, facing the fireplace, and shouts: "No, no, no, no, no, no." The room is hot with the sun, which floods in strongly from the front, south-facing windows. Nathalie shouts until it feels as if she's swallowed sand, until she is so dizzy that she half steps, half topples backward onto the blue sofa.

Lying sideways, pressing her face into the crook between the padded arm and the cushion, Nathalie is able to put a name to her misery. Dan, she sobs over and over.

She has no idea how much time passes, only that particles of lint are making her nose twitch; her right cheek is reddened from the rubbing of the sofa cushion. She hears the knock at the mudroom door and someone calling, "Nathalie? Nathalie, are you there?"

Pat Bonacio is standing over her, then bending to wipe her face with a dish towel dipped in water. "How long have you been lying here? Where's Josh?"

"I don't know. I don't know." The same answer to both questions.

"I didn't hear you shouting till after I shut off the mower."

"Shouting? Me?" Nathalie has no memory of it.

Pat asks if she's eaten anything and Nathalie says, no, I don't think so. When Pat sets a cup of tea and a slice of toast down on the wobbly side table next to the sofa, Nathalie is still lying in the same position. Only now she's sobbing ceaselessly. It's as if the internal plug has been pulled and the sobs might go on for hours or days.

Eventually Pat reaches Joshua on his cell phone and he hurries back. When Nathalie sees him she begins to cry again.

Joshua, too, sleeps fitfully, leaves the house early. How many times has he retraced the miles up and down Route 33A, hard by the meandering river, convinced against the growing evidence of his own eyes that the clue to Dan's disappearance lies along this road? Lately he has taken to stationing himself in the middle of the road when a pickup or jeep roars into sight.

He flags down the vehicle, brushes aside the anger of the driver at having his morning commute interrupted. "My son is missing. He's been missing for two days (or three days, five days, soon 10 or 15 days: how long can he keep doing this?). Were you driving on this road on Thursday, August 10th, sometime in the morning? Did you see him? Did you see anyone, anyone at all? Let me give you a picture." He has made hundreds of blowups of a 4 × 6 print showing Dan in shorts, bare-chested, flopping on the ground by the net after an hour of killer badminton with Joshua.

The motorists are taken aback by the sight of this orange-haired man in the Izod shirt and jeans, waving his hands and blocking their passage. Some snarl and curse, refusing even to hear what he has to say, until Joshua reaches in, grips the steering wheel and brings his face close to the driver's. Shouting. "Listen, we're talking about a missing boy who happens to be my son. He may be injured or kidnapped, he may be dead, but we need to find him."

75

Usually the motorists calm down but occasionally a driver, spooked by Joshua's intrusive, manic behavior, says angrily, no, I haven't seen him and then roars off, tossing the crumpled photo into the road. Yesterday the fellow who works at the lumber yard in Hartsfield called Sammons to complain, which is why he comes by the house early on this cool, overcast September day to talk to Joshua.

"Josh isn't here," Nathalie says. "He's probably having coffee and donuts at the general store in Smithfield," the one at the crossroads of Main Street and Route 57. A few regulars hang out there every morning, plus whatever newcomers or itinerants show up, and Joshua questions each of them, shows his photo, pleads for their help.

"He's been stopping motorists on the road. It's not a good idea. He could hurt himself."

As he talks to her, Sammons is taking in Nathalie's appearance. He hasn't seen her for a few days and is shocked at how she looks. Her forehead is smudged with dirt from the garden; her cheeks are the dull white of faded porcelain. She stares at him out of eyes that burn brightly, like tapers at an open window. The thinness of her face, the pallor and exhaustion, have the effect of intensifying her beauty.

"How are you coping? You don't look as if you're sleeping."

"Sleeping?" She tries to chuckle but what comes out is like the rattle of a sardine key in an empty can.

"It seems so hard for you to be here. You're cut off from your family and friends, your work, your music. Your everyday life."

She looks at him with her stricken face. She wants to say, Daniel was my life, but she doesn't say it, because it is not true, not literally true. Dan is one person and she is another; how can he be her life? Sammons looks at her with more sympathy than anyone has ever looked at her, more than her own father and mother, but sympathy doesn't cut it, sympathy leaves her cold. She wants this big policeman to be out finding her son, bringing him back to her. She wants him to be driven, tenacious, ferocious, relentless. She wants him to get to the bottom of whatever has happened. Now, today. Sympathy she can get from mother. Advice she can get from friends.

Sammons is no dope, he senses something of what is frothing inside her like steamed milk in the cappuccino machine. "Tell

Josh to give me a call. He can't be standing in the middle of the road, someone's going to run over him. Have him call me. We need to talk."

But Joshua doesn't come home from his visit to the general store; he goes across the street, finds Sam Bonacio and says without warning, "Tell me about the Preserve, Sam."

It's hard to get Sam talking; usually you have to dance around the subject for a while, warm him up the way you do with the starting pitcher, tossing the ball back and force, easily at first, then harder, till the arm is loose and the mind is focused on one thing only, getting the ball over the plate. But Joshua has no time for warmups, and so he plunges in.

For two days he's been thinking about Irina and her report of seeing the kids hang out at the Preserve. How else to get to the bottom of this but to go to the source? He crosses the street and walks the 50 yards up the road to the Bonacios' house. Pat is out, and Sam is in the back shooting arrows at a fir tree whose gnarled and banded trunk gives evidence of the many Massachusetts winters it has survived.

From 40 feet away Joshua can see Sam raise the bow, then shoot the arrow. It lands cleanly in the thickest part of the tree, where the boy has hung a tattered fragment of once-white terrycloth towel on which has been drawn, in magic marker, a red bullseye. When Sam notices Joshua his eyes immediately swivel to the ground, the boy's body inclining away from him as if repelled by a reverse magnetic force.

"Sam. I really need your help. Tell me about the Preserve. How often did you kids go up there?"

"What's this about?"

"Sam, how can you ask that? You know Dan is missing. We need to find out what happened."

The boy considers this. He has turned sideways so as not to face Joshua head-on, and Joshua realizes this must be the way he deals with a lot of things in his world: sideways.

Finally Sam nods. "Okay."

"So, did you go there often?"

"A couple of times a week."

"And the other kids?"

77

"About the same."

"Who else came?"

"Melanie. Her friend Kristen. Tony. Bobby."

"What did you do there?"

"You going to tell my mom and dad about this?"

"Sam, I'm not here to tell your parents anything. This is about Dan, not you."

"My mom'll kill me if she finds out."

"Finds out what?"

If it is possible for a boy to look even further away from the adult who is addressing him than he's been doing up to now, Sam does so at this point. He leans back against the tree with the bullseye on it, as if he's become the target.

"Stuff we do up there."

Drinking, mostly beer though once someone brought some bourbon. Cigarettes. Pot.

When Joshua asks if they smoke a joint every night, Sam says, "No. The stuff's expensive."

Who brings it?

Sam shrugs, figuring it has to come out anyhow. "Tony, Tony Bentley. Bobby's friend."

"All right," says Joshua. "Now tell me about Dan."

A wary, alert look, like a squirrel about to dart left or right. "What's there to tell?"

"Sam, how can we look for someone who's disappeared without knowing absolutely everything there is to know about them? Good and bad, Sam. We need to know the good and bad."

Still, he has to pull it out of the boy. No, Dan never smoked cigarettes. Yes, he drank beer, though he didn't like the taste.

"What about marijuana?"

"He'd never tried it before. Said his parents would go ape if they knew. So we said how are they going to know, it's not like you're bringing a stash home with you. Melanie used to dare him, kind of teasing him, she's such a little cocktease, and so he said okay, why not."

Joshua moves closer to Sam until he too is resting against the tree, with the knobs and whorls of the bark poking against his back through his thin shirt. The lowest of the big limbs of the fir tree sway out over the lawn barely half a foot above his head. He and Sam are side by side and both of them are talking to a point about 18 inches in front of them, as that way neither has to look directly at the other. Tell me about it, he urges Sam.

"It was kind of a cool night. We were all wearing T-shirts and shivering a little, and Tony pulls out this stash and we all start smoking. And then Melanie is teasing Dan, and going on and on, how just a little puff and you won't feel cold or anything. So just to get her to shut up he tries it."

"What happened?"

"Oh, he says he doesn't feel anything, so Melanie says, you got to try it again, don't be so cool. And she passes the joint around and Dan takes another puff and when it comes around again he takes another, and pretty soon he's giggling like the rest of us."

"He ride his bike home that night?"

"We walked our bikes home together. I cracked up once when I was high and it was a pain to put the bike back in shape without setting off all kinds of alarms with my mom."

Joshua realizes, in that moment, how easy it is for kids to get away with this kind of stuff. Vanish silently up the stairs, hop in the shower for five minutes until they've regained a modicum of lucidity, brush their teeth furiously until all traces of the odor have vanished. And then, as always retreat to their rooms, from whence communication proceeds through closed doors, in muffled half-sentences or monosyllables.

If Nathalie had breached the closed door of Dan's little room that night, he wonders, would she have noticed eyes that were a bit bloodshot, pupils that were still too dilated? Or, with Dan on the lower bunk of a bunk bed, no light except the cheap black table lamp with the flexible neck, turned to the left so it directed its beam on the pages of his Tolkien trilogy, would she have blown a kiss in his direction and retreated without detecting anything?

"So, was that it for Dan? That one time?"

From his hesitation Joshua can hear what the answer will be.

"No, there were other times."

Joshua hears something in his voice that wasn't there before, a hint of mirth.

"What's funny, Sam?"

"He had this crazy idea," Sam says, laughing now. "The pot Olympics, he called it. We'd smoke a joint or two and then we did these stunts that Dan dreamed up. How many seconds you could stand on one foot before you toppled over. How long it would take you to strip your clothes off, run down the hill to the bend in the road without anyone seeing you, then run back up and get dressed again."

"You did this every time you smoked?"

"No, once or twice. Bobby tried to put it down, said it was dumb but Dan called him a wuss, so Bobby said, what the hell, and he did it and then Dan did it and then the rest of us."

Joshua shifts subjects. "This Melanie. She have a boyfriend?"

All he gets from Sam is a shrug.

"Were the two of you. . . ?"

"No." Emphatic.

"Bobby Dawes?"

Sam doesn't answer but the angle of his shoulders and neck says yeah, okay.

"They have sex?"

"Come on, Mr. Sandler. I don't know that. We don't talk about that kind of stuff."

"Doesn't Bobby talk about it?"

"What if he does? It doesn't mean anything because he makes half of it up anyway."

Joshua asks about Dan and Melanie but gets no answer, asks about the other girl, Kristen and again there is silence.

"What's she like? Kristen?"

All of a sudden Sam is blushing. "She's a sweet kid who, I mean, she wants the guys to like her. You know." And he clamps his mouth shut.

"Sam, who could have done this to Dan? Who could have kidnapped him or hurt him badly or killed him? Who?"

Sam shakes his head, as if even touching the question will cause pain. Joshua sees a flash of something in Sam's eyes. What is it, Joshua asks himself: a fear of speaking his mind, an instinctive need to hide what may come back to bite him?

"Is there anything, anyone you can think of?" he asks.

Eyes downward, lips pursed, Sam says no.

Later, he and Nathalie talk about Sam as he cleans the outdoor folding chairs with a damp, ammonia-soaked rag. She watches as he wipes them with a second rag, then hangs each one on a wooden peg in the shed, there to gather dust and cobwebs and black spots from spider depredations.

Joshua relates how Sam looks away, looks down, anything to avoid facing you. "He hurts," Nathalie says. "Do you think he's capable of lashing out and hurting others?"

"I thought he and Dan were friends."

"Friends? They live across the street from one another. They hang out together."

As he dips the rag in a pail of cold water and begins to wipe the last two lawn chairs she recalls, "Remember when I talked to him that Fourth of July at the Bonacios'?"

It was 15 months ago, a big Italian family get-together: lots of beer, lots of arguments. Steve's mother had presided over the pasta, the salads, the plates of pineapple, peaches, cherries and German chocolate cake, while Steve's uncle Frank, a year younger than his father, stood by the grill with a spatula, dishing out burgers and relishing the role of family patriarch. Steve's father had died of a heart attack three years earlier. Other uncles and aunts and half a dozen of Sam's and Christina's cousins all showed up.

In the midst of all the family hubbub Nathalie was eyeing Sam, who kept his distance from everyone else. She sensed that his discomfort at these social gatherings might take the form of a bared-teeth antagonism to those around him; from Pat she'd had inklings of his occasional fits of rage against classmates, cousins, kids he barely knew.

Sam was standing apart, throwing pebbles into the stream that bordered their property to the south, and that joined with the main fork of the Northway River as it curved around the Sandlers' house. Nathalie came up to him carrying a paper plate. The hot dog on it gave off a charred odor that rose from deep within the folds of a toasted roll. A moist paw of cole slaw trickled juice that soaked the bottom layer of a pyramid of potato chips.

She held out the plate to the boy and he extended his man-sized hands to accept her offering. Shyly he mumbled his thanks.

"I didn't know you had all those cousins. What about Joey, is he your age?" Joey, oldest son of Steve's sister, wore a cut-off T-shirt that showed shoulders and biceps toughened by weights. His short dark blond hair rose in aggressive spikes from his scalp.

"He's a jerk, always trying to push you around."

"Does he try to do that to you?"

"No way." Sam paused to take a large bite of hot dog, then scooped a fingerful of chips into his dirty palm. "He used to give me rope burns on the wrist or punch me in the back with his knuckles, or try to stuff ice cubes down my shirt. Last time he came over and tried that I smacked him in the side of the head with a hardball."

She looked at Sam and what she saw was an ordinary boy with a physique that was beginning to lengthen and toughen, a boy with a stubborn neck and hands with long fingers. She'd heard that he played outfield and had a strong arm. She imagined the right hand clasping a baseball, thumping his cousin on the temple.

There was a sudden intake of breath as she said, involuntarily, "I hope he was okay. He wasn't hurt, was he?"

"Yeah, he was fine, just this red bruise on his cheekbone. His mom gets all upset and then my mom starts in on me. But he was fine."

Sam took another bite and the hot dog was gone. He ate another handful of chips and then said to Nathalie, "A kid in my class had a bad accident. Another kid hit a line drive, a really hard one, and it hit him in the head. They took him to the hospital but he died."

In spite of the heat Nathalie went cold all over.

"You were there? You saw it?"

"No, I was in school but I didn't see it happen. It was during 10th grade gym. The kid who hit the ball was really shook up. He's going to a doctor for therapy."

"A psychiatrist?"

"Right, a shrink." Sam was staring at the stream, occasionally popping a potato chip into his mouth with blackened fingers. Now he turned to Nathalie. His expression conveyed self-sufficiency, a kind of stoic acceptance of the need to fight, along with—or was she imagining this?—a naked vulnerability. The mix of emotions frightened her.

"I think if a kid is in trouble," she said, "it's a good idea to be able to talk to someone."

He looked at her as if she were babbling an oft-repeated advertising message.

"Of course you can always talk over your problems with your mom and dad. It's just that, at times, it's good to talk to a grownup who's not your mother or father."

Even as she said these words, Nathalie thought, I'm going to turn him off completely. Neverthless, Sam nodded in apparent agreement.

"My dad is like, 'do this, do that, when I was a kid, blah blah blah.' My mom is okay; she doesn't try to put me down like my dad." Sam had resumed his careful flicking of pebbles into the stream. "When he comes home everything better be the way he likes it or there'll be hell to pay. That's what he says, 'hell to pay.'"

"Your dad is just using an expression. He doesn't want to send you to hell."

"Who knows what he wants? I mean, my dad, he doesn't have a clue. Not a clue."

They sat together a while longer. Nathalie was clasping her hands across her drawn-up knees, feeling the grass both warm and slightly moist under the tightness of her shorts. Something about the boy eluded her, something more than the barely tamped-down anger, the growing rift between father and son. Idly, she asked about what he liked to do most.

"Draw."

"Draw what?"

"The river. The hills when they're full of snow or when the leaves are off the trees."

What about people? she asked. Ever draw your family or friends or teachers?

No, he said, I like to draw nature, not people.

Joshua listens as she tries to articulate how she sizes up Sam.

"He's baffling," she says. "He can be so tough, and yet at the same time there's such sensitivity. I'd love to see his drawings, see what kind of talent he has."

"Smacking his cousin in the head with a hardball doesn't sound too sensitive."

"I'm telling you, Josh, this is a kid who's vulnerable. I bet he doesn't have any close friends. I hate to think what he might do—or what others might do to him."

83

That night when Joshua calls Sammons, the policeman admonishes him: "Listen, no more stopping cars on the road. Do we agree on that?"

"Do we agree on the need to do whatever it takes to find Dan?"

Chapter 10

The next morning Joshua is still thinking over the story Nathalie told about Sam as he was cleaning the lawn chairs.

She was acutely focused when she told it—unlike the day before, when he'd rushed home after Pat's call to find her lying curled up on the blue sofa, its lumpy cushions wet with her tears. Each time he tried to get her to sit, her body would slip back, like a sack of rice when you try to prop it upright.

When she finally stopped crying and could raise the mug of tea to her lips, her words came in a croak that was nearly unrecognizable.

"My son, my son, my son," she kept repeating.

Our son, Joshua thought. Our son. It was painful to look at Nathalie in this state. Her hair was matted against her left temple and cheek, her eyes dull. He stayed with her the rest of that morning, cutting up little triangles of toast, dipping them into the tea and feeding them to her as if she were a kitten learning to take solid food.

"Tell me the truth," he'd said then, "you're not thinking about taking your life, are you? Promise me you're not thinking about suicide?"

"I'm not thinking about anything but Daniel."

The answer left him unsatisfied and when he pressed her again she says, "I'm not thinking about that. I'm too much of a coward."

"Don't ever think about it, and if you ever do, promise you'll tell me. You have to live. For when Dan comes home."

Her brittle laughter, which broke off after a couple of seconds, rebuked him.

This afternoon Joshua drives to the house on the Northway Road where Melanie lives; her very pregnant older sister tells him that Melanie is taking care of two little kids belonging to a working couple on Old Route 57, in the middle of The Hollow. He tracks her down to the kitchen where she is preparing SpaghettiOs for supper. The kids, about two and four, are on the

85

floor of the kitchen playing with plastic action figures and occasionally reaching up to grab a fistful of cheese crackers.

Everything about her is sharply etched: her needle nose, her small eyes, which bore in on Joshua's chest, as if there is some hidden insignia beneath his shirt that holds the key to his identity; her high, pointy breasts that strain against her halter. Her dark hair bulges out from her scalp in all directions.

"Hi Mr. Sandler," she greets him, as if she knew he was coming.

"Are you Melanie?"

"That's right. Is there any word about Dan? God, it's so awful, so awful for you."

"I don't have any word, but I'm hoping you can help."

"Mr. Sammons already talked to me. I told him I didn't see Dan that day, so I don't know anything."

"Melanie, I'm not asking about the day Dan disappeared. What I want to know about is your little group at the Preserve."

If Melanie is surprised at this she doesn't say.

"How often did Dan come there?"

"Gee, I don't know. A couple of times a week, maybe more."

"And you?"

A quick grin. "A couple of times a week, maybe more." It depends on whether her mother—who often works late—needs her help with cooking or cleaning. Or if she has to babysit her 18-month-old nephew. If neither mother nor sister needs her, she can go out.

As for the two kids crawling under the table with orange cheese doodle dust scattered across their palms, she babysits them most afternoons until Mrs. Peterson comes home.

"Where does your mother work?"

"Where else? The mall in Hartsfield. In the music store. It's kind of a joke; two years ago my mom didn't know the Stones from Aretha Franklin, or Prince from Garth Brooks, I mean, she was clueless. But I have to hand it to her. She's learned enough to actually talk to the kids now."

Melanie reaches out a long arm and catches the boy through a loop in his shorts before he can tug open a cabinet door and spill its contents onto the floor. She scoops him up as easily as if he were a packet of noodles.

"Supper time," she announces, plops him into a high chair and swipes his hands with a length of moist dishtowel. A minute later she has served the SpaghettiOs in a blue plastic bowl. Her fingers are slim, the nails tapered almost to a point, and painted red.

She calls to the girl, "Come on, young lady, wash up, time to eat."

Melanie gets the girl seated and then feeds the boy, encouraging him to wield the spoon on his own and maintaining a relaxed good humor as sauce-coated SpaghettiOs plop here and there on the high chair tray, on the boy's bare chest and on the floor. Melanie explains to Joshua that their mother wants them at the table and eating when she rolls in at 6:15 and indeed, Melanie is right on schedule. On the surface at least, Melanie is turning out to be a responsible, articulate teenager, nothing like the pimply pothead he'd imagined.

On the other hand, why should he be surprised? Don't all teenagers lead this dual life, acting one way in the adult world, another way in their own culture? Are they any different from visitors who come to the States, find work, adapt to American ways but then maintain a whole separate identity in their cramped but homey apartments, cooking ethnic food, playing Arab or Indian music, even marrying brides picked out for them by an aunt in the old country?

To his shock he realizes that all these observations apply to Dan. He must have had, did have a secret life—a communal secret life, involving a whole other cast of characters, a performance place, a range of behaviors that Joshua and Nathalie knew nothing about.

At that moment the mother comes home, a tall nurse in white with a sagging mouth. Sorry to trouble you, he says, introducing himself. He can see Mrs. Peterson already knows who he is; she looks at him with that mixture of sympathy and horror—oh God, let it not be me—that he has come to recognize. Meanwhile, broom and dustpan in hand, Melanie is making short work of the cheese cracker dust and wayward SpaghettiOs on the floor.

"Bye, Mrs. P, see you tomorrow."

Melanie is about to walk home, 20 minutes up the Northway Road so Joshua offers her a lift. As they drive slowly up the long hill she answers his questions about Dan, but the words come out too quickly; there's a brightness in her voice that doesn't seem genuine.

The paved part is ending and she is staring straight ahead, at the section of dirt road that she must know by heart.

"Were you and Dan, you know, together—like boyfriend and girlfriend?"

"Oh no," she says. "Just friends, that's all."

It's as if she's had this conversation in her head a few times, rehearsing what to say. Beyond her disconcerting poise, Joshua wonders what she is holding back. Sex? Sam Bonacio had said no one wanted to talk about that, except for boasters like Bobby Dawes, and half of what Bobby said was invention, anyway. Arguments? Violence that flared from nowhere?

He asks about the pot-smoking and she confirms what Sam told him. Yes they smoked, not every night because they couldn't afford it. Tony would show up with a stash and they'd all chip in. If there were arguments about who paid how much, they'd turn to Sam.

"Sam always knew. Whenever we had an argument he'd be like, 'No, it wasn't like that, this is the way it was,' and he'd be telling who paid and who didn't."

They are at her house; under the living room window he can see red splotches, which look like long fingers from somebody's Halloween painting of devils and spirits.

"What are those?" he asks as he turns into the driveway.

"My big sister thought she'd decorate the place with new paint but she fell off the ladder and that was the end of her painting. Mom gets mad at her and says, you paint that over but then she gets pregnant and just points to her belly and says, 'I'm pregnant now, can't you see? I can't be climbing on ladders or getting down on my knees to scrub floors.' Mom says, 'Yeah? Can you blow your own nose or do you want someone to do that for you, too?'"

He's about to lose her to a home life that sounds oddly appealing for its very chaos. In the week and a half without their son, the quiet in their house has come to feel like a military siege, every day ratcheting up to a higher level of tension. Even breathing takes an act of will.

"Can you wait a second?" he says.

"Sure." Again the rapid answer, easygoing but a trifle anxious. This Melanie, seemingly so upfront, is nothing like the spoiled suburban brats that friends in Mamaroneck talk about when they fret over their teenagers hanging out with the wrong kids. Someone else's kids: It's always someone else's kid who comes home from high school to get wasted every afternoon; or who borrows the car, picks up a friend and then cracks it up against the concrete abutment on a treacherous curve of the Hutch. It's always someone else's kid that stuff happens to, Joshua thinks, until it happens to your kid.

"What about Kristen? Was anything going on between her and Dan?"

"Nothing with Dan. She was in love with Bobby, poor kid."

"Why 'poor kid'?"

She shrugs. "You've got to know how to handle Bobby."

Like you, he thinks. I bet you know how to handle him. "So, were there any fights? Any arguments between Dan and the other boys? Between Dan and Bobby?"

"Nothing special. The usual stuff, guys trying to put down one another."

He asks for details but she offers none. Her eyes have shifted again, and he can't read the meaning behind her opaque gaze. Why so cool, he thinks, so controlled, so prepared?

"Was Dan afraid of anybody there? Nervous about anybody?"

"Not Dan," she says. "He'd just speak up and say what he thought."

Talking to Sam and Melanie has unsettled him, as if he'd been given access to snippets of Dan's life from a hidden video camera. Instead of viewing the tape himself, however, he had to rely on others to tell him what Dan had said and done. Were their accounts accurate? Did they themselves have something to hide—another piece of tape that he could never see?

He thought he recognized his son from their words: his playfulness, his sense of humor, the rebelliousness that Joshua had experienced with heightened acuity in this past year. Certainly they'd had their run-ins, he and Dan. More often than he cared to admit, Joshua had found it hard to contain his anger at his son. Joshua had sensed the need for confrontation in Dan's interactions with him, but perhaps he had misread the clues, not understanding the role of biological predestination in his son's behavior.

Melanie grasps the door handle to let herself out. From the movement of her lips, he thinks she's on the verge of a further confidence, but she merely thanks him for the ride and goes into the white house with the dagger-like red streaks under the windows. Joshua, driving back slowly now, because it is nearly dark and he is very tired, can't stop thinking about Sam and Melanie and about Daniel.

Dan did have this way of speaking up for what he thought was right. Funny how early that trait surfaces in a human being, Joshua thinks. He can recall Dan at age three and a half, insisting on treatment that he felt was his due, not the typical "I want my chocolate ice cream now" but something more nuanced: I've put away the toys and washed my face and eaten my supper and NOW I want my chocolate ice cream. Most of the run-ins he'd had with Dan this past year, year and a half had to do with one of them taking offense at something the other had done, for no other reason than this highly developed sense of justice.

Joshua recalls an early meeting he, Dan and Nathalie had with Rabbi Hirshfeld. Dan was just embarking on the preparation of his Bar Mitzvah portion, Shofetim, Judges, from the Book of Deuteronomy. The text included the exhortation, "Justice, justice shall you pursue."

What does that say to you? the rabbi had asked.

It would have been easy for Dan to respond off the top of his head, Always do the right thing, treat others the way you want to be treated, follow the golden rule, but instead he was silent for a long time. Finally he spoke.

"Well, Moses at this point is talking to the entire Israelite people, if you can believe that hundreds of thousands of people could hear him. I mean, no sound system, not even one of those little mikes that you clip onto your shirt so how COULD they hear him? But anyway, he's talking to all of them, a lot of stuff about when you come into the land, do this, when you come into the land, do that. So I guess God wants us to have a society that is based on justice."

"What do you mean?" asked Hirshfeld, a stout man with wavy black hair and a predilection for three-piece suits that encased his rounded belly.

Dan thought some more, and said, "A society with laws and judges and, you know, a way of finding out the truth so the guilty get punished and the innocent go free. So Moses is telling the Israelites to set it up this way and then they can pursue justice."

Rabbi Hirshfeld broke into a smile, and the smile broadened and became a grin, and he reached across the round table in the synagogue library to give Dan's hand a vigorous pump.

"Congratulations," he said. "You've got an amazing future ahead of you, young man. As for you, Mr. and Mrs. Sandler, I'm sympathetic to what you will go through with Daniel as he grows and matures even more. A child like this is a special responsibility."

Chapter 11

Joshua speaks to Sammons every day, but today, two weeks after the disappearance, he specifically asks to see both Sammons and Ford. The two of them show up at 7:45 A.M. It has turned hot once more, summer's last gasp, and Ford is wearing his short-sleeved summer uniform with dark tie, his shirt still crisp despite the prickly humidity. Joshua can see the furrows in his scalp where his short hair has receded, leaving patches of tan and pink from the sun. Sammons looks uncomfortably hot; tiny dots of perspiration are beginning to break out across the back of his neck, just above the shirt collar. The big man has his hair carefully brushed, his broad face lumpen with concern.

"Coffee?" Joshua offers; Ford says no, Sammons, yes, thank you. When the two mugs are positioned across the table like opposing bishops, one in front of him, the other in front of Sammons, Joshua forces the words into the steamy morning air.

"I don't understand where this investigation is going. Why haven't you found our son?"

Ford bristles: imagine, a citizen daring to tell the police they have failed. His long nose quivers; his thin face seems to sharpen. "Look, this guy's been knocking himself out on this," he says, referring to Sammons. But Sammons takes no offense. Together Ford and Sammons go over with Joshua the results of their investigation. They've talked to a dozen kids, not only the ones Irina had mentioned—Caroline, Doug, Melanie, Sam, Tony and Bobby—but classmates of those kids, as well as their parents. No one claims to have seen Dan that Thursday morning.

Joshua already knows that the search by volunteers up and down Route 33A, Route 57 and the Northway Road for three miles from the Sandlers' house has produced nothing. Neither has broadcasting Dan's picture throughout Massachusetts, Vermont, Connecticut and New York. There were a few phone calls, yes, but not a single lead worth pursuing.

The two policemen figure their best bet is to find an eyewitness, so working from a computer printout with the names of every resident of The Hollow, they've interviewed almost all of them. The only exceptions are one neighbor in the hospital with a broken hip, three couples away on vacation, a woman visiting her daughter in Indianapolis and the Blakely's, Joshua's across-the-street neighbors who were at a dog show in Harrisburg, PA.

That leaves 44 other residents. Four are kids under the age of five and three are over 90 and spend their mornings immobilized indoors, sometimes dozing in front of the TV. Greta Wilding, deaf and a shut-in at 80, falls in the same category. Eighteen of the 44 were at work; another seven left early that morning on errands of one sort or another. So only 11 people—adults under 80 or children older than five—were in The Hollow that morning and could have noticed something.

Sammons has already told Joshua about his conversation with Mildred and Horace Wister, who live near the bridge in The Hollow, an eighth of a mile north of where Main Street and the Northway Road meet. They saw boys going by on bikes but weren't sure what day. Mildred thought two of the bikes were red; Dan's bike is blue. When Sammons showed them the boy's picture, neither of them could say whether they'd seen him, or when.

Joshua shakes his head in frustration. He knows the Wisters, a couple in their early 80s, round-faced with thinning white hair and serene smiles. A year ago a man had assaulted his wife in the four-family house known as the Hunter's Lodge, located only a hundred yards from the Wisters' front door. It happened on a July night as Horace sat outdoors on his lawn chair to catch the evening breeze. No, he'd said afterwards, he hadn't heard anything. Oh, one or two loud bursts of sound, he'd assumed it was one of those TV programs.

"It was worth a try," Sammons says about the Wisters. "Everything's worth a try."

Janie Foster, who lives across from the community house, saw a sporty, silver-colored two-seat coupe heading toward the bridge that morning. It was going fast, she told Sammons, faster even than some of the 18-year-olds drive around here. They show her pictures of car makes—Mercedes, BMW, Porsche, Audi, Corvette. Nothing clicks, but she is emphatic about her recollection: a silver-colored, two-seat sports car whose engine roared like the crowd at a football game. The police have put out a bulletin all over the five-state region to try to identify such a car, without success.

Pat Bonacio has been interviewed twice. She has anguished over whether or not she saw Dan on the side lawn that morning, though she's pretty sure that as she pulled out of her driveway, she saw a large white vehicle, a truck or a van, come through the Hollow. Sammons went to see Alice Fickett, who runs the Smithfield hardware store. In summer she volunteers once a week to use her white van to drive residents of the Smithfield Senior Center on an excursion to Lexington Park, but she remembered nothing out of the ordinary on her route that morning. "I go by a lot of houses and a lot of lawns on the way to the park," she reminded Sammons. "I keep my eyes on the road. The last thing I want is an accident with half a dozen 80-year-olds in back."

Joshua tries hard to keep his equilibrium but toward the end of the recitation his resentment breaks out. "How is it possible," he demands, "that no one saw anything? Anything? Somebody's lying to you."

Sammons nods. "People will always lie. Sometimes it's because they were playing hooky from work, or because they were in bed with someone else's husband or wife. Those are the little lies that don't matter. Then there are the big lies, the relevant lies: 'I wasn't there, I didn't see him, I didn't hurt him.' We'll figure those out. We'll get whoever did this."

"When?"

Two days later, after a phone call from Len Stern paves the way, Joshua is in Collegeville to see the district attorney for Adams County. Frank Shaughnessy is a glad-handler with a paunch, a large black-eyed man with thick features: puffy cheeks, as if stuffed with popcorn, soft lips whose reddish tinge hints at the pickling effect of a nightly double whiskey.

He listens as Joshua recites all the things that have gone on in Smithfield since the beginning of the year: the flyer in the mailboxes, the threatening telephone calls to Bob Franco, the killing of his dog, the vandalism at Tall Pines, now Daniel's disappearance. Shaughnessy is sympathetic but points out that his office must leave the investigating to the state police. They're on the case; they're the professionals.

"There must be something you can do," Joshua insists. "Something! It's been two weeks; do you have any idea what that does to a person? Your child missing, almost certainly dead and you don't know how or why."

Shaughnessy wants to know if there's any evidence of a connection between the other crimes and Dan's disappearance.

"Do I have to spell it out?" Angrily, Joshua points out that every one of these crimes has been committed against outsiders, people new to the area or who don't live there full-time.

Can't Shaughnessy put the matter before a grand jury, subpoena some of the adults and teenagers and begin to get at the truth?

No grand jury, Shaughnessy says, not while the police are gathering evidence and conducting interviews. But he promises to talk to Charlie Burns, to see if he can put even more resources into the case. "Burns is a good guy. He won't let you down."

"Everyone's let us down so far. Until we find out what happened, everyone's let us down."

It is a little before noon; Joshua decides to have a stroll along Main Street before driving back to Smithfield. The sun-dappled aisles of the bookstore are nearly deserted this last week in August, a few days before the tide of college kids washes back into town. Joshua meanders from history and biography to travel to the baseball section, with its picture books, the inspiring stories of team triumphs, the warts and all biographies of superstars whose drug addictions, mafia connections or wife-beating propensities serve to pull them rudely from their perches. Then, as he is heading back to his car, he stops to look at the menu in the restaurant next door.

The restaurant, Café Rustica, is inviting in its simplicity: inside, about a dozen tables are set on a floor of dark red Italian tile; outside, more tables with white and yellow striped umbrellas give a seaside air to this downtown corner of a landlocked college town.

The aroma of olive oil and garlic, of sautéed chicken breasts marinated in rosemary draws him in and soon he is sitting at a table for two, directly opposite a low counter and a pane of glass through which he sees the cooks at work. A single waitress, loops of reddish hair flopping over her glistening brow, glides from table to table, swooping down with her long arms

95

to deliver plates of pasta primavera, veal scaloppine, lemon sole, tricolor salad.

Almost all the tables are filled, and there is something hypnotizing about the slow-paced way the other patrons raise or lower their white wine or dab at their cheeks with napkins.

Joshua orders a grilled vegetable plate and in a few minutes is eating roasted peppers, zucchini, onions and tomatoes, along with a small salad of arugula and goat cheese and walnuts, and thick slices of crusty pane rustica, the special bread that gives the restaurant its name. What a pleasant spot for lunch, he thinks, and though guilty thoughts come swarming around his head, he does his best to swat them away.

This hour in Café Rustica is the first time he has taken for himself in the past two weeks. What a relief, he thinks, that Nathalie is not here with him. The tension between the two of them, which erupted when his mother was visiting, is always present now. When they talk he hears the censure in her voice; when they don't he imagines the reproach in her silence.

Joshua peers through the glass partition to see a woman with bushy black hair, pulled back from her face; she is working a skillet and from the aroma drifting over the glass and into the dining room he is imagining mushrooms, fennel, leeks. There is a barely perceptible stiffness to the way she turns to the left.

This limp gives her away. Even though he can see only her profile, his mind fills in the shape of the face, long and oval, the right eyebrow slightly higher than the left, a pair of blue eyes that hint at secrets not to be spoken. It is Irina, the woman who was plucking chicken feathers the day he drove up to her house.

A tall fellow with a ponytail is speaking to her as she works. He wears neither apron nor cap; something about the way he stands there, balancing on the treads of his running shoes, with his air of business casual, tells Joshua that he is the owner. A low chuckle escapes Irina's lips. They banter easily for a minute or two. Then the ponytailed man goes back to his work station at the tiny bar in the rear of the dining section, surrounded by the tools of his domain: a green phone, a credit card reader, a computer that records orders and spits out bills.

Irina empties the contents of the skillet—shallots, not leeks—into a white mixing bowl. She cascades angel hair pasta into a pot of boiling water and then, when she has a minute of leisure, she peers through the glass partition toward the diners. For a second her eyes meet Joshua's, and he thinks he sees in them a reflection of his own stare, a tiny burst of recognition.

Strange to encounter her in this communal setting, amidst the saucepans with their burden of fresh pasta, the hanging wire baskets with their Spanish onions, their gleaming white cloves of garlic and their hothouse tomatoes. How utterly alone and self-sufficient she seemed on that hot day two weeks ago, as she kneeled in her sandy yard and talked about Dan.

He finishes his meal, signs a credit card chit and as he gets up to leave he stands at the glass partition to watch Irina. Intent on her skillet, she doesn't acknowledge him again.

There is a park on the western-most outskirts of Collegeville, a sprawling green expanse of soccer fields, baseball diamonds and basketball courts, biking paths, a petting zoo and a long rectangular pool where kids are splashing and shrieking with the desperate abandon that can only foreshadow next week's return to school. As Joshua is driving home something impels him to lift his foot from the gas pedal, to turn into the wide curving road that leads, some 300 yards further on, to the parking lot.

In the back of the Jeep is his cracked brown leather gym bag with the basketball sneakers—in the absence of running shoes these will have to do—and the blue and white striped shorts, and he finds himself seizing the bag, climbing into the back seat and wrestling himself out of shoes, formal socks, long pants, shortsleeve shirt with tie and into the shorts and sneakers.

He is in a hurry, as if the park in its green loveliness will be denied him if he dallies, but there is no way to accomplish this change of clothes quickly, no way to escape the bondage of the uniform he wore to the DA's office without grunting and sweating and banging his knee against the left door handle from the rear seat.

Now, T-shirt flapping at his waist, he begins to trot along one of the broad bike paths, moving away from the swimming pool and, as he had hoped, his eyes take comfort in the sturdy, leafy normalcy of this urban park. He loops around a vast oval lawn with soccer goal posts set at each end, and when he reaches the far side he turns onto a narrower jogging trail, a dirt path covered with wood chips that are easy on the feet and have the smell of a redwood forest. Both the broad path and the narrow trail are nearly flat, much kinder to ankles and thighs than the hills of Smithfield and Northway and Cliffmont, with their monotonous rises and falls.

The trail leads through a wooded area; on his left side are exuberant rhododendrons, dark green and wild looking. They are long past flowering, but some of their shriveled brown blossoms line the path, as if strewn upon the feet of a returning hero. Pools of sunlight appear and disappear as he moves from shadow to shadow. He is running toward the light, not the limpid golden teardrops of morning sunlight after the rain, but the pulsating warmth of the summer sun. The trail opens onto another green expanse, wilder and less manicured than the empty soccer field and it is in the middle of this space that he hears the sounds.

What first comes to his ears is a whining, keening noise, punctuated by a series of higher-pitched cries, and Joshua wonders if this can be some ugly swooping bird calling to its mate. But there is something human in these frightened calls, and as he draws nearer, for the noise is coming from the end of the field, behind an enormous spreading beech that blocks his view, he hears other sounds: grunts, curses, the clap of wood against bone and skin.

Joshua abandons his effortless lope and begins to sprint. Under the dark upward sloping limbs of the beech, he comes upon two boys beating a third with a baseball bat. The victim is a chubby red-haired boy who looks to be 11 or 12; it is hard to see his face because blood has smeared his cheeks and lips with what looks like war paint.

The boys doing the beating are older, perhaps 15 or 16. They've been taking turns smashing the younger boy around the shins and arms, though some blows have obviously landed on his head. Thrown against the ground like a projectile hurled from space is a new mountain bike, one end of its handle bars poking downward into the leaves.

When he is four strides from the pile of boys, he launches himself into a low leap, like a head-first base-stealer, and his shoulder crunches against the left knee of the nearer attacker.

He and the first boy crash to the ground; the bat flies up in the air. The second attacker, stunned, crouches there motionless for a second or two as Joshua encircles the first boy around the waist, slams him to the ground and begins punching him in the chest. One, two, three blows land square on the boy's breastplate and Joshua hears oomph as air is expelled through the boy's teeth. Joshua raises his fist to strike him again, and then sees the second boy turn and begin to run across the field.

Don't let him get away, he says breathlessly to the victim. Sit on his belly. The boy with the bloody face complies and his attacker is instantly quiescent.

Though the second attacker has a 50-foot lead, Joshua catches him before he is halfway to the trail through the woods. The boy scratches at Joshua's eyes, tries to knee him in the balls. Joshua seizes his arms and bends one of them behind the boy's back. He slaps him hard about the face, using his right hand like a pingpong paddle, four, five, six, seven slaps, each louder than the last.

He arrives at the swimming pool with all three boys in tow. The boy he punched hard in the chest shuffles meekly at Joshua's side, coughing and gasping for breath. The other one, tougher, angrier, is doing his best to sneer, though the redness of his face from Joshua's slaps spoils the effect.

Joshua has the wrist of the bigger attacker imprisoned in his fingers. "Don't even think about it," he says, warning him not to try to wriggle free. Still, he's more than a little agitated to realize that he came within a few blows of breaking the first boy's collarbone, or, had he hit him higher, of causing a concussion.

As for the boy who was beat up by the other two, he is walking on his own shaky legs, though blood continues to ooze down his cheeks and onto his green T-shirt.

After the police have come and taken the two teens into custody, Joshua waits with the injured victim in the hospital emergency room. His name is Billy West, Jr.; he tells Joshua in the calmest of voices that they knocked him off his bike and when he refused to give it up, began to smash at him with the bat. William Sr. shows up; he is a vice president and loan officer at the local bank. Horror-stricken but grateful, he takes Joshua's phone number and hands over a card with his own. At the police station, a sergeant tells Joshua, "It's not the first time we've seen these two." Both boys are 15 and must be charged as youthful offenders.

On his way home to The Hollow, Joshua sniffs at his sweat-stained T-shirt and then at the knuckles on his right hand, raw and bruised like twice-thawed steaks.

When he tells Nathalie what happened she is sympathetic, in a clinical way, to his own bruises but frantic for the victim. "How did you know he wasn't hurt so bad that he should have been tended to immediately?"

"I thought he looked all right, despite the blood. He could talk and listen to instructions. Kind of an okay, together kid, if you know what I mean. And I really, I mean really, didn't want the bad guys to get away."

"The poor kid," she says. "The poor kid."

He mentions that he may have to go back and testify, although the cops explained that often these incidents get settled between prosecutors and defense lawyers, in which case there will be no need for witnesses to appear in court.

"Incidents? They call beating up a younger boy with a base-ball bat an incident?"

In fact, the sergeant at the police station, a blond man with the flat face, close-cropped hair and snub nose of a movie tough guy, had become furious when Joshua described the cries of Billy West, the way the blood had been streaming down his face to soak his T-shirt.

"They're a couple of no-good punks," the sergeant had said. "And just you see: if it ever gets to a judge, some lawyer will be going on about their tough childhoods, the single mother, the absent dad who used to smack them around before he split for good." Then he turned philosophical. They're going to wind up in jail sooner or later, he said. With these two it's only a matter of time.

The older one is Jason Lamb: an echo of a connection sounds in Joshua's head but he can't remember where he's heard the name before.

Nathalie is still thinking about Billy West. "Was any-thing broken? Did he need stitches? Oh, his parents. His poor parents."

Will he be okay, she asks again, and Joshua tells Nathalie that Billy West, Jr. was very lucky, no broken bones, no disfig-uring scars. The poor kid, Nathalie says again, and suddenly she is sobbing furiously, crying for Billy West who was beaten so cruelly in a park in Collegeville. Joshua knows why she is weeping; knows, too, that he cannot comfort her. He lets her cry for a long minute. At last the tears run dry and she looks at him, her face haggard and spent. His own heart is sheathed in concrete, like a radioactive element that must at all costs be walled off from other human beings. His tears will not come, and so he watches helplessly until she is drained of hers.

Chapter 12

He and Nathalie suffer through another evening meal. Joshua chews dutifully on a chicken leg, eats most of a baked potato, a few slices of tomato and cucumber. Nathalie merely pushes these objects around on her plate, now and then lifting the fork to her mouth to take a bite.

Joshua forces himself to talk about everyday things—the fungus on the tomato leaves, the need to replace a broken tail-light on the Jeep. Nathalie barely responds. When the phone rings it provides a welcome interruption. First Gert, who calls to tell him about the checks that have come in to the office. Then his mother, who calls every day. Then Nathalie's mother, who says that Nathalie's father has an appointment tomorrow with the urologist at almost the same time that she is to see the endocrinologist, provoking a crisis in transportation management. Finally one of Nathalie's Philharmonic buddies, with the news that her request for a two-month leave has been approved and that they'll be auditioning half a dozen cellists to stand in for her.

Nathalie hangs up from this last call and in silence she and Joshua wash up the dishes.

"What do you say to a walk? Into town?" Town is nothing but the collection of half a dozen houses straggling along old Route 57 just before and just after the Northway Road.

"Okay, into town." They cross the bridge to the left of the house; in the dark he takes her hand, which lies there inert between his fingers. They walk until they see the lights from Norm and Ada Simmons' house; then they turn and plod back home.

For a few hours that night—worn out by the early-morning visits to the general store, the fruitless searching, the scuffle in the park—Joshua sleeps hard but sometime after midnight he wakes to the creaking of the old walls and the sound of something flicking against the back of the house. He goes to have a look. The trees along the river embankment shield the light from the stars and the moon so he can't see much but his ears tell him that pine needles are being flung against the weathered clapboards. The wind has come up strongly from the northwest. No rain is falling nor has the air suddenly turned cold, as sometimes happens at the end of August, just these roundhouse gusts of warm air, and in the sky to the west, the black and blue-edged white clouds, folding and refolding upon themselves as if being lassoed by celestial hands.

Joshua flicks on the bedside light and reads a few pages, all the while listening to the muscular power of the wind. After a time, the monotony of the storm causes his eyes to close; the book slips from his hand and thuds onto the wooden floor.

When Joshua wakes at 6:30 the sun has risen over the bridge and the wind has returned. It is blowing steadily from the west, lifting everything in its path—maple leaves, the small rotting and fermented apples, tufts of grass, the plastic lid of a coffee cup—and whipping them together into whirlpools of debris. Joshua has too much to do to let the wind deter him, and in a few minutes he is out the side door and, mounting Dan's blue bike, he cruises into the center of The Hollow, and then left and up the Northway Road.

He's forgotten how quickly the road steepens; at this early hour his legs are soon spastic and trembling. How long has it been since he's ridden a bike? He bends as far over the handlebars as he can to cut the wind resistance. The road is in shadow; the sun has yet to edge above the spruce and hemlocks that line its border.

After seven or eight minutes of relentless climb, just as he is at the point of dismounting to catch his breath, the road levels. Pedaling more easily, he passes the narrow track that winds to the right, into the hemlock grove known as the Preserve. He keeps to the Northway Road, which in a hundred yards begins to ascend once more. Another 10 minutes' pedaling brings him to a house he recognizes; the dagger-like red splotches on its white siding recall Melanie's sister's aborted paint job. In the clearing the sun is illuminating the red paint, which stands in an accusing finger like the character of a Chinese warlord. Joshua checks his watch to note the time from the house to the Preserve, from the Preserve to Melanie's home.

His spiky ginger hair is already wet with perspiration, despite the coolness of the morning, and the wind is furrowing his scalp so that the hair joins in two scalloped tufts, each flopping over his ears. Joshua bends to his task once more. In three-quarters of a mile, the road reaches a high point at Alpine Meadow farm: a wind-blasted barn glowing pink in the rising sun; a long field of corn, tassels and leaves bending and twisting under the assault of the wind.

Another five hundred yards of pedaling brings him to a trailer set parallel to the road. Narrow, vertical bands of gray are spaced at irregular intervals across its faded metal exterior, as if a giant shutter has opened and closed randomly during the sun's transit across the sky; nevertheless there is something self-respecting about this unadorned dwelling, with its neatly spaced azaleas and its homemade walk fashioned of irregular slate stones. In the side yard, a trio of gloomy spruces cast uneven, elongated shadows through the sunshine that is lighting the southern end of the trailer. With their tangle of low-swooping branches, the trees form a barrier that even the ferocious wind cannot push aside.

This, Joshua has learned, is the home of Melanie's friend, Kristen Larsen, she of the big boobs and the puppy dog willingness to do what pleases the boys. He doesn't want to stop here now, he has another goal in mind. Back on the bike, he pedals hard for an uphill stretch, then he slows as the road begins to snake downward, a hundred yards to the right, then straight, then a hundred yards to the left, all dirt, and in the late August dryness, all dust. The wind has come back with a vengeance and is tossing the dust into his face in clumps. Finally, after a last uphill around a bend, here he is at the entrance to Tall Pines: its metal fence locked, its massive front door repaired and repainted. He hasn't been here since a week before Dan's disappearance and is astonished at the changes. Most of the surrounding cabins appear finished, neatly stained a woodsy brown; gleaming stovepipes from the new fireplaces thrust upward through the steeply pitched roofs. A pristine Swiss village, transplanted intact and set among these rough and twisted Massachusetts hills.

Joshua is a building buff; he loves everything from simple A-frames and ramshackle beach houses to multi-tiered Frank Lloyd Wright creations and midtown skyscrapers. He loves the activity, the human contact, the complexity of construction, the way that something new emerges after the chaos of excavated cellar holes, acres of mud, piles of bricks and concrete blocks, stacks of wet lumber, the intricate choreography of men in short sleeves, hard hats and bulldozers.

But this building, to which he has devoted so much thought, and not a small amount of money, stirs conflicting emotions. He admires the soaring chimney of the lodge, the way the cabins snake along a winding gravel path, the sign pointing optimistically toward the Woodlands Circuit Trail at the perimeter of the woods. And yet he feels estranged from it, as if it has nothing to do with him, as if the last thing he would want would be to set foot inside.

As Joshua stands straddling his bike, too tired to dismount properly but not quite ready for the ride home, a pickup truck roars up the road, pulls around him until its nose is touching the gate. Out steps the job foreman.

"Everything all right, Josh? Car repossessed by the bank?"

"Traded in for this. Gets better mileage."

They banter back and forth for a while. Again checking his watch, Joshua figures it's 17 minutes from their house to Melanie's, 23 minutes to Kristen's, about 45 minutes in total to Tall Pines. The ride back is mostly downhill and takes barely a half hour. If Dan had set out on this journey, or some part of it, shortly after he and Nathalie left for the dump, he could have been safely back home before they returned. Of course he might have encountered trouble anywhere along the way, but in that case his bike wouldn't have been in their garage, leaning against one of the massive sills on the raised stone foundation.

Back in his kitchen he gulps his coffee and bagel, and then sets out again, this time by car. In a few minutes he has pulled off Route 57 onto the grass-covered driveway leading to the buildings he remembers from last time: the snug shed, the rebuilt front porch, the peeling clapboards on the main part of the house.

The front door is still shut tight; the same dogs are yelping and scratching at his approach. But he walks around the back, to an entryway leading to a suite of three rooms—kitchen, pantry, dining room—that appear, through the window, to be cozy, inviting.

"Oh it's you," Irina says when he raps sharply on the old wood frame door. "I've been wanting to talk to you."

Before he can ask her why, she emerges from the kitchen wearing jeans and a scarlet shirt. Her glossy hair sways like a pennant in the wind; she wears it back in a ponytail, tied loosely with a piece of clean but fraying red cloth. Her lips are unpainted but there is a dab of color in her cheeks.

"I've been so distressed about your son. There's no word, is there?" Again he is struck by the cadence of her speech; he can't imagine her shouting or hurrying her words.

"No—and until there is, one way or the other, I've got to keep looking."

"It must be hard to search when you're so fearful of what you will find."

She lowers her voice and her head and she reaches out a hand to cover the back of his palm. Joshua feels the warm presence of her fingers, moving ever so slightly across his hard flesh, trying to balance the bluntness of her speech with her touch that is meant to soothe.

"What is it you wanted to tell me?"

"Just this: I've been by the Preserve a few times. I don't think a soul has been there since your son disappeared. It's almost as if the place is off limits. Like a shrine or a place of danger."

Joshua says he's mentioned the Preserve to the police, that undoubtedly they'll check it out.

"What gives you such confidence in the police here? One overweight guy with thick black shoes riding up and down the roads of Smithfield?"

"If you mean Sammons, he has help, you know. The state police. The FBI if they need them."

She looks at him as if he has just bought a three-legged cow. Talking to this woman makes him feel agitated, witless and nervous, all at the same time.

"The Preserve," he says again. "How far is it to there from here? What's the quickest route?"

The narrow path climbs steeply up the hillside into the woods and then angles further north and west, around a huge boulder embedded in the earth.

In the woods it is easy to forget about her slight limp. Irina moves quickly, darting over rocks, deftly leaning sideways and bending to avoid a branch as Joshua hurries to keep up. The trees behind her house are scraggly, with stunted pines and many boulders. Brambles from the wild raspberries pluck at his jeans. The sun is higher now, the air moist and heavy; the woods provide insulation from the wind but not from the low, ominous rumble in the air. A 10-minute scramble brings them to the Preserve.

Here the pines stand taller, mingling with smaller clusters of ash and maple, birch and oak. As they approach the intersection of the Northway Road the land flattens and they can see a grassy clearing. In a minute they are standing near a warped cedar picnic table, its lengthways planks cracked and pitted from winter snows. Close by are a brick barbecue and the semicircular stones of a campfire. The wind is blowing hard against the westward border of trees, but inside the grove it is nearly still. Ashes of the most recent fire are cold, hardened into snaky carbon rods crisscrossing each other, with bits of unburnt log sticking out at odd angles.

Irina crouches by the fire. "This is old," she says, "A couple of weeks, probably."

In the area around the blackened stones, Joshua registers the artifacts of teenage visitation: cigarette butts, Twinkies cellophane wrappers, empty beer cans crushed into odd shapes by 15- or 16-year-old males demonstrating for one another the power in their wrists and forearms. Here and there are shreds of paper, rain-moistened and matted to the ground, that might be from hand-rolled joints. A certain staleness that stabs at the nostrils: one part dried beer, one part marijuana, one part tobacco, one part urine and feces, no doubt from raccoons that have scavenged the site for any edible remains.

Joshua sees only the disorder of the abandoned site but Irina is busy pacing the outer limits of the clearing, then moving inward in concentric circles until she rounds the picnic table and returns to squat by the remains of the last camp fire. There she pokes at the blackened debris with a stick, nudging aside charred aluminum and blackened glass to uncover sodden scraps of paper, torn into irregular pieces and burnt to a feathery lightness. What fire hasn't consumed, the wind and rains have nearly finished off.

107

Kneeling at her shoulder, Joshua wonders aloud if they ever wrote each other notes or if anyone kept a diary recording who said what to whom.

"The young are not like us," Irina tells him. "No written record, no minutes of meetings. You have to listen hard to what they say. And what they don't say."

"Maybe it's time you told me just what you've seen here."

Irina complies. She tells how once or twice she saw them gather in that half light of dusk when the sun, low in the northwest, filters through the trees here creating an eerie presence, as if the tech crew at a college theater company has figured out how to flick a switch and light the woods. It's the magical hour when day turns to night, a time in the woods when the warmth of the day lingers in the leaves, in the woody plants, in the ground cover, until all the light has faded. That's when the kids would make a fire and break into the six-pack they've brought with them, or else pull out a stash of marijuana and joke roughly as they passed around a joint.

His conversations with Sam and Melanie should have prepared him for this picture but he realizes that they didn't, because now he is seeing his son through Irina's eyes, as part of a clan or tribe engaged in a ritual of assembly and passage. He is sad, angry but most of all embarrassed that this jettisoning of everyday standards of conduct, this . . . this disrobing, for want of a better word, took place with her watching.

Sensing his thoughts, she tries to reassure him. "I wasn't there to snoop, merely to gather my berries or my wild mushrooms. Nobody saw me, I can move through the brush without making a sound. When I saw them I gave them a wide berth and disappeared into the woods."

Irina has backed up a few paces and is resting against the short end of the picnic table; one of the planks is pressing just where the curve of her buttocks starts, pulling the jeans tight across her thighs.

"I wonder if the police have been here," he says. "I wonder if they've looked through this stuff"—he gestures at the remains of the last fire—"to see if it can tell us anything."

He sees the skepticism in her eyes when he mentions the police as he wonders again what she knows that they don't know. Now he's the one circling the site in an elliptical orbit, eyeing bits of fabric, a discarded lipstick, a slick, coated wrapper, torn into small strips, that could be the carrier for an After Eight dinner mint—or a condom.

"Did you hear the kids talking? Do you know what they said to one another?"

"All I heard was the buzz of their voices, sometimes laughing, sometimes arguing."

"Arguing? What kind of arguing? Who was arguing with whom?"

She doesn't know, Irina says. She wasn't close enough to tell one voice from another.

Irina and Joshua stand at arm's-length apart on ground covered with tamped down pine needles. High over their heads branches bow and curtsy to the rhythm of the unyielding wind, but here everything is shady and nearly still.

"Even if you didn't hear what was said, you must know some of these kids just from living in The Hollow." And when she nods, yes she does, he asks for her opinion of each of them.

"The big kid, Bobby, has to be the alpha male, tougher than everyone else, boastful, looking for someone to pick on. The girl with the wiry curls and the pointy nose . . ."

"Melanie."

"Melanie. She's always three steps ahead of you, figuring out what you want to hear. Her friend with the bleached yellow hair—Kristen, is that her name?—is terribly shy and self-conscious. She probably thinks if she lets boys do stuff to her they'll like her better, which of course is the opposite of the way it works. She hasn't been around lately."

Really? Why not? he asks, but Irina doesn't know. She thinks Kristen may have been gone since before Dan disappeared, but she can't be sure.

"What about Sam?"

"The kid who lives near you? Dark hair? Black eyes?"

Joshua nods.

"He doesn't say much. I'd guess there's a lot bottled up inside."

The other kids, Doug and Caroline, were around earlier in the summer but she hasn't seen them lately. Doug Wright, Joshua remembers. He asks if the boy is related to the Selectman. Irina shrugs. Everyone's related to everyone here, she says.

That leaves only Tony among the regulars, but here Irina is no help. He's not a Smithfield kid and though she could probably pick him out, she has no idea what he's like.

"Except for his expression," she says. "Kind of self-satisfied. Maybe his parents have money and have indulged him, or maybe he's just one of these guys who thinks he's so good-looking that he doesn't have to worry about anything else."

Joshua asks again if she saw anything at all that might explain Dan's disappearance. She says no, she didn't.

"They were in their own little cocoon here, hidden away from the rest of the world."

There's nothing more to be done at The Preserve and she leads the way back. Once they leave the cover of the trees the wind buffets them, blowing even harder than before. As they move through her yard to the area behind the entry to the kitchen, it swirls and dips, raising bits of dust and twigs and tufts of milkweed. A speck of bark, shaped like a miniature arrowhead, lodges in his right eye and he raises a finger to tug at it, rubbing the eyelid and pupil until he sees a dusky blackness. A sharp pain in the lower hemisphere of his eyeball makes him dizzy.

When she sees what happened she says, "Come inside, I'll help you with that eye."

She guides him into a kitchen whose blue and white gingham curtains and scrubbed pine table are at odds with the rest of the house. He sits in a plain oak chair, and with his good eye peers through the kitchen to a small room with a floor to ceiling fireplace and opposite, a brick alcove that holds a day bed. With its simple cover and pillow, the bed has the hastily tidied look of a lair that has been slept in recently. And beyond that, a closed door and the barking dogs.

Now a great weariness takes hold, spreading over his body the way water let through a sluicegate fills the next chamber, rising, rising until it reaches the high mark on the wall. He feels her fingers tugging at his, uncovering his right eye, and then a washcloth against his cheek from which lukewarm water seeps into his lower eyelid. She moves the washcloth around the eye, and the contrast between the roughness of the cloth and the suppleness of her hands has a soothing power. His body goes slack.

110

"Don't open it," he hears her saying, in a voice meant to be minded. "Keep it closed a bit longer." Her voice comes from far away, and he wonders how long he has slept. Ten seconds? Ten minutes?

He does as he is told, as she busies herself at the stove. When he opens his eye a cup of herbal tea greets him, the steam bathing his face in an aromatic mist; tears seep out of the corner of his eye.

"It's a life-saver," he says, sipping the tea. "Or an eye saver."

The tea is her own concoction of mint, chamomile and ginger. She learned to make it the way she learned to cook: by trial and error, with a little help from books and friends. What about your mother? Joshua asks. Didn't she teach you? Not my mother, Irina says, laughing. She was an actress, then a drama teacher, much too artistic a woman to be chained to a stove.

Because Irina had no experience and no formal training they were reluctant to take her on at Café Rustica but she offered to do a week's internship, unpaid of course, and at the end of the week she had her job. Now she divides her week between the early shift, 10:30 A.M. to 6:00 P.M., and the dinner shift, which starts at five and doesn't end until one.

Joshua asks how she gets to Collegeville.

"Drive, like everyone else," she says, pointing through the window at her beat-up Jeep. "The bus doesn't come too often."

He smiles; there is no bus. Joshua notes the dented door on the driver's side, the rust eating away at the rear fender, the worn tires.

"I've got four snow tires, I put them on in November," Irina says, anticipating his question. "My mom sent me a check for them a few years ago—a Christmas present."

Agitated barking reminds Joshua that they aren't alone in the house. "Why the dogs?" he asks in a teasing voice.

"They scare people off."

"I'm sure they do."

The way he says it makes her laugh, then he laughs too, his thigh nudging the front leg of the pine table and spraying a few drops of mint-chamomile-ginger tea on his jacket.

He tells Irina how he came to be doing what he is doing: improbably, he began his working career with a leading strategy consulting firm, putting in 80-hour weeks and traveling the country. Dan was less than a year old and Joshua was coming home so late that four nights out of seven his son was asleep when he made it back from Manhattan or flew in from Chicago.

Then came his father's heart attack. When Sam got out of the hospital his mother was adamant that he could not go back to the warehouse, it was too dangerous. Joshua thought hard about it—and decided to chuck the consulting game and take over the business.

"We got rid of the warehouse, so there was no more chance of my father being robbed at gunpoint, and I got to come home and put my son to bed every night."

Next came real estate, first in White Plains and surrounding towns, then in Smithfield. If only he'd turned a deaf ear when he first heard about Franco's plans, he says bitterly.

"I knew there'd be problems with Tall Pines, but this?"

He tells Irina about the personalities on the Board of Selectmen, about the violence on the job site. She is aghast to hear about Franco's Lab, Arthur. But when Joshua suggests that the opponents of Tall Pines may be behind Dan's disappearance, she says, "No, that can't be." Surprised at her vehemence, he wonders what—or who—can account for such strong feelings.

He sips the last of the tea and asks how she wound up here.

"I went to school in Collegeville. After graduation I married my English professor. I enrolled in the master's program but I got tired of it, then we got tired of each other and called it quits. I borrowed a little money from my father and bought this place."

"How little?"

"Thirty-five hundred. And borrowed $11,500 from the bank."

"You overpaid."

Once his eye is clear and his teacup empty, he asks to see the room off the kitchen, with its huge fireplace and curving brick alcove. It's apparent that she sleeps here, on a day bed with a spongy mattress and a checkered blue cover. As they stand in the space, which has a narrow window in front and another in back, and the cool, cloistered feel of a monastery storeroom, she tells him she redid the brick walls and wideboard floors.

"You redid them? How?"

"Oh, I had help pulling up the boards but I refinished them and nailed them back in place. I got the fireplace repaired, though the mason cut the cost because I was willing to help with

112

the pointing up. I also helped lay the brick for the wall. In the kitchen I rewired the circuits and hung the lights and replaced the sheetrock."

Why do you sleep down here? he wants to ask, but she's moved back to the kitchen, to the window. He comes and stands there, looking beyond the garden to a long woodpile, held in place by stakes. Many of the logs have been gathered from deadwood, then cut to a uniform length; others have been split and sawed before stacking.

She tells him that she's slowly redoing the rest of the house; she'd take him there but it's a dangerous mess, with broken lath littering the floors and plywood insets in the windows.

"There's a lot to do," he says: the renovations, the garden to plant and tend, the woods to roam for herbs and berries—all this, plus the job in Collegeville.

"For one person, you mean?"

Yes, he nods. On the other side of the door in the room off the kitchen, the dogs, sensing an unknown visitor, are scratching and whining.

"They can't accept that there's someone here they don't know."

"Do they have a veto?"

"I do the vetoing," she says with a chuckle. "It's up to me who comes and goes here."

Irina goes around to the front door to let the dogs out. They bound into the yard, a fierce black terrier and a dirty blond German shepherd. For a few minutes they halt their scratching and barking to scarf down the food she puts out for them.

Joshua says it's time to go, that he has other places to stop.

"I'll keep an eye out for Dan. I'll be hoping for good news."

"None of us expects good news at this point."

From the house Joshua reaches Sammons on his cell phone to say he was up at the Preserve today and to ask if they've done a thorough search of the place.

"Of course we've been up there. It wasn't any help that I can recall." Sammons seems to have less patience for Joshua than usual; he's at work and can't talk long.

Joshua mentions some of the things he saw today—the bits of fabric that might have once been a shirt sleeve, somebody's pink lipstick, the twisted, blackened beer cans—but Sammons says there's no telling how long some of that stuff has been lying there.

"Kids have been hanging out there for years and years. God, I used to do that myself when I was 16 or 17—mostly in the summertime, though sometimes on those autumn evenings when the moon is huge."

Still, Sammons tells Joshua he'll come by around 4:30 on his way back from Hartsfield. It'll be a chance to bring Joshua and Nathalie up to date on everything the police have learned.

With the afternoon to kill, Joshua decides to walk up to Albie Moreau's place by way of the Hawes Hill Road, past Grace Flint's trailer. It's about two and a half miles one way, and a steep climb. The road is eroded, nearly washed out in several places, and strewn with fair-sized rocks. He hasn't been up there since the pastor died more than a year ago. Moreau's widow, a water-colorist, is spending most of her time in Tarpon Springs, leaving the house in the care of her granddaughter, Ariel.

At the Moreau place Joshua observes that the driveway has been tended, the gravel raked carefully out of the grass on either side, the weeds down the middle neatly trimmed just the way Albie did. For years Moreau would be out there with sickle and trimmers in hand, disdaining the gasoline-powered weed whackers.

"Good for the body, good for the spirit," he'd say, clutching the sickle when you caught him in the middle of this chore, bare-chested, wearing the fraying khaki shorts that were spotted with bleach stains. "Good for the thirst, too." Albie's favorite time was late afternoon, lying in a chaise, reading Thomas Merton or Ross Macdonald and sipping a beer.

Joshua is surprised to see that the vegetable garden is lush with tomato plants, zucchini, late summer corn. It was Albie who fought the good fight against aphids, Japanese beetles and funguses; the minister was soft on human sinners but implacable when it came to nature's pests.

There is no sign of Ariel, but it must be she who is keeping up with the weeding and harvesting. He recalls Ariel as a compact young woman with wild hair the color of golden raisins. Once a political activist in Nicaragua, she now lives here with a boyfriend; the boyfriend makes music, she sculpts.

"It's me, Josh Sandler," he calls. His answer is the wind, howling in the humid air.

There is always something unexpected about coming upon the clay tennis court here, pristine and untouched, bordered on three sides by green meadow, and on the fourth by a stand of white birch trees. He plops on the lawn behind the far service line, halfway up the grassy slope.

Too many memories in this spot: memories of Dan running up and down this slope as a five-year-old, and soon thereafter, pleading with Joshua to be allowed to swing the racket himself, in a hurry, as always, to try something new.

"Let me Dad, let me," he would urge. "I can do it." And in fact even at a young age he had the essentials: the eye-hand coordination, the instinct to place himself where the ball was heading, the self-control to meet the ball rather than try to wallop it. Within a few years he was swatting tennis balls back and forth with Joshua before Joshua's partner showed up.

On the way down from the Moreau place, he finds himself thinking about Irina. Every time he visits her he has this feeling that she knows more than she is telling him. He sees her face in front of him as he quickly descends the precipitous Hawes Hill Road, banging his toes on the stones as he steps sideways to avoid the craters. Already the first angry spits of rain have begun falling on his neck and ears.

Joshua goes faster, then faster still but he cannot outrun this storm. Long before he reaches Grace's trailer the rain is falling in dense swells; it deafens and surrounds him like an angry New England sea surging round an open boat. It feels as if he is wearing a helmet of rain instead of his own hair, as if his shoes are filled with wet cement.

Unable to see, Joshua slows to a step-by-step walk, picking his way around the rocks. The rain is shucking the weeds and greenery from the road, uprooting them ruthlessly, sending mud and small stones coursing downward. His walking shoes ooze with muck as foaming, muddy water rushes by.

He staggers into the mudroom and there he peels off everything. Sammons will be here in 15 or 20 minutes but all he can think of is a hot shower to warm his chilled bones.

"My God, where have you been?" says Nathalie, seeing him naked and dripping.

"Caught in the storm. I'm home now," he says, as if she can't see. "Safe and sound."

Chapter 13

"Time to go home," Joshua says, a journey that Nathalie both longs for and dreads. It's 157 miles from Smithfield to Mamaroneck; every mile is a dull blow to the belly. That is where she feels Dan's absence, inside her, like an assault on her womb. When she was carrying him she had a miracle pregnancy, a few days of nausea at the outset and then, for months, this wonderful feeling not just of well being but of biological destiny, as if everything in her body, every organ, every locus of sensation— her mouth, her nose, her fingertips, her breasts—were tuned to a single frequency, an overture to beginning life. And now, this emptiness, this anti-life eats away at her insides, leaving her raw and shredded.

Joshua packs their things, fills the cooler with the odds and ends left in the fridge, carries her soft-sided overnight bag to the Jeep. She doesn't try to help; it is all she can do to put one foot in front of the other, to keep her arms very straight at her sides as if she is sidling along the walls of a narrow tunnel.

She sits in the car and as Joshua is giving the house a last run-through the phone rings.

It's Bob Franco, wanting to know how they're doing. When Joshua says he's worried about Nathalie, that she won't even pick up the cello bow to draw it across the strings, Franco offers to talk to her. Thanks but not now, Joshua replies. I'll call you when I'm back.

At that moment Nathalie comes into the house; she has roused herself from the front seat of the car and come in to see what's taking Joshua so long. She stands in the doorway, her face frozen, devoid of purpose. He takes her by the shoulders and steers her to the car.

They pull away from the house in bright sunshine. Nathalie can't bring herself to talk. She hates the sound of her voice. She'd prefer listening to Joshua's voice with its low rumble, its occasional eruptions of laughter or anger, but for the first 60 miles Joshua drives in complete, forbidding silence.

They drive through the high, windswept center of Cliff-mont, the fading white church like a well-used prop against the curtain of gray cloud-flecked skies and waving cornfields. They float along the main street of Hartsfield as if what surrounds them is not 3-D life in its odd rhythms (yellow light, slow, red light, stop, car door thunked shut, from a narrow side street a young voice, male, impatient, yelling, 'Come on, Bud'), but a washed-out color billboard of small-town main street.

"Mind if I put on the news?" Joshua asks when they reach the Taconic Parkway.

"Okay, let's hear the news." Her tone of voice, forthright against all reason, belies what she feels: a choking sensation, as if she cannot breathe, as if she may never breathe again. They listen for 20, 25 minutes, hear the White House hail an agreement with the allies on Bosnia, as the killing goes on, hear the baseball scores, hear reports of a typhoon in Guam. They drive south, Nathalie willing the membranes in her ears to contract to shut off the awful roll call of tragedy from around the world. When Joshua switches off the radio she is hard-pressed to recall a single fact, a single name.

One hour and eight minutes on this bucolic parkway, lushly green against all the odds of late summer; even with windows shut Nathalie can imagine the sweetness of the grass, the perfume of the roses and phlox. Far from soothing her, today the beauty around her inflicts pain in tiny, repetitive pinpricks that end up numbing the senses. By the last graceful turn, the last vista of gentle green hills against the perfect end of summer blue, the sun beginning to diffuse as it descends toward the meridian, her mind is in rebellion.

So little traffic on such a fine day, Joshua says just after pulling off the Taconic. Nathalie's response comes swiftly. "It's not a fine day. It'll never be a fine day again."

As they pull onto their street, the sight of their house, a tall white colonial with black shutters, eases the strain on their faces, and for a few minutes they bathe in the comfort of the familiar. They unload the car, open the windows to air out the musty house and sort the mail. Other, sadder emotions crowd in as Nathalie steps gingerly through the rooms like a sapper looking for land mines.

117

No sooner are they home than the phone is ringing: Nathalie's mother, Robin.

"How are you, dear? I'm so glad you're back home. It must be such a relief. I know that you'll sleep better in your own bed." As if a change in mattress will make any difference.

"Mother, what is it?"

"What do you mean?"

"I can hear it in your voice. What's the matter? I know that something's the matter."

"I wasn't going to tell you, not with everything going on."

Nathalie teases out the details. Her father's been experiencing shortness of breath, fatigue, chest pains that his internist said must be checked out. The thallium stress test shows a blockage in the left anterior descending artery. They want to do an angioplasty right away, Thursday.

Of course she must go. At first she dreads the idea of the trip; every aspect of it overwhelms her. She has to force herself to call the airline and demand a special fare. She sleepwalks through the upstairs rooms, packing clothes suitable for Florida (90s outside, freezing in the over-airconditioned hospital waiting rooms). As she neatly folds the beige summer sweater and the black nylon slacks into an overnight bag, Nathalie has an unanticipated moment of engagement as she realizes that this family medical crisis is occupying her energies in a way that has been lacking for these past three and a half weeks.

In the midst of her preparations her friend Sonya, who plays viola in a string quartet and also acts as its de facto manager, calls to see if Nathalie will sub at an upcoming rehearsal. Nathalie says she can't. Sonya persists. "It'll be good for you."

"Don't tell me what's good for me. I can't do it. I can't."

The next morning Joshua drops Nathalie at Kennedy and drives into midtown. Gert is manning the phones as he comes in. She's been with Joshua for seven years, a slender woman with sharply defined features and hair that reminds him of that tangle of unruly cables spilling out from the back of the TV.

No sooner has he stepped through the doorway then she comes to give Joshua a hug. Two of the lines are blinking on her phone and Sean, a poet and part-time telesalesman, is on the third line. The fax machine is spitting out paper. To his chagrin and relief, Joshua finds the activity, even the quiet hum of the airconditioning, to be comforting.

"Is there any word? The poor boy." There is pain and sympathy scored across her face.

"No word. They're looking high and low and haven't found a trace."

"Don't lose hope," Gert says, fiercely, grasping Joshua's waist and looking him in the eye, willing him back into a semblance of normality.

Gert is a single mother, fanatically devoted to her 11-year-old daughter.

"Hope?" The word comes out very flat. "No," he says, "of course not."

Gert recites the checks that have arrived and hands him a list of upcoming auctions from a fax service they subscribe to. Joshua barely looks at the list. It's the White Plains office project that's on his mind; he makes a couple of calls to his partners and to the architect to see how they're dealing with the town's demand for a park-like plaza that will add more than a million dollars to the cost. The personalities involved are a lot tamer than in Smithfield—as far as he knows no dogs have been poisoned—but the issues of irascible neighbors, local politicians with prickly egos and the tug of war over money, money, money are just as acute.

"Oh, we'll get it approved," says the architect, a laidback fellow whose elaborate, frilly shirts and tight-fitting designer jeans are spotted with green tea stains, and who keeps telling Joshua that he'd be more relaxed—or is it more alert, Joshua can never remember which—if he took gingko biloba. The architect practices what he preaches; he smiles and smiles as the project costs mount. What does he care if the plaza in question will cost his clients an extra $1.2 million; a bigger budget only means a bigger fee.

He recalls the phone message at home from yet another Democratic county committee member. They're still dangling the possibility of a race for county legislature, hoping to entice a newcomer into a hopeless contest against a well-entrenched incumbent. If Josh won't run himself perhaps he'll write them a check to help subsidize someone else's candidacy? What if he gave in and said yes, he wonders; what if he won? How would it be to sit on the other side in these meetings, voicing objections and driving developers crazy with one proposed change after another?

For the next three hours Joshua goes back and forth in his mind between the here and now (office furniture, real estate, local politics), and Smithfield: heavy-set Art Sammons, the touch of Irina's fingers on his cheeks and eyelid, the palisade of steep hills surrounding The Hollow, the green lawn with its shimmering curtain of heavy late-summer dew, the photo he distributes showing the tanned face of their missing son.

Gert is bugging him about upcoming auctions; she wants him to go to Long Island City on Friday and Bethlehem, PA on Monday. When Joshua says Bethlehem is too far, she's insistent.

"Two hours each way, max. You can do that."

Three auctions a week with his margin of 10% give Joshua a gross profit of $350,000, $400,000 a year to work with. Deduct rent and electric and phone, the salaries of Gert and Sean the poet and the wear and tear on his Jeep and Joshua can clear a hundred twenty-five to a hundred fifty, even one seventy-five in a good year. He's always liked getting out of the office, touching merchandise, likes the feel of a real product that people sit at or on. But he's getting bored with it; real estate has more risk, more unknowns, more of a rush of excitement—or at least it had until Tall Pines came along.

The phone rings, another call for him, and when he picks up the receiver a woman's accented voice says, "This is Marie-Therese Etienne from the Bronx Academy."

"From where?"

"The Bronx Academy. It's a brand new charter school with 82 fifth and six graders who need your help, Mr. Sandler." She explains that the mission of her school is to snatch up poor kids from the Bronx, give them a quality education and get them into good colleges.

"School opened last week," Marie-Therese says, "and we're short a dozen desks. And some file cabinets, a couple of computer workstations, and storage cabinets."

When Joshua points out that he carries no inventory of office equipment, Marie-Therese persists. "I'm told you are the most capable guy in the city when it comes to finding used office furniture at a great price. Won't you help?"

"Who told you that?"

With a laugh, she names one of his customers. It's hard to resist this woman; she is charming, single-minded.

"All right," he says, "let me see what I can do. What's your budget?"

"Nothing."

"Nothing? As in zero?"

"Mr. Sandler, a charter school is for kids whose talents are being suffocated in the public schools. We have motivated teachers and kids. What we don't have is money."

"How many desks did you say?"

"A dozen. Listen, come and see the school. You'll see the layout, get some ideas."

He figures this is a throwaway offer, but she insists: "Come this week if you can."

Wednesday he takes the afternoon off and drives to a forlorn brick building on a dusty lot in the shadow of the Cross Bronx Expressway. Across the street is a car wash, in front of which two skinny Dominicans, stripped to the waist, are lounging by the raised door, and next to it, a bodega. The bodega's windows are filmed over with the grime of years; its rickety outside table is sagging badly under the weight of a pickup truck's worth of plantain bananas.

It is late August, cool, humid, gray. He walks down the hallway past six classrooms, each full of kids, each in perfect order. Regular school doesn't start till after Labor Day but these kids are already at work. All the teachers are in their 20s or 30s; half are white, half are black. He finds Marie-Therese sorting papers on a card table wedged into a 6x8 closet. "Welcome to Bronx Academy," she says. "And welcome to my office."

She straightens up and extends him a hand. She is dressed in tapered silver pants with a purple jacket, a slender woman whose glittering black eyes and laughing mouth are in constant motion. He hears construction noises as workmen patch and spackle the walls on the third floor, getting the music room ready for use.

Marie-Therese shows him around. The building used to be a parochial school but it ran out of pupils. Bronx Academy made a deal to lease it from the parish for a dollar a year.

"A dollar a year? Oh, so you have money after all."

Joshua asks Marie-Therese about her background. She grew up in Haiti, taught public school there, then came to New York and spent two exhausting, punishing years teaching in a Bronx middle school where no one cared: not the principal, not the teachers, not the pupils.

She was on the verge of switching careers, moving to Lehman Brothers to peddle stocks when she saw an ad for teachers for Dare To Succeed, a new charter school: "Long hours, mediocre pay and that priceless feeling that you're making a difference." After two years at DTS they made her associate principal. Then came a chance she couldn't turn down: a $50,000 foundation seed grant to start her own school.

By this time they are down the block at China Latina, a tiny restaurant with four metal tables where arroz con pollo costs $1.95. Over fried rice, Marie-Therese talks nonstop about the need to raise math test scores, about the plans for a music night, about volunteer projects for the kids.

"I'm not just looking for desks. That I can get anywhere. I'm looking for people who will be friends and sponsors. We need all kinds of help, and I'd like you to be part of that."

As they walk back to the red brick building, they are trading personal details.

"My wife is a cellist. With the New York Philharmonic." He tells her how disciplined Nathalie is, how hard she works. He and Marie-Therese are standing in front of the school, and Joshua can hear the whine of a floor sander.

Her question is innocent, natural. "Children?"

"Well, we have a son. But he's missing and we're afraid they won't find him alive."

On Friday Joshua is waiting at the gate as the passengers from Nathalie's plane disembark. First comes a deeply tanned young man with tangled hair, jeans and a $2,000 leather jacket slung over his shoulder, someone who could be an actor, a music industry executive, even an importer of Colombia cocaine. Then a pair of ice-blonde stewardesses pulling their wheeled suitcases behind them, followed by a fleshy, white-haired gentleman with a huge pinky ring. Looking around him, Joshua sees five wheel-chairs waiting, each with its attendant; after all, this is a Florida flight.

"Did it go all right?" he asks Nathalie when finally she comes out the exit.

"I don't know how they'd have managed without me. Mother had no idea how to get to the hospital and no idea where to go when we got there. Dad was weak and tottery but yes, it went fine."

He sneaks a sideways glance at her as he edges onto the Van Wyck, maneuvering the Jeep past a streaked and dented white van, its tailpipe held precariously in place by means of a twisted coat hanger. Nathalie's face has a look he hasn't seen in weeks, a look of exhausted calm brought on by exerting herself for others. Her thick hair is electric from the Florida humidity and in her cheeks there are bands of color from the sun. She has freshened her lipstick on the plane. Her dark eyes are staring ahead, seeking him out.

When Nathalie tells Joshua about her parents—the weakness of her father, the fussy ineffectiveness of her mother—Joshua suggests one or both of them will have to go down there more often. Every couple of months, he offers.

"Every couple of months?" She turns to him with anguish breaking out across her face like a rash. "How? How?" And she says no more.

When they reach Mamaroneck at 1:30, Joshua takes her to lunch at the tavern. It's a town landmark: a single cramped room next to the bar, with half a dozen tables. Homemade soup and a meaty sandwich with a slice of fresh pickle costs $5.95. They grab a table near the window where the sun sends an oblong splash of light across the scarred wooden top.

"Just a cup of soup," Nathalie starts to say, but Joshua is ordering two specials plus a side salad. She looks as if she lost five pounds in Florida. He insists that she have a glass of Merlot, too. When the waitress brings the food she eats with appetite, saying little. The sadness has returned to her eyes, like the shadows dogging the late-afternoon hiker.

That afternoon he works the phone and fax machine from home. An associate tells him about a building for sale in the Bronx—northern Bronx, another world from Bronx Academy. He fends off the committee chairman who's been pestering him about the county legislature. Personal reasons, he says, without elaborating.

They eat supper late. Nathalie has showered and has changed into a white T-shirt and a pair of tan slacks that are now a little loose in the waist; she has removed her makeup and Joshua can see how thin her face looks. They clean up the dishes together and take a stroll in the late-summer night, with a half moon glowing fuzzily as they walk up and down the hills around their street. Nathalie slips her hand in his; he grasps her right shoulder and pulls her close.

Is it his imagination, or is her body more yielding, more feminine? When he comes up, toward 10:00, Nathalie is reading a magazine. She is wearing one of her cotton summer nightgowns, a light blue one, and her thighs are dimpled ivory against the sheets. Now he is lying next to her in his underpants, brushing his shoulder against hers, then taking a finger and tracing the line of her waist and ass, the indentation of her hip, the ribs just below her breast. She does not touch him, nor does she move away but her breathing comes just a tad quicker. Joshua turns off the light. He kisses her on the ear, burrowing deeper into the crook of her neck and shoulder, stroking her flank with his fingers. His tongue laps at her ear lobe. She sighs, and then he is tickling her lips, brushing them lightly with his own. The street lamp near the window sends its pale beam through the grill of the open blind to cast a patchwork of dark and light across the softness of the nightgown.

Joshua is aroused now. He lies on his side and pulls her toward him. He can feel her hesitancy as he presses against her. When he reaches a finger between her thighs she starts. He persists, slowly, through the tangle of her pubic hair, sensing the nightgown rise and fall with the motion of his wrist. Now he is touching the lips of her pussy, but the flesh is cool, almost rubbery; the wetness he seeks is absent. He feels Nathalie's body tense. Though she doesn't move, something in her resists and then recedes from him, inch by inch like a tide running out. Joshua rolls away from her and, lying on his back, brings his hands back to his stomach, folded there in a dejected little heap.

"Don't go." Her voice is a whisper. He lies there and doesn't answer.

"It's not that I don't want to. It's just that there's a part of me that won't relax, ever. It's as if something in my mind says to me, 'You're not entitled, you don't deserve your own moment of pleasure.'"

"Does that make sense to you?"

"We're not talking about sense. This is not logic, this is not some problem to be analyzed and discussed and then a decision reached."

He interrupts. "Okay, okay. It's feelings, it's instinct, whatever it is. But at a certain point you can put these feelings aside, just overrule them and . . ."

"Overrule them?" Resentment creeps into her voice. "It's so easy for you. Maybe other people can turn their feelings on and off like light bulbs but I can't."

"You're putting words in my mouth. Who's talking about light switches?" He can hear his tone grow colder, more distant. His erection has shriveled; the two of them lie on the bed, not touching, not talking.

Sleep does not come to Joshua for a long time. He picks up a biography of Grant, reads a few pages. He plugs the earphones into the radio to catch a Yankees game from the West Coast. It is the fourth inning, the Yankees' third basemen fouling off pitch after pitch and finally lining a double to deep right field that scores two runners. The Yankees go on to add seven more runs. Joshua switches off the radio and reads to the end of the chapter.

The baseball scenes stay in his mind; he marvels at how the words of a sportscaster 3000 miles away can put him in the ballpark. Nathalie has turned on her side and with her eyes closed is breathing evenly, sleeping or pretending to sleep, he can't tell which. The annoyance Joshua feels toward her dissipates, leaving in its place a heaviness that seems to clog his heart and constrict his breathing. He switches off the light for a second time and draws the air into his lungs in long, slow waves that lift the muscles of his chest up, up, up, and then down as he exhales. Joshua wriggles his toes and then tells them to be still; he does the same to his fingers, to the tips of his ears, to his knees, elbows. He has slipped into a long narrow box, not a terrifying one but somehow oddly comforting because its walls lie so close to him.

What comes to mind then is not a dream but a memory, a memory in sound and motion. He is recalling Smithfield on a summer evening a year ago; all day it was rainy and gray and then at six it cleared and by 7:00 it was glorious, a freshening breeze had cleansed the sky, turning it a deep blue with a few daubs of whipped cream clouds. The sun was already heading down in the west, it was late August and the days were shorter. He and Dan put their supper plates in the sink and headed out to the side yard with their baseball mitts and Dan's new white Spalding hardball to play catch. They threw hard strikes, then looping sidearm pitches, then long lazy fly balls that sent each other deep in the yard or a step or two beyond the lawn and into the gravelly road to haul them in. On these high flies the ball hung in the sky at the uppermost point in the arc and then descended like a stone into the fielder's mitt, making a sharp, satisfying crack against the small bones in the hand.

At 7:45 they were still throwing to each other. Nathalie came to stand on the front step, to watch them, Dan's feet taking him all over the green lawn, his sneakers making a swishing noise in the dampness of the evening dew. The only other sound was the smack of the ball hitting the mitts. When the last streaks of sun had vanished from the sky and the evening star had appeared in the east and was sprinkling its brilliance like glitter, Joshua and Dan trooped in, tired and smelling of perspiration, their feet trailing bits of clover and grass from the lawn.

He remembers looking at Dan, his right hand trailing across his son's shoulder, and Nathalie at the table, glancing up from a magazine at the two of them.

Recalling that moment, he feels a tingling high up on his cheeks as if he must give in now, reach for a tissue and dab away the moisture. He bears down hard on the inside of his lower lip, mashing the soft flesh between the pincers of teeth. The lawn scene fades from his mind, pushed aside by the determination to return to The Hollow, to find answers that will lay memory to rest.

Chapter 14

In late afternoon in Smithfield, as an enervating humidity clings to his shoulders and thighs, Joshua stops at the general store. He's only come to buy bread, some local peaches and blackberries, and is annoyed that he has to push his way through the crowds: people ordering grilled chicken sandwiches, grabbing bags of chips, cans of coke, fruit juice and beer, bottles of water, oversized brownies wrapped in plastic. It's the weekend of the Smithfield Fair, always a big draw. He finds himself fuming as he listens to the questions with which these visitors, some from as far away as Springfield, pester the high school student at the register: how many miles to the fair, do they take credit cards, where can I buy fresh corn, no, not corn that was picked this morning, corn that was picked five minutes ago.

Until four years ago this place used to be windowless, dirty, stale-smelling, a typical country store. Then the Rosenscheins bought it. Steve gave up his partnership at a Manhattan law firm; he handles the merchandising and is always out front with customers. His wife Deb does the books and bakes the blueberry muffins and the apple crumb cake. They sank a quarter of a million into the place and it shows: skylights and picture windows that bring in the sun; an eating area with tables; five kinds of olive oil; goat cheese, sundried tomatoes; a whole aisle—four shelves, two sides—devoted to domestic and imported wines.

Traffic is always good, but today is ridiculous. Finally Joshua hands over his twenty and collects his change. In the time it has taken to make his purchases and stand in line to pay for them, the west-sinking sun has heated up the steering wheel and driver's seat of the Jeep; Joshua shifts his thighs this way and that to avoid scorching his flesh on the hot plastic. Where did this heat come from, four days after Labor Day? This must be a last gasp before the chill of autumn, this sultry weather that makes him weary and out of sorts.

Although he drove up two days ago because he had to, because he couldn't stay away, at this minute he doesn't want to be anywhere within the geographical limits of Smithfield. He longs to be someplace cool and dry, to shoot baskets for hours, to run for miles with a breeze tickling his bare arms, and then to sit on a porch with a fat, sprawling book set in a time he knows nothing about: the Middle Ages or ancient Rome would do fine. The desire for a way to tune out the nightmarish daily reality has flickered more brightly in recent days as the awful finality of what he and Nathalie are facing begins to sink in. Joshua finds himself wondering, with some dread, if and when these thoughts of escape will become more insistent. So much of his daily routine now seems an effort to stave off the feelings of futility. Escape, the allure of being in another, more peaceful place—he recognizes this longing as a trick of the mind, an attempt to substitute physical removal for emotional imprisonment.

Leaving the house at seven in the morning to traipse around another area of Smithfield, to talk to another neighbor, to once more walk the couple of miles up Route 33A as it follows the course of the river—this is his life at The Hollow. The chores are fraught with foreboding, and yet they occupy his body, they distract his brain. What else does he have but the chores and the phone calls: the two calls a day to Sammons, the daily calls to Gert and his real estate partners about business? Joshua sees himself as plying a narrow track on the edge of a precipice; if he stops moving he might tumble down.

Not Nathalie. Whether in Mamaroneck or Smithfield she has no desire to leave the house, even for the simplest errand. Instead she sits at home, within arm's length of the phone. She never wants to be out of the range of its peremptory summons, even though the news it bears is more likely to be catastrophic than soothing. Though he too leaps for the receiver when it rings, Joshua knows that the phone is bound to be their enemy.

He wishes he could do something to shake Nathalie out of the fog that has settled around her, robbing her of speech and ambition and pleasure. Any mention of the cello incites her to an icy fury. He stops suggesting it. She broods, I dash from one activity to another, both of us struggling against the blackness of the moment, Joshua thinks.

Enough daydreaming; Joshua chases away the thoughts of breezy hilltop retreats, of swaying hammocks and stacks of books to read. He starts to pull out of the parking lot, then holds up as a sports car swerves around the corner from Route 57, crossing momentarily into his lane before regaining the right side of the road. It then roars off toward the fairground. Through the window he sees three teenagers whooping it up. One is Bobby Dawes; another is Melanie; and the third, at the wheel, is a well-groomed boy wearing a more expensive, tailored shirt. Joshua supposes this must be Tony Bentley, whom he has never met.

On a spur of the moment, Joshua decides to drive up this same road. Fifteen and 16-year-olds, even 18-year-olds like to mill around at the fair, one of the few places outside school where small bands of teenagers can check each other out. Seeing that many kids in one place might give him some ideas, some new leads, Joshua thinks.

The road takes him into the high pastureland south of town, on the same escarpment that leads to the summit of Allen Mountain. At 2250 feet it's just a bit higher than Miller's Needle, on the Tall Pines property. After a steep climb the road levels off. Hundred-year-old sugar maples line both sides of the road, with gray, gnarled, upright trunks and branches thick enough to support the weight of an army personnel carrier. Here, with a commanding view to the southeast, is the Armstrong Brothers' farm, a hill resplendent in late-summer grass and clover, and dotted with black brindled cows. Most are sitting with legs folded under them, in the shade of the beech and poplar trees that meander along the electric fence; against the green they are in sharp relief, like a chain of life-sized cutouts.

Joshua takes the next turn and now the red silo of the fairgrounds comes into view. After he has handed over his ten-dollar bill to a strapping woman in her early 50s, trailing wisps of silver hair, she date-stamps his wrist with a fluorescent dye, then directs him to the back reaches of a vast and rutted parking field. The Jeep jounces to a halt about a hundred yards from a series of fenced enclosures and three-sided sheds where the 4H kids, each with piles of straw, buckets of water and bristle brushes, are feeding and grooming their animals for tomorrow's competition.

Joshua ducks under the railing and walks the length of the sheds, past the cows, the year-old lambs, and, new this year, the black and brown llamas with their habit of contorting their ugly faces to spit at a passerby who ventures too close. He reaches the main fair building, where he knows he will find display after display of perfect cucumbers and tomatoes, pears, plums, peaches and early Jonamac apples; and then, on the second floor, a section devoted to the home crafts—needlepoint, weaving and embroidery. All through the hall the ribbons have already been awarded: blue with three chevrons for first place, red for second, white for honorable mention.

Outside the building he runs into Rosa Puckett. "How many did you win this year?" he asks Rosa, a famous gardener and weaver who competes with her giant sunflowers, her floribunda roses and occasionally with her quilts.

"Oh never mind about that," she says. "What is new about your son?"

He gives the familiar response.

"Your dear wife," Rosa says. "How is she doing? Shall I call or come by?"

"She's down in Mamaroneck. She isn't seeing many people these days."

"Oh I understand. I understand completely."

They are standing on the lowest step of the two-story, forest green building when Joshua sees Tony Bentley and Melanie Roberts go by, talking in low voices, their faces serious. Tony and Melanie head toward the long aisle of food stalls, separated from the main building by a smorgasbord of offerings: food processors and steak knives, machines that bale hay, homeowners' insurance, vacuum cleaners, tractors, encyclopedias, college loans. The hucksters are a mixed bag: thin, sweaty men with oily skin and faces that are scraped and bristly from their early morning shaves; housewives with broad come-on smiles and strawberry blonde-dyed hair done up in frizzy perms.

Joshua can smell the burgers crowned with fried onions, the sickly sweet tang of donuts whose glaze is puddling in the sun; can see a looping trail of kids coming his way, dripping vanilla and chocolate down the backs of their hands as they clutch melting ice cream cones.

"Excuse me," Joshua says to Rosa Puckett as he hurries off to follow Tony and Melanie. Before he can catch up to them he nearly bumps into Bobby walking in his direction, hands in his back pockets and eyes looking skyward, as if to mark something extraordinary: a solar eclipse, a supersonic Concorde overflying the Smithfield fairgrounds.

Joshua forces himself into the boy's field of vision.

"Hello, Bobby."

Bobby reacts as if a bird is diving for the corner of his eye; he snaps his head away, then recovers. "Oh, hey Mr. Sandler."

Joshua has never stood this close to the boy before. Now that they are face to face, he can't help noticing how fully formed Bobby is: he has the build, the thick lips of a Marine recruit. His shoulders are massive, well-proportioned buttresses. The boy mumbles something incoherent; the only words Joshua can make out are "Dan" and "like, too bad."

They are almost at the food stands, where the grease of hamburgers and frankfurters coils upward in the humid air. At one counter, a teenage girl with a pudgy roll of flesh around her neck is selling rings of fried dough; to sell it you've got to eat it, Joshua thinks.

"Something to eat?" Joshua offers. "A coke? An ice cream cone?"

Though he and Bobby are about the same height, the boy seems to be straining to look over Joshua's head, seeking someone, anyone to rescue him. There is no one.

"Okay," Bobby says, stymied.

"Chocolate or vanilla?"

"Chocolate."

He collects the cone for Bobby; buys himself an iced tea. They are opposite the entrance to the grandstand, and the loud-speaker is blaring the news that the horse draw is about to start. Joshua takes a step onto the concrete runway that angles down past the opening in the grandstand, toward field level. With a touch of his fingers on the boy's elbow he steers Bobby in the same direction.

"Ever seen the horse draw? Let's go watch for a while."

His tone leaves Bobby no choice. The boy looks confused, trapped. No doubt he came to look over the girls and as darkness comes on, to sneak off to drink beer between the rows of pickup trucks in the parking field, not to sit next to Dan's father on a wooden bench in the grandstand. He mentions hooking up with his friends.

"Come on, let's sit for a little while. Maybe you can help me with something." He leads the boy on a climb up the steps to a spot in the fourth row, near the stanchion that rises to the roof of the grandstand. The announcer, a gravel-voiced woman named Martine, is introducing the first team of horses, from Manchester, VT, and their trainer Hank Wigman. Hank's bare arms stick out of his overalls, as he talks to his pair of liver-colored geldings. He steadies them. The chain, anchored at one end to a sledge with 5,000 pounds of concrete blocks, is quickly hitched to the wooden and canvas harness frame, and now Hank is shouting and flicking his whip. The bodies of the horses lurch forward, but their shoes seem stuck to a powerful magnet. For a long second the sledge sticks and vibrates and finally begins to move, six inches, a foot, a couple of yards, till it passes a mark in the sand. Hank is cooing to his team as a second man unhooks them from the sledge, and off they prance, dropping yellow-brown clumps of horseshit from beneath their twitching tails.

Joshua keeps his eyes on the show below them as the second pair of horses comes out, this one led by Bob Buxton of Canaan, CT.

"You know," Joshua says, "this whole thing has been incredible, a bad dream from which you never wake up. Every morning you think, today will be different, Dan will be home, and of course nothing changes. Three and a half weeks ago he was here and now he's just vanished. And no one can say where or why, or who might have wanted to hurt him."

He looks sideways at Bobby. "You must have some idea what happened."

Bobby has dark brown eyes and long russet hair whose ringlets wind around his ears and flop down over his right temple.

"No," he says, swiveling his large head from side to side, as if this could be answer enough. "Not really."

Why so awkward and uncomfortable, Joshua wonders.

Team two, a matched pair of black geldings, has come and gone, easily hauling the sled far enough to make the next round. Now the third pair is on its way in; one of the horses, a dappled gray and white, is pulling this way and that as if to shuck off the harness.

"When did you see Dan last?"

"I talked to that policeman dude," he says. "I told him I didn't know anything."

"Okay, then tell me. When did you see him last?"

"One of those nights."

"The night before he disappeared, right? Up at the Preserve?"

"Yeah, I guess."

Martine comes on the loudspeaker to announce Doc O'Shea and his team, from nearby Collegeville. "That is, if Doc can ever settle them down enough to get on with business." There are catcalls from the crowd. Doc, who has the grizzled look and sure hands of a retired GP, tugs the gray and white horses into line but when the payload is anchored to the harness one horse refuses to budge. His companion tosses his head and kicks. A shirt-sleeved teenager darts in to unhitch the pair from the sled, and quickly jumps away, as one of the horses aims a shoe at a sensitive spot. Every team gets two tries and after the others have had their go Doc's will be back.

"So? What did the two of you talk about?"

"I can't remember."

"Try."

Bobby lifts his shoulders in annoyance. "Mostly we'd just crack on one another."

"About what?"

"You know, if one of the dudes has a rip in his shirt or his hair looks real bad or . . ."

"Or what?"

"You know, stupid stuff, like if he just laid down a fart and grossed everyone out."

At this Bobby allows himself the ghost of a smile. He doesn't want to look at Joshua; neither does he want to watch horses straining at a huge weight, something inexplicably lame to him.

"There must have been something that happened that night. Something between Dan and the other kids, or one of them."

"Maybe the police dude knows. He must have talked to everyone."

Around them the benches are beginning to fill up as working men and women drift into the grandstand after a day of farming or waitressing or working construction or mopping floors in one of the nursing homes in the hills on the outskirts of Hartsfield. These evening fairgoers are hungry, hungry for food and companionship. They've loaded up at the food stalls, and are carrying 24-ounce cups of soda pop and plastic plates with kielbasa, burgers, fat french fries with thick squirts of ketchup. Some of the men are lugging coolers and now, as they take their seats, they pull out a cold beer.

The crowd cheers lustily for Hank Wigman and his pair of brown workhorses as they lug 7,000 pounds. Doc O'Shea and his team fail to nudge the sled at 6,750. Hooting and laughter break out as Martine tells him over the loudspeaker, "You've got the wrong horses today, Doc. I guess this is one of those times when a guy just can't perform the way he's supposed to." The biggest cheers erupt for Buddy Hitchcock, a crowd-pleaser who wears a white stetson with a red feather as he trots in with his team of gigantic black geldings.

No one pays the least attention as Joshua quizzes Bobby Dawes. No, Bobby says, he didn't see Dan the day he disappeared. He was home looking after his little brother until his stepfather got up.

This is a big kid, Joshua thinks again, as Bobby shifts this way and that on the hard bench, his sunburnt face caught in the pink-violet glow of the late-afternoon sun. Bobby's long arms have an arc and heft to them, like the bottom limbs of a pin oak. Joshua asks Bobby about why his father sleeps late, and Bobby reminds him that Tim Bartlett works at the factory up in Rollins.

"Night shift," Bobby explains. "Doesn't get home till one or so."

"What's he do during the day?"

"Sleep, watch TV, drink beer. Leave the cans lying around so I get blamed for them. Sometimes, he'll get the truck and go cut some firewood and then I have to help. Like today. Too hot out there." Joshua sees the traces of dirt in the lines of his hands; this is a kid who can wield chainsaw and shovel and trudge through the woods with a heavy load of wood.

"Want another ice cream? A soda?"

"Thanks, I'm okay."

"Ever have any fights with Dan?"

"Fights? You mean fighting with our hands?"

Joshua keeps his voice even. "Could be that. Or just a big argument about something."

Now he looks Joshua full in the face, as if to convince him that he's telling the truth.

"There wasn't any fight. I told you, we would crack on each other, the way guys will do. That's all it was." Bobby's annoyance has turned to nastiness now.

Maybe, Joshua offers, maybe one of the other kids got into an argument—even a fight—with Dan. Sam? Tony? Someone else? Nothing, nothing like that, Bobby says.

Buddy Hitchcock's team is coming up for its last try at 7,500 pounds. If they fail, the cash prize of $2,000, will go to Hank Wigman. Hitchcock acknowledges the importunings of the crowd, touching his fingers to the red feather in the band of his stetson. His good luck feather, he calls it. Hitchcock, a lefty, has the whip in his hand, raised almost to shoulder height. He gives a shout and lays the whip sharply across the back of one of the horses. For the longest time, perhaps 25 hundredths of a second, the sled doesn't budge. Then there is a tremor and it begins to slide along the sand. Hitchcock applies the whip a second time, and the sled grinds on, a few inches, a foot, a yard and a half.

"Come on, Bobby, what's the story. There has to be an explanation. Somebody had it in for Dan. Somebody did a terrible thing to him. You must know something. You must."

"I said no. I don't know."

At 8,000 pounds neither Hank Wigman's nor Buddy Hitchcock's team can budge the sled. "That's a tie for Hank and Buddy," Martine's voice crackles. "We're done here, folks."

Bobby is done, too. He bounds down the rows of grandstand benches, hopping from one to the next as Joshua watches the fairground crew—the wiry teenage boy who ducked away from the kicking horse, and a man who looks old enough to be the boy's grandfather—make ready for tomorrow's tractor pull by shoveling off fresh mounds of horseshit and putting down more sand.

Joshua strolls the fairgrounds for a half hour or so, peering through the dark at teenagers balancing drinks and plates of food, watching the preening of the girls and the slouch of the boys. On the way back to the car he spots Melanie and Bobby gesturing to a third figure. Tony, Joshua thinks, but on closer look it is not Tony; it's Sam. Bobby, Melanie, Sam; something tells Joshua he should remind Sammons to have another go at these kids. The three of them have ducked into the shadows on the back side of the main fairgrounds building. He sees them indistinctly, as if through a streaky windshield, and any sound they make is too far away, too muffled, like the faint buzz of a radio under a blanket at the beach.

135

Chapter 15

He knows what she looks like before he speaks to her on the phone. Melanie has shown him a picture of Kristen: a comfortably rounded girl, busty, with puffy arms, soft, somewhat heavy legs, straight yellow hair, teased up into a beehive atop her head, and on her face one of those excuse-me-if-I'm-in-the-way expressions.

It takes him the better part of a week to locate her. Her mother was a Beaulieu who moved from Quebec to Massachusetts with her parents in the 50s, when jobs in the Belle Province were scarce. For all Joshua knows, they're still scarce.

Grace Flint, who lives alone in the trailer on Hawes Hill Road, helps Joshua find Kristen. Grace's husband Walter Flint was a second cousin to Kristen's father, who died in a peacetime army helicopter crash at Fort Devens in the mid-80s. Once a week now, Kristen's mother sends Kristen up to the trailer with meals for Grace—a tuna casserole, half a roast chicken. Even though Grace insists she's fine with her mayonnaise and sardine sandwiches, or her canned salmon—which she shares with the cat—she eats whatever Kristen's mother prepares, washing it down with heavily sweetened tea.

On her visits, Grace fills Kristen's ears with stories. Before her marriage to Walter, Grace had a wild time—engaged to two other men, one right after the other, and then, at 19, on the verge of eloping with a third. Now she repeats the same tale for Joshua.

"It was a warm May night when the moon was full," Grace recounts, in the same ironic singsong voice that captivated Kristen. "Herbie—that was his name, Herbie Miller—had a hip flask in his jacket pocket and we were sitting under the big elm tree in back of the church, sipping whiskey and loving it up. He was a handsome boy with a new Ford car and the whitest teeth, like something out of an Ipana toothpaste ad. Finally when I'm as hot as a bitch in heat he says to me, 'Grace let's go get married.'"

She pauses, forcing Joshua to ask, "Well? What happened?"

"We get into that Ford car, kissing and feeling each other up the whole time and he misjudges the curve on Church Hill Road and bounces off the road into a tree stump and busts an axle. And that was the end of our elopement."

Grace laughs and laughs. "Kristen loved that story."

"I need to find her," Joshua reminds Grace. "Do you know where she is?"

"Of course. She's at her uncle's house, somewhere up near Ottawa. She went there to have an abortion."

Grace writes down for Joshua the name and address of Kristen's uncle. The address turns out to be wrong, and it takes half a dozen phone calls—there are a lot of Beaulieus—but eventually Joshua reaches the right one. Kristen herself answers the phone.

"Oh my gosh," she says when he introduces himself. Her voice is self-effacing, flighty, as if she is trying to talk through a constant siege of hiccups. "Oh, Mr. Sandler. Oh my gosh." And then she starts to sob.

She's been away since before Daniel's disappearance but she knows all about it. Was it one of the kids who filled her in, Josh wonders. Was it Grace Flint?

"I'm so sorry," she keeps saying. "I'm so sorry. Oh, Mr. Sandler, I'm so sorry for you and Mrs. Sandler."

"Do you have any idea what happened to Dan? Any idea who might have hurt him?"

"Me? Oh my gosh, no."

"How did you hear?"

"Melanie called and told me."

Joshua recalls asking Melanie where to reach Kristen, and being told she didn't know.

"When was the last time you saw Dan?"

When he'd talked to Melanie and to Sam he'd had the feeling that they were playing mental chess with him, working out in their heads, if I answer this way, then he'll ask that, but if I answer that way then he'll ask such and such. But Kristen seems incapable of subtlety.

"I guess it was the night before I left," she says.

"Which day was that?"

"It was a Sunday night because Mom and I left on Monday morning. A couple of the kids came over the house to say goodbye."

137

Dan, Melanie and Sam came, she tells him. Tony? No, he wasn't there. Bobby? At the mention of his name Joshua can hear her tense.

"No," she says. "He didn't come."

"So you didn't see him at all before you left? Bobby, I mean."

"Maybe I did. I just don't remember when it was."

For the first time she is being evasive, not so much to deceive, as because the truth is painful.

"Kristen, I thought you and Bobby were close. Wasn't he your boyfriend?"

"Well, I thought so. I guess he didn't."

"Did he treat you badly, Kristen?"

"Yeah." The burst of anger, when it comes, stings his ear. "Yeah, he did."

The hurt that she has suffered is still very raw. Joshua realizes that this line to a Canadian telephone is his only connection to her, a connection that can be cut anytime Kristen hangs up. He switches tone and asks her about something that he's been curious about.

"Dan was younger than you, wasn't he? He was almost 14 and you're, what? Fifteen?"

"I'll be 15 in December."

"Gee, you sound older."

"I do?"

"You do. So how come you and Melanie would hang around with a boy a year or two younger than you?"

"He doesn't . . . he didn't seem younger. And I mean, this is The Hollow. It's not like there's tons of kids around. Besides, he'd help me with stuff."

"What kinds of stuff?"

"School things. I had to take math in summer school. He'd help me with homework."

"Homework."

"The night he came over, I gave him my phone number up here. He said he would call."

"He did?"

Joshua has trouble keeping the surprise out of his voice; the revelations about Dan are coming too rapidly to absorb, too rapidly to make sense of.

138

"He said he would. But after that night I never talked to him again." She is sobbing again but talking through the sobs, like a voice in the kitchen with rain coming down everywhere, on the walk, the corrugated tin roof, the window sill.

It all sounds pretty harmless, he thinks, unless there was something between his son and Kristen, something that provoked a fit of violence against Dan. Even as he tries out the idea he dismisses it. How could anyone have been jealous of this simple girl with the straight blond hair and that flat face?

He asks her about Sam, Bobby, Tony. Did they get along? Did she see any fights? Was Bobby really a tough guy or was it all bluster?

"He's always saying he's not going to take any crap from anyone, that nobody's going to, you know, dis him."

"Did Dan dis him?"

"He cracked on him. I mean, you know, made fun of him. But it's not like I saw Bobby punch him out or anything."

She stops, makes a strangled sound, like someone gulping a mouthful of ocean water and trying to expel it.

"Oh Mr. Sandler. I can't believe it. I can't believe that Dan is gone and that someone would do such a bad thing."

"Couldn't he have just run away? Kids do that, sometimes." Joshua knows this is impossible, but he wants to hear what Kristen will say.

No, she says, not Dan. He has a normal home, a mother and father. "My dad died when I was real young. Melanie's lives in New York. Bobby's real father is in prison."

"What about Sam? Sam's father and mother are together."

"Sam hates his father."

"Tony?"

"Yeah," she says. "Tony is different. His dad is rich—he drives a Mercedes and owns a lot of things."

What's Tony like, Joshua wants to know, and she says, "Like his dad. Smooth, like he knows where he's headed in life."

They've been talking for 20 minutes and Joshua is no closer to knowing what happened to Dan, or how Kristen figured in it. As gently as he can, he asks again about her and Bobby. I heard, he says, I heard you were pregnant and decided to have an abortion.

Yes, she says, about three weeks ago.

139

"I'm sorry, I hope it wasn't painful."

"Not the thing, the operation itself. Everyone was very nice, the nurse was so nice. They put you out and you don't feel a thing. But afterwards, afterwards, it's . . ."

He waits, lets her catch her voice.

"It's so hard. I must have cried for a whole day. I kept thinking about it, thinking I'd done the wrong thing. After a while my mom got angry at me and said, stop it already. But my aunt Louise was, like, amazing to me. So understanding. She said to me, you go ahead and cry, cherie. It means sweetie in French. And she told my mother off. Said she should just let me alone."

"Was it Bobby's baby? Was he the father?"

He hates himself for hitting her over the head like this, but what choice does he have? When Kristen doesn't answer he thinks, that's it, she's going to hang up. Instead her silence lengthens, and he realizes that what he thought would be anger is something else. She is too drained to cry, too beaten down and ashamed to tell him what he wants to know.

As softly as he can, he repeats his question. "Was it Bobby's?"

Before she can answer, Joshua hears through the telephone line the creak of a wooden door opening, a woman's voice calling to Kristen and then the girl starting to explain. At that moment she leans into the receiver, almost pressing her lips against the handset, or so Joshua imagines, because all the chirpiness in her voice has vanished. She speaks in a throaty whisper, sharing her secret with this man she has never met.

"I don't know," she says, and the next thing he hears is the click of the receiver as the line is closed.

Chapter 16

From Mamaroneck Joshua calls Sammons every morning, usually before the policeman has left for his job at the mall in Hartsfield. From day to day Sammons has little to report. The police are still looking for the silver sports car that Janie Sargent says was going fast, even though there is no evidence it exists—or if it exists, that it bears any relation to Dan's disappearance. They are still focusing on the dozen houses closest to Hunter's Lodge, where Main Street in The Hollow joins the Northway Road—but except for Janie, none of the occupants can offer any clue as to what happened. A search of the registry of known child molesters in western Massachusetts and adjoining New York and Connecticut also proves fruitless. Of the three men in the area who ever served prison time for such a crime, one is back in jail, a second is dead and the third has moved to Georgia.

For the past three weeks, Sammons and Ford have been tracking down Smithfield residents who drive west through The Hollow every morning, an effort that means many dozens of phone calls. No one can pinpoint Dan's whereabouts on the morning of August 10th.

Now the policemen are branching out to residents of the other hilltowns—Northway, Woodfield and Cooperville. Joshua thinks it's futile. After all, it's been weeks since volunteers rode up and down putting handbills with Dan's picture in every mailbox for 15 miles around. There've been appeals on radio and TV, full-page ads, articles and pictures in the *Collegeville Times*, the *Hartsfield News* and the local hilltown paper. At this point can there be anyone who doesn't know that a 14-year-old has vanished?

"The answer is in Smithfield, in The Hollow," Joshua insists. The kids, he says, the kids know.

After Kristen and her mother return to Northway the policemen interview them, then follow up with a second visit to a weepy Kristen. At Joshua's urging they go back to see Sam Bonacio, Bobby Dawes, Melanie Roberts. No one can tell them anything.

"What about Tall Pines," Joshua says, as he begins to recount all the threats and sabotage against the resort.

"We're not investigating Tall Pines. We're investigating your son's disappearance."

"Yes dammit, but what if they turn out to be related?"

"If there's a connection we'll look into it. But so far I haven't seen one."

The weather turns rainy, blustery. Joshua is preoccupied with Nathalie, but whatever he does to reach out to her falls short. Sometimes he looks at her and wonders if she can move anything except her eyeballs, swiveling the pupils from side to side, blinking the eyelids, making just the slightest movement of the jaw up or down to change the angle from which she views the world.

At work Joshua cannot sit still. He grabs for the phone before he is even seated. "Sal? Sal, it's Josh Sandler," he yells; Sal Costantino runs a vast office furniture basement in Brooklyn. "There's a big auction next week and I can get you a hundred desks."

"You should pay me to take them off your hands," Sal says. They yell back and forth about whether Sal should buy 50 desks or 80 desks; now he breaks off to take a call from a developer who needs computer carrels and insulated room dividers to convert warehouse space into office suites. Another phone call to Sal, another barrage of abuse but in the end they make a deal for 75 desks.

On Saturday he bursts out the front door to drive to the gym to play basketball; an hour and 40 minutes later he bursts out of the gym, orange hair wet with perspiration, to drive to the supermarket. Everything he does, everywhere he goes, is at double-time.

This frenetic pace frays at Joshua's equilibrium, and over several weeks, a period of spasmodic dissonance occurs: his hands and feet twitch, stop and start, flutter, but the driving energy is dissipating with nothing to replace it, like a giant clock that can't be rewound because the special one-of-a-kind key is lost. The pockets under his eyes deepen and sag.

He and Nathalie are both nearly bowed over from the weight of remembering, a weight that seems to grow rather than lessen day by day. And yet Dan's name goes unspoken even as it reverberates in their ears.

For Joshua, back-to-school days were nearly intolerable this year. Seeing the kids on line for the bus, backpacks sagging with books; watching them make their way home, in clusters of two's and three's and four's in that milling, half-sideways, half straight-ahead gait that they have—these things tear open his chest as deeply as any thoracic surgeon's knife.

He recalls how often the three of them, Joshua, Nathalie and Dan, used to appear magically on the front step, each emerging from that grainy autumn dusk, each home from a different gig: Nathalie from rehearsal, Joshua from the office, Dan from cross country practice, a run along the twisting trails of Saxon Woods on the border of Mamaroneck and White Plains.

None of Joshua's hyperactivity, his dashing to and fro, can still these memories. One morning at 7:15 he is bent over in front of the fridge when a bottle of cranapple juice slips from his hand and shatters on the floor. Nathalie comes down to find Joshua pounding an oblong plastic container against the edge of the counter, hurling curses into the air, as a red tide filled with glass shards laps around the vibram soles of his shoes. When Joshua sees her he lets out a final "fuck you" directed at the high hat lights overhead, and lapses into embarrassed, sputtering silence.

Silently they kneel on their hands and knees with sponges and paper towels and eventually the whisk broom and dustpan, bumping foreheads as they clean up the mess.

"Thanks. Sorry," is all Joshua says, as he heads off to work. On the train he thinks, Am I'm losing it, losing control? In Saturday's basketball game hard passes bounced off his stiff fingers, opponents stole the ball off his dribble, he missed an easy layup.

He tells himself the answer is even more activity. For a few days he gets up at 5:00 to run five miles and is at the office by 7:30, makes more phone calls, scouts more real estate deals. Exhaustion stalks him; one day he oversleeps and doesn't arrive until ten. No longer is he waking at 2:00 A.M. to circumnavigate the first floor of the house or to settle into an armchair in the living room with a book of history. Now nothing disturbs him; he clings to his bed like a tightly cornered sheet. The dreams come at him in swarms of images and snatches of dialogue, images that he can never recall. More and more he sleeps through the sunrise.

When the 11 desks for the Bronx Academy arrive, Joshua spends most of a Sunday man-handling them into place with the help of one of his regular delivery guys, an unshaven Israeli named Roy. Over another plate of fried rice he and Marie-Therese argue over money. She wants to pay him the wholesale cost, $22 per desk. He refuses. "You offered me nothing, and nothing is what I'm going to take."

Now, two weeks later Marie-Therese has recruited four of the kids as volunteers and on a Saturday afternoon Joshua arrives to help them paint the walls of the music room. In the hallway, Marie-Therese introduces him to her crew.

"This is Mr. Sandler. Mr. Sandler, this is Joycelyn, Amika, Marcus and Alejandro."

The girls blush and look away; Marcus is too flustered to speak. Alejandro, the smallest of the four, has lively black eyes and a smile that spreads across his squarish face.

"Hi, Mr. Sandman."

Joshua smiles. "Not Sandman," he says, gently correcting the boy. "Sandler."

"Alejandro, what you messing up Mr. Sandler's name?" Amika is chunky and outspoken, a natural leader.

"Alejandro, you didn't do anything wrong," Joshua says. "How do you spell 'Sandler'?"

Alejandro gets the S A N D but then begins to go astray.

"LER," Joshua prompts. "How do you spell 'LER'?"

"What kind of word is 'LER'?"

"It's not a word, it's a syllable."

"What's a syllable?"

"Part of a word. So, how do you spell 'LER'?"

Alejandro sounds it out, and then repeats his question: "What's a syllable?"

"Every word has syllables, depending on how many different vowel sounds there are. House has one syllable; Marcus has two syllables. And Alejandro . . ."

"Has four," the boy says triumphantly.

Upstairs, paint, drop cloths, paint thinner, brushes and rollers are waiting for them. Joshua takes the biggest wall; the

144

kids divide up the other three. When they're done he takes them to the McDonald's down the street, a place with a spotless parking lot, a scrubbed yellow sign and order takers whose cardboard caps stand straight and proud under the manager's watchful eye. Here in the south Bronx, the streets shadowed by grimy public housing, McDonald's seems like the Four Seasons.

Marcus is a fifth grader; Amika, Joycelyn and Alejandro are sixth graders. Joycelyn wants to become a singer. "I want to be a doctor," Alejandro proclaims. "For children."

"A pediatrician," Joshua says.

Alejandro repeats the new word. "Pee-dee-a-tri-shan. Five syllables," he says, grinning.

Marcus, younger and less sure of himself, still can't utter a word.

Joshua drops them back in front of the brick school building where Marie-Therese is on the sidewalk, speaking French with another Haitian woman, regal in her yellow and blue print dress. After she thanks Joshua for all his work, she asks what else he can do for them.

With Alejandro looking on, he mentions math tutoring, a chess club and basketball.

"Basketball?"

"I know, white men can't jump, but actually I can."

She points out that there's no gym, nothing but the low-ceilinged basement, already over-booked with lunch and African dance and whatever P.E. they can squeeze in.

"Okay, then, math tutoring," he says. "Just get me the books."

Chapter 17

It pains him to see what is happening to Nathalie. He'd thought being back in Mamaroneck would be good for her, that she would break out of the cycle of sleeplessness and self-absorption, that colleagues from the orchestra would be in touch and that she would begin to play again. But week after week the cello stays in its case in the upstairs closet.

They are flood victims. She lets herself be carried willy-nilly by the foaming current, barely clutching at the branches rushing by, while Joshua fights to make shore. He fills his time with real estate, auctions, customers. He makes long phone calls to Sammons or Ford, demanding particulars—whom have they talked to, what have they learned. He needs to personify the disappearance, to feel that it is not an accident but the deliberate work of a cabal of evildoers.

Sometimes he drives to Smithfield for the day, headlights knifing through the blackness of these chilly autumn mornings. He'll arrive there by 9:00 A.M., spend the hours talking to neighbors he knows or strangers he doesn't know, walking round and round their property, the roads, the woods of The Hollow— until at 4:00 or 5:00 he climbs back in the car to fight through the darkness to home. Nothing could be more heartbreaking on such a trip than the sight of the surrounding hills—red and green and yellow, as if lit from within, on a bright day, or gray, sodden, dull and hopeless under the drip drip drip of a cold autumn rain.

These trips leave him trembling with anger—at himself, at this town with its mysteries; the word 'why' screams in his head for what seems like hours. Once he pulls over to pee at the rest stop on I 84 and as he is coming back to the car an older man with one of those gray crewcuts and a nose the shape of a peanut rolls down his window.

"'Scuse me, but are you all right?"

"Sure. What's the matter? Who are you?"

"Just now on the road, I pulled even with you to pass and when I looked across you were banging your forehead, seemed

146

like it was almost hitting the steering wheel. I waved and honked but you didn't notice. I thought you might be having some kind of seizure."

Joshua, embarrassed and a little frightened, says, "I'm okay. A lot on my mind, I guess. Hey, thanks for stopping."

And for the last half hour Joshua holds the wheel with both hands, shoulders straight against the car seat and tells himself as if to a small child, it's going to be all right, stay in the middle lane, no sudden swerves, you'll be home soon.

He thinks of Dan in that moment and as often happens, a soothing calm—the calm of cloistered monastery walls, of shady hideaways in meandering gardens—takes hold. It's as if Dan has been gone on a long trip and the distance between them is teaching him to understand and cherish his son. In his brain he knows that, like any 14-year-old, Dan was a hormonal, secretive teenager. Surely Dan must have resented Joshua's oversight, benevolent or not; when he got together with his buddies surely he must have articulated the common disdain for cloddish parents and their hopeless ways. But in Joshua's memory the specifics of family discord soften, and the Daniel who emerges is mature and self-aware.

Joshua does not wallow in these edited memories but merely accepts what they grant him, a brief respite from the agony of uncertainty. It is uncertainty that bears down on him like a rock from which he cannot extricate himself, an uncertainty far worse than whatever horrible thing transpired. What happened, happened, Joshua tells himself over and over; it's in the past. Not knowing what happened contaminates the present as well. And yet, uncertainty also allows him to entertain the possibility of a miracle that will restore their son to them. He will never speak of such an eventuality, won't even let his mind entertain it and yet, absent proof, it exists as an incalculably small possibility, as if he could sift every grain of sand on a wide beach and find the one that bears the singular ivory white hue he seeks.

Once a week he comes to Bronx Academy to tutor three fifth graders: the tongue-tied Marcus and twin sisters from Santo Domingo, sweet-faced and well-meaning but very slow. Every time he explains something to one of them the other giggles.

The regular math teacher, a leather-voiced ex-wrestler named Chris Swift, has briefed him on how to proceed. "Drill and practice, drill and practice," he says. "Teach them the method, the steps to solve any problem, don't let them guess or stray from the method." Multiplication tables, long division, fractions: always the method. They tackle the day's homework, problem by problem and before Joshua knows it his watch reads 5:30.

He bumps into Alejandro, who shows him his science notebook, a unit on the human body. When Alejandro asks what pediatricians study, Joshua urges him to ask his own doctor. Alejandro explains that his mother takes him and his sister to the community clinic whenever one of them is sick; it's always a different doctor that they see.

"I know a pediatrician," Joshua says. "Maybe he'll come and talk to your class."

A few days after the episode with the crewcutted stranger, he leaves the office early. Daylight savings time has ended and he walks in the door at a quarter past five to find Nathalie in the kitchen in the gray-black of late-afternoon becoming evening. She is staring at the backs of her hands and he is sure she has been sitting there a long time.

"Were you out today?"

"Yes." Her voice lacks timbre; it is the voice of a tollbooth attendant.

"Where were you?"

"At the store." She points to dishwashing liquid, yellow liquid cleanser for floors and countertops, a bottle of disinfectant, bleach, soap pads; they stand ranged on the counter like stage props. She has this fetish now about bacteria; everything must be spotless.

"Why don't we go out for supper?" He mentions a Szechuan restaurant she likes.

Which is worse, he wonders; to bustle around the gloomy kitchen or to sit her in a restaurant, trying to elicit a chuckle from her as he comments on everything, the skinny blond hostess, incongruous in a Chinese restaurant, the early-bird special (do people still eat this column A, column B stuff, chow mein, spare ribs, won ton soup; thank God we got here after six), the unsmiling waiter with the lank of dark hair brushing his right eye, whose guttural Hong Kong-accented English seems to be pulled, a word at a time, from deep in his throat.

If they stay home Joshua will cook. He prepares simple meals, poached salmon, rice and broccoli; linguini with a red sauce. He does the shopping too, often at ten at night when the supermarket is empty. He'll ease the car out of the garage, letting it roll down the three percent grade, waiting to switch on the ignition until its wheels are in the street, so as not to wake Nathalie. At the supermarket he skates up and down the aisles, swinging the cart in front of him for balance. Minutes afterward he is marching to the car, the weight of two plastic bags—meat, potatoes, grapefruit, apples, tomatoes and carrots—cutting into his palms. Sometimes he'll start cooking after he comes back from the market; the aroma of roast chicken or brisket fills the house as he brushes his teeth upstairs.

Nathalie accepts his new role as a matter of course. Her delightful laugh, which crinkled up her face in merriment and came out in trills like the echo of a bell high on a mountain, has vanished. In its place is the look of the somber, unsmiling Dutch girl in the Vermeer portrait.

On this night they drive to the Szechuan restaurant and there they run into their good friends, Bill and Sandy Cohen. Sandy waves them over.

"Come and celebrate with us."

Bill has just learned that come June he'll be supervising principal (the high school, middle school, two elementary schools) in a small town in northern Westchester. The promotion means a nice raise but now, he jokes, there'll be even more people to drive him crazy.

Their food comes quickly, heaping plates of rice noodles, chicken with garlic, sautéed duck, a whole baked fish surrounded by scallions.

As Bill orders another martini, he entertains them with stories about pushy parents and interfering school board members.

Joshua sips his beer and nods. "I know about local boards," he says. "You should see the Smithfield selectmen in action." Soon he is describing Albert Sims and Carl Puckett. Bill is laughing, Sandy is laughing. Nathalie picks with her chopsticks at the flaky white flesh of the fish, barely responding as Sandy tries to get her to talk.

The next day Sandy calls Joshua at work to say how worried she is about Nathalie. "I'm doing everything I can," Joshua yells.

"I'm telling you, Sandy, I'm at the end of my rope. I can't take it any more."

"Easy does it, Josh," Sandy says, and a few days later, she takes Nathalie to lunch and listens to her plaint.

"I don't deserve to live like other people, to love and work and be useful. To enjoy myself. I don't deserve any of that."

"That's awfully selfish of you," Sandy snaps. "So many people are worried sick about you: your husband, your sister, your parents, your friends. How can you let them down?"

"Don't put any guilt trips on me, Sandy. You have no idea what I'm going through."

"No I don't, but I'm dead serious, Nathalie. You can't do this alone. Get help."

Joshua drives Nathalie to an appointment with Dr. Joan Meyerson. From her booklined office in Edgmont, Dr. Meyerson and her patient can look out onto an arc of perfect lawn, bordered by lilacs and rhododendrons.

Joshua has briefed Dr. Meyerson and at her first visit with Nathalie, the psychiatrist says, "I know there's been a terrible tragedy in your family. Please tell me about it."

"They don't know where our son is. They haven't been able to find him."

"In Smithfield. Smithfield, Massachusetts," Nathalie says, when Meyerson asks where this happened. "I don't suppose you've ever heard of it."

"Actually I have," Meyerson says. "Years ago we visited friends in one of the nearby towns. We even went skinny-dipping at the quarry."

Nathalie smiles to think of the large, broad-beamed Dr. Meyerson, now attired in dark skirt and jacket, swimming nude in that rocky gorge. Meyerson smiles too.

Meyerson has Nathalie tell the whole story. Okay, she says, how have you dealt with it?

Nathalie forces her words out. "When this first started," she says, "when Dan disappeared, I felt as if I was three feet underwater. People would talk to me and by the time I had figured out what they'd said the conversation had moved on."

"And now?"

"Now I'm not underwater, I can hear what's being said, but it's as if it's nothing to do with me. Josh talking on the phone to his office about those stupid desks. My Dad with his cardiac condition, my mother with her laxatives and her worries about driving to the supermarket and back without hitting anything. I know there's a world around me, full of people with their own lives, but I don't want to be part of that world."

"We can't help being part of the world," Dr. Meyerson observes. "How we engage with it, that's the issue. That's the choice you have to make."

Then she asks, "Do you feel singled out in some way to have had this happen?"

"Singled out?"

"Do you ever feel, 'Why me? Why not them?'"

"All the time I feel, 'Why me?' I never feel, 'Why not them?' How could I ever wish this on someone else?"

"Why not? Because you think it wouldn't be nice, it wouldn't be proper? What I'm asking is, are you stopping yourself from having feelings that it would be natural to have?"

"How can I know what feelings I'm supposed to have? I only know the feelings I have, and those are difficult enough."

Meyerson steers the conversation to music, and Nathalie says she is pained that she can't pick up the cello and play it. After all, she has been in love with the cello much longer than she has known her husband, much much longer than she has been a mother.

"It's as if I'm on strike against it. Or against myself, I don't know which."

Meyerson writes her a prescription for Prozac, 20 milligrams a day, and says she wants Nathalie to go back to playing the cello. Nathalie balks at this; finally she says she'll try.

Dr. Meyerson says she's not much for the words 'I'll try.' "I want you to commit to playing the cello every day. Fifteen minutes, that's all. Come back in a week and tell me how you are feeling."

A week later Nathalie says she's feeling no worse, maybe a little better. Meyerson bumps up the dosage. Asked about the cello, Nathalie shrugs. She's playing, dutifully, but without confidence in her own talent.

Keep at it, Meyerson says. Don't give up. Then she asks, "Is Dan an only child?"

"Yes."

"Why didn't you have other children?"

"What difference does that make?"

"Anything and everything can make a difference. So, was it a conscious decision not to have more children?"

"Conscious, no. A few years went by and the topic sort of dropped off the table. We were both so happy with Dan; we didn't see the need for another child. He was everything a parent could want. Maybe I thought another child would only take away from that."

"Did your husband agree?"

"Joshua wanted another child. I was the one who was ambivalent. I don't know, there were lots of reasons. My career . . ." She stops. "That's not right. It wasn't my career. It was that everything was just in such . . . in such harmony. The three of us just fit together. I was afraid something might go wrong." She tells Dr. Meyerson about her sister's childhood illnesses, about her fears during her pregnancy with Dan.

"Fate had been kind to us. Somehow to have another child seemed like challenging fate."

"And now fate has turned on you so cruelly. Is it any wonder you have such anguish?"

"I'm a mother who's lost a child," Nathalie says sharply. "Any mother would react the same way. It has nothing to do with my conception of fate."

"Any mother might," Meyerson agrees. "But we're trying to get at *your* feelings. The better you understand them, the better you'll be able to cope with them."

"I'm coping, in spite of myself I'm coping. Can't we leave it at that?"

Chapter 18

Nathalie is better one day, worse another; without any special mention she begins to take charge of a few household chores, straightening up the kitchen, making the bed, a trip to the ATM machine. She won't hear of traveling to The Hollow; she all but plugs up her ears at hearing it named. For his part Joshua cannot stay away. Week after week he is compelled to return, no matter Nathalie's mood, no matter how often he telephones Sammons.

He is no thrill-seeker who visits the site of a catastrophe—a house fire that kills a family, a bridge that collapses, plunging motorists to their death. Instead he is an actor in the ongoing docudrama. All he wants is to ring down the curtain on act three once and for all, to liberate himself from the haunting uncertainty of its ending.

If someone were to call this a quest for his son, Joshua would shake his head impatiently; a quest sounds voluntary but he has no choice. An obligation to Dan urges him on, even though the Dan to whom he owes this obligation can never return.

This Friday in November he starts the drive up the Taconic under a benign late-afternoon sun but somewhere past Hartsfield gray clouds smother the light and soon swirls of fog engulf the Jeep. On the tricky climb to Cliffmont, he peers through the gloom of the approaching night, trying to pick out the headlights of the oncoming cars as they sweep around the bend. Just as he is turning into the driveway at The Hollow, he realizes that he forgot the milk for tomorrow's coffee and decides to get it now. He cruises through the village slowly, foot barely on the gas pedal, and turns east. Everything here is black, black with a ghostly white mist that forms where cold air from the north meets the warmer road surface.

In the parking lot at the general store, mist washes over him like a sea spray, pinging against his cheeks; the faces and limbs of people are blurry in the fog. Inside, one woman is buying hamburger meat and Oreos while another clutches a container of Deb's homemade dinner special, which tonight is lasagna. Two men in dusty workclothes are grabbing sixpacks of Bud with tortilla chips.

Clutching his pint of milk, Joshua considers staying and eating here. The room is warm with laughter and the bustle of small-town commerce; he is tempted to have his supper at one of the cozy tables between the low stand of newspapers and the spinning rack of work gloves and winter caps. Except that conviviality is a burden he is loathe to shoulder just now. He is about to climb into the front seat of the Jeep when across the parking lot he sees a woman coming toward him. He recognizes the slim figure, the suggestion of a limp, the rope of black hair hanging down her back and then she is slowing her pace and coming into focus, as if emerging from a veil of water.

"What brings you out in this weather?" Irina asks.

"Good question. I came up by myself a little while ago and I realized I'd forgotten milk. You?" Why this need to tell her immediately that he was alone?

She names a few things that she has come to buy. He wants to know more—what *kind* of cooking oil—but his fingers are closing around the door handle and like a skater attuned to the slightest movement of her partner this barely perceptible act seems to set her in motion again, gliding toward the store.

"Well, be careful on the road," he calls.

"You too."

Then he is driving back through the mist, which seems alive, exhaling tendrils of frost into the blackness.

In the kitchen he unpacks his leftover roast chicken and potatoes, bread, a grapefruit and now the milk. As he deposits his backpack at the foot of the stairs, he flicks on the hall light and looks up. The yellow light seeping out of the bone-white, slightly fly-specked globe catches the gold paint on the treads, their edges worn to a polished curve by a hundred years of feet on these stairs. He glimpses, at the top of the staircase, the polished balustrade, the slender oak uprights in parade formation along the upstairs hallway.

Joshua suddenly has a picture of his son in a characteristic pose, lying on the bed in his cave of a bedroom, pillow propped up behind his head, and in his hand the latest *Sports Illustrated*. He'll still be in shorts and gray T-shirt—except for muddied sneakers, tossed just across the threshold of the room—and the mosquito bites, dirt and sweat from the day's exertions will be caked along his arms and legs. When Nathalie calls him for supper he'll ignore the call once, twice, and then the third time he'll shout, wait, I've got to shower. Why now? Nathalie will yell up. You want me to eat in these dirty clothes? All right, be quick. Okay, he'll yell and then read another five minutes before hopping into the shower.

As Joshua stands there the whole scene unfolds so believably that his mind can't possibly be playing tricks. If he runs up the stairs, with no hesitation, without putting the milk in the fridge and scraping the chicken into a pot to heat up on the stove, if he does all this this second Dan will be there. His brain tells him he is a pathetic fool but in an instant he is up the stairs and flying along the corridor, and then he is through the door into Dan's bedroom where he flicks on the floor lamp with its goose neck pointing toward the pillow.

The room is empty. The bed is made, the blanket stretched tautly over the mattress. The floor is clean of soccer shoes, dirty socks, magazines and books. In the half-height closet he can see Dan's shirts, jeans, sweat pants, the pajamas he never wears, a gortex windbreaker, and the single pair of dress-up clothes—pressed chinos, a striped short-sleeved shirt with collar. Everything is as neat as in one of those historic 18th century homes where you stand behind the rope, peer in at the study and see the pipe rack, the inkwell, the blotter on the desk, lifeless objects, without the ragged edges of human to- and fro-ing.

The police borrowed a bunch of Dan's clothes and took pictures and did fiber analyses, then returned them to Nathalie, who washed and ironed everything. In the three-shelf bookcase she's arranged the magazines, the Travis Magee paperbacks, the *Lord of the Rings* trilogy, the favorite children's books from years ago.

Joshua switches off the light and from the hallway he hears the phone.

"Hello?"

"Hi. I should have asked you at the store." He recognizes Irina's voice by the lazy way she talks. Does she have something to report, a new discovery in the woods?

"I have a stew simmering on the stove. Do you want to come and have some supper?"

"Supper?"

He can hear the smile in her voice. "Yes, supper. You do eat supper, don't you?"

Joshua is bewildered by the invitation, disoriented by his own behavior. His wacko vision of Dan on the bed, then the empty room, and the closet of neatly pressed clothes—it all makes him wonder if he can tell what is real and what is not.

What time, he asks.

"Come as soon as you can."

As his Jeep bounces up the incline to her house he runs his fingers through his thicket of orange hair. He comes around to the kitchen window to find her standing at her little stove. When she opens the door the rich odor of beef stew surrounds him like a tent.

Joshua hands her the only thing he could find on short notice, an unopened bottle of sherry that a house guest once brought. Though he wiped it hastily with a dishtowel, he notices a long triangle of dust on the back of the bottle.

"Thank you," Irina says, with a low laugh. "This'll be just fine."

She hands it to Joshua, who wields a paring knife to cut away the plastic seal, and works the cork back and forth until out it glides.

Irina reaches up to unhook the apron from her neck, sliding her fingers under the blue tie that holds her hair in a ponytail. She is still wearing her work uniform from the restaurant: black pants, a long-sleeved white shirt, sleeves rolled up to below the elbow.

Irina puts two short glasses on the table and he pours out a few fingers worth of sherry into them. She has set out two place mats, and on each a large earthen soup bowl sits atop a blue-rimmed dinner plate. She turns off the flame under a pot on the stove, and he inhales the aroma of slowly simmered beef stew, onions, red wine and mushrooms.

He hands the glass of sherry to Irina, the tips of his fingers brushing her open palm.

"Your hands are cold," she says. "Did you drive all the way through that fog?"

"Only the last 40 minutes, but now it's everywhere." He motions toward the window and together they look through the blackness at the white mist hiding the trees. How quiet it is here: no radio, no music, no voices, just the breathing of this woman next to him.

At the table in the kitchen they sip the sweet sherry and eat her stew, sopping it up with chunks of chewy Tuscan bread. She smiles as Joshua cleans his plate and asks for seconds.

"Did you like it?"

"I loved it. You should get a job as a cook."

"I bet you'll say anything when you're hungry."

They look at each other, neither knowing what to say. She begins talking about the storm that hit a week ago, five inches of rain in 24 hours, flooding sections of Route 57. Instead of braving the drive home that night Irina stayed over with Barb.

"Barb?"

"A girlfriend in Collegeville."

The existence of this person takes Joshua by surprise; how idiotic of me, he thinks, to imagine she has no life except this house, the dogs, the restaurant. He tells her about his buddies at Saturday basketball, about the White Plains city council and its demands.

Nothing new is there? she asks, not mentioning Dan's name. No, he answers, nothing.

She brings him a salad of greens and avocado. When Joshua finishes it, he studies her face, calculating the arc of the thin, very black eyebrows over her astonishing blue eyes. Under his gaze, her face relaxes into a smile. Her lips twitch, then open to ask a question.

"How long are you going to be up here?"

"For the weekend, at least. Tonight and tomorrow night. Then we'll see. What about you? Are you around all weekend? No special plans?"

Irina has to work tomorrow night till late, then again Sunday from noon until eight. That's a heavy schedule, he says, somewhat relieved to hear that she won't be out with friends. What can you do, she replies; weekends are make or break time for restaurants.

He starts to clear the plates but she stops him. "Forget about the dishes. Let's just enjoy the moment. More sherry?"

"Just a drop." Joshua really doesn't want any more sherry. His mind is an untidy grab bag of longings, obligations and fears. He tips his glass toward Irina.

"To the moment," he says.

When he leaves soon thereafter he reaches for her hand, she rises up on her toes to give him a chaste goodbye kiss. Her lips miss his cheek as her chin bumps his shoulder.

As Joshua pulls into his driveway, the phone is ringing and he dashes to get it.

"Where were you? I called an hour ago and got no answer." Joshua tells Nathalie about the lengthy drive, the mist on the road, the excursion to the general store.

Silence at her end. "Is everything all right?" he asks.

"Fine," Nathalie says, meaning not fine at all. She tells him who called: her mother, his mother. "And Bob Franco. I told him you were up in Smithfield and you'd get in touch."

Joshua is up at six the next morning. He drags himself downstairs to sit motionless at the table, remembering the aroma of the stew and the way Irina smiled. Now he has no thoughts, only reflexes: sip coffee, toast a bagel, push my body upstairs, into the shower. As he leaves the kitchen he can see the first snowflakes swirling in the back, as if giant hands have seized the branches of the pine trees and are shaking tiny bits of confetti from them.

When he calls a little after eight to thank her for supper she sounds out of breath: "I was outside, exercising the dogs and feeding the chickens."

The snow or sleet or whatever it is will be making her black hair all wet and tangled; he pictures Irina striding around in worn jeans and a fleece pullover.

"Nice weather for it," is what he says, wincing that he is beginning to sound like someone whose great grandparents were born in Smithfield.

"So you're working tonight?" he continues. "You won't be home till late?"

"About one."

"Is it too late?"

"Too late? For what?"

"Nothing, I just thought you might like some company." Her silence is assent so he asks, "Do you want to call me when you get home?"

"No. Why don't you wait for me here?"

It is as if he is energized, as if in one long pull he swallowed a bottle of adrenaline. He laces on hiking boots and heads for The Shadows on foot. When he is halfway up Route 33A the snow gives a final swirl and then stops. The sky lightens a shade. At the swimming hole he picks his way across the shallow, icy river, stretching or jumping from stone to stone. Then he turns north toward the state park following the line of the hills, a couple of hundred yards away from the river, where the ground is marshy, tough going. The iron gray heavens crack open for good and the sun appears, as perfect as an egg yolk. The brambles have died back and he pushes steadily through the withered yellow grass, admiring its headdress of tiny beads of snow as they twinkle and vanish under the distant sun.

This is new territory for Joshua—away from the house, away from The Hollow. It seems anti-intuitive, except that all previous directions have turned into dead-ends. Joshua plods through the wetlands at the bottom of the hills, mashing down the seeds deposited by the birds, stepping over fox droppings. Here is an oxidized bottle cap, there, a pair of pliers, rusted beyond use. He finds a scrap of soggy, tattered material, perhaps from a jacket collar. It's nothing Dan could have owned, let alone worn on a sunny August day.

After a slog of 50 minutes he leaves the marshy fields to vault onto a dirt road that leads to a white farmhouse, sitting on a spread of watercolor quality: two barns, a pond, three horses grazing in the pasture. This is Edward Torvald's place; the horses belong to his wife Betty Sue.

Torvald, an icy-veined 70-year-old, with a stringy neck and a croak of a voice, has been gradually selling off some of his many hundreds of acres. Torvald has a poker player's sense of the market. He waits until the economy is perking, until out-of-towners are looking at property here because all the prime locations in the Berkshires have soared out of sight. Then he tacks up his For Sale signs along the road. When he gets a bite he attaches himself to the caller with such courtly persistence that he rarely loses the sale.

Joshua recalls an autumn day as cold as this one, sitting in Torvald's kitchen with its '50s look, the yellow and white linoleum, the florescent ring fixture. Torvald took a call and before his eyes Joshua saw this frosty businessman turn into a saccharine-tongued salesman.

Torvald is not the sort of fellow you drop in on, so Joshua hurries home via the main road and gives him a call.

"I heard about your son," Torvald says on the phone. "Damn shame. We live out here to get away from that sort of thing. No chance he just ran away, is there?"

No, Joshua says. And then he asks Torvald whether he's noticed anything strange, anything at all, when he is out walking his land. "We're still looking for him, you see."

Would Torvald know where on his many acres someone might bury a body?

"They probably wouldn't pick the deep woods. Too hard to drag a body there, too hard to dig. Oh, I suppose you can always dump something into one of the crevasses and cover it with dirt and leaves. But the best bet would be the meadows and bogs."

"Where?"

"Problem is, there are dozens of places. We're talking almost 800 acres in Cliffmont, Smithfield and Northway."

"Mark them for us," Joshua says. "Give us copies of your maps and show us the spots."

Torvald says he'll do it. Take him a day or so, but he'll drop it by the house.

Next, the Bentleys. He drives to their spread in Northway: a big yellow house, outbuildings, a swimming pool. Joshua finds Tony alone there. From the kitchen entrance where Joshua stands talking to the boy, he can see construction going on behind the barn.

When he asks about it Tony waves a hand in that direction and says, "Oh, the tennis court," as if everyone is building one. "My dad plays a lot of tennis."

With his thick hair in casual disarray, the jeans that look like something out of a *GQ* ad, Tony has a seen-it-all manner, like so many of the suburban teens Joshua knows in Mamaroneck. He wonders what Tony sees in Bobby, Melanie and the other Smithfield kids, why he drives them around in the red TransAm coupe that his father gave him. Is it slumming or pity or something more complex, crueler that explains his choice of companions?

On the subject of Dan, Tony has little to add. "Dan was more buddies with Sam and Bobby than me," Tony says. Sure he was there at the Preserve the night before Dan disappeared, he acknowledges, but nothing special happened. When Joshua asks whether he is the father of Kristen's child, Tony gets a nasty edge in his voice.

"There's no way that kid could've been mine."

"How can you be so sure?"

"Because I'm careful. Always."

"So whose was it?"

"For that you have to ask Kristen."

"I did. Maybe she knows you weren't as careful as you say."

"That's bull."

What a prick, Joshua thinks: not a word of sympathy about Dan, not even the gesture of lowering his eyes so as to not to stare at the missing boy's father.

"Think you've got it all figured out? How to protect yourself while screwing a sweet kid who probably thought you cared about her? She's not the loser, you little shit, you are."

On the short ride to Tall Pines to visit Franco, his anger turns coldly analytical. This Tony is the type who likes to pull strings. What if he put the others up to something? What if they hurt Dan to satisfy Tony's warped sense of mastery over them? The thought is so disturbing that he almost misses the turn into the Tall Pines parking lot. Once there, he is astonished to realize that Franco's word picture of three years ago has come to life. The sun is glinting off the fresh paint on the beams around the main lodge, highlighting the snug cabins, their redwood porches, the dusting of snow across the new roofs. The only thing missing is guests—Joshua counts barely a dozen vehicles in the parking lot.

Six, Franco confirms, when Joshua tracks him down in the kitchen where he is going over menus and food bills with the chef. Six guests.

"How are you Josh? Man, what you've been going through. You hungry?" He turns to the chef. "Charlie, make us a couple of specials, and have Audrey bring them to the office."

They sit across from one another at Franco's desk, sipping bottled water and eating Charlie's lunch special, a juicy steak sandwich with fried onions and shoestring potatoes.

"Fill me in, okay," Franco urges. "Have they found anything at all?"

"Nothing. Nothing." He tells Franco the police have talked to dozens of people, he himself has run around all over Smithfield, but so far it adds up to a big zero.

"The whole thing is like an endless tunnel, with no going back and no way out. But I need to hear about something else. How are things here? Are we going broke?"

"Of course we're not going broke." They've been open three weekends, Franco says; on the first the place was operating at half capacity. Last weekend there were seven cabins occupied; this weekend it's six; for next weekend they have already eight reservations.

Joshua has all kinds of questions. Is it couples or families? Are the guests from New York or Boston? What do they say about the rooms, the food, the staff? The wine? Finally he asks, "Have you gotten any more threatening phone calls? Any more sabotage?"

"Nothing in the lodge or the cabins, we've got full-time security," Franco says. "But my guys have noticed stuff in the woods. Trees felled, the trails torn up in a couple of places. And strange phone calls. No threats, no voices. Just a lot of clicks and hang-ups. And dozens of calls tying up the fax machine. I've already changed the number twice."

The police still don't have a clue who's responsible. "Sound familiar?" Franco asks.

This time he calls Nathalie at ten, as she is about to climb under the covers. He feels worse than a schemer, more like a thief creeping from house to house in the night. After they say good-night he sprawls fully clothed on top of the bed, nearly falling asleep; then he remembers Irina and bolts awake. At midnight he makes coffee—black, extra sugar—before climbing into the Jeep to coast through Main Street: nearly every house dark, here and there a blue TV screen squawking silently behind windows pulled down tight against the cold.

A clear, frigid night. In her driveway Joshua sits in the front seat, arms wrapped around himself, looking up, open-mouthed at the Milky Way. When he hears the car make the turn onto the long driveway he leaps out of the Jeep. She comes around to the kitchen door where he is waiting, his dark shape pressed against the clapboards.

"Who's there?" she asks.

"Who do you want to be there?"

Neither of them turns on a switch. As he follows her inside, she stops, then moves backward half a pace. She does something with her shoes and she is leaning against him, her back

162

tucked into his chest and her now-bare feet on top of his instep. He cinches his arms around her waist, tight as a parachute belt. Joshua can see only the back of her neck and her black, black hair, which smells of lemon. And then she slowly turns into him, raising her arms lazily, with exaggerated emphasis, like an actress waking up on stage, until finally her fingers join behind his neck and she pulls his head down to hers.

They move across the floor to the alcove, clutching each other; shed outer clothes quickly at first, then quicker still. Please, she says to Joshua, please, and at first he doesn't understand the urgency of her need. Her long fingers reach out like snakes in a slow, twirling Eastern dance, drawing him close. His ears, his chest are burning; the ends of each strand of hair on his head jab outward.

He searches out her face, licks her lips, finds the curve of her belly, new and strange but also familiar. In the gray no-light he trusts his fingers more than his eyes.

She moans, a low impatient moan: Now her legs are around him, pulling, anchoring him to her, and she gasps as he slips inside her, and they are rocking one another gently, and now urgently. Wait, wait for me, she cries, oh that's it, that's it, that's it.

After a time, when his eyes are still closed, she begins to kiss him, slowly, touching his tongue with hers; her mouth is every flavor of sweetness; raspberry, cherry and honey. She presses him onto his back; on all fours she bends over him, her fingers stroking his limp penis until he is stiff and she can lower herself onto him. He moves in her as if in a warm bath, ever so gently, feeling the tide of her lap around him; seeing her face taut with longing.

They sleep. Later he wakes with a start, his eyes seeking contrasts in the blackness. His watch reads 3:30. I should go, he whispers. Don't go, Irina says, I don't want you to go. Outside, leaves skitter against the old clapboards as the wind rises and falls, asking a question over and over. Her arms clasp him to her as if the answer is only this, only this tight embrace.

He comes back the next three weekends. She has given him a key, and on the following Friday he waits until after midnight, lying in the dark on the blue-checkered cover, listening to the rustle of sleet against the propane tanks outside. He has the thief's routine down pat; he always calls Nathalie at ten to say goodnight.

As if to justify his nights with Irina he pushes himself during the day, climbing up and down the hills, doing an inch-by-inch inventory of both sides of the river in back of their house. On gray days the cold seems to seep inside his black cotton work gloves as he lifts up fallen branches and upturns piles of leaves, looking for something, anything.

Working his way through the list of residents that Ford and Sammons compiled, Joshua revisits them. Ada Simmons, a plain-faced woman in her 60s who wears her gray hair in a top knot, pours him coffee and cuts him a slice of apple cobbler. Norm comes in and they talk about the coming Selectmen elections. Both Ada and Norm say how sorry they are but their words are unnecessary, because Joshua can see the pain in their faces.

The day Dan disappeared, Ada was babysitting her seven-year-old granddaughter, doing the wash, hanging the sheets out-side on the line while the girl sat in the kitchen filling in her coloring book. When she was outside, she's sure, there was no sign of Dan, no kids on bikes, no slouching teens with puffy faces and uncombed hair, the way they look when parents yank them from their beds and send them off on errands or to work.

Joshua goes to see the Wisters, husband and wife who look like brother and sister: identical faces, fine white hair combed across pink scalps and synchronized smiles. When Joshua pulls out his photo of Dan, Mrs. Wister starts to cry.

"Is he the one who's missing? The dear boy, the poor boy." They don't recall having once told Sammons they'd seen him on that distant day.

"August? My goodness, was it that long ago?" Mrs. Wister says. "You know people go up and down this road all day long. So many people; who can keep track of them?"

Horace Wister smiles his warm, vacant smile and nods his agreement.

He heads back to the house in late afternoon, the hardest time for him, with the light gone and the sky the color of empti-ness. Curled-up brown leaves blow across the road and crunch under the tires. Each time the sun dies it reminds him of Dan's absence. He paces the house, unable to read or think or doze, until it is time to go to Irina's.

When Joshua is back in Mamaroneck he can't think about anything else but this: the slow drive to her house, the quiet minutes after midnight, listening for her car, the feel of her hair in his face and her hands around his waist, how they make love quickly, the way they lie together afterwards, whispering to each other.

One Monday on her day off, he calls her from the office; it's late, after seven. When she picks up, Irina is guarded. He hears someone in the background.

"Who's there?" he says, accusing her.

"A friend."

That Friday Joshua thinks he won't come up; then he arrives at the house and tells himself, I won't go to her. He watches the minutes inch by: 11:00, 11:30, 12:15. Furious, helpless, he drives the mile and a half and lets himself in. When Irina arrives a little after 1:00 A.M. she finds him in the kitchen.

They look at one another without a word. On the bed in the alcove, he pulls at her clothes, stripping away blouse, bra, panties, until she is lying naked against him. Long seconds pass, and there is just the expanse of her ivory limbs and the agonizing progress of his fingers and the way her stomach rises and falls with her breathing. He flips her over roughly until she is on all fours and he is behind her, hands fastened to her hips, sliding her back and forth, up and down on him like a painted horse on a merry-go-round pole.

Afterwards he lies with hands clasped behind his head, in absolute silence.

"What is it?"

"You know."

She strokes his cheekbone, his ear, his lower lip with her supple fingers. "It's complicated," she says. "Life is very complicated sometimes."

"Was it Tom Robinson?"

"Yes."

He asks how long they've known each other.

Almost three years, Irina says. They met at a Town Meeting, not the one at which Tall Pines was a topic for public discussion, but two years earlier. Irina had got to her feet to complain about commercial signs cluttering the main street of Smithfield. Afterwards this lean and leathery man came up to her and began

165

stammering about how he agreed with her. A shy man, Irina explained, younger than she thought. A good-looking man, too.

They ran into each other here and there, and one day when Irina was getting the bad news at the garage about the cost of rebuilding her car engine, Robinson overheard and offered to fix it for nothing. The whole thing cost her a hundred eighty dollars for used parts.

They saw each other half a dozen times over the next few months.

"Eventually it just happened. Not right away. I told you, he's a very shy guy." She tells Joshua that Robinson's wife walked out on him five years ago, taking their 10-year-old daughter and moving into Hartsfield.

"You say shy. But he strikes me as someone who's tough, who has a mean streak."

"You can be shy and tough at the same time." She pauses. "The other night. Tom stopped by here, said he hadn't seen me in a while. We talked. I asked him to supper."

"And?"

"And nothing, dammit. We ate, we had a few laughs, he went on his way."

"Am I supposed to believe that? How do I know what you really want?"

"What I really want? You have some nerve. Why don't you figure out first what it is that you want, and then maybe you can ask someone else what they want."

The next afternoon at day's end they sit together in her kitchen, watching the sun as it fades to red. It splashes off the solitary leaves that remain on the trees—one or two stubbornly green, the others a mottled, tawny yellow, like mustard that has been too long in the jar. Night waits to take possession of the woods that surround the house, the dark descending early, mercilessly, like the executioner's blade. Irina gives him a wan smile.

"It's nearly time. I have to be there at five."

He leaves before she does. Back in his own dark house, Joshua feels he understands nothing—not himself, not his surroundings. He and Nathalie came to this little corner of the world to have a refuge, and for years that's what it was, a refuge. But always something about the place disturbed him: the secrets hidden in the woods, buried in the rocks and gnarled roots that lay just below the surface of the earth. Not Nathalie; she seemed truly at peace working in the garden, practicing the cello in the big empty living room. He wonders why he never told her about the leap of relief he feels when they set out in the car after a weekend here.

Going home, he thinks, going home to what? Civilization is the word that comes into his head, but that isn't it; not civilization but predictability. In New York he is among people whose motivations he can fathom, even if he doesn't always agree with them. To fully lease the new 48-story office building; to have the biggest house on the hill; to exercise and practice and starve yourself enough to become the prima ballerina; to brave bullets and the stench of death in order to win a Pulitzer for coverage of a distant war—these are the ambitions of his neighbors in Mamaroneck, people he knows, people who live all around him.

In Smithfield there are no such ambitions; those who have them leave. For those who remain a living is hard to come by. Many here struggle through the month until the next Social Security or disability check arrives. Is that the measure of their lives—to make it through? Is it challenge enough, the endless cycle of the seasons, each with its implements: the snowblower in January, the garden rake in May, the riding mower in July? Those outdoor obligations set boundaries to life and reduce its dread to a series of battles to fight: against the snowdrifts, against the wayward leaves, against the weeds, against the relentless sprouting of the summer grass.

Yet someone among these people has this unfathomable need to destroy, even to kill. Did Dan fall prey to the same brutes who poison a dog and take an axe to a resort lodge? To a twisted teen for whom the shedding of blood is a bizarre rite of self-affirmation? Joshua is sure he will find the answer, but despairs that he will ever understand it. Sammons and Ford, the professionals, and he, the amateur, are all in the dark together.

He craves light now, goes from room to room switching on the lamps. When the house is ablaze he picks up the phone to call Nathalie. "Nothing new to report," he says. "To tell the truth I'm sick of Smithfield. I'm going to leave early tomorrow."

Two days later, Art Sammons calls him at his office.

"Sam Bonacio has run away."

"Run away? Where? Does this have something to do with Dan?"

"I don't think so. He and his father had a huge fight. I talked to Steve and he wouldn't say much. Apparently the two of them were screaming at each other and Sam said he wouldn't be in the same house with Steve. After school he just took off. He hitchhiked down to Yonkers, to his grandmother's house. Pat is going down to get him. I'll talk to him as soon as he's back."

Sam, Joshua thinks. He's always the one I can never figure out.

Chapter 19

Now the bitter winter comes: an early December snowstorm, then two days of thaw followed by a cold snap that freezes everything. Furrows of sculpted snow snake up and down the streets of Mamaroneck; cars skid on manhole-cover-sized patches of slick ice as they make their turns.

Joshua tosses restlessly for most of a Thursday night, his blood boiling, thinking of the weekend, thinking of Irina. Despising himself but unable to chase away the thoughts. Twice he gets up to pace around downstairs. When he returns to bed the second time, it is after four. Nathalie turns to him, eyes closed, exhaling her warm sleeper's breath.

"Everything all right? What's the matter?" she asks.

"Nothing, everything's okay." How can I be saying this, Joshua wonders, the absurdity of his response smacking him in the face like a dead fish. Everything is upside down, nothing is as it should be.

Four hours later Joshua is finishing his coffee, preparing to toss his khaki backpack in the car. His plan is to spend the morning at work and then drive straight to Smithfield. Then comes the phone call from a frantic Robin in Florida: an ambulance has taken Nathalie's father Dave to the hospital with chest pains. The cardiologist recommends immediate bypass surgery at a hospital neither of them has ever heard of.

Joshua puts down the backpack, shucks off his jacket. In spite of everything he wants to be in Smithfield, but the absurdity of this impulse overwhelms him with shame. As Nathalie lifts the phone to make travel plans he says, "Wait. Wait. I'm going with you. Get two tickets."

For the next five days they take turns shuttling back and forth between the hospital and the condo in Boca. On one of these trips Joshua glances over from the wheel at Robin. She is shrunken and haggard, the folds in her neck as rippled as corrugated packing cartons. Fatigue has nearly shut her eyes; she peers up at him out of tiny slits behind her bifocals.

At the condo he insists that she lie down, swatting away her concern that there may be a call from the hospital. He takes her by the hand and leads her to the bedroom.

This is a dark lair whose ugly matching brown bureaus are crammed with photographs. The procession of images is like a diorama of Dave and Robin's lives: Dave's parents in the Bronx, standing in front of their mom and pop grocery store in their heavy immigrant clothing, wedding pictures of Robin's parents, Robin as a baby, as a girl in pigtails, at high school graduation. Dave as a boy in knickers, Dave with his newsboy's bag slung over his shoulder as he delivers the *Bronx News*, Dave with his CCNY diploma. On and on the saga goes: Nathalie's girlhood, the wedding pictures of Nathalie and Joshua, finally an entire row devoted to Dan.

Nathalie is tireless and exacting when it comes to dealing with the surgeon, the residents and the nurses. She fills in Dave's menu slips and complains when they bring jello instead of rice pudding: she arranges for the home health aide who will visit three days a week when her father gets home. Still, her exasperation with her father seems to grow by the hour as he lies in bed or shuffles up and down the hall, obeying the surgeon's mandate to walk.

When Dave begins to explain in minute detail about the box on the closet shelf in their bedroom that holds every important paper in their lives—the deed to the condo, years and years of tax returns, up-to-date wills, cashed-in life insurance policies (why keep them if they're cashed in?), receipts for burial plots, old cancelled checks—she lashes out at him.

"I can't believe this. When you get out of the hospital you've got to go home and throw out half of those papers. It's ridiculous to be keeping them."

Joshua tries to put Dave's mind at ease, telling him don't worry Dad, we'll look after your papers. It's not until they are sitting on the plane home that he says to Nathalie, "It's as if you had a grudge against him, as if you resented his needing the operation, the hospital stay and everything else."

She is silent for a long minute, then says, "It's not fair, that's what I kept thinking. Here's this 76-year-old man who's lived his whole life and then there's Dan practically at the beginning of his. He's the one who deserves to live, not Dad."

The strength of her feelings unsettles him. Then he thinks, perhaps this anger can help shatter the passivity that has encased Nathalie these past months. Perhaps it can do some good.

Joshua skips the following weekend in The Hollow as well. He calls Irina from the office late one night, and though she understands perfectly—illness in the family, out of town trip—he can hear the questioning in her voice. Are you coming back, her silence accuses him. Where do you belong, there or here?

Where do I belong, there or here?

He goes through most of a day asking himself that question. He asks it over morning coffee, sitting alone at the kitchen table before hurrying to catch the 7:37. Nathalie is washing her hair; he can hear the jet of water, then the whoosh of the hair dryer. Where do I belong, here or there? Is my job to pursue this search for Dan forever, or to resume what there is of my life? Nathalie enters the kitchen as the winter sun clears the line of trees in the backyard, dissolving the red-tinted clouds. It pours through the window behind the sink, backlighting her neck and shoulders, her gleaming chestnut hair. The sadness is always in her eyes, but she is standing straighter, walking with more purpose. Now and then he hears the cello early in the morning or when he returns from the office. Joshua goes to her, kissing her cheek and then her mouth, feeling his lips press a few wayward grains of toast against her soft skin.

"What's that all about?"

"Just loving you."

The words sound strange to his ears but he repeats them, "Just loving you." And then he is out the door and picking his way over the ramparts of snow on his way to the station. He settles into his window seat and stares at his *Times*. Where do I belong? What do I do with my life? Whatever I do will it come down to a bedroom in Florida with a hundred family pictures, a box in the closet with the yellowing papers of 70 years?

Later that afternoon, Joshua shows up at Bronx Academy for his weekly tutoring session. The Dominican twins, Rosa and Rita, are still shaky on their multiplication tables but they giggle at all his jokes. Marcus is making progress; now and then this shy, self-conscious soul will even string together an entire

171

sentence without blushing. But what's with Alejandro? As always Joshua waves to him when they pass in the hall but today there's a dullness in his eyes, a slowness in his step. As he is leaving, Joshua mentions this to Marie-Therese Etienne.

"His mother," she explains. "His mother has breast cancer and is undergoing a mastectomy tomorrow." She's 36 with no husband at home, and Alejandro and his eight-year-old sister to look after. Neighbors and teachers are pitching in as best they can. "For now there's nothing else to do except wait."

In the office Gert has been pestering him to make a doctor's appointment. You're much too thin, she says, and in fact he's down to 155 pounds, 15 pounds less than normal. He fends her off. "No way. I'm not going to the doctor."

Yet he can't be annoyed with Gert, a loyal woman who has never uttered a word of complaint about her life. Her husband was killed in a car crash at 38, no insurance, no savings. She hoards paper clips, recycles file folders, saves supermarket coupons in a plastic case. Her daughter, Jenny, whose 11th birthday is this week, is a rabid Knicks fan. On impulse he strolls down to the Garden and buys her a birthday present: two tickets for the Saturday afternoon game against the Lakers.

"For you and Jenny," he says, presenting them to Gert, but she has a different idea.

"Listen, Josh, why don't you take Jenny? She'd get such a kick out of going with someone who knows basketball like you do."

The day of the Knicks' game, Joshua picks Jenny up in Astoria and after a 20-minute subway ride they emerge from Penn Station onto the escalators of the Garden. She walks confidently at his side, a girl with skinny arms, long curly brown hair and rimless glasses. When they pass a food stand she pulls out the ten-dollar bill Gert has given her to buy a coke, a hot dog and a bag of cracker jacks.

"Jenny, your money is no good here," Joshua tells her.

"It's not?"

"It's not, but luckily, mine is." He loads her up with a box full of food and they find their seats high up in the mezzanine. Jenny has come prepared, with binoculars and a program full of photos and stats. When he asks who's her favorite player, she looks at him like someone who doesn't know the price of a hot dog at the Garden.

"Patrick Ewing," she says. "Of course."

Jenny knows everything about Ewing: his age, his weight, his lifetime averages (points, rebounds, assists per game). The night before, Ewing bruised his knee when he slipped after coming down with a rebound. In practice before the game it was hard to miss the mammoth bandage, looking as big and white as a pillowcase. When they announce a starting lineup without Ewing, Jenny reassures Joshua that it's a smart move.

"He'll get some rest, scope out the Lakers. The injury report said it wasn't serious. I bet we'll see him after the halfway mark of the first quarter." Sure enough, at 8:02, Ewing lumbers off the bench to a roar from the crowd. Within three minutes Ewing has hit a short jumper, blocked a shot at the other end and tipped in a rebound.

"He's on," Jenny tells Joshua. "I say the Knicks by five."

They win by six, the first time they've beaten the Lakers here in three years. On the way down the escalators, Joshua and Jenny are surrounded by boisterous, beery, disbelieving fans. Jenny slips her hand in his and he holds on tightly. Seventh Avenue at 5:00 P.M. on a frigid Saturday in December, under a sun fast dipping toward the Hudson, is all purple and black and yellow, a jumble of cabs and limos, delivery trucks, even a few carts laden with men's suits, being pushed by swarthy men in windbreakers. A breeze clutches at their necks.

Joshua steers her to a diner. "Best ice cream in New York," he tells her as he orders them a banana split with double chocolate, cherry vanilla and butter pecan ice cream, chocolate syrup and enough whipped cream to fill one of Patrick Ewing's sneakers.

"Patrick was baaad," Jenny tells her mom when they get back to Astoria. "The Knicks beat the point spread by 11." Joshua could have won a bundle if he'd followed Jenny's early hunch.

"Jenny, can we do this again?"

"You bet. I had an awesome time. Thanks." She reaches up to plant a kiss on his cheek and waves goodbye as he clatters down the staircase to his car.

Chapter 20

It's not enough, she knows, not enough to haul out the cello a few times a week to play scales and exercises and bits and pieces from her repertoire, until an hour has passed. As Josh would say, to do only that is to be a pitcher who forever warms up but never throws his high hard one, never faces a real batter with men on base and the game at stake.

True, Dr. Meyerson challenged her to play again, shamed her the way you might lift a reticent child, throw him into the pool and say, "Enough of holding back. Swim, you know how." But these sterile practice sessions do not count. She has gone nearly five months without performing; five months could stretch to 12, a year could stretch to two, three, five.

Perhaps what she told Dr. Meyerson is the truth: she has been on strike, withholding her ability to make music in a protest against the universe. But the universe takes no notice, and every strike must eventually end if the striker is to reclaim his job. This willful abstinence sometimes cudgels her with physical force, bringing on numbing headaches, dizzy spells or sharp, unexplained pains in the stomach. She keeps these episodes to herself; only her pallor gives her away. She is extraordinary to look at these days, her face drawn but still unlined, the striking face of a model in jeans on some windswept Irish hill. Her chestnut hair, longer than usual, is pulled back, accentuating the paleness of her cheeks. She wears no makeup except for a thin swipe of lip color.

Her great friend Sonya, the viola player, calls her every week or so but this Saturday, in January, she has a special request. The cellist in Sonya's string quartet, a diminutive Korean, has bronchitis and won't be able to perform at NYU that Sunday night.

"I know it's short notice but can you help us out?"

And then, hearing Nathalie's hesitation, Sonya says, "Don't say no. We need you."

We need you: words Nathalie hasn't heard in a while.

"You'll get paid, too."

"Sorry," Nathalie says. "I don't think I can do it."

Sonya urges her; Nathalie demurs. At this moment Joshua comes back into the house, his gloves smudged and dusty from carting trash out of the basement—sticky, empty paint cans, rusty nails, a bent and battered storm door hinge.

"What was that about?" he asks.

"That was Sonya, she wanted me to sub tomorrow night." A wistful echo in her voice, as she remembers the days when the only reason she turned down a gig was because she was already booked, not because she was afraid to play.

"You didn't say no, did you?"

"I can't do it. Can't you see that?"

"You know what I see? I see a brilliant cellist who won't play, who's lost the will or the self-confidence to play. That's what I see."

Angrily, she bats aside his words. "You're not a musician." She fastens in on this statement and repeats it. "You're not a musician. I've lost two children, Dan and my cello."

"Dan we can't do anything about. But your cello is something else. Your musical ability is a gift from God. How can you ignore it? How can you leave it to languish?"

"My ability to play the cello is a gift from God? Then what do you call the disappearance of our son? When are you going to get it through your head that we don't have any gifts from God, only curses? If God wanted me to play the cello he wouldn't have taken away my son."

At her outburst Joshua's eyes widen, as if he wouldn't be surprised to see her throw herself on the floor, pounding the linoleum surface with the fleshy part of her fists. All her frustration has been reduced to a single laser beam of rage.

"Is that the way you want to live, defined by those feelings?"

"Oh stop it. Stop talking to me in that tone of voice. You sound like a cop with a psychology degree. Like the guy they send out with the crisis team when there's a hostage situation, or some nut who wants to jump off a bridge."

Joshua tries to calm her. Don't make this any more than it is, he says: a chance to play the cello and get paid for it.

"We need the money, is that it?"

"I think you need the money. I think you need to feel productive, and getting a paycheck is one way to accomplish that."

She watches him clatter down to the cellar to deposit his gloves on the shelf where he keeps the hinges, springs, nuts and bolts. Then he is off to Saturday morning basketball, leaving Nathalie alone to sip her coffee. She doesn't remember eating, but the bowl in the sink tells her she must have. Even though her mood is better, she still takes only enough to keep going: for breakfast, yogurt and a banana, for lunch, a cup of soup.

Now she sits, disconsolate, at the kitchen table. She can feel the bow in her right hand, the neck of the cello in her left, can feel them as surely as the plain white mug in the crook of her forefinger.

Dr. Meyerson has helped rouse Nathalie from utter immobility. But her blunt advice, like the 50-milligram Prozac tablets in Nathalie's medicine cabinet—a hefty dose, Meyerson says, but worth a try—are only palliative. For what I have there is no cure, Nathalie tells herself.

She sets the mug down and goes to the upstairs closet where she keeps her treasure, the Italian cello from the 18th century. Just to hold it used to take her breath away. For her 30th birthday her father gave her this prize. They drove to Philadelphia together to try it out and when he saw the look on her face he said, okay, we'll take it. Dad, how could you, she said, breathless, her face hot with joy, embarrassment, pride and love.

"Some parents give their kids a house. We gave you a cello," her father said, shrugging. Nathalie thinks about all the driving to lessons, all the recitals, all the outfits her mother bought her—or made with her own hands—all the checks written to teachers and conservatories and competitions, and blushes for shame that she has ever criticized her parents.

She brings the cello down the stairs to the sunroom, which is bright and warm, the long radiators pulsing with heat, and there she plunks herself in the straight wooden chair and begins to play: scales, exercises, a Bach cello suite. Her own ear hears the rustiness but unless she is kidding herself, the essential sound, rich with longing, is still present. She plays for 45, 50, 55 minutes, the familiar routines, loosening the fingers, feeling the arm grow warm and heavy.

After an hour she sets down the cello and bow in hand, does the circular walk that is her way of relaxing the body, three times around the music stand, flexing the shoulders, waving the fingers in the air.

There is a phone extension in the sunroom; she has schooled herself never to pick it up when practicing. Now she reaches for the handset and dials a familiar number.

"Sonya? It's me. Your gig—is it still available? I've changed my mind. I'll do it."

The program is Mozart, Prokofiev and Ginastera. She gets to work on the Prokofiev. Midway through the first movement she thinks about Dan, waves of emotion crashing over her, and her playing becomes ragged, the strings growling under the punishment of the bow. But she refuses to stop. She does what she trained herself to do as a 13-year-old in the Julliard weekend program when her teacher, the crotchety Mr. Saperstein, scolded her in German-accented English for gazing at a spider crawling down the wall in the middle of a lesson.

"Miss Lindner," he said, "stop looking at that insect. For you that insect doesn't exist. The heat or cold in the room don't exist. The only things that exist are you, the cello and the music, and of course in the back of your mind, your teacher and how you are going to please him. You must fix on those three things; you must have a picture in your mind of you serenely playing, playing quite perfectly, the elbow held just so, the arm relaxed but strong. Every great cellist has such a technique of shutting everything out to concentrate only on the music."

Nathalie caught on quickly, just as she caught on to everything Mr. Saperstein taught her. In her picture she was taller—she always wanted to be taller—with long flowing hair that fell almost to her waist, and a full, womanly figure; she was alone on stage in a concert hall with majestic, oversized leaded windows; sunlight filtering through those windows bathed her in amber. She played and played, never tiring, every note perfect, and though she couldn't see the audience in her picture, she knew that the music she was making held them spellbound, and that she existed for one purpose only, to keep playing. She called her picture The Cellist in the Amber.

Whenever she had trouble learning a piece, or when a difficult passage gave her fits, she would sit calmly, evoking the cellist in the amber, and then set anew to practice.

She plays. When the thoughts—the look of the lawn on the day Dan disappeared, the months of searching, the cruel emptiness in her stomach at no news, every day no news, even though they know what the outcome must be—she pushes them away and brings back the cellist in the amber. Throat dry, hair sticky, armpits dripping with sweat, she plays.

She hears Joshua back from basketball, rooting around in the fridge for a muffin. His constant activity astounds and annoys her. Already at 7:00 A.M. he was making his daily call to Sammons; she heard his familiar questions, his barely contained frustration. In a few days he will drive back to Smithfield for more searching, more questioning; he will come back 24 or 48 hours later, scarcely able to speak. He goes alone; Nathalie can't bear to accompany him.

Now he is tiptoeing through the living room to stand in the doorway, his head cocked, breathing in quietly so as not to interrupt.

She stops playing, lays the cello on the floor. "Josh, is that you?"

"Didn't mean to disturb you. I'll get out of your way."

"No, it's okay." She stands facing him, flushed, elated. "I'm going to do it. I've been practicing since you left."

A pause, and then she says, "You're right. I was wrong. I have to do this."

"It's about time. Did I tell you we could use the money?"

They have a bite of lunch together and he tells her he wants to hear her play tomorrow. "We'll go out for supper afterward, it's been ages since we've been in the Village."

"No," Nathalie says, automatically. "I mean, I don't know if I want you to come."

"Why not?"

"It'll be boring for you."

He looks at her. "You're nervous, is that it?"

She is touchy. "Of course I'm nervous. I haven't picked up the cello in months and here I am playing before a real audience. It's not like the Philharmonic where you can be anonymous, hidden among all those faces and instruments. Four people on stage and if I screw up everyone'll know who it was. And you there to see my embarrassment."

"You won't screw up. But you decide—I won't come if you don't want me."

She spends four hours that Saturday afternoon on the music, and after supper another hour. Before she goes to bed she sits at the dressing table and brushes her hair, 15, 20, 25, 30 strokes, something she hasn't done in many months. Lying on her back after she turns off the light, she thinks not about the black hole at the center of her life, but instead about tomorrow's performance. She has a flutter of nervousness and excitement—what if I screw up, two of these guys I've never played with before, what if our styles don't mesh—and in the midst of these concerns, everyday concerns, not like the anguished thoughts that have been tormenting her for months, her head flops to one side and she is fast asleep.

Sunday she is up at six to practice again. Soon she can hear Joshua rattling around. He pours himself a cup of coffee and there he is standing outside the door of the study, listening.

Nathalie puts down the bow. "Josh," she says.

"Sorry, I just, I mean, it sounds great. I'll get out of your way."

"That's not, I mean, you're not bothering me. I was just going to say that I'd be happy for you to come today."

They have to get there at five so Nathalie can do a run-through with the other musicians. When it's time for her to march out on stage, holding the instrument, taking her seat, adjusting her music on the stand, tuning the cello and limbering up her arm, the pressure between her ears almost causes her to lose her balance. The temperature in her chest soars until she fears her blood will vaporize. Panic smothers her; I can't do this, she thinks, I'm going to faint, I'm going to choke, my throat is like a sandbox.

Next to her Sonya gives Nathalie a big wink. Simeon, the first violin, raises his bow to signal they are ready and then he begins to play, followed by the second violin, Sonya on the viola and then Nathalie. Seconds after she draws the bow across the bridge the pounding between her ears ceases, her air passages open and she breathes as if for the first time. Now she is at home on stage, with the air going in and out of her lungs, the cello held just so in her left hand, the strong right arm and the bow caressing the strings. She glances at the music but she doesn't need the music, she knows every note by heart. Halfway through the Mozart she closes her eyes for a fraction of a second and in her mind she sees the cellist in the amber.

At the concert's end one of the NYU music students comes to the edge of the stage with flowers for the performers. To her astonishment, Simeon swoops down to pick up the first bouquet and delivers it to Nathalie's arms. Unprepared for this kindness, and for his murmured words of praise—"you played masterfully, Nathalie, masterfully"—Nathalie's eyes fill with tears. Joshua has leapt onto the stage and is embracing her, as Sonya and the second violinist crowd around to offer their congratulations.

Afterwards Joshua and Nathalie make their way to a favorite haunt on Bleecker Street, a trattoria with round metal tables on a floor of black and white tiles. Over the remains of a thin-crust pizza, a salad of arugula and artichoke, Nathalie turns to her husband. Her cheeks are flushed from a glass and a half of wine, more alcohol than she has consumed in five months.

"Tell me the truth. Did I play that well or was everybody just giving me a free ride?"

"A free ride," he says with a straight face. "Actually you stunk, as they used to shout at me in pickup games of hardball when I gave up a homer or a game-winning hit."

Her face falls, and Joshua takes her hand and brings it to his lips. "My dear," he says, in an imitation of Simeon, "you played masterfully, just masterfully."

Simeon, with his curly black-gray locks and deep voice, fancies himself a lady's man, and Nathalie bursts out laughing at Joshua's imitation.

"I didn't know you heard that."

"There's nothing I don't hear. Just remember that when these musician types are trying to get into your pants."

She is laughing again. "Was I really all right?"

He grins. "Masterful, just masterful."

He pours the last of the Chianti into their glasses. Later, the jerk of the car as Joshua shoots down 14th Street toward the West Side Highway makes her dizzy. Nathalie opens the window a crack. The rush of cold air helps, and by the time they reach the city line she is fast asleep.

The next day she wakes later than usual to find Joshua gone: an early appointment in the office and then an auction in New Jersey. She thinks of her success the day before and then, once again, the absence of Dan settles over her like a suffocating tarpaulin from which she cannot fight free. What is the point, she asks herself, over and over, sipping a glass of orange juice and struggling to hold herself together. What is the point?

Today is gray, wintry but not cold, more like March than January, and Nathalie has chores to do, the fridge is bare, the laundry and ironing have piled up, one of her blouses and two of Joshua's shirts need buttons sewed on. It's the kind of mindless work that she used to plow through before 8:00 A.M., leaving the rest of her morning free for practicing. Today the hard part is getting started. She lingers over coffee and reads her list a second and third time and finally she climbs to the spare bedroom where she piles the shirts and blouses needing mending over the fraying silver cover of the ironing board. The blond pine desk that holds her sewing supplies is under the window. She slides the center drawer open, selects needle and thread from one of the compartments in the plastic tray and picks up the first of the shirts.

Her fingers, supple and practiced, are made for this kind of work. Sitting at the desk, watching the garbagemen dash to and fro from the back of the truck to the curbside for the Monday morning pickup, she is aware of two intersecting dramas in progress: these stocky men with their windbreakers and padded gloves and the legs in constant motion are in one play, and she in her contemplative sewing repair mode is in another. If they could look up and spot her through the window, nod at the accomplished way she threads the needle and cuts and ties the thread and anchors the button to the cuff of the shirt—would they see her as she sees them, as someone at one with her vocation?

What if they saw her playing the cello as she played it yesterday? Would they have the all-encompassing sense of performance, not performance as the actor on a stage and the audience in the seats, but performance as life enlarged, as humans engaged in the heroic, death-defying acts of everyday existence?

The exhaust of the garbage truck coughs, its revolving drum noisily sweeps the trash into the maw of the vehicle; the men hop on and it turns the corner. Moments later she finishes the second of the shirts. The sky is a bit lighter and she sees a seam of yellow to the northwest, above the trees: clearing weather, perhaps colder but cleaner, brighter.

After the sewing, she hurries to bring the cello downstairs, nearly catching her heel on a tuft of carpet. Slowly, slowly, she tells herself, if you go too fast you'll be sweeping up a pile of splinters. She waltzes the cello into the sunroom. With no stress, no impending concert looming, she plays the exercises surely, confidently, then goes back to a tricky part of the Prokofiev. She may not play it again for five years, she may never play it again, but she is seized with the need to get it down pat.

Now she brings out the score for her beloved Dvorak. Her back is to the window but she can feel the sky lightening as she draws the bow back for the first notes. At the end of five minutes the notes are dancing before her eyes as daggers of sunlight pierce the outlines of the rhododendron outside the den windows.

It has been more than a year since she played this music; it was an early part of her repertoire, something she had to perform for many auditions. But now, after so many months of not playing, Nathalie is discovering it anew. It is like walking a stretch of beach that she knows from childhood vacations: the slope of the dunes, the hardpacked sand underfoot, the breeze ruffling her hair, make for a palpable, omnisensory encounter that awakens all the organs: eyes, ears, feet, fingers, nose. The pressure on her fingers as she angles the bow, her eyes darting ahead to the next measure on the score, to glimpse notes she knows so well, the sound that she makes registering in her ears, all give her an intense pleasure, as if she is both performing and receiving the performance, making the music and enjoying the making of it.

Nathalie realizes, with wonder, how rare these moments are. What she is conscious of is what she railed at Joshua for daring to name: the gift that the universe has bestowed on her. In her outburst on Saturday she talked about God's curse, but today, in a more reflective frame of mind, she regrets and repudiates those words. She rarely thinks of God; only in synagogue a couple of times a year, or at a funeral when heads are bowed, does she ever presume to address the Almighty, wherever or whatever he or she is, and at such times she imagines that God is too besieged with the intercessions of hundreds, thousands of others, more needy and more believing than she, to take notice of what is in her heart.   ·

But to be given this gift, this gift of making music, of taking nothing but an instrument and a bow of wood and gut and to make them reproduce the most exquisite sounds, surely this miracle must derive from some force in the universe more powerful than nature, more pure in focus than humankind. What is even more miraculous is that the gift does not come to her fully developed; instead it comes in the form of talent that must be nurtured, then worked hard if it is to reach its potential. She thinks of a field of lettuce or onions or peppers ripening in the July sun. Those straight-as-a-ruler furrows, the banked and watered earth, the weeds plucked from the soil, all bear testimony to the hours of effort by the farmer. No man-made beauty appears in the world except by the messy, unpicturesque toil of human beings; the gift, then, is to plant that idea of the finished work—which in truth is never finished—to spur on and reward that effort.

In this, she sees it all so clearly, she is nothing more, nothing better than the laborer bent over her rice plants or the mason with his trowel and his bucket of mortar. Her task is to weed and prune and develop her talent, to work it ferociously, relentlessly. And to do so knowing that moments like the one she is living must be rare.

Now, she bends to the task of practice in a way that she has never done. At Curtis when she was 19 she put in hours and hours, but that was driven by some external need: to satisfy a demanding teacher, to get ready for a recital. But now she practices for no reason other than to practice. This is her dusty row to hoe, her metier, her purpose.

So she plays, through the morning, through the noon, until the sun has arced from its position low above the rooftops to the east of the sunroom, to its zenith above her roof peak. She plays until her fingers are wood, until it is as painful to lift her right arm as it would be to heft one of the huge concrete planters on the rear patio, just beyond the double doors.

It is 2:00 and she has been playing for five hours. Too tired to carry it upstairs, she lays the cello down in the sunroom. She goes to pee and then has lunch: cottage cheese and sliced apple, banana, a cup of tea. The day has turned brighter, but even this wan, thin January sun offers enough warmth to permit her to walk with nothing but a windbreaker. She plunges down the hill to the town and picks her way along the sidewalk, past the movie house, the Italian deli with its hanging hams, salami

183

and provolone cheese; past the real estate offices with their colored placards of listings. In 20 minutes she has come to the marina; she follows the footpath around to the right until she has a view that shuts out all traffic and that fills her eyes with the blue-gray of the Sound, the few lonely boats moored in their slips, with masts down and hatches battened, as the angry tides lap at their hulls.

The wind blows strongly here. At the edge of the park promontory overlooking the water, Nathalie finds that she is rethinking her life in this wind, which is buffeting her, pushing everything out of her head. Her hair is whipped this way and that; her eyes sting from the assault of the wind, which sets the sailboats bobbing in unfriendly seas.

At the end of the contoured footpath, with its inlay of mango-colored stones and white-gray background, she slides onto the wooden bench. On a Sunday in April she might be vying for a place here with a pair of teenage lovers or a white-haired Italian man with a face crinkled and bronzed by the years, hand in hand with his American grandson. But now she has the bench, the park, the Sound to herself. She drinks her fill of the sight of the sea, with its mixture of turbulence and quietude, of upheaval and tranquility.

For months she has been alone, entombed in her house, and this sojourn in the out of doors with an ocean breeze in her face and the odor of fish and brine and seagull droppings strong in her nostrils, has an astringent, restorative power. It gives her wild thoughts, enticing thoughts: Maybe she wasn't meant to be a cellist all her life. Maybe 30 years of practice and performance are enough, and it's time she found another calling. Nathalie thinks of ships or planes that could carry her away from New York. She could travel to New Zealand and sign on to labor in the breathtaking gardens of Christchurch, working for just enough to buy her a bed and her food. She could make her way to Senegal and help out in the overcrowded, dank and malodorous clinics that care for women and children with AIDS, wiping their brows with a cool rag, helping them to a sip of water when they are too weak to lift their heads. How strange, she marvels, that my daydreams have this Florence Nightingale theme, that the missions they embody are distant and solitary—as if I were a nun, not a wife.

184

In the midst of these imaginings she thinks of Dan floating somewhere between ocean and sky, always with his face reddened from activity, from throwing a ball or climbing a mountain, and that smile that could set her heart singing.

Now comes the long winding walk through town and then up the hill to their house. Step by step her solace ebbs away, that solace she found in the punishing hours of practice, in the wind-blown stroll by the ocean. As self-aware as a discharged cardiac patient, she marches with reluctant feet to the empty house. The inspired moment has fled, and what lingers is not peace but bittersweet understanding: the realization that in the consciousness of human beings, the consciousness that gives shape to the contours of our physical universe, time flows backward as well as forward; the present laps into the past as it laps into the future, stitching today's thought to yesterday's deed, binding those remembering to those remembered.

Chapter 21

Joshua wonders how long they can avoid talking about it. His visits to The Hollow have dwindled, and now when he and Irina are together there is a kind of impermeable sadness between them, a sadness that neither words nor passion can dissolve. This time he makes love to her fiercely, as if angry at her or at himself. Later as he lies in her bed, his head crushed against the pillow, he can feel her staring, questioning. He opens his eyes and reaches up to stroke her bare shoulder, then pulls her back down until her head is level with his.

She speaks first. "Nobody's keeping you here. You can go anytime."

"You don't just mean tonight."

It is 2:00 A.M., she has come back from work later than usual, a big Friday night crowd at Café Rustica. Something strange in her eyes tonight, some cruel need that she doesn't bother to disguise. He knows this from the way she reaches for him, she way she tugs impatiently at his shirt and pants, the urgency of her mouth upon his.

"I mean that you have no obligation to me."

"Nor you to me?"

Now her voice is very low, he hears the effort she is making to avoid tears. "For you this is an interlude, something between one life and another. Honestly I wonder how you can keep coming back to a place that must represent so much heartache. You're a strong man, you are going to recover from whatever happened to Dan. When you do I wonder if Smithfield or any aspect of it will be part of your universe. That's what I am, an aspect of Smithfield."

"And you? What will you do?"

He asks this automatically, without any inkling of her response.

"I'm going to sell the place and move."

"Where? Where will you go?"

"Maybe San Francisco, where my brother lives. He's made some money. He's willing to back me if I start my own restaurant. And I won't need snow tires there."

Joshua is stunned into silence. Before he can respond Irina tells him something else.

"For a long time something has been bothering me about what's gone on, the Tall Pines business, your son Daniel. I've had the feeling that I knew something but didn't want to confront what it was. A few days ago I talked to Tom. I said, 'Whatever you know, whatever you've done, you have to tell. You just have to.' First he wouldn't respond, wouldn't even discuss it. In the end he agreed. Give him a call."

"This is Tom Robinson," the voice says. "I hear you want to talk to me."

It's a strong voice with an undercurrent of anger. He might be angry at Joshua, or at Irina, or at his wife for walking out on him five years before. Or at the world for moving at a speed and in a direction that he did not care to match.

"Yes," Joshua says. "I'd like to talk to you." It is late February and Joshua is back in The Hollow. A thaw has melted most of the snow and a few green shoots are poking through the white ground cover.

The two of them meet for coffee in Hartsfield the next morning, at a diner off Route 57. There, in a booth in back, amidst the swirl of grease from the griddle where bacon is sizzling, Robinson tells him that the idea of Tall Pines was like a stake in his gut.

"It's great hunting there," he explains. "A couple of times I took your neighbor, Steve."

"I didn't know he could keep up with you."

Robinson smiles. "The last time, I came by for him was at 4:30 on a Saturday morning. One of those really cold ones. Eight degrees. December first and it was eight degrees."

They'd driven north on the Northway Road and Robinson led the way into the woods, the black dawn wrapping them in its icy embrace. Just after the sky began to crack into yellow and pink streaks, he'd spotted the buck sheltering in a depression and told Steve to take him. They'd gutted the deer back at the Bonacio's, the blood running in red splotches across the thin patches of snow that had fallen the day after Thanksgiving. "Steve made his son come and help and the boy got covered with deer guts and blood and was mad about it."

"It figures," Joshua says. Tension between father and son has not abated. And in the aftermath of his running away, Sam has had yet another visit from Sammons and Ford. Pat Bonacio asked couldn't they leave Sam alone, saying her son was irritable, uncommunicative, barely sleeping, but Sammons insisted. We have to get to the bottom of this crime, he said. If he knows something he has to tell us.

What is on Robinson's mind this morning is not the Bonacio family. "I love to hunt and I love those woods," he says. "I've been hunting there for more than 20 years. I logged those woods for old man Watts when he was alive and then after he was gone I used to do odd jobs for his widow, never charged her a penny. It was always understood that I could hunt that land."

"Things change. Land gets sold, new owners have new ideas. You can't turn back the clock. It's not like there's no place to go hunting around here. There's all the state land just along the Northway Road. Or over toward Hartsfield, in the woods off the Cliffmont Road."

Robinson shifts uncomfortably on the bench of the booth. He picks up the coffee mug and takes a long sip and catches the eye of the frizzy-haired waitress for a refill.

"Look, what I did was wrong. I did it because of the hunting but that doesn't make it right."

"What exactly did you do?"

"Called up Franco and told him to leave the land alone, to forget building the resort."

"Or what?"

"Or things would happen to the building. People might get hurt."

"In other words, you threatened him."

"Yes."

"You didn't think this up yourself, did you?"

"What do you mean?"

"I mean, didn't other people put you up to making those phone calls?"

Joshua asks the question a few times but Robinson avoids giving a direct answer. Exasperated, he asks if Robinson knows that what he did was a crime, that he could go to jail.

"Yeah, I know that."

"Then why won't you say who it was?"

"I'm not the kind who rats on people."

"Oh, I see. You're too loyal to name names and yet it's you who calls up a law-abiding citizen and makes threats, who breaks the law, who participates in a scheme, a nasty scheme, to harass someone and harm his property and kill his dog."

"That I had nothing to do with. I didn't kill his dog. I don't go around harming pets."

"And the defacing of the property? Are you going to tell me you had nothing to do with that either?"

"Nothing at all. They got some kids to do that, is my guess."

"And just who is the they?"

Robinson won't say. But he looks Joshua in the eye and apologizes for what he did. "It was wrong. I'm ashamed I did it."

"What did you have to do with the disappearance of my son?"

"Nothing, I swear. I didn't know him. I never touched him. I would never lay a hand on a child. I have a daughter myself. If anyone took my daughter, hurt my daughter, I wouldn't rest until I found that person."

"And how do I know that the person you're protecting had nothing to do with Dan's disappearance? Just how in hell do you know that?"

"It couldn't be," Robinson says. "It couldn't be. But if I find out otherwise." He stops, and Joshua, sitting across from him, can see the power in his arms and chest.

As Joshua is getting back in the Jeep he says to Robinson, "How come you didn't ask me if I was going to tell the police what you told me?"

"That's up to you. Whatever I did, I'm responsible for."

All day Joshua turns it over and over in his mind. He knows he should fill Sammons in, but tells himself, not yet. Finally he calls Robinson again. It is 9:00 on a starlit night and Robinson answers the phone like a man with a blanket over his head. It's been a long day, he says, and he's got chores to do early tomorrow.

"I'm hoping you've reconsidered," Joshua begins. "You can help. We need you to help."

He waits. He can sense Robinson fidgeting at the other end of the line.

"It was Carl. Carl Puckett. It was his idea. Him and that guy Phil Wright, who's always running around to do Carl's bidding."

Carl Puckett.

"Why'd you do Carl's dirty work?"

Robinson doesn't answer right away. Then he says, "It's hard to say no to Carl. He always knows just the way to get you to do something. He knew how upset I was about the land being sold."

Robinson goes on. "There's work I do for the town. Mowing and tending the cemetery. Plowing the roads in winter. A big tree comes down in a storm, I'm the guy they call to clear the road. All that, it's income to me. Carl's got the power to take all that away. He knows it. I know it."

And that night Joshua lies awake for a long time. He can go to Sammons and Ford, but Puckett will deny it. It's one man's word against two others, Robinson's against Puckett's and Wright's. There's got to be another way, he thinks.

Two days later Joshua walks along Main Street heading for the little dirt lane, apprehension causing his breath to come in shallow snorts. Just as he makes the turn a red pickup truck lumbers by and he instinctively turns his face. Faster, he tells himself, faster. Further down Main Street a woman calls angrily to a dog nosing its way across her yard; the hem of her house dress whips this way and that in the chill morning breeze.

Not wanting to be seen, he quickens his pace and steps onto the wooden bridge to cross to the other side of the river. They closed the bridge to cars three years ago by planting twin curved steel plates at either end of the bridge, and Joshua, on foot in the middle of the span, can see why. Large sections of flooring are missing—weathered, pitch-covered 10-inch thick planks whose gaps have a bitten-off look. To walk across he must constantly switch back and forth from one plank to another, like an aggressive driver changing lanes.

On the far side of the bridge, Joshua lands in the parking lot bordering Route 57. Here truckers heading west from Boston sometimes pull in for an overnight snooze. A black trash barrel is overflowing with styrofoam coffee cups, cellophane from Slim Jim beef jerky and greasy, cream-colored bags from the donut shop on the way out of Collegeville. He follows the paved parking area around to his left, where it ends in a tangle of tall grass and brambles, now at the tag-end of winter, died away to withered brown vines, their stickers all desiccated and turned to dust.

Here and there near the tip of one of these stalks he can glimpse a tiny green bud, no bigger than a snipped off bit of toenail—a sign of the coming spring. At a point where only a stride separates the two banks of the stream, he hops across to face a four-foot high bluff. Here the land looks as if a giant fistful of earth has been ripped from the bank by a bear's paw, leaving clumps of raw and flaky dirt that lie thawing in the milder late winter days. Today is March first; the sun is up by well before six, to greet him after four hours of fitful sleep.

Joshua gets a handhold at the top of the bluff and pulls himself up, puffing from the effort, ears ringing from the possibility that someone will spot him here, at the far end of the property owned by the head of the Selectmen. Now, crouched low, he is in sight of the fading but shipshape barn, which sits 80 yards behind the backmost part of the house. Joshua angles across an undulating meadow that is bounded on both sides by a four foot high fence topped by a single, threatening strand of barbed wire. It is to avoid this wire, and also to avoid entering the property from Main Street, where someone might see him, that he has fixed on this circuitous route, across the bridge and then back across the water.

It is 9:15 on a Monday morning; everyone in The Hollow who works out of town has already left, for Collegeville to the east or Hartsfield to the west, or points farther away. As for the Pucketts, Rosa told him that she and Carl were driving down to Richmond, Virginia on Friday for a family wedding, and wouldn't be back until Monday evening.

Rosa has mentioned to him that Carl has an office on the second floor of the barn, a little alcove under the eaves. Joshua doesn't know what he is looking for, only that he must look. Irina has led him to Robinson and Robinson has named Puckett as responsible for a lot of the dirty tricks that took place. Now Joshua wants evidence he can take to the police.

But what if the Pucketts come back early? What if someone else in town, strolling along Main Street, happens to see this orange-haired man prowling round the Puckett's barn?

The position of the barn favors his scheme. To the right of the Pucketts' property on Main Street where an ample side yard beckons, stand three mature spruce trees, their branches sloping downward like a ballerina lowering her arms. The trees form a dense, interlocking barrier that, combined with a newer two-car garage, nearly shields the barn from passersby.

He jogs quickly to the barn over grass that an hour earlier would have been crunchy from the overnight frost. Now the sun is turning the frost to pearly drops of moisture, sprayed across the yellow-brown grass like drops of milk on a breakfast cereal.

Joshua tries the side door of the barn without success; the front doors are padlocked shut. He circles around to the back where two small windows are set amidst the lengths of red-painted, overlapping clapboards. The sash on the west side window refuses to budge. At the window opposite, he scores a line between the sash and the frame with his pocket knife, paring away a thin layer of wood and running a furrow through the moist sawdust-like insulation of generations of disintegrated flies and spiders. Hands braced against the side panels of the sash, he presses outward and upward. The panes in the old sash creak and for a second Joshua fears he will fracture the 100-year-old glass.

He takes a deep breath, then tries again. The sash loosens, coughing in its track like a phlegmy smoker, and then scrapes open. He fears the screech will echo into Main Street but it is only his ears that register the volume of the sound, which melds into the sighing of pine branches, the sputter of a car engine, the angry bark of a terrier in the road.

He snakes a leg through the opening, ducks his head and twists his shoulders sideways in order to pull his body through. For a time he fears he will lose his footing and tumble face down, imprinting the clammy soil on his forehead. But he finds his balance, plants his feet and immediately is encircled by a moist, clinging cold that rises from the dirt floor.

Straight ahead, Joshua sees the riding mower that Carl Puckett mounts to keep his four acres of grass neatly tended. His huge body astride this machine, his small blue eyes boring straight ahead out of the jowled, thick-necked head, Puckett gives the unmistakable impression of a water buffalo, pawing the ground as if to trample anything in its path.

Past the hoes, rakes, hedge clippers and gardening imple-ments, hanging from hooks, Joshua spies the stairs. They are no more than a few years old, their pine wood already tinged in spots with the green-black mold that thrives in this old structure.

As Joshua puts his hand on the railing he hears a whisking, clicking noise and ducks behind one of the three upright posts that hold up the upper story and the barn roof. A key being turned in the massive padlock? Someone in clogs or cleats tripping along the gravel driveway in his direction? As he turns his body sideways, willing himself to be no wider than the post, he sees something sinewy and gray swishing among the tines of an old-fashioned wooden rake; the noise must be this large field mouse getting its daily constitutional as it searches for crumbs that fell out of Carl's pocket after the last mowing in early November.

Joshua quickly climbs the stairs to the old hayloft. To his left is the stored summer lawn furniture, green plastic chairs from Shanghai, a striped white and green umbrella. He steps to his right into a little office tucked under the eaves. He takes a seat in the swivel chair in front of the weathered oak desk, bare except for a Mac computer. The bottom file drawer is locked; Joshua twists the awl of his pocketknife back and forth with no effect except to produce a whisking, clicking noise not so different from that made by the gray mouse.

He turns on the computer but the word processing program won't load without a password. He's come prepared with the Pucketts' phone number, each of their birth dates, their license plates (Carl's reads SELECT1). He tries the last four digits of the Pucketts' phone number, then Carl's date of birth and gets an "entry not valid" message. Outside a truck lumbers through town, a big trailer rig from the length of the rumble. Inside there is more scampering—maybe the mouse and a companion, it sounds more like eight feet than four. His watch says 9:55; he's been at this an hour. How long he can spend here without someone becoming aware of his presence?

Finally he enters Rosa's birthday in year, month, day order. Bingo, the program loads. He finds a folder for tallpines, clicks on the earliest file and sees notes of Carl's meeting with Stern and Franco. He scans letters from Carl to other Selectmen but it's harmless stuff, routine griping about out-of-towners and their plans. Still, he hits the print button. His breath is coming faster again. Can it be that this whole adventure will turn out to be fruitless, unauthorized entry, the risk of discovery, and for what?

The ink-jet printer is an old clunker giving agonizing birth to the pages at barely three per minute and making a racket in the process, and Joshua is so intent on searching the files and printing out the letters that at first he doesn't notice the crunch on the gravel outside: the sound of a large vehicle pulling up to the doors of the barn.

He freezes. He was sure Carl and Rosa wouldn't be back till late this afternoon at the earliest. From outside he hears gruff masculine voices, younger-sounding than Carl's. Joshua hits the power button to shut off the Mac, and yanks the power cord of the ink-jet from the wall socket. With the grinding of the printer halted, he can make out words more clearly.

"Dad it's locked, you got the key?"

"Yeah, that's grandpa, he locks everything; Christ, he locks the bathroom door when he's taking a crap. I've got the spare key somewhere in the truck; let me take a look."

Throwing himself onto the floor of the hayloft, Joshua crawls forward until his head is just below the arc-shaped windows over the front doors to the barn. Below him is a broad-shouldered man with Carl's block-shaped head and tiny eyes, wearing a flannel jacket and a baseball cap that says "Win with Honda" in sweeping red letters. His companion, skinnier, wearing one of those sleeveless pile vests over a white T-shirt, reaches into the pocket of his jeans for a cigarette. Joshua recognizes the older man as Carl Puckett's son, Carl Jr.; he owns an auto dealership in Collegeville. The younger man, 18 or 19, must be his son.

Joshua hears the truck door closing, a solid, final sound, and knows it's too late to vault down the steps and scram out the back window. He tiptoes back to the hayloft, turns left instead of right and burrows into a spot under the eaves amidst cardboard boxes stacked three high. Amazing how cold the floor feels against his stockinged feet; he clutches the low Nike boots to his chest to make sure he doesn't drop them. He hears the sound of the padlock being lifted from the clasp, the clasp swinging free, and now a rush of air as the two doors slowly swing open.

"There it is," says Carl Jr.

194

"Will it start?"

"Won't know till we try it, will we?"

"Jeez it's cold. Why is it always colder inside these friggin' barns in the winter?"

"I told you, watch your language."

Now there is a clicking sound as Carl Jr. tries to get the riding mower to kick into life. He tries a second and third time.

"Damn."

"Hey, you hear that?" the son asks. "That scratching noise?"

Joshua stops breathing, and as the air expands in his head, tries to reassure himself that yes, he turned off the printer, that it's not still coughing up that last page of letters.

"That? Some mouse or chipmunk, more than likely."

"Shit, there it is." And then the grandson is off chasing the mouse; Joshua hears him thrashing at it, perhaps using the rake with the wooden tines.

The next thing he hears is, "Looks like grandpa left this window open a crack," followed by the sound of the sash being pushed that last little bit into the frame.

"Come on, I haven't got all day, let's get this thing into the truck," says Carl Jr. After a pause, Joshua, still curled in a tight ball, is aware of the truck starting, backing into the barn and then the grunts as the two of them wrestle the mower up a ramp and into the back.

"Funny, grandpa leaving that back window open. I'm going to have a look around."

More seconds pass; he hears footsteps on the first treads of the stairs, imagines, if he doesn't quite feel it, the vibration caused by the grandson's hand gripping the railing. Joshua has no idea if the top of his head is visible over the cartons that shield his body. He draws his arms ever tighter across his knees, pressing them against his chest.

Then he hears Carl Jr. again, exasperated. "Jimmy, it's bad enough that today's the day I have to pick up the riding mower and get it shipshape, never mind that no one's going to be mowing lawns for four, five weeks at least. But I don't have time to be snooping around this old barn finding more mice and chipmunks."

So it's Jimmy. Joshua wonders what happened to the third generation of Carls.

"It'll just take a couple of minutes," says Jimmy, lifting his foot to climb higher.

"Yeah, well a couple of minutes is what I don't have. We're short-handed in the service department and the finance company guy is coming in about redoing our floor plan."

"Floor plan?"

"It's how we finance the cars on the show room floor, Jimmy. If you'd go to college the way I keep saying instead of messing around with those stock cars which are only going to get you hurt or killed in the end, you might finally learn something about business."

Carl Jr. tells his son to get going, in a tone that leaves no further room for discussion. The father drives the truck out of the barn and waits for Jimmy to padlock the doors. Joshua gets to his feet, dusts himself off. Restarting the Mac, he scrolls through more files. All of a sudden there it is, dated January 2, the text of the flyer that was put in every mailbox in town, opposing Tall Pines.

Joshua clears a paper jam and prints this out, along with the correspondence between Puckett and his stooge on the Board of Selectmen, Phil Wright. An e-mail with the heading, 'To: pwright@earthlink.net From: selectman#1@worldnet.att.net,' reads, "Make sure this gets delivered and don't let anyone see you having anything to do with it." Pwright@earthlink.net wrote back, "My nephew's son can do this, the kid needs bucks to help fix his '54 Chevy." To which selectman#1 replied, "Good; 100 bucks if he does all the mailboxes in town." And pwright's final word: "Carl this must mean alot if your throwing money around like that."

He also finds the text of an e-mail dated a few weeks later from selectman#1 to pwright saying, "We need a guy to make a few phone calls, to, should we say, put the fear of God into F. No money, just for the love of country."

And pwright responds, "Robinson's your guy. Got his nuts twisted because of his deer-hunting."

Standing again at the back window, Joshua jams the heels of his palms upward and the sash rides easily open. He considers strolling nonchalantly to the front of the Puckett house and onto Main Street, by far the shortest way, but opts instead to angle back across the meadow and to vault down the embankment, smacking his knee against a rock. He limps across the river and heads west on Route 57 until it joins Main Street, before doubling back to the house.

In his hip pocket is the floppy disk onto which Joshua copied a dozen files. The printouts he folded in thirds and then again in half, and wedged them into the elastic of his underpants; their sharp edges frayed against his belly. Now, hands shaking from the tension of what he has done, he lays disk and printouts flat upon his kitchen table, a pile of evidence pointing in a single direction. Though his heart is pounding with a ferocious anger at Carl Puckett, Joshua's head is full of questions.

Yes, he tells himself, the son of a bitch organized the whole campaign against Tall Pines, and surely, the break-in at Franco's house and the poisoning of Arthur. But did he kidnap and kill Daniel? Why would he? And if not Puckett, then who?

Chapter 22

What can it mean? Joshua wonders. Why would Carl Puckett make such strenuous efforts to derail a project that has already been approved by the Board of Selectmen? General orneriness? Hatred of out-of-towners? They hardly seem motivation enough to take such chances with the law.

Seeking clarity, Joshua the next day visits the Collegeville county records office, in a two-story building whose dull red brick exterior seems to drink in the sun on this March morning. He walks up the wide staircase to the second floor public room; its well-lit desks and trio of computer terminals seem out of place in this high-ceilinged 19th century building. A middle-aged clerk in white—flowing white hair, white shirt with top button fastened, white gold earring in each of his ears—shows Joshua how to use the maps to find the parcels, then how to match the parcel numbers to a database of owners.

Joshua concentrates on the larger plots of land in The Hollow, from Main Street north along the Northway Road. The state owns quite a bit of the land; Torvald has a few parcels here and there, though most of his property is on the other side of the road, on the hill that runs up behind the Sandlers. A number of parcels are held in the name of Arco Realty Partners, Carlton Partners or Cupten Partners, all at the same PO Box in Collegeville.

From the records office it's a two-minute stroll along Main Street to Len Stern's office, with its view of a mottled green dumpster in the supermarket parking lot.

When Stern has no idea who is behind those names, Joshua asks, "Len, ever play anagrams?"

"Anagrams?"

"Remember, a box full of white on black letters, you'd turn them over, one at a time, and when it was your turn if there was a word to be made from the letters in the middle of the table you made it and put the word in front of you."

"If you say so."

"Know any real estate guys around here named whose first names or last names contain a T O N or a T E N?"

"Tony Bentley, up in Northway. Owns a fair amount in town and also up your way."

"Is he a friend of Carl Puckett's?"

"How would I know? What the hell is this all about, anyway?"

"Suppose we play anagrams. Arco, Carlton, Cupten all contain letters of Carl or Rosa Puckett's name. Carlton has the C A R L of Carl and the T O N of Tony. And Cupten has the P U C of Puckett and the E N T of Bentley."

Back at The Hollow, Joshua locates a business card from the First Adams Bank in Collegeville, its corners wrinkled from being jammed into his basketball shorts. It's the card he was handed the afternoon he tackled the two teenagers who were beating Billy West, Jr. He dials the number and gets through immediately.

"Mr. West, it's Josh Sandler. You remember, your son, about five or six months ago . . ."

"Of course I remember—you saved Billy's life." West and his wife had called and written, had sent flowers; his wife had even baked them a homemade apple crisp. Now West tells Joshua how well Billy is doing: his best year at school ever, a four-game winning streak for his soccer team. Is there any news about Dan, he asks.

"Nothing good. Nothing at all."

"I'm so sorry. If there's anything . . ."

"Actually, there is."

Joshua asks him about loans that may have been made to Puckett and/or Bentley to finance real estate purchases. When West says that information about bank customers is confidential, Joshua replies, "I understand. But this is really important."

Within half an hour West calls back. "Puckett and Bentley have had loans outstanding as high as a hundred and fifty nine thousand; the current balance is ninety-eight seven. They bought a lot of land along Northway Road and some in the center of Smithfield. A few years ago they wanted to borrow an additional two hundred eight thousand to buy a larger parcel. When

Franco bought the land for Tall Pines they withdrew the loan application."

"What in the world were they buying all that land for?"

"'Future development,' they said. At the bank we're making more loans for houses in the hilltowns, including some newer, expensive ones. You've got people coming east from the Berkshires, seeking bargains, and professors in Collegeville moving west for the same reason. We've heard that one of the big builders from Worcester has been scouting sites for a vacation community, maybe along that pretty pond on the Smithfield-Northway border that the Tall Pines property abuts. And of course Puckett would be in a position to know the timing."

At 8:00 the next morning Joshua is back from jogging up Route 33A, the same route as always, past every bend in the river; these days he does five miles in less than 40 minutes, pushing himself faster than he has run in years. He takes no pleasure in the outing; he does it the way he would hit a punching bag. A pale sun barely pierces the steel-colored clouds. There is no running toward the light today; he has no hope that revelation lies in a golden pool of sunlight around the next curve. Foreboding, a cold fear in the pit of his stomach, tells him that he is closer than ever to knowing what happened to Dan. He dreads the answer even as he rushes toward it.

Joshua is sitting with the remains of breakfast, toast dust and an empty mug, when Shaughnessy returns his call of late yesterday. Within the hour, the DA is escorting him to his office in Collegeville, one floor up from the police station. On his way, he sweeps past a state police sergeant who is listening to the police radio, searching computer databanks and bantering with a trooper about what went wrong with the Patriots this year and whether the Celtics have a shot at the playoffs; past a well-worn coffee machine, its indicator light a foggy red as it reheats stale coffee to the point where the level of gassy emissions threatens to violate the Clean Air Act.

A surprise awaits Joshua; Charlie Burns, the western state police commander, is in the office. Joshua thinks he wouldn't want to be pursued by Burns, who exudes not only physical strength but also an austere, grounded sense of himself and his intellectual abilities.

"Carl Puckett's barn," Joshua says, announcing the purpose of his visit. "If you search his computer and his files you will find evidence that's relevant to the Tall Pines harassment and perhaps to Dan's disappearance, too."

He describes the e-mails, the flyer, other documents. When the DA reminds Joshua that he has to follow orderly procedure, Joshua rocks out of his seat.

"Orderly procedure? Don't tell me about orderly procedure. Has orderly procedure brought back our son, safe and sound? Every night my wife and I come home to a house that is empty. Bob Franco got threatening phone calls, had his house broken into, his dog killed, his property defaced, and orderly procedure did nothing to find the perpetrators. And you talk to me about orderly procedure?"

"You're upset," Burns says. "And of course you have a right to be."

"Upset? My son disappears, and for seven months you search and find nothing. Upset?"

Before Shaughnessy or Burns can answer, Joshua says, "Do I have to spell it out for you? There's a computer upstairs in his barn; the e-mails are stored on it. It's about as hard to find as a 100-dollar bill in the middle of the sidewalk."

Burns himself goes before a judge to obtain the warrant. By now it's the end of the first week of March and it has turned sharply colder; a nor'easter has roared up the Connecticut Valley, dumping nine inches of snow, slush and ice on the hilltowns. Residents who'd hoped they'd put away their snowblowers are hauling them out once more, cars are spinning out on the long upgrade that begins at Smithfield on Route 57 and continues past The Hollow and up to Cliffmont, where already a foot of snow has fallen.

Carl Puckett has a standing arrangement with Johnny Lambert to plow out his driveway and Lambert has just finished the 10:00 A.M. plowing when two state police cars, lights flashing, skid to a halt outside the Puckett house. Two troopers get out of the first car and head up the walk. Two from the second car make straight for the barn.

At the front door of the house, Rosa Puckett tells the troopers there must be a mistake.

"This is the residence of Carl Puckett, isn't it?" says the shorter, older trooper. "Where is Mr. Puckett?"

"He's down the street at the Town Hall."

In less than a minute one trooper is in the kitchen riffling through bills and correspondence while the other tramps upstairs, dripping water from his black boots on the risers. Rosa throws on a jacket, puts galoshes on her feet and heads for the Town Hall.

Five minutes later Puckett arrives, steaming with anger, displacing large quantities of swirling snow, which seems to gather behind him in a kind of roiling cloud. He has Phil Wright, his fellow Selectman, in tow. One of the troopers asks him to open the barn and when he balks, explains that the warrant gives them the right to enter the premises with or without the owner's assent.

Puckett protests but in the end he hands over the key. Puckett tries to step into the barn ahead of them but the bigger of the troopers, who must be six-two or six-three, restrains him. His hair is cropped very high on the back of his neck, a neck that is red and dotted with half an inch of snow between the back of his collar and the pebbly skin.

"Sorry Mr. Puckett, you'll have to wait."

"Carl, go inside the house," says Wright, "it's too damn cold out here."

Within an hour the troopers come back down from the hayloft, carrying boxes of stuff, the computer's hard drive, half a dozen floppy disks, tens of pages of printouts. Inside the house, the troopers have snatched piles of bills, folders of correspondence, two envelopes of prints with pictures of woods and hills that might represent the Tall Pines site. Puckett stands impassively on his front doorstep as they load the booty into the back of a state police van.

By this time a collection of Smithfield residents has gathered in the road outside the Puckett house: the son of Alice Fickett who owns the hardware store; sleepy-eyed Jack Cerniak who owns the B&B a few houses down; a tenant in a two-family brown wreck of a house, a rough-looking fellow with shaggy hair that looks as if he hasn't washed it since the end of daylight savings time. Through the snow, falling heavily, making a sound like coins falling on wet leaves, Puckett stares out at the onlookers. They stare back; no one says a word.

Puckett has never been a popular fellow. He is respected and feared—for his vindictiveness, for the power he wields in a small town—but not liked. There is a mixture of emotions in those looking at him now: a sense of retributive pleasure at the travails of any powerful person; a frisson of fear at seeing the police trample through a neighbor's house.

One by one the neighbors drift away. There is a burst of snow. For a half hour it comes down as thickly as if someone slit open a vast heavenly pillow, but then it dwindles and stops. Up and down the street residents dig themselves out by hand or prepare to push the snow out of their driveways with snowblowers or with pickups equipped with plows. A moment of stillness settles over the main street of Smithfield, and then the wind starts to howl.

By the end of the afternoon the troopers are back, produce an arrest warrant and take Puckett to Collegeville, where he is arraigned on a charge of threatening to injure Franco and damage the Tall Pines property.

In the ensuing negotiations with Puckett's lawyer, the DA, Frank Shaughnessy, demands that Puckett tell what he knows about the disappearance of the Sandler boy. "If it turns out that the harassment extended to physical harm or death of the boy, your client is looking at a kidnapping and murder charge."

"He knows nothing about the boy," the lawyer says.

"Then let him answer our questions."

Puckett gives a detailed account of what he did on August 10th, reconstructing his time from diaries and computer files. Never, Puckett says, never at any time during the consideration of Tall Pines, did he ever have a word or share a thought with anybody about the Sandler boy.

"To tell the truth, I wasn't even aware of his existence until afterwards. I guess I knew they had a son, but that was it. If I passed him in the street I wouldn't have known who he was."

Afterwards, when Shaughnessy asks Joshua if he knows of anything, anything at all, that links Puckett to his son, Joshua has to say no. "I wish I had some evidence, even a presentiment, but there's nothing, nothing that I can think of."

But Joshua has to give Shaugnessy credit for the way he handles things. Statements from Phil Wright and Tom Robinson both corroborate Puckett's involvement. Puckett has no choice.

He pleads guilty, and receives a fine of $3,000, six months in jail, plus another year of probation and community service. He resigns as a Selectman.

Wright gets a suspended sentence and a fine; he too resigns. In Robinson's case, the judge accepts his admission of facts and places him on probation for a year. If Robinson stays out of trouble, the charges will be dismissed.

Joshua follows it all closely, even showing up in court the day that Puckett appears before a judge to acknowledge his guilt. In their daily phone conversations and occasional visits, Sammons keeps Joshua up to date on other, surprising twists as they emerge.

Through Robinson and Wright, Sammons finds his way to Johnny Lambert, another part-time town worker dependent on Puckett's largesse; it turns out that Lambert helped distribute some of the anti-Tall Pines flyers around town. Lambert admits he also recruited two teenagers, his nephew and a friend, to break into Franco's house, poison his dog and then vandalize the Tall Pines construction site.

The nephew turns out to be Jason Lamb, Johnny Lambert's nephew. Johnny's brother changed his name from Lambert to Lamb when he settled here from Quebec. It's the same Jason Lamb whom Joshua caught that day in the park, beating up Billy West, Jr. Jason is a tough kid who's been in trouble one too many times, and the judge sentences him to four months in a juvenile detention facility.

Sammons comes by the house in The Hollow with the last of these details and Joshua has never seen the man in such a state of outrage.

"I won't say I couldn't ever imagine something like this. My job is to consider everything as possible. But these people," he says, shaking his head. "These people."

Sammons calms down. "I've already gone to see the other Selectmen. None of them say they knew anything about it. They don't see any connection to Daniel's disappearance."

He gets out his notebook and reads from notes of his conversation with Tony McMartin. "Never thought Carl could be trusted to tell the truth. Thought he was vindictive. But hurt a child? Be in on a kidnapping or murder of a child? No, not Carl."

His notes on Mary Shaw say, "The big overweight slob. All these years lording it over everyone. Serves him right."

Albert Sims quoted the Bible to Sammons. "'The inclination of man is evil from birth.' Says it right there in the story of Noah."

"Sims doesn't strike me as a religious man," Joshua says to Sammons.

"He's not. According to him, religion is all a load of crap. But he learned the Bible as a youngster and has never forgotten it."

Joshua is glad, at last, to have a few answers, but he is surprised at how little satisfaction he takes from Puckett's fall or even from the man's impending incarceration.

"Enough," he tells Sammons wearily. "It's time to find out what happened to our son."

Chapter 23

The last person he is expecting is this gaunt man with the calculating eyes. Edward Torvald stops in front of the house and gets out of a big black car, the kind of car that meant success 30 or 40 years ago. Everyone young with the down payment for a 36-month lease now is driving a Lexus or a BMW but Torvald pays no attention to fashion and still has his Chrysler Imperial. He raises his hand in greeting and starts walking toward Joshua.

Joshua, alone in The Hollow, has been working outside on this first warm spring day. It's late April and the trees are still bare. Along the edge of the road is an undulating ribbon of sand, left over from the work of the road crews as they sanded and plowed and sanded again. Now the residue lies in forlorn tracks deposited by the retreating snow. With one of those big push brooms, Joshua is sweeping the sand out from the edge of the lawn into the road and then merging it with the piles that are already there. Then he scoops up as much as he can with a snow shovel and dumps it into a big garbage can.

It rained yesterday and the day before, a steady, soaking rain that produced new green shoots of grass all over the lawn, and in their midst, like a series of explosions, starbursts of dandelions. In the air is the tang of oozing mud.

Joshua is halfway down the length of the lawn, near the second of the big maples that provides the shade on the west-facing side of the house. The door of the Imperial makes a heavy thunk as it closes and then Torvald is coming toward Joshua, walking briskly despite his 72 years. A second vehicle traverses the bridge and rolls to a stop. Art Sammons gets out. In an instant the two of them are standing in front of Joshua, each waiting for the other to speak. Joshua looks at Sammons' face, and his heart starts to pound as he leans on the long-handled push broom for support.

Torvald speaks first. "Months ago you asked me to mark on maps the locations of the meadows and bogs and places with easy access and to give a copy of the map to Art."

"Yeah, I remember." It was Joshua's idea; he'd thought such a map might help the police in their searching.

"I dropped off copies at your house and his house," Torvald reminds Joshua.

"We used those maps a lot but none of the places checked out," Sammons says.

"Two days ago," Torvald says, "I was up on the east side of Northway Road about a quarter mile beyond where the state land ends. I've got property on both sides of the road there and I was showing prospective buyers a 38-acre parcel. Maybe half a mile in from the road at the top of a steep bluff—you have to circle around a rocky formation—you come to a thick spruce grove and just beyond it a kind of broad indentation surrounded by birch and oak trees."

Joshua looks at Torvald and then at Sammons and then back at Torvald.

"The thing is, I forgot to mark that spot on the map because I've only got about 12 acres on that side of the road; the other 26 acres are on your side. It must be seven or eight years since I was up there, but this young couple looking to find a nice piece of land for their country retreat insisted that I walk the property line with them. And while I was up there I saw something."

A scrap of fabric, perhaps from a pair of green shorts, Torvald says, that's what was sticking out from under a pile of leaves. The leaves were much heavier in that place than they should have been, as if they'd been mounded up to cover something.

"I didn't come any closer. I told that young couple that I had to get into Hartsfield for an appointment. As soon as I got to my car I called Art."

"I would have told you on the phone yesterday," Sammons said, "but since you were coming up, I thought it would be better to tell you in person."

"Okay," Joshua says. "Okay."

Sammons says he and Ford hiked in to the spruce grove with a police photographer, a criminalist and another detective. Ford had already alerted one of the state medical examiners to be ready to drive out here if they found something.

In the indentation beyond the grove, they saw the oval pattern that Torvald had noticed, a bed of leaves heaped up as if covering a rough trench. They photographed the piece of green fabric and then he and Ford pulled away the leaves and began to dig down. They dug slowly and carefully, first with spades and then with their gloved hands.

Soon they came upon the toe of a sneaker and lying next to it a bit of rotted shoelace. Seconds later between the fingers of his brown work gloves Sammons was holding something that he was sure was bone, in the shape of a foot.

"What we found are the remains of a male adolescent, aged 12 to 14, approximately 63 inches in height. We need you to come to Collegeville to see if you can identify him as your son."

Joshua and Sammons and Torvald are standing there at the edge of the road with the sun hot on their necks. Except for Torvald's and Sammons' cars there has been no traffic. Now a solitary man passes by, bent over his racing bike—a porky fellow with the groaning thighs and black spandex of the weekend athlete. Joshua's hand starts to rise automatically in greeting, the way they do it around here; everything is in this motion of the hand, with the face itself offering neither a smile nor a grimace. The biker huffs and puffs his way past the three men, as, in spite of himself, Joshua lifts his hand and waves.

"When?" he asks Sammons.

"As soon as possible."

It doesn't take long at the morgue, 15 minutes or so. Joshua's heart stops at seeing the tattered bits of forest-green shorts and what is left of a Shazzam T-shirt with its zigzag red arrow. "It's Dan," he says, quickly looking away.

Joshua stumbles toward his car; as he wills himself to pull open the driver's door he hears someone behind him.

"Why don't you ride with me?" Art Sammons says. "Bill will drive your car home."

In the front seat of Sammons' Oldsmobile, Joshua keeps his hands clasped in front of him, peering dully at each twist and turn as if he has never taken this road before. He is conscious of his breathing in and out, can feel the diaphragm expelling the air, the nipples on his chest tingling as they push ever so slightly against the polo shirt he is wearing. As they climb into the hill-towns, his eyes are assaulted by the rush of the foliage coming toward them, the early green of the mountain laurel, the ribbed trunks of the maples, the fir trees hiding their mysteries under dark, dense branches. Every sensation registered by his body is an accusation: how dare he feel or experience or carry on with his life, as if consciousness itself must stand in abeyance because of what he has just witnessed.

It is warm outside the car and Sammons is fiddling with the air conditioning, trying to get just the right flow of cool air. Now he begins to talk, telling Joshua about Catherine, his beautiful 24-year-old daughter who has suffered from paralyzing migraines since high school. It took her six years to finish college but now, finally, she is settled in Boston, in her own apartment with a job as a paralegal.

Joshua listens, understanding the words but not their import. "Is she your only child?"

"No, we have three others. But Catherine is the one we lose sleep over. There isn't a day that I don't worry about our daughter—about her health, about how she is coping, about a million dangers, imagined or real. If anything happened to her I don't think I could even get myself out of bed."

He takes his eyes off the road for just a fraction of a second as he looks over at his passenger.

"I'm sorry, Josh. We'll find whoever did this. We're very close and we're going to find them."

Seeing the pain on Sammons' face forces Joshua to reach for some formula that will help him endure the next five minutes, the next hour, the next day.

I am going to live through this, he tells himself. We are going to live through this. But even as he recites this mantra, he knows it bears no relationship to what he is feeling. It is as if the mass of the entire universe has concentrated itself between his two ears. It keeps beaming him a message: nothing matters, not the sun or the moon or the tides, not an earthquake in Iran or a typhoon in Guam, not bloodshed in the Middle East, genocide in East Africa, plenty in America; not billions of people on earth looking for food, shelter, clothing, companionship, sex, laughter and recognition. The only thing that matters is me and my hurt.

The emptiness inside him seems to expand when he reaches the house, as if his body has been inflated to twice or three times its normal size but his heart and brain have shrunk; when he turns a door knob or grasps a dish towel his fingers are numb and register no sensation. He moves dully to the wall phone in the kitchen to call Nathalie in Mamaroneck.

"Where? Where did they find him?"

"In a piece of land belonging to Torvald, not too far from the Preserve."

Joshua says he'll be home in a couple of hours, but when she hears his voice she says no, he should stay put. She'll drive up there.

When she arrives he is astonished by her calmness. She sees how he is; her eyes are full of compassion. She boils water for tea and into his cup she pours a few drops of bourbon from the liquor cabinet. She makes the calls to Joshua's mother, to her parents, to her sister, to Gert, to Franco. In between the calls the phone rings: it is Sammons telling Joshua the results of their scouring the area around the meadow for clues. What they've found so far is tantalizing, if inconclusive: bits of fabric, the squashed and nearly disintegrated end of a cigarette butt, a gray button that may have come loose as someone hurried through the woods catching a shirt or pants on branches.

Later that afternoon Sammons shows Joshua and Nathalie color photos of the fabric fragments but not even Nathalie can identify them.

"What about the other kids?" Sammons presses. "Is it something that one of them might have worn?"

She turns her hands palm up: how can I know?

It is Nathalie who keeps saying no. She won't go to The Hollow for Memorial Day weekend. Go by yourself if you have to, she tells Joshua; just leave me out of it.

But in the end Nathalie changes her mind. Terry McBurnie has sent her a note on a sheet of ruled school copy paper. The letters of his words start out large but soon trail off the edge of the page, like stragglers on a western trek.

"Dear Mrs. Sandler," he writes, "I'm so sorry about Dan. They showed me the article in the paper. It was on the TV news too but I don't watch TV much. He was a wonderful boy and I'm heartbroken for you. Please tell Mr. Sandler how sorry I am." Terry adds that the flowers Nathalie likes so much are in bloom all around. "I am doing okay," he ends. "I can get around okay with the walker. They take care of us fine here, so no complaints."

The Collegeville paper sent a reporter to the funeral in Westchester, attended by more than 300 friends and relatives. In his article the reporter described how they buried Dan in the cemetery next to Joshua's father, how eight of Dan's classmates carried the coffin to the edge of the grave and how, once the box had been lowered into the earth, mourners took turns covering it with shovelfuls of dirt.

For a couple of days Nathalie leaves Terry's note on the shelf in the kitchen with the bills and announcements. Finally she tells Joshua, "I think we should pay Terry a visit. It's been so long since we've seen him."

Before they drive to the Senior Center Joshua and Nathalie stop at the house, where Nathalie spends an hour and a half turning over the garden. By noon she is drenched; the day has grown too warm for such exertions.

She comes inside to shower; she has a glass of iced tea and checks on her baking. She was up at six to assemble the batter for a banana bread, mashing the ripe bananas with a large fork, mixing in the egg, flour, sugar and melted butter, slipping it into the oven, preheated to 350. Now the loaf, moist and sweet-smelling, has cooled to body-heat temperature. She double wraps it in a sheath of aluminum foil and then places it inside a plastic bag. In a second plastic bag she puts two large California white peaches, a couple of red plums and an arrangement of local blueberries and blackberries. After lunch she and Joshua set off in the car.

When they reach the Smithfield Senior Center there is no sign of human habitation. In front of the building a row of beaten-down rhododendrons, battered by the harsh winter, offers little shade from the sun. They pull around the rear into a parking lot that is empty except for a lone, rusting Chevy station wagon.

The two-story frame structure houses two dozen residents. All but five of them are women who spend their time in front of the console TV in the living room, arguing over the soap operas or about whether they should watch the movie of the week or a repeat of *ER*.

As for the men, they seem to be playing out, on a public stage, the final act of a drama that has consumed them for much

211

of their lives. There is toothless Jack Gunderson, who'd spent 36 years working at the mill; he'll sit in front of the fireplace with its fake gas logs and begin sounding off at a foreman with whom he'd feuded for nearly two decades. There is Ernie Green, a dairy farmer with six daughters, none of whom had stayed to run the farm; he sold the land to a builder and took up Dewar's as a hobby. Every now and then he manages to get hold of a bottle. Perhaps Doris, the thin, nervous daughter who lives the other side of Collegeville, brings it in her floppy handbag; she could never say no to her father.

And there is Harold Whiting, the town intellectual; he taught English at the high school for 33 years and unbeknownst to anyone, had published more than 60 poems, including two in the *New Yorker*. He rarely speaks to his fellow residents, preferring to read biographies and to lament, from time to time, the absence of men of character in the leadership of the country.

A few of the men play cards, which Terry does not; nor does he watch TV or snooze in public in the parlor. Instead he looks over the copies of *National Geographic* or reads the tattered paperback bestsellers that townspeople donate to the Senior Center library.

Terry shares a room with Miller Shaw, the fifth man at the Center. Miller is one of the frugal Smithfield Shaws. He insisted on bringing to the Senior Center not only his string ball, 14 inches in diameter, but also his late wife's collection of 2,300 buttons, sorted by color into seven shoeboxes.

Before Joshua and Nathalie can get out of the car, a white van arrives to disgorge nine elderly residents—seven women, two men. A bit dazed from the sun, they straggle toward a side door entrance. Terry is the last to disembark and he stands by the double doors of the van, gripping the bar of his walker and locking his arms in position to inch forward. For a few seconds he is unable to generate any traction; then the woman driver, erect and authoritative, comes around to steady him and give him the gentlest of pushes.

From her trips to buy brushes and paint thinner at the Smithfield Hardware & Supply, Nathalie recognizes her as Alice Fickett, who is sharp with a cash register and even sharper to turn aside complaints about items she has sold. To Alice's way of thinking the problem always stems from the incompetence of the customer rather than from a defect in the merchandise. Yet here she is, as patient as a ewe with her suckling lambs. Every week she spends a couple of hours volunteering to drive the residents of the Senior Center to the parks in the nice weather or to the movies or library in wintertime.

Nathalie and Joshua catch up with Alice and Terry just outside the door. So intent is Terry on lifting first the walker and then his feet over the aluminum door jam that at first he doesn't notice his visitors.

"Terry," Nathalie says with a mixture of pleasure at seeing him and distress at how feeble he has become.

"Mrs. Sandler? Mr. Sandler?"

"Terry, how are you?" Joshua says, shaking his hand.

Nathalie reaches out to hug him. Her palms cup his shoulders, which used to be so strong and well-formed; now she has the impression of grasping hollowed-out balsawood forms rather than flesh and bone. He stands there with his hands locked onto the walker, blushing with embarrassment at her display of affection. Except for handshakes at the beginning and end of each gardening season, they've rarely touched. She does remember giving him a goodbye pat on his arm after she and Joshua drove Terry and his meager belongings to the Senior Center. He'd been boarding on the third floor of a house further down on Main Street but climbing the stairs had become not only painful but hazardous.

They'd helped him move one Saturday in April, four months before Dan's disappearance. She'd boxed up his underwear and socks (five pairs, seven pairs), his shirts and sweaters (four of the former, two of the latter), his work pants and church pants (two of each) and his collection of magazines and books (a Bible, a couple of *Reader's Digest Condensed Books*, a James Michener novel, a privately printed history of Smithfield and a cookbook that had been his mother's). All his toiletries fit in one cracked leather case.

As he got into the car for the 300-yard ride, he was holding onto a small photo album with pictures of his mother, his mother's sisters and himself as a child, a box of letters that his mother had written him while he was in prison, and the telegram they'd sent him the day she died, exactly one month before his release. That was it; there was nothing else.

Terry refers to the prison only as "that place." Now, as they accompany him to his room, Joshua realizes he's never asked Terry about those 28 years, almost half a life spent behind bars when the world was in upheaval: Hitler and the Nazis, World War II, Korea, the Cold War confrontations of the '50s and '60s, the birth of television, the price of a long-distance call coming down and down, until it cost less than a package of gum, the growth of the suburbs, the rise of the chain stores—all of it had passed him by. One time Terry had mentioned his shock at the JFK assassination. He'd been out of "that place" only a few months when it happened. I didn't know anyone could do such an awful thing to a president, Terry had said.

Joshua looks at the man, with his stooped shoulders, his surprisingly unlined face, his oh so serious blue eyes. Terry's gaze used to be clear as the first ice on the pond, so focused on the task at hand, whether it was weeding the flower beds or pushing the mower through the tangle of grass and debris at the edge of the property line, along the row of hemlocks. Now, peering into Terry's eyes is like staring at a light that has begun to flicker, the tungsten contacts fraying until one day the bulb will flare for a fraction of a second before going dark forever.

Terry inserts his walker through the door, maneuvers around two beds, then folds the walker, leans it against his two-drawer chest of drawers and shuffles to the far corner at the foot of the bed. Here he shifts his body and flops down into the armchair. Joshua positions the second armchair so Nathalie can sit facing Terry, while he leans against the chest of drawers.

"I brought you some goodies," Nathalie says, thrusting the two plastic bags toward him. "Would you like me to arrange these for you?" When his head moves—is that a nod, or an involuntary shake?—she places the foil-wrapped banana bread on his slender night table and positions the second bag at the end of the bed. Nathalie holds a peach and a plum in her two hands and he takes them both and begins to eat the plum, the red juice running down the sides of his mouth and onto his threadbare blue shirt.

"Here, let me get you something," she says, and she takes out a couple of tissues and gently wipes his face with them, then sets them on his lap like a dinner napkin.

214

"Where did you go today?" she asks when he finishes the plum.

"Lexington Park. If you wear shorts or a bathing suit you can dunk your feet in the water and under the trees it's cool and there are picnic tables and shuffleboard. Miss Fickett brought lunch and drinks for us." Each word takes an effort, and at the end of this account Terry is nearly breathless.

And then he adds, "That other day that you came to see me we went to Lexington Park also."

With a start Nathalie realizes he is talking about ten months ago.

"That was the day Dan went missing."

"We went right by the house," Terry says.

"Today?"

"Today and that other day."

Joshua pushes off from the chest of drawers until he is standing erect.

"You did? Go right by the house?"

"Sure."

"What time did you go by the house that day?"

Terry wrinkles his nose and eyes in an effort to remember. "I don't know."

"What was it like around our house that day?"

"The house looked nice, like always. The lawn was mowed."

"I mean, did you see anyone at the house? Near the house? Did you see Dan?"

"I didn't see Dan. I didn't see anyone near the house."

"Nobody? Nobody at all?"

"There wasn't any car in your driveway and no car in the driveway opposite. There was a car in the Bonacios' driveway."

"You remember which cars were there and which weren't?"

Terry seems surprised by the question.

"Sure I do. I think Mrs. Bonacio was getting in her car to go somewhere."

"So there was nobody near the house or in the road? No other car? Nobody on foot?"

"Well, except for that girl at the edge of the woods."

"What girl? Where?"

"She wasn't that close to the house. She was sideways under the trees, partly hidden by the rock. Like she was going into or coming out of the woods. I remember it because she had a hand touching the rock, to steady herself, I suppose. It's steep there and it's easy to slip."

"How could you see her if she was in the woods? I mean, you were in the van and it was going fast, wasn't it?"

"I always sit in the seat next to the window, on the other side from Miss Fickett. And Miss Fickett has to slow down there because of the curve in the road. The girl wasn't very far away. Maybe 25 yards, maybe less."

"What girl? Could you make out her face?"

"I could see it some, but she was facing sideways. I remember her hair, though. It was frizzy, like that girl who lives up the Northway Road."

"Melanie? Melanie Roberts?"

"Maybe. I'm not saying it was her because I couldn't see her clearly."

"My God, Terry, didn't you think . . ." And then he stops himself in mid-sentence. Terry's head is shaking from side to side, the tremors coming much faster than before.

Joshua is annoyed for being angry at Terry even for a second. Was it up to Terry McBurnie to say he'd seen a teenage girl in the woods, not a quarter of a mile from their house, on the day Dan disappeared? Or was it up to the police to knock on every door, including the door of the Smithfield Senior Center, and talk to Terry and Edith Robins and Ernie Green and 20 others? And of course, even if they had, it still would have been too late to rescue Dan from whatever fate he had suffered.

Lately, as the distance lengthens between him and that day in August, Joshua has begun to imagine snatches of conversation with his son. He'll be sitting in front of the TV watching the Yankees beat up on the Orioles and he'll hear, "Hey, Dad! We have next Wednesday afternoon off, you know, one of those teachers' professional things. Okay if a couple of us go to the day game at the Stadium?" Or there'll be the rush of feet on the stairs in Mamaroneck, like rain pummeling the car hood in an August thunderstorm. "That you, Dan?" he'll call, and the answer will come floating back, just as the door opens, "Going over to Jeremy's, see you about five-thirty, six."

Now, as Joshua stares at Terry McBurnie's blue eyes, as the legs of the armchair rock ever so slightly from the frequency of his tremors, Dan's voice is saying, "It's okay, Dad. Don't worry about me. Even when I'm not there I'm okay."

Alice Fickett, her favorite pencil sharpened to a knife point and tucked behind an ear, raises an eyebrow at Sammons across the counter of the Smithfield Hardware & Supply. Joshua has wasted no time telling him what Terry saw, and the policeman hurries over from work.

"You want me to tell you about a day ten months ago?"

"Thursday, August 10th. It was the day the Sandler boy disappeared. You drove a bunch of the seniors from the Senior Center to Lexington State Park that morning."

"Yep, that would be our Thursday excursion. A couple of them bring their fishing rods or sit under the trees and listen to the radio or play cards. Then I'll grill some frankfurters and hamburgers for lunch and then we'll go home."

"What time do you leave the Senior Center?"

"Usually a quarter to ten, occasionally 15 minutes later."

"Was Terry McBurnie part of the group that day?"

"Jesus, Art, I can't remember a specific day that far back, no way. But Terry almost always comes along. Even though the Parkinson's is making it tougher and tougher on him. Sometimes he can barely get the legs moving, no matter how hard he tries."

"Okay. Did you go through The Hollow on the way to the state park?"

"I must have—that's the way I always go."

"As you come through The Hollow, past Hunter's Lodge on your way to the bridge, you pass a quarter-mile stretch of woods. There's a big gray rock maybe a hundred yards before the bridge, surrounded by woods but visible from the road. Must be eight feet high, that rock. Know the spot I mean?"

"Sure, I've gone past it a hundred times."

"Well, on that day I'm talking about did you see anyone in the woods near that rock?"

"You've got to be kidding, Art."

"Dammit, I'm not kidding. Try to remember if you saw a female, perhaps a teenager." His eyes bear in on her as if stripping away her yellow short sleeve shirt and her tan work pants to get to the naked core of this 50-ish spinster with the lusterless brown hair and the mole at the base of her neck.

But no matter how many times Sammons asks the question, Alice Fickett cannot remember.

Chapter 24

Sammons gets right to the point.

"Tell me about the argument at the Preserve, the night before Dan disappeared."

Melanie and her mother are sitting in the kitchen of the house with the vertical dagger of red paint splashed along its left front side. Sammons has given Melanie the standard Miranda warning, advised her of her right to a lawyer, gotten Melanie's and Karla's consent to proceed. As he talks, Karla's eyes keep searching out Melanie's face, hoping to find there the answers that will set her mind at ease.

"Argument?"

"Come on, Melanie. We both know what happened between Bobby and Dan."

She is panicky, now, this girl with the springy curls and the upfront manner. The can-do expression she always wears is fading. Karla's face has gone clammy.

"Sam," she says, half to herself. "Sam." In fact, Sam has given Sammons only a tiny part of the story, but the policeman knows there's much more to come. The atmosphere in the Bonacio house is like a military stockade, the boy walled off physically and emotionally from the father, and Pat the only one who can speak to both of them.

"Bobby started putting down Kristen, saying she was too fat, too much of a loser," Sammons continues, "that she'd put out for anybody. Dan told Bobby to cut it out and that's when Bobby threatened him. Right?"

Sammons notes the surprise dancing its way across Melanie's lips, as if she's just seen something for the first time, a clown juggling six bowling pins or a young skater twirling giddily into a double axle.

"It wasn't like that. It wasn't so in your face. Maybe Dan said something like, 'that's enough, can't you leave her alone?' and Bobby got mad and was like, 'Butt out. I don't have to hang around here and listen to this crap.' So we left."

Then Sammons asks her about the next morning, when she was babysitting at the Petersons'. What time did you get there, he wants to know.

"Mrs. Peterson was on the overnight shift so I had to be there before Mr. Peterson left for work. Maybe it was 7:30 or so."

"Did somebody come by to talk to you there? Did you talk to anybody by phone?"

"No."

"Are you sure?"

And when she looks at him with a puzzled expression, Sammons says, so quietly that he can see her straining forward to hear, "There are phone records, Melanie."

"Phone records?"

"We checked the Petersons' phone. Three calls that morning—one to the Bartlett house, one to the Sandlers' house, another to the Bartlett house. All between 9:30 and 9:45."

Melanie is watching him as Sammons goes on with his narrative. "Mrs. Peterson gets off work at 8:30, right, so she's home between 10:00 and 10:15. As soon as she got there you were out the door, weren't you? But instead of walking up the Northway Road toward home, you head left on Main Street, going toward the bridge, toward the Sandlers' house. But then you change your mind, scramble off the road right where the big rock is. Why did you do that?"

Karla is becoming more and more agitated, looking from Melanie to Sammons and back to Melanie, seeking some assurance that everything will be all right.

To Sammons, Karla's expression is easy to read: let this be nothing but an ordinary disaster, one of half a dozen things that might happen to her in the course of a month—losing her car keys again, not having enough money to pay the town tax bill, learning that the 30-something record store manager with the close-cropped blond hair, the one who bought her a drink and took her for a drive, is actually married with a three-year-old daughter. Let it be anything except a terrible lie about a teenage boy who disappeared one day last summer.

This girl's mother has no guile to her, Sammons thinks. Melanie is another story. She has self-assurance; she has brains. But now her thoughts must bump up against the unmovable wall of reality. Her eyes show a commingling of fear and disbelief. It

220

often comes down to this in a small town like Smithfield; residents assume the part-time police chief isn't up to spotting the most obvious lie, let alone untangling a long-running plot.

When she doesn't answer he says, "Melanie, someone going by in a van saw you by the rock. Just about 10:15. Why were you there?"

"I was going to his house to tell him to stay put. That I'd changed my mind."

"Changed your mind about meeting Dan? So you did call Dan that morning?"

"Yes. Bobby called me at the Petersons'. I was changing the little one's diaper and had to call him back. He told me to get Dan to meet me at that spruce grove above the Preserve."

"So that was the plan, and you changed your mind and were going to warn Dan. But you didn't warn him. You changed your mind again. Why?"

"I don't know. I'd promised Bobby. Besides, Bobby swore not to hurt him."

"Not to hurt him?"

"He was going to hide and wait for him, and when Dan passed, he was going to tackle him and tie his hands up and then get the blindfold around his eyes. That was it. Not even beat him up. Just tie him to a tree for a couple of hours."

"But it didn't work out that way, did it? Were you there, too? Did the two of you tackle him together?"

"No way. I wasn't there. I didn't know what happened till later."

"Till when?"

"In the evening mom got a call from someone in town and then she called over to me and said, 'They say Daniel Sandler is missing. Isn't he one of the kids you hang out with?'"

"You could have called the police then. Or told your mom. Why didn't you?"

They both look at Karla, whose face seems to be collapsing like a snowman's in a January thaw.

"I was scared of what they'd do to me. I didn't see what happened to Dan, I didn't know for sure, so I told myself I had nothing to do with it."

She won't confront Sammons' eyes, the way she might avoid a mirror if she had taken a paring knife to her cheek, inflicting a mark of disfigurement that time will not erase.

"But you did have something to do with it. You helped plan a crime—and afterwards you knew that it had happened. You had an obligation to come forward."

Sammons asks when she heard from Bobby Dawes next.

The next morning, she says, Bobby came to her house early, saying he wanted help burying the body. Saying that what he'd dug was too shallow and he had to make it deeper.

The two of them, she and Bobby, were behind her house, where the two propane tanks sit in a patch of sand and weeds. In the woods across the road, less than half a mile away, an old logging trail led to the spruce grove. It was barely 15 minutes away.

"I told him I couldn't do it. I told him to tell the police."

She expected that Bobby would be agitated, but instead he was collected, determined—and very angry with her. It was an accident, Bobby claimed, but we can't tell anyone. They'll say we did this on purpose. Melanie protested. An argument flared but then abruptly ended. Bobby had a small shovel with him and he set off across the road into the woods, looking like a crazy man searching for a leaky pipe.

She didn't see him again for two or three days and by then it was too late.

"He'd made up his mind. He wasn't going to tell. He was going to tough it out."

"It was her idea," Bobby Dawes says, in the end.

The two policemen come for him at Tony Bentley's father's store, a richly festooned wall coverings emporium on Main Street in Collegeville. Dressed in polo shirt and shorts, bare arms bulging with muscles, Bobby is high on a ladder arranging a display of blinds. It is a gray, dull June day. Ford calls to him and when Bobby does not move fast enough he barks, "Dawes, get down here now." Ford and Sammons grab him as he backs off the ladder, swinging him so that his feet whisk through the air before coming to rest on the carpeted showroom floor.

"What the fuck?"

"Shut your mouth," Ford says. "Any personal stuff you have here, go get it. You're not coming back."

They shove him in the back seat of the police car and Ford slams the door. Barely three minutes later they pull up to the

Collegeville police station, a gray stone building with the words "Adams County, 1885" chiseled into the concrete lintel above the doorway. In a drab room with a green metal table, the two men read Bobby his rights as he nods, Yeah, I know.

"Your mother will be here soon." Sammons says.

"My mother?" At this time of day Ellen Bartlett is usually on her way to the mall for her regular shift, noon to 8:00 P.M., selling tickets at the multiplex theater outside of Hartsfield.

"She's going to have to miss work because we want her to hear you tell us what happened the day Daniel Sandler disappeared."

Unlike Ford's raspy growl, Sammons has a low voice, a non-argumentative voice, but each word counts, as if it were a round stone being dropped into a still pond.

"Nine months and three weeks, Bobby. That's how long it's taken to figure it out." Sammons has spent so much time thinking about August 10th that the day is forever imprinted in his senses: a flawless day of 80s sunshine and low humidity, the day the Sandlers drove to the dump and the hardware store, and came back to an empty house.

Ford and Sammons sit without a word, at ease with each other like two guys side by side on bar stools, waiting companionably for the Monday Night Football game to begin.

Bobby tries not to look at them, tries to keep his eyes on the caramel-colored wall, bare except for a picture of the goddess Justice. In the cheap print, hung there years ago by a chief of police with a wry sense of humor, the goddess has her hair bound up in a white kerchief and sits on a throne, eyeing the scales of justice like a housewife trying to decide how many pounds of potatoes she needs.

The room has no windows, no light except from the three fluorescent tubes overhead, one of which flickers and crackles. The chill from the gray June day has seeped into the police station and Sammons can see the tiny goose bumps developing on Bobby's arms.

There's a knock and Sammons steps outside, closing the door behind him. "She's here," says the young state policemen who collected Ellen Bartlett in Smithfield.

Facing her, what Sammons sees is a slim, washed-out blonde with deep circles under her eyes and a vulnerable look that to men constitutes her chief charm. It is a quality that might, in some women, attract the tender, protective male. But Sammons knows that Ellen enjoys no such luck, not with her first husband, Bobby's father, in prison for armed robbery or her second, Tim Bartlett, working the night shift and spending his afternoons in front of the TV, a Budweiser for companionship.

Ellen and Sammons have known each other since third grade. In another setting they might ask about each other's families. Today all he says is, "Bobby's inside. It's time for him to tell us what happened to Daniel Sandler that day."

Ellen looks even paler than usual. "What are you saying? That he was involved?"

Sammons' steady gaze tells all. "I'm going to bring you in. Tell him to tell the truth."

What about a lawyer, Ellen murmurs, should they get a lawyer.

"It's his right," Sammons says, shrugging. "Either way it's all going to come out."

As soon as they enter the room Bobby repeats what he told the two policemen: he doesn't want a lawyer. He grits his teeth, turns away from his mother. Instead of addressing her son, Ellen looks at Sammons and says, "I don't want anything to happen to Bobby."

"It's a little late for that. You know we found Dan's remains on Torvald's land. In that clearing by the spruce grove, not far from the Preserve."

"Bobby can't have had anything to do with that," she says. Bobby keeps his eyes on the wall with the picture of the goddess Justice and her scales. Sammons compels Bobby to face him. Again he asks what he did to Dan that day.

"I already told you before, nothing. I didn't do anything to him."

"You were in the woods that day. We know it because she told us."

"Who?"

"Melanie, who else."

"I didn't see him that morning, I already told you."

Sammons is watching Bobby, looking for something, some spark of doubt, some sign that his swagger is melting. Ford slams his palm down on the table.

"Stop bullshitting us. We know what happened, Bobby. We dug up Dan's body right where you buried it. Want to see the pictures? Want to see what a body looks like when it's been buried under leaves and dirt for ten months?"

Ellen Bartlett sits like a Renaissance statue, frozen in a timeless agony. How long, she seems to be saying, how long must I endure this?

Ford reaches into his pocket and takes out an envelope and lays the pictures carefully on the scratched metal table where Bobby Dawes sits opposite.

"You know," Sammons says, "for ten months I've kept asking myself why. Why this kid? Who would want to hurt this kid?"

When Bobby doesn't reply Sammons asks, "How'd you and he get to know each other, anyway? You were sort of friends, right, even though he was younger?"

"So what? Who is there to hang out with in that place anyway? The Hollow? Smithfield? Jesus. My mom had made some curtains for his mom. They were always fixing up the place. Anyway, we rode our bikes together. We went swimming. Played Monopoly. Big deal."

"You hated him, didn't you?" Sammons has dropped his voice till it is as thin as a wire. "You always hated him, this New York kid whose parents had a lot of money."

"Why do you keep saying I hated him? Mostly he was okay. One time, I think, he went on about what he was going to do, like he had his whole life worked out. Some fancy college like Amherst or Yale, and then medical school. I said some of us can't afford college and he goes on about loans, work-study programs. Loans—can you see me telling my mom and stepdad, 'Oh, I want to borrow $10,000 so I can go to college'?"

Ellen Bartlett recoils as if Bobby has smacked her with his meaty hands. "I would have done anything, whatever I could do . . ." she begins, and then appeals to Sammons.

Sammons ignores her. "So which was it, Bobby? You always hated this rich kid? Or was it that what he was doing or saying at the Preserve made you see red?"

No and no, Bobby says, his voice lower and lower. He has a mauled, chewed-up look as Ford and Sammons pummel him with questions.

The long June afternoon marches toward dusk; for a couple of hours sun chases the clouds away, then it fades and the cool air returns. Sammons and Ford take a break so Sammons can help Ellen from the chair and lead her gently to the ladies' room, where she stumbles inside to vomit. A sympathetic policewoman finds her a cot on which to rest, and then brings her some warm soup with crackers.

Sammons and Ford share a pizza, leaving the door ajar so the aroma wafts in to the 16-year-old. After a while, Sammons returns to the room with the green table and the print of the goddess Justice; he is carrying the last slice of pizza and sipping a cherry soda.

Sammons takes a large bite. The boy sits like a park bench, his feet bolted to the floor.

"I'm hungry."

"Tell me what happened and I'll get you some pizza."

"Screw you."

Sammons shakes his head. "Bobby, that's no way to talk. I'll make a deal with you. Dan's mother says the three of you climbed up to Torvald's land a few weeks before he disappeared. Tell me about that time and then I'll get you something to eat."

Bobby starts to relate the story of when they climbed to the green meadow high up in the woods. Halfway into this his voice gives out. A look of hopeless vulnerability crosses his face. It is 9:00 and outside the police station the stars are winking on one after another.

"All right, Bobby," Sammons says, sensing the change in the boy. "Let me get your mother."

Bobby is sipping the last of the coke that Sammons has given him as Ellen Bartlett is led into the room, her sandaled feet scraping reluctantly along the worn wooden floor. When Bobby says, "I'll tell you how it was," Ford goes and gets the camcorder.

"It was all an accident."

He claims it was Melanie's idea, her idea to get Dan to meet her at the spruce grove, where they'd grab him and blindfold him.

"Who's the we?"

"Me and Tony."

"Why did you want to do this?"

226

"We were pissed at him, going on and on to Kristen, trying to get her to bug me about taking care of it. Of the baby. Like she was going to have it, for Christ sake."

"Taking care of it? You mean supporting a child? You got her pregnant, didn't you?"

"That wasn't me. That was Tony."

"He says it was you."

"Whatever. I told her to get rid of it, and then he starts butting in with all these ideas. Like, I should spend my life working to take care of some kid she could just get rid of."

Ford shakes his head. "So your plan was to grab a kid in the woods and tie him and blindfold him? Then what? Leave him until he starved to death?"

No, Bobby says. "We were going to come back in a couple of hours, when he was good and scared, and let him loose. And then maybe he'd shut up."

"I don't think so," Sammons says. "I think you said to Melanie, 'I want to get rid of this prick.' This prick, isn't that what you called him?"

"I call everyone prick. And no it wasn't to kill him, it was to scare him. I didn't want to kill him. Why would I want to kill him?"

"Because you hated his guts. Because he stood up for Kristen. Because he was a rich New York kid who was going to have everything in life and you weren't."

"Come on, I had nothing against him because his parents are rich. Look at Tony. His old man has lots of money. He's going to college, and I don't have it in for him."

Ford snorts and says to Sammons, "What does this punk want, points for not killing Tony?"

And then he asks, what about Tony? Was he in on this? Did he help?

"He said he would. And then, the night before, he goes, 'Sorry, I have to work in my old man's office tomorrow.' He helps us plan the whole thing and then he wimps out."

"All right, Bobby. What happened in the woods?"

"Dan was supposed to meet Melanie at the spruce grove. You climb up through the steep part of the woods, then the land flattens out for a bit and you go over a little brook where it's very marshy. And there's a huge pine, it must be a hundred feet tall.

And next to it some bushes that form a shelter. You can crouch down there and wait."

"So Melanie was there with you?"

No, Bobby says, it was just me waiting there, then coming up behind Dan very fast and grabbing him around the neck and pulling him down. I'm bigger and stronger, Bobby explains, and once I have him down he's going to stay down. Then I'm going to tie his hands and bring him to that big pine tree.

But it didn't happen that way.

He says Dan broke away from his neck hold and veered back toward the little brook, a muddy spot, a slippery spot.

"He slips on a wet spot and down he goes, backwards because he's off balance. And his head hits a big rock. I wasn't even close to him. He was four or five yards away."

Bobby halts, takes a deep breath.

"The sound."

"What sound?"

"The sound of his head hitting the rock. It was awful. Awful. I run over to him and he's just sprawled there. His eyes are open but they don't see anything. I feel for a pulse and I feel his heart. Nothing. Nothing."

If it was really an accident, Sammons says, then you would have done something to save him. Did you try mouth-to-mouth resuscitation? Did you run to get help?"

"I didn't want him dead but he was dead. In an instant he was dead."

He takes a breath and continues.

"So I've got to move him. I can't leave him like that. I pick him up, put him on my shoulders and start climbing. I didn't expect him to be that heavy. His arms hang down onto my shoulders and below my shoulders, to my chest. Now and then his fingers flopped against my belly. It's spooky. He's heavy, so heavy. I'm stumbling from side to side, trying to keep my footing. I know I'm getting close. Finally I come to those evergreens."

"The spruce grove," Sammons says.

"The spruce grove. When I get there I can't hold him a minute longer. He sort of falls off my shoulder onto the ground. There's a little tree there, and his neck smacks against it. I think, uh oh, I've killed him. I wasn't thinking straight. I mean, he's already dead and here I am worried about hurting him. I think, maybe he's not really dead. Maybe I can get help.

"But I know that isn't true. I know it's too late. As soon as anyone saw the body they'd say I killed him." Bobby describes finding a dip in the land where the ground was soft enough to dig. He makes a hole, drags Daniel's body there, covers it up. Then he realizes the hole is too shallow.

"So the day after, I came back with a shovel to dig him out. I dug a deeper hole and buried him again. It was awful, digging him up again. I'll never forget the smell. I buried him maybe two, three feet deep. It was hard to go deeper, there's rocks and tree roots everywhere. It took me an hour and a half. I was sopping wet from the effort of it. Then I piled some dirt and twigs and leaves on top till you couldn't see any sign of it."

Sammons waits for Bobby to finish. The boy raises his eyes part way, as if to avoid the glare, but there is no glare; his face is in the shadows cast by the dim fluorescent fixture. The only sound in the room is Ellen Bartlett's sobbing.

"What time did you get home that Thursday?"

"Around 3:30, 4:00."

"Three-thirty or four." About the time, Sammons is thinking, that Joshua and Nathalie would have been feeling frantic, yielding to that despair that strangles speech.

He asks who was there when Bobby got home. His brother Timmy was out playing. His stepfather, in front of the TV, never even looked up.

"And your mom?" Sammons asks.

"At that job," Bobby says. "At the movie theater in the mall."

The way he says it brings a rush of blood to Sammons' face.

"That job? You mean your mother works hard to bring home money to feed you and your brother and buy you clothes and hope you'll go to college, while you're killing a 14-year-old kid in the woods and then lying about it for almost a year. Is that what you mean?"

When Ford asks what about his clothes, weren't they dirty, wasn't there any blood, Bobby tells how he came out of the woods by way of The Shadows. There he wet down his T-shirt and wrung it out, scraped the dirt and mud from his sneakers and cleaned his shorts.

"Wasn't there anyone at The Shadows?"

Ford poses the question idly and he and Sammons are astonished when Bobby says, yeah there was. "Sam was there; he saw me. Good old Sam, always in the wrong place."

And Sammons realizes that Sam has a lot more to tell than he's told so far.

Once he got home, Bobby goes on, he stuffed the shirt, the shorts and the socks into his backpack and went to take a shower. His stepfather left for work and Bobby made supper for himself and for Timmy.

So what did you do that night, Sammons asks.

Watched TV, Bobby says. Went outside to look at the moon, too fidgety to sit still. His mother came home at nine, and when she said she was going to the laundromat the next day and to give her any dirty clothes, Bobby realized he had to get rid of them.

"After I reburied him the next day I took a pair of her sewing scissors and cut up the shorts and the T-shirt into little pieces." He tells the policemen how he'd put the pieces of clothing in a plastic bag and stuffed it under some garbage in the dumpster at the general store and how, when he went back a few days later the dumpster was empty.

"Nothing ever got discovered," Bobby says.

"No," Sammons says. "When I talked to you that night you just gave me your 'aw shucks' look and said you hadn't seen him. And all the time your clothes that were filthy from burying him in the woods—those clothes were at the bottom of your knapsack. You told the biggest lie of your life and thought you got away with it."

How many times did I come back to interview you, he asks Bobby.

"I don't know. Three or four."

"It was seven times, seven separate times. I looked up my notes in the case file. I was trying to find the killer of this boy, who as far as I could tell, never did anything to anybody. He had no enemies. He didn't annoy his teachers or his neighbors. Just a good kid."

Sammons pauses, then asks Bobby who else knew besides Melanie, Tony and Sam.

"No one else."

Sammons takes him through the list: Not his mother? Stepfather? Little brother? No other friends? Not the minister or a teacher or any adult at all?

"No."

"No. You kept it to yourself. And you consigned that boy's parents to a living hell. May your soul burn in hell, too." Sammons unhooks the handcuffs from his belt and cuffs Bobby as the goddess Justice watches from her picture frame.

"Are you going to tell my father? I mean my real father?"

"First things first, Bobby. First I'm going to tell Daniel's father and mother. They've already lost their son. Your father will have to wait a few days longer to learn that he's lost his."

Chapter 25

"Are we done for now? Can we go home?" Only desperation could produce such a question, Sammons realizes.

"Ellen, you can leave any time, but Bobby isn't going home."

"What's going to happen to him?" she asks, her voice on the raw edge of hysteria.

"It depends," Ford says truthfully; it depends on whether he's telling the truth, it depends on what Shaughnessy decides.

The district attorney is on his way. Ford tracked him down around 11:00 P.M. at Brierly's, the darkly lit restaurant with the phony gas lamps—about the only place in Collegeville, other than the all-night donut shop, that's open this late. The DA favors a booth in the back, where he knocks down Bushmill's and water with a couple of the lawyers in town, or with the provost of the college.

Sammons and Ford, meanwhile, are speeding toward Northway, arriving at midnight to pound on the door of the Bentley home.

"You've got a hell of a nerve coming here at this hour," Tony Bentley, Sr. says to the policemen. Tony Jr., barefoot, hovers at his father's shoulder, wearing nothing but white tennis shorts and his irritating smirk.

Ford can no longer contain himself. "We've got a nerve? You've got a nerve, you stuffed shirt. Your son is looking at a homicide charge in the death of Daniel Sanders. Two of his buddies have already confessed."

Within the hour their lawyer joins Tony and his father at the Collegeville police station. He confers with Tony for a few minutes, but when he starts to tell Shaughnessy his client is innocent, the DA quiets him with a wave of his fingers.

Shaughnessy's black eyes are glittering; his fleshy lips are in constant motion as he anticipates the publicity, the attention, the buzz around town, from the night's activity.

"Innocent? Don't use that word in connection with this crime because it just makes me see red. These two guys"—he

232

points to Sammons and Ford—"have been busting their asses on this case for nearly a year and I'm going to see to it that everyone involved in this boy's death gets the punishment they deserve."

"Look, I didn't have anything to do with planning a murder," Tony exclaims. On August 10th of last year, he says, he was working in his father's real estate office. It was only the next day that he got a call from Bobby asking if he'd heard that Dan was missing and telling him in so many words to keep quiet.

Sammons shakes his head. "Come on. Bobby says you knew all about it, that you planned it, that you were supposed to help—till you wimped out, as he put it."

Shaughnessy has heard enough. He waves away the lawyer's protests as his eyes, very small and quite pitiless, bore in on the boy. "We're charging him as an accessory to murder."

An hour and a half later, Sammons and Ford have completed yet another round trip to Smithfield. This time they return with Sam Bonacio and his mother, Pat.

Sam has already told Sammons and Ford about the bitter argument between Dan and Bobby the night before August 10th. But, he repeats, he never saw Dan the day he disappeared. He was visiting a friend in Northway until late afternoon.

"You rode your bike back along Route 33A," Sammons says. "Did you stop anywhere? Maybe go for a swim?"

"A swim?"

"Isn't that where you saw Bobby? At The Shadows? You got off your bike there and had a swim in your shorts, the way you've done many times. Didn't you see Bobby, washing his T-shirt and shorts like some woman in a village somewhere in India?"

When Sam doesn't respond, Sammons asks, "Did you know then what had happened?"

"No. I just saw this guy in the bushes across the other side of the stream. It took me a minute or two to figure out who it was and what he was doing. He's carrying a wet T-shirt all balled up in his hand. His face and arms are mostly clean but I can still see bits of leaf and twig around the back of his neck and in his hair. His shorts are wet and streaked with dirt and his sneakers are covered with muck."

"'Get a little dirty, did you?' I ask. 'What's it to you?' he says to me. I just look at him some more without speaking and then I pedal my bike home."

Only when he got home and saw his mom in a state because Dan was missing did Sam begin to suspect what happened. The next day is worse, everyone talking about it, search parties out looking and he resolved to tell what he saw. That's when Bobby came by.

"He gets kind of desperate and says, 'Listen, dude, don't mention to anyone that you saw me the other day, okay?'

"I give him a look like why should I help you, and that's when he does it."

"Does what?"

Sam hesitates for barely a second, but once he starts talking Sammons realizes what a leap into the unknown the boy has taken.

"Says he'll tell stuff about me if I go to anyone."

"Stuff? What stuff?"

"Stuff about me and another kid. An older boy."

"What stuff? What boy? Did the two of you get into some kind of trouble?" The expression on Sam's face tells Sammons he has missed the point. But Sam doesn't seem to care about Sammons. In fact he is looking at Pat, speaking softly but clearly, telling her things he has never told her before as he answers the policeman's questions.

"We did things together. He had a car. He would take me places, places where we could be alone."

Sammons can't bear to look at Sam's mother. Though he has steeled himself not to show the least bit of sympathy for any of these kids, nevertheless his voice softens.

"Sam, are you . . ."

"No." The word explodes out of the boy's mouth. "It was my first year in high school and I had no friends. At home my dad was always picking on me. This guy was nice to me; he gave me things: a shirt, a wallet. For my birthday he gave me money. So I let him do things to me and I did things to him."

The two of them met in a photography club at school, Sam explains. The older boy was 18, Sam was 14. It went on for three or four months; then the older boy graduated and left for New York. But there was gossiping among the kids at school. Bobby knew someone who'd seen Sam in the older boy's car, with his arm draped around Sam's shoulder. He told Sam to keep his mouth shut or he'd put it all in a letter to Sam's father.

"For God's sake, Sam. If only you'd spoken up we'd have arrested Bobby."

"If I'd spoken up my father would have beat the crap out of me—or worse."

"No!" Pat is yelling at her son; anger, frustration, misery—they all mingle in this scream of shame. "Never, never would I have allowed that."

"Right, you'd try to stop it and that would only make things worse between you and him, and they're bad enough already. I was trying to keep all that from happening."

"Look at the result, Sam," Sammons says. "You kept your mouth shut and Dan lay buried near a spruce grove for almost a year before we found him. Didn't you ever think about his parents? About what they went through?"

Sammons is prepared for anger, or sullen acquiescence or even the prolonged silence of which this boy is capable. What he is not prepared for are the sobs that burst from Sam's throat until the boy's wiry frame heaves and shakes with the futile effort to regain composure. Pat edges her chair close to him, close enough to take him by the shoulders but he stiffens at her touch and pulls away. Even in remorse he is alone.

For many months Sammons has deliberately held himself aloof from the pain that Dan's disappearance has inflicted on others, but now he turns his face away to hide his own heartache. Finally he can give a name to the torment he has witnessed in this boy. It's bad enough that Sam and his father can't stand each other. Bad enough that Sam let himself be enticed into a relationship with an older boy. But the worst is his shame and self-hatred at keeping silent.

When he is once again composed, Sammons turns back to Sam, who is still trembling.

"You've done a terrible thing, you know. I'm not talking about your behavior with that boy. I'm talking about leaving Dan's parents in the awful uncertainty that they lived through for so long." Though his voice is almost a whisper, the words land on Sam with the force of sandbags.

"Even now you've got to try to make it right."

Sam looks confused. He says, haltingly, that there isn't anything more to tell.

"Yes there is. Of course you'll cooperate fully and tell a judge or jury everything you know. But I'm also talking about the Sandlers. I'm talking about going to them, telling them what you've done and asking them to forgive you."

How can he do that? Sam asks.

"How can you not?"

June, which began with those peaceful cool mornings, the smell of new grass, the restful sight of trees in full leaf, has, in the latter half of the month, turned unseasonably warm. Now by 8:00 A.M. in the city, the rising temperatures are roiling the tempers of both civilians and uniformed workers—policemen in blue, UPS drivers in brown, Fed Ex delivery people in black, hotel doormen in maroon jackets with gold epaulets, their upper sleeves already stained with perspiration.

Shortly after Joshua and Nathalie paid the visit to Terry, the call had come from Sammons, naming the teenagers who'd caused Dan's death.

"There's one other thing," Sammons had said. "Sam Bonacio."

"Sam? Sam was one of them?"

"He wasn't one of them, but he knew. He knew for months." And Sammons tells him the story.

Nathalie deals with the news better than Joshua. His rage is not assuaged—not by the letter from Sam, covering half a page, nor by the surprise Sunday appearance of Pat and Sam in Mamaroneck. Joshua would have kept them standing there on the front step forever, but Nathalie invited them in and brought them a glass of juice, and for a half hour Joshua had to endure a halting apology delivered by a teenage boy being strangled by his own guilt.

Rage cools, hardens into something bitter and insoluble. Three weeks later, Joshua still moves through the streets dazed and distracted, irritated by the least obstacle in his path. He resents the disorder, the continuous tossing of peach pits, newspapers, crumpled napkins, banana peels and gum wrappers, as if the morning human discharge from subways and trains is a

236

single monster with one pair of eyes, one mouth and a thousand hands and feet. He used to vibrate in sympathy with the pulsing rhythms of the city, the relentless beat of its push toward the future; now he is deaf to its discordant rhythms.

Worried about his mood, Nathalie has been urging him to take time off, to sneak away somewhere for a long weekend.

"Let's take a plane to Nantucket, stay in some spiffy B&B. Just to do it, just to have a splurge."

"We'll see," he replies. Too much on his mind right now: a final volunteer stint at Bronx Academy, business to wind up in the aftermath of Dan's death (among other things, how to dispose of a college savings account in his son's name), office furniture to buy and sell, real estate to develop. The White Plains project is moving ahead, finally, and now he's looking at one in Pawling.

In fact, the very routine of purposeless business activity that chafes at his spirit—am I really doing this, he wonders, at least once a day—also provides perverse, familiar comfort. Now, from his east-of-Second-Avenue parking garage, Joshua is borne along the sidewalk, merging into the monstrous flow of walkers and letting it carry him forward.

To get to his office, eight floors above Third Avenue, Joshua must cut through the tangle of pedestrians, bikers, cabbies, cops, newspaper hawkers and those slouching men with protruding eyeballs and rolled-up pants cuffs, each one on a different street corner snapping a 3x8-inch flyer for a topless bar between their fingers before thrusting it toward the passerby with the exhortation, "Check it out." Consummate ventriloquists, they manage to expel these three syllables through lips that appear sewn shut.

On this day Joshua steps past the second of these real-life action figures, on 42nd Street between Second and Third as he strides toward his building entrance. "Check it out," says this black man in black T-shirt and black pants. He slips the oblong flyer deftly between Joshua's fingers before Joshua can close his fist, already moist from the early morning humidity. The flyer, printed in blue with the heading Feline Felix's Cat Lounge, offers the crude outline of a female with sinuous locks and sausage–shaped breasts.

"Thanks but no thanks, buddy," Joshua says as he tries to hand back the flyer. The Feline Felix representative lets it fall through his fingers; it makes a lazy descent on currents of warm air already fetid with the odor of donut grease, taxicab exhaust fumes and stale coffee from the splattered plastic lids collecting in the nearby trash barrel. Grinding it into the sidewalk with his left heel, he snaps a fresh flyer between his fingers. In less than a second he proffers it to the next passerby, a pasty-faced Ivy League law student clasping an oversized briefcase on his way to his summer internship.

By then Joshua has reached sanctuary: the high-ceilinged lobby with its dim coolness, its background hum of murmured good mornings, the smack of a rolled-up newspaper against an outstretched palm, the rumble of the airconditioning compressors.

At his desk it requires an intense gathering of forces to actually go about his business. When thoughts of Daniel swell the cavities of his skull he resorts to pressing the knuckles of his middle fingers against his temples as hard as he can, as if what ails him is an abscess that can be drained by applying pressure.

Thank goodness for minutiae, Joshua thinks now, as he busies himself with the numbers on a cash flow statement and a quarterly sales tax return. The office is unusually quiet: Sean the poet has taken the week off to go to the beach; he got a deal on an Asbury Park cottage at pre-July Fourth rates, and lucked into this hot spell of weather. Gert leaves Joshua alone, though from time to time she peeks at him sideways from her computer screen to make sure he is not going off the rails.

The phone rings. "Bob Franco for you," she announces. Joshua was surprised and touched when Franco flew in from California for the funeral. Now back in Collegeville, he's been calling every few days.

"I'm okay," Joshua says as he lifts the receiver, anticipating Franco's question.

"We don't want okay," Franco protests. "We're not going to settle for okay."

They ease into a discussion of Tall Pines, and what Franco is doing to goose up business: a special Fourth of July package, consisting of an all-you-can-eat cookout with free soft drinks for the kids and beer for the grownups, volleyball, water polo and fireworks.

Fireworks will require a special permit from the Selectmen, which to Joshua means another opportunity for them to dilly-dally. Still, with Puckett and Wright gone there's always the chance that an epidemic of sanity will break out among the remaining three members. There's no provision in the town bylaws for special elections to fill a vacancy, so the seats will remain empty until next January's Town Meeting.

Water polo, fireworks, a keg of beer—it all sounds pretty good to Joshua that afternoon as he retrieves the car and drives to Bronx Academy for his last tutoring session. The South Bronx sidewalks are steaming in the heat; the six-block area around the school is devoid of trees, shade and the restful, cooling aspect of well-tended gardens.

It's when he takes the kids out for cokes and pepperoni pizza to celebrate the end of the school year that he hears the news. Joycelyn and Amika from last fall's painting party have come along, and when he asks where Alejandro is, they tell him: Alejandro's mother got sick after her operation and had to go back to the hospital. Alejandro and his sister are staying temporarily in New Jersey. They might even have to go back to Mexico.

Joshua gets Marie-Therese to fill him in. After her mastectomy, which went as well as these things can go, Alejandro's mother contracted a staph infection in the hospital. Her temperature shot up to 105; she became delirious. Finally the intravenous antibiotic kicked in and now she's mending, but it's been two and a half weeks, an exhausting two and a half weeks, since she first entered the hospital.

If all goes well, Alejandro's mother will be home in another week, after an intermediate stay in a skilled nursing facility. In the meantime, Alejandro and his sister are marooned in Hoboken, in the care of a distant and aging cousin. Their mother has no insurance, and is facing thousands of dollars in hospital bills. It'll be weeks before she can resume her job cooking in a neighborhood restaurant.

Joshua gets the number and calls Alejandro. Not wanting the boy to miss the year-end assembly, Joshua picks him up in New Jersey a few days later and drives him across the bridge to the Bronx. In the auditorium, Alejandro sits with his class while

Joshua finds a place next to Chris Swift, the math teacher who showed Joshua the ropes. Chris gives him a high five. Chris is wearing lemon-colored trousers, a black silk shirt and gold tie. Joshua, in blue blazer and khaki trousers, feels as boring as a hotel check-in clerk.

Ms. Etienne is welcoming the guests. The kids recite the pledge of allegiance; the school orchestra saws away gamely at the *Star Spangled Banner*. There is Puerto Rican dance, gospel singing and a pupil-written skit. Amika, who was elected sixth grade president, grasps the mike tightly as she thanks Ms. Etienne, the teachers and volunteers.

Then come the pupil awards. Alejandro snares two: a prize for the most inquiring scientific mind, and a prize for the most improved in English composition.

There are words from the Haitian-born president of the Parents Association, regal in her flowing yellow and purple dress, more songs from the chorus, a Langston Hughes poem recited by a small boy whose quavering voice gains volume as he nears the end. My God, Joshua realizes, it's Marcus.

Finally it's Ms. Etienne's turn. As always she waits for complete silence, her eyes panning across the rows of pupils, boys in navy pants and pressed shirts, girls in black skirts and white blouses.

Her message of tough love is undiluted. "If you think this year was hard, just wait. You haven't seen anything yet."

After the program, Joshua makes his way to Marie-Therese's side as the milling crowd of children, parents and guests presses in on them. She is the star; the dignitaries all want a minute of her time. He rubs elbows with the Bronx borough president, a local Congressman, the head of the foundation that put up the seed money for Bronx Academy. The latter is an unprepossessing man with a few sparse hairs on top of his head but a singular talent: the ability to write a $1 million check for a future building campaign.

Joshua interrupts her glad-handling to whisper a question: how is Alejandro's family going to manage at home, how are they going to pay the bills?

She has her public smile on, but her ironic voice pricks at him. "What are you, a social worker now?"

Alejandro holds his prizes tightly in his lap but as they speed back across the bridge, Joshua can see his joy begin to curdle. He tries to tell the boy that it'll be okay, that his mom will be home soon, words of comfort that sound phony to his own ears.

"Sure, Mr. Sandler," Alejandro says, but the only sure thing is the fear in the boy's eyes.

Chapter 26

It's a strange group that Nathalie has gathered at their home for the Sunday late-July barbecue: Gert and her daughter, Jenny; Sandy and Bill Cohen; Sean the poet and his girlfriend, a slim and slinky brunette who manages one of those shops on Madison in the 70s, the kind where they look you up and down through the glass door before they buzz you inside. Sonya the viola player comes with a tall, klutzy crewcutted guy whom Nathalie has never met before.

"This is Greg," Sonya says proudly. Within 60 seconds Greg proceeds to slosh white wine on the patio stones and to drop his wheat cracker with goat cheese into Nathalie's lap, cheese-side down.

"Another cracker, Greg?" Nathalie asks, as she scoops up the first one and folds it into a cocktail napkin. She smiles tolerantly at him, then hands him several sheets of paper towel with which to mop up the puddle of Chablis.

Her demeanor, self-possessed and puckish, bears witness to her breakthrough: first the rigorous daily practice sessions, then five or six weeks of subbing occasionally for her colleagues both at the Philharmonic and at other area orchestras and now, at the beginning of this month, she has reclaimed her Philharmonic chair. She skipped the orchestra's western Canadian tour but in the past 10 days has played a full schedule of rehearsals and concerts, earning a rare compliment from the conductor and garnering the vocal approval of her peers. Hard work agrees with her: she is sleeping better and her appetite has returned.

Everyone notices how radiant she is this day. My God, Nathalie, you look gorgeous, Sonya whispers as Nathalie provisions the oafish-looking Greg with a fresh wine glass (only a third full), and points him toward the outside trash can. Even Sean's girlfriend Clarissa, with her Connecticut prep school manners and her clear diction, the way she tilts her neck just so in order to thrust her full lips forward—even she seems awed by Nathalie. Nathalie has put on the simplest black dress, very short, and over it a sheer sleeveless white shirt; she's recently had her hair cut so that it is curling just above her neck. There is the faintest hue of pink in her skin, like the trace of a scarcely remembered blush; her face is the white of evaporated milk. Her eyes have a luminous vitality; they radiate wisdom and longing, pleasure at seeing everyone but at the same time not hiding, indeed proclaiming, a hurt that will not heal.

Greg turns out to be a jazz percussionist of awesome ability; his unseamed, sun-avoiding face, with its permanent musician's pallor, makes it impossible to guess his age; he could be 40, he could be 55. Greg has played with everyone—Ellington, Herbie Hancock, Miles Davis, Jimmy Heath, Basie, Lionel Hampton; he's on dozens of recordings, and now backs up a famous performer in thrice-weekly gigs at an East Side hotel piano bar. Greg offers to help Joshua flip hamburgers and grill the chicken breasts that were sitting all day in a thyme, olive oil and garlic marinade of Nathalie's own concoction.

"Sure, come and keep me company," Joshua says, resolved to keep Greg's hands away from any food or cooking implements. The two of them stand under the branches of a maple. From time to time Joshua lifts the barrel-shaped cover of the barbecue to turn the chicken while Greg, at his side, tells him stories about the antics of jazz musicians on the road or in the studio.

There was the famous saxophonist, getting on in years, whose afternoon naps went on so long that he often needed to be yanked out of bed by Greg in order to make it to the first set at 10:00 P.M.

There was the trumpet player who arrived at the recording studio high on cocaine, eyes bugging out of his head, pulled himself together to play brilliantly for an hour and a half, then collapsed and was rushed to the emergency room just in time to save his life.

And there was the band leader who was so incensed when a Cleveland bar owner handed him an envelope that was short $125 of the agreed amount for their gig that he threatened to drive the band's bus right through the front window unless the man came up with the cash in the next five minutes. With less than a minute to go he drove the bus up onto the sidewalk and revved the engine, until the owner ran out with a handful of crumpled bills to make good on the shortfall.

Gert arrives with her daughter and Jenny runs to where Joshua is bent over the grill and pulls him by the arm till he turns around to give her a kiss. They talk basketball and how it's a shame the Knicks got killed in the first round of the playoffs, except that Greg is happy it worked out that way because he grew up in Blue Bell, PA and is an avid 76'ers fan. Jenny gives Greg a pitying look, as if he hasn't yet learned that the world is round.

"Play any hoops when you were growing up?" Joshua asks.

"No time, I was always practicing, practicing. Too bad, 'cause I could have been great," Greg says, and Joshua cracks up.

When the meat is done Joshua toasts the buns over the coals and then sets out two platters on the big oval table, one with the chicken breasts, the other with the burgers. There's a big bowl of homemade potato salad with red onion, oil and vinegar and hardboiled eggs and green beans, and dishes of cole slaw, tomatoes, pickles and onions.

Joshua keeps circulating with the Chablis and the bottles of Mexican beer and when everyone is very mellow they set up the croquet set and bang away at their own and each other's balls, sending them skipping over the bumpy and very lush grass in the backyard. Jenny, her eyes fixed on the basketball hoop attached to the garage, enlists Joshua to locate a basketball for her.

It's a bit flat. "Got a pump?" she asks, and when Joshua produces it she expertly wets the valve, inserts it into the ball and pushes the handle up and down till the rubber is hard and tight. While the others are playing croquet she stands in the driveway, 12 feet back of the hoop and shoots free throws.

She raises the ball to her chest, steadies it there and then lunges upward, as if her entire body is attached to the ball and only when she has extended her toes and her arms are over her head does she release it, her torso falling back to earth like the booster rocket in a satellite launch. Joshua comes over to watch.

"I'm practicing as much as I can," she tells him. "I'm going to try out for the school team next fall."

"Your first time trying to make the team?"

"No, I tried out this year and didn't get on. But next year could be the year."

She holds the ball in front of her, passing it from one hand to the other. "Want to play some one on one?"

"Sure."

They play for 10 minutes or so, and Joshua is impressed by how she harries him on the dribble, her hands reaching in to try to swipe the ball away. When finally she hits a basket after Joshua has sunk seven or eight jump shots, he pats her on the butt.

"Way to go, Jenny. Nice shooting."

She gives him a serious look. "I've got to work on my shooting," she explains. "I keep telling myself to shoot from close in, the odds are so much better but sometimes I forget and shoot from too far away."

"You're going to get taller, you know. Then you'll have more range."

"I know, but now's the time to develop my shooting eye."

"Want to play some more?"

"Thanks," Jenny says. "It's okay. You can go back to being with the others. I'm going to work on my free throws."

He leaves Jenny to hoist up one free throw after another, and when he heads back to the spirited croquet game, Gert comes up to him. She has a beer bottle in her hand and she points it at her daughter.

"Sorry, I know she can drive you crazy."

"She's amazing. I'd hate to be in the way when she decides she seriously wants something."

"All kids want something badly, don't they?" Gert says.

"Yeah, all kids want things, but the number who are disciplined and organized and dedicated to getting what they want—that's another story. There aren't that many of them."

I should know, Joshua thinks, as Gert squeezes his shoulder.

They are all gone by nine.

It is one of those midsummer evenings that seem to grow even milder and more entrancing as night falls. The late afternoon breeze dies away; the scent of the roses creeps into the air and hangs there as if suspended in an aromatic band between Nathalie's shoulders and the top of her head. As she and Joshua walk to and fro cleaning up outside, their feet can still feel the afternoon sun on the patio stones. The house itself, seen from the patio, is a shadowy thing, hulking but strangely insubstantial; it only becomes real from inside, so that every time Joshua walks from the patio into the kitchen there is the sensation of passing from the mists of a dream into the harsh, unwelcome light of wakefulness.

"I'll clear, you stack?"

"Sure."

So he and Nathalie work silently, in the intricate, wordless harmony that graces long-time comedy teams and married couples. First he brings in and scrapes the plates and she rinses and puts them in the dishwasher. Then without a word they switch; she goes out and clears all the wine glasses and platters, while Joshua takes his turn at the sink, washing up the serving dishes and all the wine glasses and the delicate bowls that held oversized radishes, green and black olives, celery stalks or wheat crackers and goat cheese.

Now and then, as she brushes by him, she will trail her fingers across his shoulders. It is a long time since he has seen this look on her face, the smile of satisfaction after a party, the sign of remembered companionship, the ease of once more being alone together.

"That was so nice. Such a nice afternoon."

"Everyone got along," Joshua says.

"More than got along. They had a great time. Did you like Sonya's friend?"

"Greg? What a hoot he is."

"You know what was so nice? No one said a word."

"No, not one word."

She looks at him with cheeks that are flushed from wine; a few tears are glistening in each eye. "It was so normal. Just so normal."

Nathalie is standing there inches from him. She pivots around to pick up two of the wine glasses, which are sitting upside down on a dish towel on the table. Her strong fingers flip the glasses right side up and then she goes to the pantry. He hears her putting them away, hears the solid clink of the glass as she settles it firmly against the wooden shelf.

Joshua turns up the hot water and works the brillo pad into the corners of a rectangular pyrex pan and then, when that is shiny clean, he picks up the last of the serving dishes, a silver candy plate with scalloped edges, its burnished platform sitting on a delicate fluted column. This he cleans with the sponge; no scouring pads, Nathalie always reminds him, be gentle with it, grandma brought it back from London.

The front door of the house is half open and he can hear the agreeable rasp of the cicadas, the scuff of a tire as a bicycle is ridden up the apron of a driveway and laid against the garage door. A stern and commanding voice begins to berate a woman, a wife or girlfriend, for some shortcoming. Joshua doesn't recognize the voice and when he sticks his head out the front door and twists it to the left he realizes the noise is coming from Mrs. Morris' house. He can see the bluish glow of the TV set as he peers up at her second floor bedroom. She is hard of hearing, and the sound, turned up loud, is pouring out of the open window.

He shuts the screen door and there is Nathalie passing behind him, carrying another two wine glasses. She comes back for two more wine glasses, and then another two. Joshua hears the sound of each glass being set down in its place, and another sound, a scuffling noise as her foot hits the floor, this as he dries the candy dish and maneuvers the pyrex pan into place in a corner cabinet. Finished: he dries his hands, leans back against the cabinet, and through the open window listens to the night sounds, the insistent cicadas, the leaves stirring in the boughs of the maple trees.

"It's so still in the backyard," she says when she comes back in. "Let's sit out for a bit." Nathalie is wearing the expression of a little girl who wants to keep a secret but knows it will come out.

He follows her through the door with its stiff border of weather stripping and the tiny crack in an upper pane, and out onto the patio. The chairs and chaises longues are flung a bit this way and that from the guests. In the sky there is a single bright star, no clouds, no moon.

She sits on the chaise longue and Joshua, coming closer, sees the small goose bumps forming on her upper arms.

"You're cold, aren't you?"

"Just a little. But it's so beautiful out here."

"Want me to bring you a sweater?"

She shakes her head. "Nothing, nothing at all."

Nathalie turns to the right to peer at the southeastern sky where Mars is burning brilliantly, like the red bulb in a darkroom. As she swivels, Joshua marvels at the line of her hair moving like a living curtain across her graceful neck.

247

She seizes his hand and pulls him closer and then down, until he has squeezed onto the chaise-longue next to her. Through the shorts he is wearing, Joshua can feel the warmth of her ass pressed against his thighs; no chill here.

Now Nathalie is reaching a hand under his blue polo shirt to trace a faint circle in the middle of his chest, and then to stroke the ribs of his flank and his hard stomach. She is wanting him to turn more toward her, a message she conveys without a word, just by the pressure of her hand, the way she kneads his flesh with her fingers.

He lies back against the chaise and she lies back too, pulling him toward her, her fingers now squeezing his buttocks. His lips are pressed against her neck, his right leg inserted between her thighs. She brings her fingers around to unbutton the shorts and now she is caressing his prick, which is pressing furiously against his underpants. Her short black dress is up around her thighs and when he probes with his fingers he learns that she is wearing no panties, that she has shed them somewhere between the putting away of the wineglasses and this journey to the patio. Then he remembers the sound of her foot coming down hard in the pantry; so that's it, he smiles, that's the secret that you couldn't keep.

In the darkness he knows her face so clearly, can feel the hunger in her eyes, her mouth, her hands. She is pressing him down against the fabric of the chaise, tugging his underpants down around his knees, then reaching down to take hold of him. He hears her gasp, hears the rush of breath into her mouth and throat. She strains upward, as if to bury him as deeply as possible inside her.

Oh yes, oh my God, oh yes, she says, as she rises and falls like a dinghy bobbing in ceaseless seas, up and down, up and down.

Now, she urges, now, please now. She doesn't want him to wait; she wants him to finish, to finish her, and when he does she sprawls against him and her breasts, her thighs, her arms, her face are warm.

"You'll get chilled if you stay like this," he says after a while, and his voice sounds muffled and far away.

"No, I won't."

Minutes go by as she snuggles against him. "I'm getting cold," she says, and giggles.

Told you, he says, so softly that she hears only the caress of his words, feels the warmth of his large hands cupping her shoulders.

The night is fixed around them, like the background of a Flemish landscape in which every element is perfectly proportioned, expertly shadowed: the graceful overhang of the spreading beech with its canopy of dark leaves, the outline of the rose bush winding lazily beyond the stone bench, the gurgle of the fountain, the dim, ghostly trail of starlight reaching down from eternity into the ordered precincts of human habitation.

The night breeze tickles their bare arms and legs. Now Joshua leads her inside, the two of them creeping naked up the stairs, carrying their clothes in their fists like thieves. He folds down the sheet and blanket and inserts her in the bed, like a pet that has been left out in the rain and now needs to be cosseted and pampered. He drops his shorts and shirt on the floor and climbs in beside her.

Neither of them wants to let go of the other, and for long minutes they lie entwined, nuzzling each other's neck and cheeks and lips.

"Let's just stay like this, let's just always stay like this."

"Mmmm," he says in response.

"No, I mean it. We'll order a lot of food, a week's worth at a time and put a little fridge in the bedroom and quit our jobs."

"Will we get up to pay the electric and phone bill? To answer the phone?"

"Only what we have to. Survival mode, that's what it'll be. And we'll screw all day long, and then again at night, until we fall asleep."

"Mmmm."

Her hand is tickling his flank once more, and then she is reaching around to cup him and he is hard again.

"What's this?" she asks.

"I don't know. Do you know?"

"Why don't we find out? Why don't we see where it goes?"

She lies on her back and he is on his knees, kneeling between her legs, and she is raising up her hips, grabbing the pillow and putting it under her ass, and now he is on top of her and in her and they are looking in each other's eyes and kissing.

"Don't hurry."

"No."

"Go slow. I want to feel you there. I want to feel you for hours."

"Yes."

She is panting and sighing and gasping but she giggles nonetheless. "Can't you say anything but yes or no?"

"No."

They are like this for a long time, not hours, but a long time, until her hair, her neck, her belly, her breasts are all moist, until her gasps have died away to just a sweet and exhausted moaning. When finally he comes, it is as if something precious has passed from him to her.

Side by side they lie, breathing easily.

"You know we could . . . we could . . . we could. . . ." Nathalie stops.

"We could what?"

"We could make a baby like this."

Chapter 27

Thirteen months later, on a breezy day in August, they come back to The Hollow. When they get out of the car Nathalie is carrying the baby in a reinforced plastic seat. Dana is four months old now; she was born the first week of May when the air was fragrant with the early lilac blooms. She's an alert young thing with a head of fine, shiny light brown hair with threads of gold. Her eyes follow her mother and father everywhere, and when Joshua comes into sight after an absence of even an hour she greets him with a smile and an excited gurgle.

They've stayed away from the house ever since Sammons found Daniel's body up on Torvald's land and Terry McBurnie gave Joshua and Nathalie the information that led to uncovering, finally, what had happened.

Of course they came and went in a single day in January for Terry's funeral. It was the day after New Year's, the coldest day of the year: one degree Fahrenheit at half past six when they climbed into the car in Mamaroneck. Still, that was mild compared to The Hollow. Here the thermometer hanging outside the kitchen window read minus 11 Fahrenheit; the wind moaned against the panes in an eerie warning that wild beasts—in that frigid weather you could almost imagine polar bears—were on the prowl. Soon after they arrived, Joshua and a five-months'-pregnant Nathalie stood warming themselves over mugs of tea in the kitchen, waiting for the forced hot air heat to kick in. Even Nathalie had eaten a donut that morning, an oversized one with a honey glaze.

The funeral service took place at 10:30 in the white-clapboarded church opposite the town hall in Smithfield. Snow was heaped in glistening piles all up and down Main Street. It also lay in irregular cones and peaks about five feet out from the foundation of the church building, in a ragged perimeter formed when Art Sammons and two other volunteers had shoveled it off the roof. They'd climbed up there a few days before just to make sure that the rafters didn't give way under the weight: 23 inches of snow just in December. Too much snow too early, the old-timers said; it looks to be a bad one.

The minister of the Congregational Church officiated. A painfully thin bachelor, he's been here five years, ever since Albie Moreau passed away. The locals still can't get used to his West Virginia mountain twang. The minister hardly knew Terry, so it was left to the retired principal of the elementary school to speak about him—his punctuality, his work ethic, his affection for the kids.

"At the end of each school day no matter what he was doing, painting or putting a new lock on the front door, he'd stop to smile as the kids streamed out of the building to walk home or to wait for their mothers to pick them up."

Among the couple of dozen mourners were Rosa Puckett, Mary Shaw from the Board of Selectman and Alice Fickett, who still takes the residents of the senior housing on their weekly excursions. A dozen of those residents gathered in a little group in the fourth row pews. Further back, sitting by herself, was a lady in her 70s, her gray hair in a topknot, her large, plain face wet with tears. At every word from the principal she sobbed louder.

"Who was that?" Joshua asked afterwards.

"Edna Foley, one of the teachers," Nathalie said. "She was sweet on Terry. She'd bring him little treats and invite him to dinner but he was too shy to go. I think he couldn't imagine feminine charms directed at him. What a shame. She lived alone, he lived alone; they could have shared some laughs, could have warmed each other's bones on the awful winter nights."

"Too bad Dan couldn't be here," Joshua said as they drove home to Mamaroneck. Even to his ears the words sounded bizarre, but Nathalie understood.

"I know. They were so close. The way Terry used to talk to him, so seriously, treating him like an adult even when he was only seven or eight—it was something to see."

Joshua was back at Bronx Academy this past school year, working with a new group of tutees. Amika, Joycelyn, Alejandro and even Marcus still begged to come along when he took the kids for burgers or pizza. The girls were growing up faster than the boys, especially Amika, taller, fuller of body, aware of how the boys looked at her, seeming to disdain them while enjoying the attention. Don't let her get into trouble, Joshua tells Marie-Therese.

"If any of those girls gets pregnant I'll boot them out of Bronx Academy. That's after I beat them with a hair brush so hard they won't sit down for a month. They know I mean it, too."

Too bad no one delivered that message to the girls in Smith-field, Joshua thought.

Alejandro took his place with his seventh grade class. His mother came home after another two and a half weeks in the hospital, and by mid-July she was able to go back to work. Joshua negotiated with the hospital to cut the bill by two-thirds, and he and Nathalie said they'd pay off the balance.

They promised themselves and Ms. Etienne something more: that they would keep adding to Daniel's college savings account and use the money for Alejandro's college tuition.

Now, on this summer day, Joshua and Nathalie park the baby in her chair outside the shed door. Keeping her always in sight, they stroll around the lawn to the west of the house where, in late afternoon, the sun lays down its gentle kiss on the green expanse. Joshua has his sneakers off, enjoying the feel of the blades between his toes, cool and squishy in the shade of the trees, as warm as bread from the oven where the sun strikes the lawn full on.

Should we sell the place, should we keep it, do we really want to be going there—this has been the on and off discussion for the better part of a year. Joshua is usually the one saying, "Let's be done with it, let's get rid of it and move on, it's not a place for us."

"Why pretend we never lived there, never had fun there?" Nathalie responds. "It was Dan's place as much as ours. He loved it there."

And Joshua has to acknowledge that yes, he did.

But circling between the trees and Nathalie's plantings, meandering to the far corner where the land rises to a bluff from which, through the vines and branches of the river bank, they have a fine view of the stream below, Joshua has a different feeling. His heart is at ease, a strange sensation here where they knew such pain. Would it be mad to stay?

At the end of the morning they drive to Tall Pines. Bob Franco gives them lunch in the dining room and tells them his news: he's bought an old farmhouse just north of town, about two miles from the resort and is fixing it up.

"I'm spending so much time here that I don't want to drive back to Collegeville all the time."

Franco has turned things around since last summer. How? "Hard work and marketing, marketing, marketing," he tells Joshua.

"Just when you think you've tried everything you discover there's all kinds of things you haven't tried." He's made deals with the ski shops in Collegeville, Hartsfield, Hartford and even with a couple of big sporting goods places in Manhattan: with each package of cross country skis, boots and poles comes a coupon good for 25% off on a weekend at Tall Pines.

"When a customer books two room-nights using one of those coupons, the store and the salesperson each get a twenty."

Franco and his sales manager have also reached out to groups, all kinds of groups: "Rotarians, Shriners, Reconstructionist Jews on a Sabbath retreat, the association of Massachusetts judges, alumni picking a place for their 25th high school reunion." Even the Smithfield Selectmen held a dinner here for town employees (all three of them, part-time), themselves, spouses and kids, the first ever, and it was such a success that the Selectmen from Northway and Cooperville may do the same.

"We're buying lamb and milk and fruit and vegetables locally," Franco says. "That's money in the pocket for area farmers. We're a source of jobs—a dozen Smithfield people are on our payroll, from assistant manager to waiters and cleaning people."

The resort has hired a crackerjack bake-chef whose cakes, pies, brownies and custard tarts are on sale at the Smithfield General Store, alongside Deb Rosenschein's muffins and apple crumb loaf, introducing Tall Pines to a stream of potential new patrons.

"People stop me in my car now to say hello," Franco says. "One old-timer said Tall Pines is the best thing to happen to Smithfield since Mrs. Roosevelt spent a night here in the '30s."

Are you going to keep the place in The Hollow? Franco asks. When Joshua says they don't belong here and wonders aloud how they could stay after all that's happened, Franco shakes his head.

"I never took that outsider crap seriously," he said, "not even when your buddy Tom Robinson was making those phone calls. I figured it was a couple of assholes with their own agenda. It's a beautiful place to live and work. I'm having a lot of fun with Tall Pines. I'm here for a while."

I'd love it if you guys stayed, he says to Joshua.

"Running into any of those kids would be really hard. I'm still full of hatred for them."

The teens involved in the disappearance have all been sentenced. Melanie Roberts received 18 months' detention, of which six months was suspended subject to her performing 400 hours of community service. Tony, sentenced as an adult, also got a year and a half in jail—with good behavior he could be out in half that time. Sam Bonacio was not charged with any crime and has only the burden of his conscience to carry. In the family tumult that followed the revelations, Steve got violent with his son and Pat threw him out. Now she manages the house alone and holds a full-time job at the general store.

As for Bobby Dawes, the DA charged him with kidnapping and first-degree murder, on the theory that the crime against Daniel Sanders was premeditated. The lawyer assigned to his case protested this vigorously and although the DA didn't budge, the judge had a few skeptical questions for the prosecution at the pre-trial hearing. No witnesses, no clear forensic evidence, and a statement from the defendant saying it was an accident—do you really think you can get a murder conviction, he asked.

At that first court date, Joshua took a seat near the front and when he looked across the aisle there was a woman wearing a long black skirt and high-collared beige blouse, both a little too big for her. She looked as if she were interviewing for a job in clothes she borrowed from a cousin. It was Ellen Bartlett, even thinner and paler than usual. The courtroom in the old county courthouse, with its warped wooden floor and tall windows, was full of reporters: the Boston, Springfield, Albany and West-chester, NY papers, the local radio stations, a couple of area TV crews.

Three weeks later, Shaughnessy and Bobby's court-appointed lawyer had reached a deal. Bobby Dawes pleaded guilty to manslaughter. The judge ordered him to jail for 18 to 20 years, the maximum penalty. There'd be no possibility of parole until at least 12 years had been served—and even then parole was iffy.

"Twelve years doesn't seem like much of a price to pay for taking the life of our son," Joshua says to Franco. "That bastard could be out walking around by the time he's 30."

Nathalie, however, offers a different opinion. "Hatred doesn't do me any good. I just pray these kids never get over what they did—that it haunts them forever, spurs them to do something positive with their lives."

Maybe that'll be true for Melanie or Tony or Sam, she adds. But Bobby Dawes, in her opinion, is doomed to go from one jail term to another. Like father like son, she says.

As they finish lunch, Dana, who'd been napping peacefully in her seat, wakes up and begins to fuss; she's hungry. Nathalie finds a quiet space in the lounge outside the ladies' room, and when she has finished nursing the baby she and Joshua drive back to The Hollow.

They'd thought to spend the afternoon quietly, sitting by the river, perhaps strapping Dana into her sack and strolling up Route 33A as far as The Shadows. But Nathalie can't resist picking up the long-handled, six-prong cultivator to clear the neglected, overgrown, weed-entangled rectangle that used to be the vegetable garden. With Dana napping nearby, Joshua grabs one of the hoes and begins working at the same task from the other direction.

Only when they are sweaty and tired and thirsty do they stop, and sink into the lawn chairs that Joshua has liberated from a pile of outdoor furniture in the shed. Nathalie fetches tall glasses of iced tea. Joshua plays a game with Dana, showing her a shiny sixpenny nail and then hiding it in his closed-up fist; opening his fingers to reveal the silver-gray nail and then, as she laughs with excitement, making it disappear again. He holds Dana close to him to tickle her and make her laugh some more. After a while Nathalie says it's time to get her inside, she's had enough sun, it's suppertime for her, 5:30 going on quarter to six.

"I'll come in soon and give her her bath," Joshua says.

"It's a deal."

He rotates the lawn chair so it is facing west and the lowering sun is warm on his face and arms. His eyes close. He opens them with a start to see the broad lawn, the shadows of the fruit trees. It's so quiet here, he thinks, and though his eyes are open, he is imagining, dreaming, inventing a scene that runs into another scene that runs into another; not just one scene succeeding another but an entire story.

It is an August day in the early afternoon. He is hopping down from the jeep, his foot landing in the soft sand that gathers at the verge of the driveway, between the gravel bed and the lawn. Joshua hears a rhythmic, melodic sound coming from the far side of the house. He unloads his bale of chicken wire and V-shaped nails and stows them in the corner of the garage.

Setting these few items in their place—the nails, the motor oil, the round metal gas container, a hand-scythe—brings to mind a painting he once saw of a Shaker barn, everything so simple, each tool beautifully made, wiped clean, hanging on its own wooden peg. You could tell the care these people took with their tools from the painstaking way those pegs had been fashioned. You could stare at this painting for hours, absorbing the lesson that the Shakers left as their legacy: that simple doesn't mean easy, but its opposite.

Nathalie is busy making lunch: a salade nicoise with its puckered black Greek olives, Sicilian tuna, anchovies, bits of red pepper, celery, capers, slices of hardboiled egg.

Joshua exits the garage and follows the sound, angling across the front lawn, skirting the large fir with its knobbed, ringed trunk, smelling the tang of its needles baking in the sun.

The shed door is open and there in the half-dark, half-light, a spray of sawdust covers the floor. Daniel has upended the old wooden wheelbarrow, and is redrilling a hole underneath the flat platform where the bolts had come loose. Joshua sees that he has also cut a new front piece to replace the one that had buckled and cracked.

"Need a hand?"

"Hi Dad. Just hold the brace still while I put the new bolt in. Well, not a new bolt, but one I found when I was rummaging around for parts."

Joshua straddles the platform with both legs and pushes the brace hard against the platform as Dan drives the one and three-quarter-inch bolt home. Nice job, Joshua says. How come today?

257

"Aw, you know, mom has been yakking about this all summer." He shrugs, his tanned forehead moist from exertion. "So I found some scrap wood and did it."

"Looks great. How about lunch?"

"Yeah, but first I'm going for a swim. No, not at The Shadows, right here, under the bridge." Daniel is wearing his blue and yellow swim trunks and a pair of gray all-terrain running shoes, no socks, no shirt.

"I'll join you?"

"Sure."

The two of them are still lazing away in the middle of the shallow stream when Nathalie calls them to lunch. "That was so nice, how you fixed the wheelbarrow," she tells Dan.

"Aw, well, it was nothing."

"Better than some people I could name, who say they'll fix something and then six months later it's still sitting there, broken and shabby-looking."

"Oh God," Joshua exclaims. "Protect us from the broken and the shabby."

Her laugh comes naturally, a chug-chug-chug sound rising higher and higher.

After lunch Joshua issues a two-part challenge to Dan: a tennis match, preceded by a race up the Hawes Hill Road to the Moreau place.

As they jog up the steep, twisting hill, with Dan in the lead, Joshua marvels that it can be so important to him to beat his soon-to-be 14-year-old son. Is this what has been going on in their household for the better part of a year—a pentathlon consisting of a long footrace, a swimming meet, a debating contest, a wrestling match, a battle of wills?

Dan strains upward and steps out of the crumbling, eroded ruts of Hawes Hill Road onto Blueberry Glen Road, a broader, flatter, quite deserted road. Three seconds behind, Joshua leaps onto that same road. Midway up Blueberry Glen Road Joshua thinks he will pitch forward and impale his forehead on the fingernail-sized stones embedded in the packed dirt surface of the road. He gulps for breath. With the driveway of the Moreau place in sight Joshua's hands are reaching forward, they can practically flick the dust off the back strap of Daniel's cap. They

258

race for the driveway, stride for stride; their toes cross at the same instant.

Joshua is winded by the jog up Hawes Hill Road. Dan wins the first set easily but a couple of hard serves in a tie-breaker enable Joshua to even the match after the second set.

"What do you say, Dad? One more?"

When they start the third set, the heat is already ebbing and the pine branches begin the rhythmic rustling that signals the hint of the evening breeze.

Dan leads the set 5-4. It's 40-30 on Joshua's serve when Dan hits a cross-court floater toward the baseline. Joshua lunges, the ball squirting beyond his racket head.

"Out."

But was it out? The ball bounced low and skidded; Joshua doubts he had a clean look. "Dan, I have to change my call. I think it was good. Deuce."

And then Dan wins the next two points: game, set, match.

"Way to go, Dan. But you were lucky. Next time . . ."

"I know, next time you're going to whip my butt," the boy says, laughing.

They are walking down the meadow, and as they turn onto the path that leads back to the house the barn looms up at them, as red as the cinders that sputter and glow from under the grate of a winter's fire.

"Dan, how about we race down?"

"Sure, Dad," he says, tolerantly. Joshua tries to remember his attitude toward his own father when he, Joshua, was 14 and his father was in his late 40s, a bear of a man with that barrel chest and the oversized arms and the surprisingly slender legs.

Joshua never recalls Abe doing any exercise at all, no hand-ball, no tennis, not even a brisk walk around the neighborhood, so there was never any question of challenging him to a footrace. But his father had amazing strength; he'd rearrange the furniture in the warehouse by himself, if Benny and Isaiah (honest to God, those were their names, a couple of Old Testament names for a couple of young black men from the projects in Mt. Vernon) didn't show up to work in time.

"Count to three when you're ready," Joshua says.

"Ready, set, go." Dan starts off fast. Joshua takes a couple of painful strides, feeling the muscles in his thighs sing, not again, not again. At the point where Blueberry Glen Road makes its big turn to the right, descending toward Hawes Hill Road, Dan is 25 yards ahead.

By the time Joshua reaches the upper gullies of Hawes Hill Road he has lost sight of Dan. He steps quickly over the rocks and washed-out trenches, and ahead of him he can hear Dan, the crunch of his tennis shoes on the stones and on the hump of hardpacked sand that runs down the center of the road.

Only as they turn onto Main St. three-eighths of a mile from home does he finally have Dan in sight. His son is 100 yards in the lead; Joshua is out of breath and out of time. Dan touches the big maple with his left hand, raises his right in a sign of victory and crosses the lawn to throw himself onto the white millstone in front of the front door. When Joshua totters up, Dan is holding out a tall glass of lemonade to his father.

"You okay, Dad?"

"What do you think, a few sets of tennis and a run up and down a hill are going to do me in? Anytime you want a repeat, I'm ready."

"Dad, give it a rest."

They sit side by side on the millstone, listening to the sounds of Nathalie on the cello pouring out into the late afternoon; the sweet-smelling grass seems to be alive with the music. The sun has sunk to a line even with the neighbors' trees, and there are bands of shadow unrolling across the golden green lawn. All day it has been cloudless and still, the sun glowing like a jewel, but now a breeze starts from the west, drying the sweat on Joshua's neck and legs, lifting the orange hairs along his arms.

Supper will be hamburgers and hot dogs on the grill. Nathalie reminds Joshua that he was going to wash the jeep today; there it sits in the driveway, under a sheen of brown dust.

"Oh, yeah, the jeep."

He attaches the hoses and brings a pail with cleanser and sponges. They wet the car down and then soap and rinse, soap and rinse. At one point Dan grabs the hose from where it is lying under the front wheel and turns it on his father, not full force but with one of those funnel-shaped fine sprays. Joshua wrenches the hose away and does the same thing to Dan, who ducks away, and they chase each other round and round. Before supper they hop in the river once more, letting the bubbling

260